POSSESSION

POSSESSION

A GREYWALKER NOVEL

KAT RICHARDSON

A ROC BOOK

ROC
Published by the Penguin Group
Penguin Group (USA) Inc., 375 Hudson Street,
New York, New York 10014, USA

USA | Canada | UK | Ireland | Australia | New Zealand | India | South Africa | China

Penguin Books Ltd., Registered Offices: 80 Strand, London WC2R 0RL, England
For more information about the Penguin Group visit penguin.com.

First published by Roc, an imprint of New American Library,
a division of Penguin Group (USA) Inc.

First Printing, August 2013

 REGISTERED TRADEMARK—MARCA REGISTRADA

LIBRARY OF CONGRESS CATALOGING-IN-PUBLICATION DATA:

Richardson, Kat.
  Possession: a Greywalker novel/Kat Richardson.
    p. cm
  ISBN 978-0-451-46512-2
  1. Blaine, Harper (Fictitious character)—Fiction. 2. Women private investigators—Fiction.
3. Psychic ability—Fiction. I. Title.
  PS3618.I3447P67 2013
  813'.6—dc23   2013007272

Printed in the United States of America
10 9 8 7 6 5 4 3 2 1

Set in Adobe Garamond
Designed by Alissa Amell

PUBLISHER'S NOTE
This is a work of fiction. Names, characters, places, and incidents either are the product of the author's imagination
or are used fictitiously, and any resemblance to actual persons, living or dead, business establishments, events, or
locales is entirely coincidental.
  The publisher does not have any control over and does not assume any responsibility for author or third-party
Web sites or their content.

In memory of:
Arthur Carpenter and Lois Alnutt

ACKNOWLEDGMENTS

Seems there's always something crazy happening the past few years, and this book had to dodge a lot of angst and problems to get into your hands, so I'm indebted to a lot of people for various chores in that respect. Many thanks to: minions Thea and Eric Maia (Thing One and Thing Two); Nancy Durham and Elisabeth Shipman; the fabulous Cherie Priest; Robin MacPherson; Rhiannon Held, who provided all sorts of information about archaeology in Washington, and the tunnel and seawall projects, as well as beta reading, advising, and being a stellar friend and wonderful writer; Mary Robinette Kowal for writer hangouts online and encouragement in person even in the face of freakish weather and cross-country moves; Dr. Martha Leigh for medical information; Sally Harding and the whole crew at Cooke International— you guys rock; my long-suffering husband for sticking with me through all this; my totally amazing team at Roc—especially Anne Sowards and Rosanne Romanello—for continuing to make these books such a success; Anton Strout, who made me laugh at Comic Con when I wanted to scream; Paul Goat Allen, who continues to say nice things.

And to my mother-in-law, Sandra Carpenter: Thanks for being here—I love you very much.

POSSESSION

PROLOGUE

I don't like dying. No one does and no matter how many times I've done it and how much I know about what lies beyond that thin edge of existence, I still dread it enough to wish for no more—or at least only one more and stay down for good. I've died three times that I'm sure of and that's enough for anyone. I shouldn't complain—I'm still alive at the moment. I seem mostly normal, I suppose—I have a boyfriend and a pet and a job—but even those things aren't quite ordinary: The boyfriend is an ex-spy, my pet is a ferret, and I work as a private investigator. I sometimes think it would be nice to just be normal and have a normal job and a normal family, but that isn't going to happen. I have been down to death and back and whether that is the reason or whether it's the other way around, I am a Greywalker—one of the rare few who can move through the overlapping fringes of the world of the normal and that of the paranormal. That here/not here world is the Grey and it lies just beside everything you see and contains everything you don't and never want to. Magic streams and sings through the darkness and the mists of the possible as hot neon light in lines and tangles that burn with power; spirits, monsters, and nightmares are its native inhabitants and I am one of its naturalized citizens. I have been called the Hands of the Guardian—the eldritch creature that prowls the borders of the Grey—and the paladin of the dead. I remain in the "real" world as the go-between, negotiator, troubleshooter, and general fixer for all things Grey. I dance on a hair-thin high wire, balancing between the uncanny and the mundane while trying to keep myself alive a little longer, because I'm sure that my next death will be my last.

The thing about this twilight freak show is that I sometimes know more about the dead than I know about the living, and the ghosts and monsters just keep coming around. They all have problems and the problems seem to be stranger with each new case. Sometimes the Grey things impose themselves on my life with such force and vehemence that the world changes, even if only a few of us can see it. It's part of my job to make sure these changes don't destroy the balance between this world and the next without destroying myself or the people I hold dear.

ONE

I don't usually acquire clients in secondhand stores. Books, jackets, furniture, knickknacks—yes. Clients—not so much. I was lurking in the nook at Old Possum's Books 'n' Beans where the volumes about music, theater, and philosophy were currently kept—more a comment on the owner, Phoebe Mason's, sense of humor than any practical filing system—when a woman approached me. Even before I saw her, I felt the touch of her desperation and fear like a cloud of bad perfume.

Her footsteps stuttered as she walked across the scarred old wooden floor, and I looked around and down to find the source of the uncertain sound. Thus, the first thing I actually saw were her shoes: good-quality leather loafers with low heels that had become unevenly worn so each step wobbled just a bit, the dark brown leather scuffed along the sides and toes as if they'd been scraped repeatedly through rough stones. Her designer jeans were baggy at the knee, cinched in at the waist with a belt that didn't match the shoes, and fit like they'd been meant for a curvier body, while her blouse was so rumpled it appeared she'd misbuttoned it.

I looked up to study her face and saw a once-lovely middle-aged woman with shoulder-length black hair, the gray roots leaving an undyed band about an inch wide along her part. Her cheekbones stood in high relief, hinting at some mix of Asian ancestors with taller Europeans, under skin that was dry, fine-lined, and too tight, as if she'd given up eating and was subsisting on nerves and dry toast. She stopped, her eyes widening as she bit her lip and stared at me for a second. Then she drew a deep breath and asked, "Are you the detective? A friend of Phoebe's?"

Her question seemed to hang in the air and I took a beat before I replied, frowning a little at the weight it seemed to add to the room. Phoebe had been my first friend in Seattle, but I answered hesitantly, not sure which role this woman expected me to fill: detective or friend. "I . . . am." The fading ghost of a former customer wafted obliviously down the aisle and through the pair of us as we stood there.

The woman didn't see it, but she twitched at its cold passage and gave me a deer-in-the-headlights stare, while a drained shimmer in shades of olive and charcoal around her told me she was terrified. For another moment we just blinked at each other, until I prompted her to tell me what she wanted.

"What can I do for you?" I held back my desire to frown or look sideways at her to see whether she was entangled in the Grey, since I thought either would seem unfriendly and drive this skittish creature away.

"I need—um, I have a sister—" She stopped and shook her head as if she could shake her words into the right order. "I need help. I came here because I'm desperate to find out what's happening. I was told I should talk to you—" She wrung her hands as she babbled, her body slightly bent, stooped forward as if her chest ached.

I touched her hand and felt a chill of distress twine up my fingers like the tendrils of a climbing vine. I didn't jerk away, though that was my first impulse. "It's all right," I started, patting her hand very lightly and then closing mine over it to stop her churning motion. "Let's sit down and you can tell me about it."

She returned a jerky nod, her hands stilling as she let her gaze slide away from mine. I led her down the aisle and around the corner to the coffee nook, where there were a few cushy armchairs set between a fake fireplace and the espresso counter. A one-third-scale replica of a Triceratops skull looked down on us from the wall above the espresso machine, just a few feet from a round traffic mirror that showed the alcove to whoever was manning the front desk. We were alone, but not unobserved, and that was fine.

One of the chairs was occupied by a massive golden feline that laid claim to being a house cat only because we'd never been able to prove it was a mountain lion. "Hump it, Simba," I ordered, with a dismissive jerk of my head.

With impressive languor and a yawn that showed off white fangs and a long tongue of barbed pink velvet, the cat flowed out of the chair and prowled off to intimidate one of the lesser cats from its sleeping spot. I waved to the two now-empty chairs nearest us and watched the woman stumble and nearly fall into the one just vacated by Simba.

I got a cup of water for her rather than coffee, since I figured that although she looked exhausted, she didn't need to be any further wound up. She clutched the cup in both hands, her shoulders hunched. Her skin had a sallow cast over its natural lightly bronzed color, and blue shadows of worry smeared her eye sockets. She peered at me like a frightened cat from under a bed.

I sat down and started the conversation since it seemed like she wasn't ready to. I did my best to give the impression I was earnest, honest, and safe to talk to. "I'm Harper Blaine and I am a friend of Phoebe's. I'm also a private investigator and I help people with problems. What's your name and what can I help you with?"

"I—my name is Lillian Goss," she said. "Lily. Phoebe says . . ." Her gaze darted around, looking up at me, then down, then side to side in nervous jumps. "She says you see ghosts."

I was a little surprised: Phoebe hadn't seemed entirely convinced when we'd had "the talk" about my weird abilities and the grief that they had caused her in the past. Of course, she might have still been mad at me; it was hard to tell precisely what Phoebe was thinking when she was displeased. "Do *you* believe in ghosts?" I asked.

"I don't. Or I didn't. Or—I don't know. But I believe in God and I believe in the Devil and I believe that whatever has my sister isn't either one of those."

I blinked, but I didn't balk. " 'Has'? I'm not sure I understand. Something . . . that isn't God or the Devil has . . . taken your sister? Is your sister missing?"

"No. Or yes. She's . . . not home anymore. But someone else is."

"Someone else is in your sister's house?"

"Not her house—her body."

"You're talking about possession."

"Yes."

I felt . . . well, the British would say "gobsmacked," but I wasn't sure that was quite right, either. I just sat still and tried to get my brain around it.

She watched me absorb the idea and took my well-schooled poker face as rejection. She looked at the floor, her hands squeezing the cup so hard that the plastic sides deformed with a popping sound that made her start and gasp. "You don't believe me!"

"Yes, I do. But why have you come to the conclusion that someone or something other than her own self is occupying her body? That's quite a leap for most people. In fact, most people wouldn't even consider that it might be the action of demons or the Devil. . . ."

"It's not the Devil! God—*my* God—wouldn't let that happen! He doesn't just—just throw people away. He is loving and forgiving and Julie loves him just as I do. He wouldn't—"

I stretched my hand out toward her, placating. "Ms. Goss, it wasn't my intention to offend you. I'm only surprised. Please tell me what makes you think some entity has control of her body."

She bit her lip, clamping down on sobbing breaths. She wheezed and snorted for a moment before she regained some control and was able to speak. "My sister is in what they call a persistent vegetative state—a PVS. She's not really awake, even when she has her eyes open and seems to be looking around. She breathes on her own and sometimes she laughs or cries, but the doctors and nurses tell me it's not real joy or sadness, just an involuntary function of whatever's still working in her brain. She can't do anything but lie in bed or sit in an armchair. The doctors say if her state doesn't change soon, it never will; she'll just deteriorate slowly until she dies.

"But a while ago she sat up on her own and she started drawing or painting something on her bedspread—"

"With what?" I asked. "With her fingers?"

"Yes, at first. I thought she was getting better, but that's not it. She just paints. She doesn't improve. The machines indicate that she's not doing anything—that her brain isn't sending these signals that move her body—but she's sitting up and painting. I started bringing her brushes and supplies so she wouldn't use food or blood on the bed. . . . Now she just sits up at random times and paints. And then she lies down and whatever spark she had in her goes away again. The machines say she never did anything. Her blood pressure and breathing go up, but that's all. But these paintings . . . they're real paintings— not crazy smeary things."

"Is it the paintings themselves that distress you?"

"No. She paints landscapes but they're . . . they're odd. Someplace you almost know but can't name. She paints them—it's not a hoax or a prank. But it's not her . . . it's not her doing it." Goss gulped a sob and tried to drink from the crushed cup, getting water down the front of her blouse for her pains.

I took the cup from her hand and fetched her a new one along with some paper towels to mop up the mess. Flustered, she patted at herself, looking embarrassed and finally hiding behind her cup of water for a few sips. Once she'd settled down again, I encouraged her to continue her tale.

"You've seen her do this?" I asked. "The painting."

"Yes. She lives with me now—if you can call what she's doing 'living.' I sit with her all the time. Night and day. Everything is falling apart, but I don't know what else to do. Nurses come twice a day to help me, but she doesn't move or do anything unless she's painting. There are so many machines . . . but they all just beep quietly away as if she's only lying there like always. And now it's getting worse."

"In what way?"

"She paints all the time, so many hours, and not all the same kind of paintings anymore. Now it's like there's more than one person painting. Even when she should be sleeping, she sits up and paints.

If I take the brush away from her, she just grabs something else—or uses her fingers—and goes back to painting. Some of the nurses don't want to come anymore—it freaks them out to be with her. The doctor said I was imagining things, until she started doing it in the exam room. Now even he's spooked. And all the time she's doing it, it's as if her arm is moving without the rest of her doing anything. She'll move her head around, open and close her eyes, laugh, cry . . . wet herself . . . and keep on painting. It's like *she* isn't the one painting at all. It's just her body being moved around by someone else. Like a puppet."

"Does she finish the paintings?"

"Not always. But she paints faster now, like she's racing—or whoever is inside her is rushing to finish before they have to leave again. If she doesn't finish one the same day she starts it, she'll never finish it at all. She just goes on to the next painting. Sometimes she'll do three in a day."

"I think I need to meet your sister."

Lily Goss's face seemed to flower with hope. "Then, you'll help me? You'll find out who or what is possessing Julianne?"

I had to shake my head. "I can't guarantee that. I don't know what's happening to your sister or if it's really in my purview. There are some things I can't do anything about. If this really is some kind of possession, then you need to talk to your priest."

She gaped and looked on the verge of crying, her aura turning a bleak, muddy green that seemed to drip downward like rain. "No . . . I already talked to Father Nybeck! He can't help me! It's outside his role or something. He said he can't help me . . . won't. Don't—don't say you won't, either. Please."

She crushed the second plastic cup, sending a gout of water into her lap. She jumped up with a sob and I think she would have bolted if I hadn't caught her shoulders and steadied her. She felt like a bundle of dry twigs barely held together by her rumpled clothes, and I was too conscious that I loomed over her, but there was little I could do to make myself smaller. I braced her and held her still, saying, "Miss Goss, I didn't say I wouldn't help. I said I might not be able to."

She looked back up at me, her lip trembling and her jaw twitching as if she wanted to say something but couldn't remember the words.

"It's all right. I'm not saying no. I'm saying let's go see."

"Right now?"

"If you're comfortable with it, sure."

She didn't hesitate. "Yes. I live just up the street and we can walk it in a few minutes."

I convinced her to ride with me in the Land Rover—I didn't want to have to walk back to the bookstore later in the chancy weather we'd been having.

Fremont has a lot of condos these days, but there are still plenty of single-family dwellings on the narrow streets of Seattle's former homegrown Haight-Ashbury. Lily Goss lived in a freestanding house that was tall and narrow and very, very modern with a lot of steel, glass, and bright red exterior panels mixed with sections of horizontal wood strips that sported big black bolts holding them to the structure's surface. Somehow neither the wood nor the red panels made the house look warm; it just looked expensive.

The interior was stark and seemed empty—as if things were missing. I glanced quickly at the entry and the living room as we passed through them. Goss caught me at it as she stopped in front of a tall

wall of frosted glass and steel. "My ex-husband took half of the furniture and I had to sell the remaining art," she said.

Part of the frosted wall slid aside, revealing a surprisingly large
elevator. "So, you're divorced," I said, following her into the glass-
and-chrome box.

Goss heaved a sigh and looked embarrassed, pushing the top button of four on the control panel. "Yes. The church frowns on it, but
they don't prohibit it anymore and I . . . I'm glad Teddy left. He
didn't have a generous nature and he wouldn't have coped well with
my sister living here, dependent on us for everything."

"How long have you been on your own?"

"A little over a year. I hadn't been . . . alone for very long before
Julianne got sick."

The elevator came to a smooth, quiet stop and we stepped out
onto a wide, wood-floored landing at the top of a staircase, with
three doors facing us. Goss stood still for a moment and I could hear
a susurrous, mechanical mumble coming quietly from our left. Grey
mist boiled out from under the double doors on that side.

"I had the master bedroom converted for Julianne. I wasn't sleeping in it anyway."

She opened the door that leaked ghost-stuff and showed me in.

I could tell it had been a sumptuous suite originally, but it now
more resembled a hospital room. The thick white carpet was covered
with heavy, flexible plastic like the material used for floor protectors
under office desks. The primrose yellow walls on two sides were almost hidden behind various pieces of medical equipment and monitors. All that remained of the original furniture were a white
table—stained with paint and spilled brush cleaner—and a couple
of yellow armchairs, one of which was pulled up next to the hospital-

style bed near the far wall. A bed table with art supplies and a stretched white canvas standing on a small easel had been placed nearby. A stocky middle-aged woman in nurse's scrubs and practical shoes occupied the chair, but she jumped up when we came in.

"It's all right, Eva," Lily Goss said, waving her back. "Sit down. If Julie doesn't need anything, you might as well rest." Goss looked at me. "This is one of Julianne's nurses, Eva Wrothen. She was kind enough to come early today so I could go out for a while. And that is Richard Stymak. He's a medium."

I turned my head to look down the table at the man who had just come out of what I guessed was the bathroom. He was a burly, bearded guy with a geeky air to him, wavy red-blond hair brushing his collar, and a T-shirt with a logo I couldn't identify peeping out from under his unbuttoned dress shirt.

He raised a hand in a token wave, seeming a bit embarrassed to have shown evidence of bodily functions—as if those who commune with spirits don't do that sort of thing. "Hi. Um . . . I've been monitoring and recording Julianne's activities for Lily and trying to contact whoever or whatever is doing this."

"Any luck?" I asked, hearing Wrothen snort in derision behind me.

"Depends on how you define that. Lots of ghosts around, but they aren't talking to me." Then he drew an excited breath and perked up, staring over my shoulder toward the bed. "Oh! She's up!"

"No, she's not," the nurse snapped, looking at the monitors and making rapid notes on an electronic clipboard. "Her blood pressure is up, and she's upright, but she's not awake."

"I didn't say she was awake," Stymak objected.

Ignoring the argument, Goss rushed toward the bed and I followed her.

The patient—sickeningly thin, her dark hair hanging limp around her head—was sitting rigidly upright in the bed and staring straight ahead as her left hand groped across the bedspread for something.

Goss snatched a flat paintbrush from a jar on the nearby table and put it next to her sister's seeking hand. Julianne grabbed it, but nothing else in her body or face seemed to react. I could see the silvery mist of the Grey coiling around her in a thick, moving mass. A clutter of shadows pushed and boiled near the bed, then began to draw aside as the patient started painting on the bedspread.

Goss pushed the table with the easel over to the bed and into place in front of Julianne, who transferred the brush to the canvas. The patient daubed at the canvas with the empty brush for a moment before she swung her arm suddenly to swirl it in paint from the art supply table. She moved no more of her body than her arm, not turning or looking at what she was doing. Then she went back to the canvas, painting with rapid movements.

I drew closer, peering at her. Her aura hadn't changed since I'd entered the room, but something opaque and dark now hung over her left arm and side, wrapping around her back. Her half-open eyes were focused not on the canvas or the supplies near her, but slightly upward and far away. Her mouth was slack. Goss and Wrothen stood on either side of the head of the bed while I moved closer and then past the foot of the bed, more interested in watching Julianne than seeing what she was painting. Stymak was somewhere behind and to my right, but I didn't spare any attention for him.

The unconscious woman hit me in the face with the paintbrush. No one really expects a vegetative patient to flip a brush loaded with sage green paint into their eye from six feet away, but I suppose I should have seen it coming—I'm a ghost magnet. I wasn't sure who or what might be in charge of Julianne Goss's body at the moment, but it seemed to have a juvenile sense of humor; right after the paint came the babbling.

I reeled back a few steps.

"Turn on the recorder!" Stymak yelled.

"I can't see it! You turn it on!" I shouted back, swiping thick, sticky oil paint off my face and hoping nothing else was winging my way while I was temporarily blind. You wouldn't think oil and pigment would sting so much. . . .

I could hear Stymak and Goss scrambling around me to get to the table where the digital recorder lay. An alarm was going off from one of the machines monitoring Julianne's bodily functions. I held still in spite of an urge to help—which in my state would be no help at all; I didn't want to blunder into the machines by mistake and I could feel the paint starting to burn my eye. I really needed to get to the sink without falling into anyone's path or crashing into anything vital, but I couldn't find the bathroom without aid. I cursed my inability to get out of my own damned way, much less get a look at what was happening to Julianne Goss. I squeezed my eyes closed and took a deep breath, shutting out the distractions in the room as I sank into the Grey.

Even with my eyes closed, the ghost world lay bright before me, all white fog and colored light reflecting on clouds of lucid steam. I wound around the churning movement of people and the bright tangles that were ghosts in the room, heading toward the dull heaviness of man-made walls, searching for a sink. The uproar and activity distracted me a little, so I stumbled a bit, hearing the bustle and chatter of the people behind me as I searched for the bathroom. Julianne Goss continued to speak flowing, foreign-sounding words while her sister and the medium argued with the nurse.

I bumped through a doorway into a room that felt much colder and harder than the bedroom, found a sink by feel, and washed off as much of the oily goop as I could, wiping more of it away with a towel. I blinked and looked up into the bathroom mirror, seeing moth-wing streaks on my cheekbones that my swiping with the towel had left behind. My eyes were watering and I blinked some more to clear my vision. It didn't help much, but I could at least see somewhat more normally. I'd still have to rely on my Grey sight to see any details, though, and that wasn't usually an accurate view of the world. But it might be helpful, since, after all, it was ghosts I was here to see.

When I got back to the bedroom, the hubbub had died away. The alarm was no longer squealing and no one was shouting. Julianne had flopped back into her bed, silent and sleeping, the paintbrush she'd wielded now dropped to the floor, leaving a new blob of color among the others on the plastic sheeting under her bed. Lily was hovering close to the bed as the nurse took Julianne's temperature. Stymak leaned against a table nearby, wearing headphones and poking at his digital recorder. Between and around them all lay a swarming sea of ghost-stuff boiling with faces that appeared and dissolved again, and sudden extrusions of body parts that fell away into silver mist after a moment's manifestation. I wanted to see the people in the room better as well, but my left eye stung too badly to make the strain of peering at them seem fun, so I resigned myself to looking primarily at the ghosts.

There were quite a few, mostly the sort of thin, colorless things that haven't much will of their own left, if any—repeaters, I call them—who continue to go through the same loop of memory over and over endlessly. I was surprised to see so many of them, since they aren't the sort to go wandering around looking for someone to talk to; usually they just sit in the place their memory loop had lodged and run through the motions until something wipes them away. These had moved from wherever they were usually stuck and clustered around Julianne Goss, continuing their endless loops—walking, talking, and gesturing out of context. There were a few brighter, more colorful ghosts in the misty sea of spirits and I knew they were more likely to have some information I could use—if I could get them to talk to me. So far none of them had turned any attention my way, which was unusual, since specters are usually attracted to me. But these just pressed close to Julianne.

"Someel vague . . ." the ghosts muttered.

"What?" I asked.

Someone touched my shoulder and I jumped, turning away from the voice and squinting to see who in the normal world had grabbed me. The nurse peered at my face from a few inches away, her breath smelling of lemon-flavored candies and the glimmer of a gold chain peeping from under her collar. "What happened?" she demanded. "Your eye is red and irritated and it looks like some swelling is coming on." She hesitated before she asked, "Did Julianne hit you with something?"

"The paintbrush," I said.

"Eyewash."

"No, really, the paintbrush," I repeated.

Wrothen gave an irritated sigh. "Back you go to the bathroom. You need to rinse that eye properly or it'll get worse. You have any idea what nasty chemicals are in paint? Come on."

She wasn't anywhere near my height, but we probably weighed about the same, and she had no difficulty turning me around and dragging me back to the sink. Stocky, bossy women have a towing advantage over bemused beanpole chicks like me. I also couldn't get over feeling it's just wrong to belt a nurse in the chops.

Wrothen pushed me down to sit on the edge of the bathtub, draped a towel around my shoulders, and did mildly uncomfortable things to my eye involving a lot of liquid that managed to dribble into my ears, the corners of my mouth, and down onto my shirt and jeans in spite of precautions. But it did take the worst of the sting away.

"Well," she huffed as she puttered around me, "at least we don't have to listen to Mr. Stymak's 'ghost recording' while we're in here."

"You don't want to hear it?" I asked.

"I do not. I hear quite enough from him and his digital recorder as it is."

"So you don't believe Miss Goss is, umm . . ."

"Possessed? Frankly, I don't know what's going on and I certainly won't go flinging words like that around in a sickroom. It only makes people upset. There's plenty of things to worry about here without adding demons into the mix."

"What do you think is causing Miss Goss's unexpected activity?" I had to splutter around a fall of bitter liquid.

"Sorry," Wrothen said, patting some of the eyewash off my face. "I said I don't know and I don't. If I had any idea what's going on with any of the patients that are experiencing this, I'd do something about it. But you see I'm not able to. In Miss Goss's state she shouldn't be able to sit up and start painting or babble crazy words that mean nothing."

Was she implying there were more PVS patients like Julianne? I wanted to ask, but I didn't want to shut down her current chattiness on the case at hand. "How long has this been going on?" I asked as she poured more liquid over my eyes. I couldn't decide if it was terrifying or just creepy.

"I can't discuss it."

"I'm not interested in the case details, just how long she's been doing odd things."

"I'm not sure. I haven't been here the whole time. She was already painting when I started on the case."

"What about the other patients?"

"What other patients?" she replied, sounding defensive.

"You said other patients are experiencing this. What other patients? How many?"

She hesitated, scowling.

"I'm not asking for names or details, but surely the fact there are other patients going through what Miss Goss is experiencing is unusual. How many are there?"

Wrothen looked stormy, but a tiny spark leapt off her aura. "I've only heard of two." She gave me a quelling look so pointed I could see it even in my bleary state. "And it's not something I'll discuss further."

Chastened, I changed tack. "Well, then, how long have you worked for Ms. Goss—for the patient's sister?"

Wrothen patted at my face again, wiping off excess eyewash. "A little more than three months. Blink, please. How does that feel?"

I blinked and my vision cleared a bit, but it was still a little blurry and some of the irritation remained. I told her so.

"You need to see your doctor. He might want to give you something in case there's some damage." She whisked off the towel and started to shoo me back into the other room.

I stopped and turned back. "Wait," I said. "These other patients—"

Wrothen gave me a hard look. "I can't give you any information about that."

"I just think it's interesting that there are others. I thought this sort of thing wasn't supposed to happen."

"It *doesn't* happen. Vegetative patients don't just sit up and start . . . painting pictures, or writing nonsense, or speaking in tongues. Or talking. Now excuse me. I have to mark up the chart and send a note to the doctor about this incident. Don't put too much store by what that 'medium' says—or Ms. Goss. She's under his spell and I think it's terrible the way he's preying on her fears." She brushed past me, leaving me in the bathroom with a wet face, stinging eyes, and a host of questions.

In a moment I returned to the bedroom. Things were still a little blurry and the Grey persisted more than I liked, but I could see the living people in the room a bit more clearly. Wrothen had gone to a small desk on wheels near the monitors and was working at a computer keyboard. Lillian Goss and Richard Stymak were bending over the white table, listening to the digital recorder through small headphones. I wondered why they weren't using earbuds, but I suppose some people don't care for sticking things in their ears—or they'd been intimidated out of doing so by Wrothen, who I imagined wouldn't approve of earbuds just on principle.

I went to the table and loomed until they noticed me and looked up from their concentrated staring at the recorder—the way one does when there's nothing to look at and too much to hear. Lily Goss glanced up first and motioned at Stymak to stop the playback. Then they both pulled off their headphones and blinked at me.

"Have you . . . got any idea what's happening to my sister?" Goss asked.

"Well, not really. Not yet. I need to know more—to observe more—which is not possible at the moment. The paint that got into my eye seems to have messed up my vision. I'd like to come back after I've seen a doctor and discuss this with you both. And I'd like to hear that recording." I doubted it was going to be case-breaking—since that kind of thing only happens in TV shows—but I wanted all the data I could get.

"I can make you a copy," Stymak offered.

"Could you e-mail the file?"

He nodded. "I sure can. It's large, but if I can't e-mail it, I'll send you a secure link you can use to download it. I've got more if you want them."

Yep, he was definitely a geek. My turn to nod. "All right. But let's start with just the one, thanks." I turned back to Lily. "I'll call you to coordinate a time to return, if that's OK with you."

"Oh. Yes. Of course. I . . . I'm the only one here from four to midnight. . . ."

"I understand. I'll be in touch, but probably not tonight. Get some rest, Ms. Goss." I found myself patting her shoulder—a ridiculous gesture I didn't usually indulge in—and turning away to let myself out, but she rushed to walk with me.

As she opened the front door, Lily Goss touched my arm in a hesitant fashion. "Umm . . . I'm sorry . . . about your eye."

"I'm sure it's not a major injury and it was an accident."

"I'm not. Sure, that is. Julie's been . . . unpredictable lately. She didn't used to talk. Now she babbles like you heard today. And she's never thrown anything before. I am—truly—sorry."

I wished she'd mentioned the talking and throwing things earlier, but I only said, "Nothing to be sorry for. I'm not quitting. I'll be back."

She bit her lip and nodded, frowning and disbelieving me. But I would be back—I wanted to know what was going on with Julianne as much as she did. There were ghosts, and there was something guiding her actions—if not actually possessing her body, which I wasn't quite sure of.

I did, however, need to do something about my eye. The longer I let it go, the more the sting came back. Unlike another Greywalker I'd met, I had no desire to give up my sight—either Grey or normal. I'd gotten used to seeing the invisible, but it was not an adequate substitute for the normal view.

My eyes were watering badly by the time I got in to see my doctor, who sent me to an ophthalmologist for some kind of chemical test, who in turn sent me back to Dr. Skelleher with the results—dealing with the labyrinth of health care and insurance can be a royal pain in the ass, not to mention the time it takes.

Skelleher's an odd young duck, but he understands my situation as much as any medical professional is ever likely to and he doesn't believe there's a pill for every problem. He gave my eyes a good looking-over and read through the ophthalmologist's report. He always looked rumpled and sleepless, though a bit less so than usual today—his spiky hair might actually have been styled that way rather than having happened by accident. He had a small following of ghosts standing just behind him everywhere he went. They didn't seem hostile and he was oblivious to them and any dampening effect they might have had; his aura was bright and colorful, shifting through gold and pink and shimmering, pale blue. Maybe he finally had a girlfriend—or a boyfriend; I had no idea what revved his engine. Whatever it was, he was tired, but pretty content with his life, which is something I rarely get to see.

He plopped onto the backless stool and took a deep breath before giving me the news. "You have some chemical irritation to the lid and sclera. It's fairly mild, but it's going to feel uncomfortable and itchy for a few days and may cause you to have some minor vision problems—blurry vision, watering, and so on. Like the ophthalmologist, I'd advise you to rest your eyes as much as possible, but I know you'll ignore that. Try anyhow. Dr. Michaels prescribed some drops for the pain and some ointment to clear up the irritation, which you need to use twice a day, as I'm sure he told you. If the irritation doesn't clear up with these meds, I'll have to insist on your going back to Dr. Michaels. And I know you don't like to do that. Also, don't rub your eye. At all. Use the drops and make sure you *pat* any excess or tears off with a tissue. No wiping with your fingertips or the corner of your shirt or stuff like that.

"If you start seeing anything weird . . . Well, that's pretty much normal for you, so let me rephrase that: If the irritation gets worse or you seem to be losing sight, seeing dark spots, having an unusual degree of tearing or blurring, bloody tears, literally seeing red, or the eyelid swells significantly, take yourself to Emergency. And I mean it. You do not want a major eye infection—at least the green pigment wasn't radioactive, so you missed that complication. But I will bust your chops about it if you don't do as you've been told."

"Whoa, Skelly! Nice bedside manner."

He shook his head. "Seriously. This is not something you can ignore. Chemical burns create conditions that can lead to severe infections and we don't do eyeball transplants. And I shouldn't have to remind you that your eyes are in your skull, very close to your brain, and you really don't want massive infections anywhere near the blood/brain barrier."

"I'm sorry I sounded flippant. I understand the implications." I didn't have to pretend to be abashed. "And I know I'm a difficult patient."

"Actually, you're not. But you are stubborn and prone to extraordinary accidents."

I couldn't argue against that. After all, Skelly had treated me for monster bites, ribs broken by ghosts, and any number of more usual injuries from physical confrontations. Not to mention a small case of being dead once or twice.

"I promise to do as instructed. I'll go straight home and rest my eyes. But can I ask you a question first?"

Skelly pushed his hands through his hair and gave me a tired smile. "Sure."

"What can you tell me about persistent vegetative states?"

"PVS?"

I nodded. "Yeah."

"Why do you ask?"

"I have a case that touches on it."

"Ah. Well, I can't talk about specific cases and I'm not a neurologist but I can give you a broad rundown. Do you know what a PVS is?"

"It's like a coma, isn't it?"

"No. It's a separate thing. Coma is a short-term state that mimics very deep sleep—it only lasts hours to a few days while the cortex of the brain is severely traumatized. Then the patient either dies because the brain can't survive the trauma, or they move on to a vegetative state where they may respond to some stimuli, may seem to be awake for a few minutes at a time, but they aren't actually aware. Usually that state lasts a few days—a couple of weeks at most—while the brain heals from whatever trauma caused the initial coma, and after that the patient wakes up and resumes normal response to stimuli—or as much as they can.

"This kind of thing happens in . . . say, meningitis cases or head trauma cases and usually resolves one way or the other very quickly. But if the patient's state doesn't change—if they don't wake up and start responding to stimuli after four weeks—we call it a persistent vegetative state, or PVS. To most people it still looks like deep sleep, but the patient may seem to respond to some stimuli and to do things like sigh, laugh, or cry. It may seem like they're aware, but it's just autonomic function. They are actually nonresponsive because the brain stem is functioning but higher functions are shut down."

"So, is this common?"

"Oh no. PVS is rare. Comas aren't common, so the states that evolve from them are even less so, and most—as I said—resolve long before a persistent state occurs. I've never actually seen a case of coma or PVS in my career. Most non-neurologists don't unless they work in emergency or trauma. And then there are fugue states, which are psychiatric cases of personality disassociation in which the patient has periods of amnesia and denies actions they undertook at that time—not just don't remember, but actively deny doing them. Fugue states can be related to temporal lobe epilepsy, schizophrenia, and multiple personality disorder," he added, ticking them off on his fingers.

I shook my head. "That's not the situation here. The person in question is literally bedridden and seems to be asleep, but she keeps sitting up and painting compulsively. But I have to say, she doesn't really seem to be 'there' when it happens."

Skelleher stared at me. "You saw this?"

I nodded.

"When?"

"Today. That's how I got paint in my eye—the patient flipped her brush at me while she was painting, but it was more like she was a puppet being operated by someone else because she didn't actually open her eyes or seem to respond to anyone in the room. And then she started babbling and lay back down."

"That's . . . that's impossible. Not even in a minimally conscious state would that happen. It has to be a hoax."

"Unless the home care nurses are in on it, I don't think so. I hear there may be other PVS patients in town who are doing similar things. . . ."

Skelly seemed appalled. "Really? That's freaky."

"You haven't heard about them?"

"I'm a GP. When would I have *time* to hear about even the weirdest case that's not on my ward or watch? I didn't know there were *any* PVS patients in the city until you mentioned it. It's really that rare. If they're all doing strange things I'd expect the neurologists to be in a lather over it. I'm surprised they haven't called a conference."

"Do you think I could talk to the other people involved with those cases . . . ?"

"No. Not through me or any other medical professional. Patient confidentiality is sacrosanct. If you think it's true and connected to whatever case you're working, you'll have to find another way."

He looked uncomfortable; I understood his position and didn't push him. I shouldn't have asked in the first place, but the coincidence of three rare cases that might all be doing the same impossible things set off every investigatory instinct I had, and I had to understand what was usual before I could reasonably judge what wasn't. I'd have to find the others by myself somehow and determine what was going on, because one strange manifestation is just a case, but three could be, as Auric Goldfinger said, enemy action. And I didn't have any living enemies that I knew of. Dead and restless ones . . . *that* I wasn't so sure of.

TWO

I did get home all right, in spite of my eye. The itching, aching, watering aspects weren't the worst of it; my left eye simply would not banish the Grey from sight, even when I was surrounded by the filtering effects of glass and steel in my truck. When I'd first become aware of the Grey it had, for a while, been persistently visible until I learned to filter it out. At the moment, no amount of trying would allow me to see without a flickering, color-tangled overlay of the ghost world so long as I had both eyes open. If I closed the injured eye, the vision merely changed intensity, but at least my eye was less raw. I hoped this wasn't going to last too long. . . .

I felt like a slacker coming home so early, but I wasn't going to get anything done at the office or on the street with my eye objecting nonstop. As I opened the door to my condo, a furry little blur raced out, crossing my boot and streaking into the hall.

"Ferret!" came a warning cry from inside. Apparently Quinton— my . . . "boyfriend" doesn't quite cover it, but it's close enough for most applications—had been hanging out at my place. He often did, but there had been some risky circumstances in his life recently and the frequency and duration of his companionship had become unpredictable.

"Too late," I called back, dropping my bag and spinning around, hoping to catch the fuzzy miscreant before she managed to get outside, underfoot, or into one of the neighbors' homes. Visions of the Grey and the normal slid and tipped over each other, making me dizzy, and I wobbled, stumbling into the wall and sliding down to my knees.

"Sneaky little carpet shark!" Quinton charged out and tripped over me, falling face-first onto the carpet outside my door. "Blast!" We both scrambled around, getting only semi-upright before lurching farther along the hall like a pair of gorillas as we tried to snatch the ferret from the floor.

Chaos, the ferret, flipped around, dancing backward out of our grasp, chuckling and chattering at us as if we were the funniest show on earth. Until she backed into a door and her progress came to a sudden halt. For just a moment, her back end attempted to climb vertically up the door, but gravity was still operating and her butt slipped back down, piling into her middle. She sprang up, swiveling to face the new threat, and smacked her nose into the immovable object. With a chirp of surprise, she leapt away from the door, showing it her teeth by waving her open mouth in its direction, and backed straight into Quinton's scooping hand.

"Got ya! Victory is mine—because I have thumbs and you don't!"

The ferret stuck her head out of his fist and licked her nose as if this was all very boring.

I put out my hands. "Do you want me to take her?"

"Nope. It was my miscalculation that let her out and I'll be the one to put her back." He blinked at my face. "Umm . . . did you have one of those 'interesting' days today? Because you look like someone clocked you."

"Painted me in the eye actually. And yes—a little too interesting. I'll tell you in a minute. Maybe over a drink."

Quinton raised his eyebrows.

I nodded. "That kind of day. All right—you carry the furry offender back to ferret prison."

Chaos was not pleased to be returned to her cage so I could put my things away without tripping over her on my semi-blind side. Ferrets tend to want to dance right in your path and I didn't want to fall down again or—worse—step on her. But she was tiny, warm, and fuzzy, which went a small distance to making me feel less annoyed.

Quinton let me retire to the couch while he dug up a couple of beers as well as a cool, wet cloth to put on my irritated eye. I did my impression of a slug and slumped on the cushions as if my bones had dissolved, closing my eyes and letting the half-Grey effect of my injury reel forth in silver streamers against the darkness inside my eyelids. I heard Quinton bumping and rattling in the kitchen and saw a glowing energetic mist-shape moving in the persistent Grey that had invaded my mind's eye. There were several other odd shapes floating about in the limited vision that played out behind my closed lids, but I couldn't identify who or what they were—ghosts, neighbors, random knots of energy . . . ? They weren't really doing anything that I could understand, just moving here and there. Only Quinton's shape seemed to be operating with conscious intent. It drifted over and I felt him nudge my hand with something cool.

"You said you'd like a drink."

I opened my eyes, finding that the lids seemed heavier than usual, and glanced first up at him, then down to the glass he was holding next to my hand. The small glass had half an inch of amber-gold liquid at the bottom. "Whiskey?"

"It didn't sound like a mystery beer sort of day," he replied, alluding to his habit of accepting payment in beer for odd jobs done for various street people we knew around Pioneer Square.

I took the glass. "Definitely not." While the drink was welcome, I would rather have had the energy to ravish him. A warm sensation in my chest and a wicked glint in his eye gave me the impression he was thinking the same thing. Oh well . . .

He sat next to me as I sipped and covered my free hand with his. "So, what about this day of yours?"

"Well, a client's sister flipped a blob of paint into my eye. Turns out oil paint has quite a few nasty things in it—before you start: I already saw the doctor—and I need to give the eye a little rest. But I also need to figure out what's going on with the sister."

"In what way? She has a habit of flipping paint at people?"

"No. This is kind of delicate ground since I'm breaking confidentiality to discuss it, but I don't know how else I'm going to get to the bottom of this if I can't talk to a few people about the case—or cases—but I'll get to that bit in a minute."

"I won't discuss it with anyone."

I nodded before going on. "OK. The sister is in some kind of vegetative state—kind of like a coma but not. Anyhow, she shouldn't be doing much of anything beyond lying still, but in the past few months, she's started sitting up and painting. Even more recently she started babbling. She doesn't appear to be doing this on her own but rather seems to be either under someone else's control or channeling a ghost or something that's using her body for a few minutes at a time before it drops out or gets pushed out. I don't know anything else yet, but the home care nurse let slip that there are two other cases like this—vegetative patients doing strange things—and Skelly was surprised to hear there were any vegetative patients at all in the area, since it's very rare, much less that they were doing impossible things." I paused to sip my drink, appreciating the warm sensation of the liquor making its way down and expanding the calm and security that spread from Quinton's touch on my hand.

"Now," I continued, "you know me. I can't swallow that all of the rare cases in the area are exhibiting the same strange behaviors for unrelated reasons."

"Mathematically unlikely," Quinton agreed.

"So there has to be either a link or a related cause. And before I got paint in my eye, I could see that the room was pretty heavily haunted. Most of the ghosts weren't of the willful variety—there were a lot of displaced repeaters there. I'd like to get in contact with the families of the other PVS patients and find out what's been happening to them, maybe get to see them and evaluate the ghost situation. The client initially broached the subject as a possible spirit or demonic possession. She's religious and apparently this is causing her more than the usual crisis experienced by the haunted. Her priest isn't being very helpful—something about the limits of his role, which is frankly beyond my knowledge and probably not germane."

Quinton made a disgusted face. "Is he blaming her in some way? Making the situation out to be some kind of punishment for sin?"

"I don't get that sense, but apparently he, or the church in question, doesn't support the Catholic idea of demonic possession and exorcism, so she's mostly been told to sit tight and pray. Which hasn't been helping, that the client can see. So she's desperate and very upset and she's hoping I can figure out what's going on. What she expects to happen after that is anyone's guess. I suppose she'll want to get rid of the unwanted visitors, but she hasn't said that or how she'd prefer to see it done. She has hired a medium to sit with her sister and try to converse with whoever or whatever is coming around, but the medium hasn't had a lot of luck. The babbling appears to be the only communication they're receiving and that seems to be in a foreign language."

"Wow. Does the sister know any foreign languages?"

"I don't know, but if so, I'm guessing either it's not one her sister also knows or it's not a language at all." I took another sip of whiskey and sighed, closing my burning eyes again and tilting my head back against the sofa cushions. "The medium took a digital recording of today's outburst and said he'd send it to me—"

"Wait," Quinton interrupted me. "A male medium? Isn't that a bit unusual?"

"I don't know. As far as I've ever seen, mediums are universally charlatans, regardless of gender."

"Do you really have room to make that accusation, Harper?"

I pressed my lips hard together and didn't say anything until I'd thought about it first. "I'm not a medium. I don't act as an intermediary to spirits or wandering souls—which is what a medium supposedly does. I don't act as a conduit for their voices or actions, either. I don't even talk to them in that context. So, no. I'm not a medium. But you're right. My experience isn't everyone's and it's unfair of me to assume that there aren't people with other skills related to the Grey. I know witches, shape-shifters, necromancers, sorcerers, vampires, shamans, and plenty of others who have some touch with the Grey that is unlike mine. So I should keep an open mind about whether there might be such a thing as a legitimate medium or channeler." I opened one eye and peered at him. "And that being the case, you should be equally open-minded about the gender of any mediums that might be running around this case. This one is male and blond and a bit on the pudgy side, none of which is part of the stereotype, anyhow." I closed my eye again.

"And he uses a digital recorder?"

"Even TV ghost hunters have moved on to high technology."

"Yeah, but they aren't likely to be hanging around you while I'm distracted by ruining my dad's career."

"Is that your latest project?" I asked.

"It's a frequent enough accusation that I've decided to make it my life's work, if I have to." He didn't sound at all jocular about it. Quinton's relationship with his father was even uglier than mine had been with my mother until a couple of years ago. James Purlis was an unrepentant manipulator and a professional liar—he was a spy, after all. He worked for some covert branch of the government, running the sort of bizarre and creepy projects featuring alien autopsies or psychics attempting to kill goats with the power of their minds that you usually see only on cheesy documentaries running on late-night TV. Except, in his case, the "Ghost Division" wasn't a scam or a joke and he was deadly serious about it—whatever it was. He had also seemed set on sucking Quinton back into the espionage business ever since he had confirmed that his son wasn't dead.

That was my fault. If I hadn't gone off to get myself killed, Quinton wouldn't have broken his cover and ended up asking his father for help. I tried not to feel bad about it, not because I wasn't guilty but because Quinton didn't like it and tended to tell me off. Aren't we a fun couple? Though I will admit to a certain degree of sinful glee anytime a wrench was thrown into the elder Purlis's works—more so if I got to throw the wrench, since I'd disliked him from the first moment we met and he knocked me down.

"Your dad's a jerk," I said. "And I promise not to fall in love with any pudgy blond mediums or their digital recorders while you're busy reminding him of that."

"All right, then."

"Hey," I added, peeling open my eyes again and looking at him. "Can I get a promise from you, too?"

His slightly stiff expression broke and he smiled. "Sure. I'd promise you anything."

"I only want small things. Don't let him snatch you and if you have to run, let me know you're not dead. Oh, and that, too."

"What too?"

"Don't get dead. I'm the only one in this family who's allowed to play that game."

He leaned over and pulled me into his arms. As he spoke, his voice trembled just a little. "That's a lousy game. Let's not play it at all." He squeezed me and I squeezed back, breathless. "And . . . uh . . . what do you mean 'family'?" he asked. "Is there something I don't know?"

I puzzled that one for a moment and gasped once I got it. "Oh. No. No imminent pitter-patter of little geek-feet. Just you, me, and about three million ghosts."

He laughed and I thought he sounded relieved. "Damn, this town's got more dead people than live ones."

"Most do."

"Then we shouldn't add to the population."

"I wasn't planning to."

He kissed me. "You never do."

"Hey, the last guy I shot was already dead."

"Come to think of it, the last guy I shot was, too. Although he was a zombie, so does that really count?"

"I vote no. Doesn't count."

"I vote for dinner."

I wriggled a bit in his arms, but didn't have the energy to push away and look at him—I couldn't even get my eyes to open properly. "Dinner? How romantic after zombies."

"I was thinking more of the fact that you sound like you're about to fall asleep and food might be a good idea."

I gave up resisting and put my head on his chest. "OK. It is a good idea. Whiskey was probably not. But I still appreciated it. You're my knight in silicon armor."

"I think I'd rather be the frisky rogue in stealth motley."

"How can motley be stealthy?"

"How is a hipster like a cheap hot pad?"

"What?" I asked, not sure I'd heard that correctly. I felt very sleepy. . . .

"I asked you how a hipster is like a hot pad."

"Umm . . . they both look ridiculous with a mustache?"

"No. They both only think they're cool."

"I'm not sure that explains how motley can be stealthy."

"It doesn't, but I need to get up and find some food for you. If you're laughing, it's easier to change the subject."

"Oh. I hear there's some food hiding in the fridge."

"Was it Chinese food? Because if so, its hiding place was discovered and ravaged by terrorists."

"Terrorist forks, I presume."

"Chopsticks. I would never send a lone fork against Chinese leftovers. Totally against all conventions of food warfare."

I started giggling and could barely say, "So you're the food terrorist."

"I admit it. And I'd do it again—for Queen and Country. Or at least for lunch."

I kept giggling and Quinton let me slump back into my corner of the couch with my eyes still closed while he picked up my whiskey glass and returned to the kitchen. I could follow his movement through the Grey fog version of the room and was content with that, not even sure I was going to be awake whenever food was ready to eat, and pretty sure I wasn't going to care.

The smell of food perked me up a bit. Quinton persuaded me to move to the kitchen table instead of trying to eat while sitting on the couch on the supposition that I was less likely to suffocate in my dish if I was upright. The ferret was not invited to join us for dinner and she snubbed us by sleeping in her cage the whole time instead.

Quinton brought the case up again once I'd gotten a few bites down. "Do you think your case is a legitimate haunting?"

"Not a haunting, a possession. Although they do fall into the general category of hauntings, in this particular situation the possession doesn't appear to be related to the location or to an object—which is usually the case with classical hauntings. I'm not that familiar with haunted houses, since I've only seen a few personally, but this doesn't have the same feel at all."

"Is that why you want to talk to the other patients you heard about? After all, they aren't your clients."

"That's exactly why. If the cases are significantly similar, then I'll have more information to give my client. It's really weird that there are so many to begin with and that these are all demonstrating aberrant behavior. Skelly said even one normal PVS case in an area the size of Seattle is rare. So this is freakishly beyond statistical probability. I'm not sure how I'll find the other patients, though. Skelly had no idea and warned me off of asking anyone to violate patient confidentiality. Which is fine, but it does leave me unsure how to get the info I need."

"Can you ask the ghosts?"

"Which ghosts? I'm not sure who or what is controlling my client's sister and I wasn't able to make any contact in the time I had in the room. They seem very concentrated on the patient. That may be the same problem Stymak—the medium—is having. He may not be able to break into their communication with the patient long enough to get any useful information and has to try to pick through the bits that he can capture on the recordings."

"Yeah, but he's at least getting that much. You could try working with him to get the ghosts' attention and find out who the other patients are. As you pointed out, it's unlikely that the cases are unrelated, so there should be information about the other patients in the collective knowledge of the ghosts hanging out around your client's sister."

"Interesting idea. Can't hurt."

I finished up my dinner and felt much better, if still a bit blind. While I was doing dishes, Quinton checked something on the tiny palmtop computer he'd started carrying around and began packing up his things.

"Hey," I said, "you going somewhere?"

"Yeah. I have to get out and rattle some cages, create some uncertainty, undermine some progress. . . . I may need your help later, but for now I'd better get to it."

"Will you be back later tonight?" I hoped I didn't sound too wistful.

"Not tonight. If you get any odd phone calls, act normal and pretend you've never heard of me."

I raised my eyebrows. "Okaayy . . . I can do that, stranger."

He put on his jacket and slung his backpack onto his shoulders. "Thanks, beautiful." Then he kissed me and hurried off to wreak some havoc, I supposed. I hoped it wouldn't come home with him, whatever it was.

It was still light outside, so once I was done with the dishes and had let the ferret out again, I went ahead and called Richard Stymak, who seemed less surprised to hear from me than I might have liked. He offered to meet me at the Goss house the next morning, saying Julianne tended to be less dramatically active in the mornings than she had been today. I decided I'd keep a much closer eye on her nonetheless. Ghosts are unpredictable and I didn't want to end up with something worse than paint flung at me.

THREE

As he'd expected, Quinton had not come home and I slept alone and got up in a strange mood, as if I'd been emotionally disconnected from the world and was floating along waiting for some feeling to rush into the void. Outside, Seattle was experiencing the usual "June gloom" of weird overcast that would give way late in the day to cool sunshine until the clouds slid back in for the night, the pattern seeming unbreakable even on the last day of the month. It made my city seem a little detached from the rest of the country, as if it just couldn't make up its mind about summer.

When I reached the Goss house and Lily had escorted me back up to the former master bedroom, I saw that, once again, Julianne was painting. Lily left me to go and sit by her side. She seemed to have as little interest in Stymak and me as Julianne did at that moment. Stymak was doing something with his digital recorder at the white table again and no nurse was in evidence. I'd been left momentarily alone just inside the room's double doors. I took the chance to look the room over, since there seemed to be no threat of flying blobs at the moment, and see what I'd missed the first time.

I started with Julianne's latest painting on the easel—a rough cliff with some kind of low, rambling building along the top. The strokes were soft and yet precise, in spite of the speed with which they were being made. I almost recognized the place, but not quite. It didn't look like a modern location; it looked more like something old and almost forgotten. I turned aside and surveyed the next piece, which was leaning against the wall nearby: a huge, rugged mountain of sharp sandstone-colored bluffs and smoky shadows rearing up against a lowering charcoal sky—draped in soft white scarves of cloud—from a foggy forest of tiny pines that clustered at its foot like anxious pets. My breath caught in my throat as I studied it. I didn't exactly recognize this scene, either, but for a different reason—this one didn't seem to be a real place so much as one that recalled real Washington places; it was strange and familiar and powerful, glistening with paint still wet a day later and the threads of some passing ghost form that had caught and lingered in the moisture. I turned slowly around to look at the other paintings in the room—most hung on the walls around the main doors and leading toward the bathroom, others just leaned against the wall. Dozens of paintings.

They were not the same. Some shared a similar style, but the rest varied as widely as an art school exhibition. There were some with strong colors and blocky forms; others were almost photo-realistic in their detail, picked out in clear shafts of sunlight and minuscule brushwork. Still others were more like sketches, lines of color roughly brushed to create just a shape or suggestion of a scene. This could not be the work of a single person—certainly not a bedridden, nonresponsive woman with the muscle tone of a limp towel. And over and over, the same scenes: the cliff, the mountain, a long beach of rock-strewn sand bordered by soaring pines in shades of green and gray marching up steep slopes to higher ground.

And all around the bed pressed a susurrant surge of spirits, like flotsam circling round and round the center of a maelstrom, drawn to the way out but unable to escape. I'd seen ghosts pulled to an object before, but I'd never seen this sort of expression. If I stared very hard, making my injured eye water, I could perceive among the dark shapes and writhing scribbles of energy individual ghosts reaching toward Julianne, or bending down to whisper into her ears and being swept aside again as the next moved closer. They kept circling, whispering, reaching. . . .

"I've never seen anything like this," I said.

"Automatic painting," Stymak said. "Like automatic writing. The spirit is channeled through the subject's body and produces the work independent of the channel's abilities, often while they are unconscious or in a trance state. Though I've never heard of anything on this scale."

His voice jarred me out of my staring and I turned to him, letting my gaze pull back toward normal, though the Grey vision lingered, shading the room in silver and smoke. "Nor have I, though I do know what automatic painting is, Stymak—but you knew that, since you say you talk to ghosts."

Stymak glanced away for a moment before he looked straight into my eyes. "I don't quite *hear* the dead—I certainly don't *talk* to them. I *feel* them, really. I can't say I *see* them so much as I experience their presence. They whisper to me and I know they're here."

"You can get information from ghosts that aren't in your immediate area?" I had a rusty memory of being told that mediums somehow talked to ghosts in the Grey in such a way that they didn't have to be in the same literal space, unlike me.

Stymak nodded. "They compelled me here a few weeks ago and I met Lily and I saw Julianne and I knew the ghosts were here, that they are trying to tell us something through Julianne, but I can't understand what it is they're trying to communicate this time."

"Why not?"

He shook his head. "It's too loud. It's like . . . there are a hundred people in a tiny room, all shouting different things at the same time. They press in and they recede again like a furious tide, but I can't sort them out. It's like trying to catch a fistful of seawater and separate a single molecule of salt. It's an allegory, but it's real. I can't make it any more clear than that. Not to myself, and probably not to you, either. But you know what I mean. They indicate you do."

"They? The ghosts?" I cast a glance back at them, clustering around the bed, but they didn't seem to pay us any attention.

"Well, the ones that can hold a thought together at least. Your identity is like a thin, clear current in the river of their babble. It was hard to pick out at first, but I finally got it and when I got here and experienced the turmoil around Julianne, I thought I should mention you to Lily."

"*You* mentioned me to Lily? She said she heard about me through Phoebe Mason."

"The owner of Old Possum's?" Stymak asked. "Yes. See, I didn't have your name or know where to find you. I only knew who you were to the ghosts. They knew that you and Lily both knew this bookstore owner—"

"Phoebe."

Stymak nodded. "All right: Phoebe. They let me know the connection, so I told Lily to ask Phoebe about you. And that's how it works for me—strings of connections and associations and ideas, but not anything as easy as a voice saying 'Hey, stupid, go talk to this lady at this address.' Ghosts are kind of slippery and obscure most of the time, but I've learned how to be patient and put it together. Sort of decode them, I guess you could say."

"But you haven't decoded what's going on with Julianne."

"Oh, I have. But I don't know *why*, or what they're trying to tell us."

"Have they let you know there are others?"

"Others like Julianne? Unconscious channels? I'm not sure. . . . The information I've been gifted with is confusing at best and . . . very noisy."

"I'm given to believe it's true. Can you confirm it with your ghosts?"

"Can't you?"

"I haven't tried yet."

"You haven't tried," Stymak echoed, incredulous and staring as if he'd never seen so odd a fish as me. "What sort of medium are you? I mean, I don't have a choice about hearing them. They're in my head, like pieces of my own mind. I can't not try because I don't try to begin with."

I had experienced the inability to tune out Grey voices for a while and it had nearly driven me insane, but I'd died again and the phenomenon had ceased—I was grateful for that, especially since the voices I'd heard had been part of the Grey itself, not just ghosts. "I'm not a medium," I said, shivering at the idea of going through that all the time. "I'm more of a . . . fixer. I work out problems between the normal and the paranormal." Stymak nodded while frowning as if he wasn't sure he saw the distinction. "My contact with the paranormal is less mental and more physical than yours," I explained, but I had the impression he didn't understand that any better.

"I'm sure we all experience it differently," he said.

Of that I was certain, but there was no point in saying so. I glanced around and noticed that Lily was watching our conversation from the corner of her eye as she looked after Julianne—who had stopped painting once again and lain back down. The ghosts had ceased circling the bed and seemed to be moving back, separating, and loosening their bonds to float out and fill the whole room in drifting clouds.

"There," Stymak said. "The ghosts are moving. It's like their attention is changing. Now might be a good time to try and talk to them, before they wander off."

A dark form pushed forward to hover over Julianne, cutting off most of the other spirits. A few of the more self-aware ghosts did seem to be drifting away, as if they were tired of waiting and had decided to go elsewhere, but the repeaters and the barely-there lingered, stuck or unable to leave and moving neither toward the bed nor away from it. They wouldn't be much help.

"Do you want to give it a go together?" Stymak asked.

I was eager to see how Stymak operated—and if he was for real or was just jerking my chain. Not to mention, we'd get more information from the stronger ghosts, who were now starting to pull away. "Sure," I said. "How do you do this?"

"I usually just close my eyes and concentrate on drawing them to me and when they get close enough, I guess we 'talk,' though it's not talking really. What do you do?"

"Kind of similar, except I go to them."

"I'm not sure how that would work."

"How 'bout you take my hand and we'll see what we can do."

Stymak frowned as if he wasn't sure of my sincerity, but he moved closer and put out his right hand. I gave him my left and took a deep breath, waiting for him to close his eyes and do whatever he did.

I let the Grey sight flood over my normal vision as I slipped a bit closer to the land of ghosts, watching Stymak. The distant buzzing, muttering sound of the Grey swelled and, with a jolt of unpleasant surprise, I could hear voices. I hadn't heard voices in the Grey in quite a while and I didn't like the episode they reminded me of, but these weren't quite the same and after a moment's panic I settled myself down and let whatever was happening come to us.

Which was just what it did. The ghosts gathered around Julianne's bed and some of the stronger ones that had started drifting away turned toward Stymak, fixing us in dead gazes. The voices grew louder.

I slid down lower into the Grey, looking for the brightness of the energy grid of magic and finding it suddenly in a swarm of color and silver ghostlight. A bright rope of twined blue and gold energy spun out from Richard Stymak's bright white shape beside me. I'd never seen a living person with a pure white aura before and I wasn't sure what it meant. I watched the rope weave and wave, luring the ghosts toward it, toward Stymak, while a crystalline voice nearest me—Stymak's, I realized, though it sounded different here—called softly, "Hello, hello, I'm here. Come here. Hello . . ."

Three ghosts moved toward him, slowly at first, then rushing as if each wanted to be the first to arrive. Far away I heard a strained voice whispering, "Go away," and the rattling, distant roar of the Guardian Beast. That particular monster that patrolled the borders of the Grey wasn't coming closer, but I suspected it knew we were here. It's an uncanny and unpredictable beast and, for lack of a better description, it's my boss in the Grey, so I wasn't sure if its attentive distance gave me comfort or scared the hell out of me.

The first of the ghosts, a coal gray form with a midnight face, its energy a tangle of fading blue light and dim red points, pushed against Stymak, brushing against me and leaving a scent of burned flesh in its wake. I shuddered at the smell and the strange sensation of jagged bones poking into my skin as if I'd embraced a fractured skeleton. It made a keening sound as the other two rushed up, pressing close to Stymak and jostling for his attention.

The three ghosts babbled in a squealing cacophony that set the rest of the ghosts to howling and jabbering like a mad chorus behind them. I tried to listen, but the words were a jumble, diced into useless sounds.

"One at a time, please," Stymak said, panting. That at least was understandable, though I still wasn't used to the violin-sharp clarity of his Grey voice.

The ghosts didn't listen but continued to push and shove to get his attention, chattering incomprehensibly. I heard Stymak grunt as the darkest one of them shoved unusually hard, rocking him. Stymak's energy dimmed and took on a greenish tone. "Stop! One at a time!" he said, sounding distressed.

I snatched at the pushing spirit and crooked my fingers in its tangled energy, pulling it away from Stymak. "Back off, jerk," I hissed at it, giving it a shake. Flame flashed up my arm and I felt a jolt as the ghost fought back, then faded to a dim shape.

"Someel otsu vagueish . . ." it muttered, crumbling into black ash and blowing away in the swirling of the Grey, not destroyed but exhausted for the time being.

"What?"

But that ghost was gone and another one had pushed itself up to Stymak, talking so low and fast I could barely hear it as more than a chatter of teeth and a clatter of consonants. The last of the three ghosts had something more like a recognizable human face and form over the knot of pale blue energy at its core. It whispered and hissed with the other, the sounds of their voices harmonizing with each other and mixing with the background chorus of ghosts in a quavering dissonance that almost brought sense to the noise, but not quite. I could feel it, like pressure waves, trying to fall into a recognizable pattern but never quite matching up.

I let go of Stymak's hand and reached for the two ghosts. The Grey wavered and shimmered, then realigned itself with a jolt. Stymak shivered, shedding his brightness for a moment before it flared back, not so bright as before but without the green tinge. "Who else is like Julianne?" His voice sang on the Grey.

The ghost chorus replied. "Jorvin. Stermar. Kadon. Derling." Stymak shuddered, but I resisted touching him again. I brushed my tentative fingers against the ghosts and they flushed with a fleeting spectrum of color, whining like an ancient crystal radio. With a sudden pop, the ghosts sang back: "Kevin Sterling. Jordan Delamar. Sterling. Delamar. Delamar. Sterling. Kevin. Jordan . . ."

The ghost voices faded as the two primary singers slid away from Stymak, back toward Julianne again.

In the Grey I saw the dim form in the bed flare into color. The ghosts rushed toward her, swirling again into their desperate, dancing gyre.

I pushed away from the Grey, coming back into the normal as much as I could. The silver light of the world between still lay over everything in my left eye, but I could see the rest of the room normally. I glanced quickly at Stymak, who looked all right, if a bit pale and shaken, and then toward the bed.

Julianne sat up like a marionette being raised by a careless puppeteer, her limbs oddly flopping as her head lolled. She picked up the brush she had recently put aside and brought it to the wet canvas with strokes so harsh and slashing that they pushed the built-up paint aside and left a smear across the painting: "DelamarSterling."

Then she fell back onto the bed, the heart and blood pressure monitors blipping faster for a few seconds before they reverted to their usual low, dull murmur. Eva Wrothen rushed into the room— I hadn't realized she was even in the house and her appearance startled me for a moment. Then I turned to Stymak again.

He was blinking at Julianne. "That's what the ghosts said."

FOUR

"Kevin Sterling and Jordan Delamar. Do you recognize the names? Could they be the other patients?"

"I'd guess," Stymak replied, shrugging. "That is the information you were after, isn't it?"

"Yes, but ghosts don't always give the answers you ask for." I looked away from him and back to Lily Goss by the bed. "Do those names mean anything to you? Either of you?" I added, turning to fix the nurse in my gaze.

She blanched, but Goss just looked confused and shook her head. "Nothing," Goss replied. "I don't recognize those names. They aren't anyone I know. Or that Julianne knew, so far as I can remember."

I looked harder at Wrothen, and said, "But you know."

Wrothen shook her head, conflicted, but what she said was, "I can't—I can't tell you."

"You don't have to. But do you recognize either of those names?"

Trembling, she nodded, her aura glowing a sickened shade of yellow-green as she said nothing.

"Patients, like Julianne," I guessed.

She nodded again, breathing a little easier, as if I was taking some weight off her.

I put my hand on her shoulder and offered a grateful smile. "Thank you."

I don't think I have a movie-star smile, but I guess it was good enough. Wrothen seemed to sag, sighing out the last of her confusion as she slid from under my hand, her head bowed. "I'm supposed to help people. . . . I hope I haven't done the wrong thing."

"You haven't done anything wrong. You're helping us find out what's happening to Julianne. You haven't said or done anything to harm anyone."

Lily jumped up and ran over to hug Wrothen. "Thank you! Oh, God, thank you, Eva!"

Wrothen looked almost comically startled and stiffened in Lily's embrace before she put her arms around the other woman and returned a weak hug. I turned away from them, wanting to give them a moment's privacy, and focused on Stymak again.

"You OK?" I asked as he plopped into a chair.

He blew out a breath and pushed his hair back from his face. "Yeah. That wasn't quite what I'm used to."

"I think that was my fault. I was afraid the first ghost was hurting you and I pushed it away."

"It was. That's—I mean the whole thing was just wrong from the beginning. That was just really, really weird. Usually I just get impressions, ideas, a few words, but this was . . . painful. Scary. I've never been afraid of a ghost in my life and that was . . . really scary. What happened at your end?"

"It was . . . very loud. There are a lot of ghosts in here and they're clustered around Julianne, waiting for an opportunity to . . . use her, I guess. But they were very interested in you once you started calling to them. And then they were babbling and it sounded like a bunch of pieces trying to make one whole or . . . well, more like a jumbled signal that needed to be adjusted. So I tried to 'tune' the ghosts a bit, I guess you'd say, trying to get the bits of the noise to line up into an intelligible sound. It was just a guess, though."

"Seems to have been the right one. But, man, that was really unpleasant."

"Ghosts generally are."

He frowned at me. "I don't find them to be. They're just . . . needy. Scared. Lonely. Like the living."

"That's a nice commentary on your fellow man."

"I mean the things that make them seek help are the same things that make living people do it. And like us, they sometimes do the wrong thing or don't know how to express themselves. People don't get wiser when they get deader."

"That's the truth."

"So, now what do you plan to do?"

"I need to find those other patients and see if they truly are manifesting anything like Julianne's behavior. With three cases, I might find something they have in common that could tell me what's happening."

"I'd like to come along."

I hesitated. I wasn't keen on having an impromptu partner, but I had to admit Stymak had been able to make contact with the ghosts in a way I couldn't. I wasn't certain I'd have been able to get any information out of them on my own. "I'm not sure it's a great idea . . ." I started.

"It's a better idea than keeping our information to ourselves. We both want to find out what's going on with Julie and I'm not sure what would have happened if you hadn't been here to push that ghost off me. I'm scared, to be honest. But you're not scared."

I made a face. "Oh, I'm scared. I just know it doesn't help, so I'm going ahead anyhow."

Stymak brightened up. "Good! Then I'm sticking with you."

Whether I liked it or not, it appeared I had a sidekick. Or something like that. "It may take a while to track these guys down," I said. "I can start on that. Could you get started deciphering yesterday's recording?"

"Oh, crap! I forgot to send it to you. I knew I'd forgotten something." He looked abashed. "I'll get it done today. I still haven't figured out what language it is—if it is a language."

"Don't worry about it. Once you get it to me, I'll have a friend of mine work on it too. It'll go faster that way."

Stymak nodded. "All right. I'll stay with Julianne for a while and then head back to my place to work on the file. She usually gets pretty quiet in the middle of the day."

"Maybe she's exhausted by then."

"Could be. . . ."

I turned back to Lily Goss and Eva Wrothen, who had settled down near the bed. Julianne was apparently asleep—or whatever one called the state she was in. Wrothen kept shooting me furtive glances. I wondered what she thought I was going to do. Maybe she'd noticed my tendency to become a bit see-through when I dropped toward the Grey. Most people ignore it, but those who do notice are often a little freaked out at the sight. I hadn't been too hard on her . . . had I?

I frowned and turned my attention back to Stymak.

"All right, if we're going to work on this together, you stay here and observe Julianne or work with the ghosts—you know better what's yielding information in this situation than I do. And be very careful—I don't want you to have another problem with a ghost trying to harm you. I'll get started finding those other patients. Send me the audio files as soon as you can and I'll send you the information I dig up. When we're both up to speed, we can get together and decide how to proceed."

Stymak nodded. I started to leave, pausing for a moment by the bed. The dark shape that had descended over Julianne wavered and heaved like a sail in a gusty wind and as I listened, it sighed and groaned, "Leave, leave, leave . . ." No one else seemed to have heard. I wanted to touch the dark form and see if I could communicate with it, but I was afraid the motion might seem sinister to Goss and Wrothen.

"Ms. Goss," I began, then turned my gaze to include the nurse. "Ms. Wrothen, would you mind if I touched Julianne?"

Wrothen scowled. "In what way?"

"Just my hand on her hand."

Wrothen looked at Goss, who bit her lip but nodded assent.

I drew as close to the bed as machines and rails would allow and reached out to take Julianne's left hand. The first thing I felt was wet paint and I realized she'd been using that hand to paint with. Then I felt a cold jolt that traveled up my arm and zinged across the back of my eyes, warping my vision into a static-filled haze of darkness shattered by jagged curtains of shifting colors. The shock stole my breath and I gasped, taking in air gone ice-sharp. There was no summer here. The darkness hovering over Julianne lashed at me with thin whips of silver mist that left a howling despair and anger behind as they passed through my flesh. "This is mine! Go away!" They weren't so much words as they were the strongest mental impression of a shout.

I held out for a moment against the pressure, pain, and cold, trying to see the shape of whatever held sway over the body of Julianne Goss, but all I could make out with either eye was a dull, unbroken blackness that cloaked her form like a drenched blanket. No more enlightened than I had been before, I broke the connection and pulled my hand away from hers, easing back from the edge of the Grey.

The two women beside me stared at me with expectant expressions—Lily's more hopeful than Wrothen's.

"What did you see?" Lily asked, hesitating as if she wasn't sure she wanted the answer.

"Just darkness."

"Is that . . . bad?"

"I don't know."

"Does something have possession of my sister?"

"In a way, but what it is and why it's acting like this is still a mystery to me. It doesn't seem to be harming her . . . any more than she's already been harmed, but it's not helping her heal, either. It's a lot of angry and confused something—it might even be Julianne herself."

Goss grabbed the hand I'd laid on her sister's, her head enveloped in hopeful shades of blue with white sparks. "Can you help her? Can you figure out what it is?"

"I will, one way or another, with Mr. Stymak's help. You and Ms. Wrothen need to keep her safe and well until we do."

Wrothen made a soft snorting sound in the back of her throat, but didn't say anything while giving me the evil eye, her aura spiking out in an annoyed shade of pumpkin orange. At least she seemed to be back to her normal grumpy self—which was better than con-flicted and confused—and I had the impression she didn't like me much. Not that that's new: A lot of people and things don't like me.

FIVE

I didn't see Quinton that night, but I did talk to him on the phone while the ferret played the clown and tried to hide one of my boots under the living room bookshelves. I had been poking, searching, and sneaking around databases trying to get information on Kevin Sterling and Jordan Delamar, so while I was pleased to hear from he-who-dislikes-the-phone, my mind was not quite on his track at first.

"Hey," he said. "Just a heads-up: Your friends with long teeth might have attracted unwanted attention."

I puzzled over it for a moment before I connected what he was saying to what he meant. Quinton was busy making trouble for his father's project because he didn't want to be sucked back into the covert machine; he was also dead against the project on moral grounds, since it had something to do with "investigating" paranormal creatures and using them in horrible experiments for purposes that I wasn't quite clear on. Among other things, Quinton didn't want his father to discover that I was a sort of paranormal creature myself, because the gods only knew what James Purlis would do if he thought he had a "freak" so close to hand, much less one who had access to monsters and the deep secrets of the Grey. He was still thankfully ignorant of it, though he must have been close to figuring out that there was an interface between the normal and the paranormal. So if Quinton was warning me about trouble for folks with fangs, Purlis must have been close to or actively targeting vampires.

The local blood-sucking society wouldn't like that and since they were still making the transition to new management—the fall of the old regime was three years ago, but vampires don't like change—and if Quinton's father was messing with them, that would put certain people on the spot, which could upset the current calm among the life-challenged and lead to a hell of a lot of mess that would spill out into the normal world in the guise of gang violence and murder. I hadn't heard anything about this from them, so it might not be an issue yet, but with my almost-father-in-law involved it would come my way eventually.

"Great," I muttered. "Any idea what the problem is?"

"Not in a position to discuss it. If they don't know, they will soon." He sounded harried and nervous.

"OK. I'll look into it. And you do remember there's a meal-thing in a couple of days, right?"

"Meal . . . ? Oh. Right. I'll make it."

He disconnected without further conversation. I sighed—I hadn't mentioned Stymak's digital recordings to him. I wouldn't be able to run the same sort of high-end analysis on them that Quinton could have. I'd have to muddle through it on my own, since it sounded like Papa Purlis's plans were dangerous and advanced far enough to require a lot of Quinton's monkey-wrenching to derail. I hoped he'd be safe and that he would actually show up for our dinner with

Phoebe and her family—it had been planned for a while and I wouldn't be forgiven easily for missing it. Quinton, though, usually got off the hook of Phoebe's ire through sheer charm. Still, I'd rather be chasing my comparatively mild case of possession than dealing with James Purlis and whatever gang of human spooks he had with him.

I couldn't talk directly to the local vampires during the day and in this situation I thought it best not to leave a detailed message with their daylight assistants, but I left call-back requests and hoped for the best. No one called back.

Frustrated, I put that task aside and tried to listen to Stymak's recordings, but they were static-filled and confusing. I don't know how it happens, but electronic voice phenomena, or EVP, is always lousy—full of background noise, electronic feedback, pops, hisses, dropouts, and overlapping voices that have to be filtered, isolated, and pulled apart for analysis. I didn't have those skills or the right tools on my computer even if I knew how to use them. Stymak had filtered quite a bit, but Julianne's voice was still broken and difficult to pick out and the only thing I was able to hear consistently was a sudden clear voice that said, "Beach to bluff," which put me in mind of Julianne's paintings but didn't clear up any of my questions. The whispering of ghosts overlapped Julianne's strange mutterings and the sharp screech of electronic feedback in the presence of the uncanny marred the playback, making me wince. After an hour of gritting my teeth and trying, I had to give up and put it aside for Quinton when he had time.

I went to bed that night without having heard more from Quinton or gotten any response from the vampires. I'd keep trying on both scores, but the most pressing thing was finding the other PVS patients. In the morning I went back to tracking Sterling and Delamar through cyberspace.

It's easier to get information about politicians' questionable funding and personal activities than it is to get information about medical patients—which is as it should be. The back door to this stuff, however, is insurance. As a private investigator, I've done my share of personal injury fraud investigations and while medical records may be protected by HIPAA, billing records—especially disputed or defaulted bills—aren't quite as hard to get. I didn't need to know what the bills were for or what treatment the patients were getting, only that they were being billed and where the bills were being sent. I'm not saying it was easy, but it's an even bet that anyone who's been sick long enough will have a bill they can't pay or that the insurance company has refused, and those bits of business are the crack in the wall through which sneaky bastards like me can creep. It took another day of digging, but I finally found mailing addresses for Kevin Sterling and Jordan Delamar, which was a good start. And I wasn't distracted by Quinton's presence while I was doing it—more's the pity—because he didn't come around. I assumed he was busy making his father's life difficult and I was fine with that.

Delamar's address was a private mailbox company in Capitol Hill. It would take a little more digging to find the actual address, but I kept that working in the background. Sterling's address was a single-family house in Leschi.

Leschi households ran pretty much the whole range of the middle-income bracket, with a few folks struggling to keep up balanced by those having no problems even in a bad economy. The usual mix of condos and houses, a smattering of older apartment buildings, and a long stretch of Lake Washington shoreline kept the area diverse and a little hard to peg culturally. Unlike some parts of Seattle, there wasn't one strongly defined ethnic group or neighborhood feel here, so I arrived in the area without much idea about Kevin Sterling.

The house was on one of the curving streets on the north end of the hill that overlooked the shoreline and Leschi Park. Not as swank as the south end of the hill near the marina, but certainly not a slum. The Sterling house was one of the few that had no lake view to speak of, being set back on the slope by a twist in the road. There wasn't much parking to be had on the street, so I ended up a few blocks away and walked back. My eye was still giving me some trouble and I appreciated the leaf-dappled shade on the streets, since the sun had decided to pop in for a short visit to un-sunny Seattle that afternoon, just to prove that it was, technically, summer. I could hear distant children in the park and down the shore, though I couldn't see them, and the Grey's energy grid shone through the landscape in pulsing lines of azure and jade, frosted here and there with the memory of old trolley lines that had cut imperiously over the hill until 1940.

I came up the driveway and looked at the house. One end was unsided and looked as if a renovation project had been given up in midwork and temporarily weatherproofed until it could be completed at a future date that had come and gone some time ago. The Tyvek and plastic were beginning to fray from friction under wind and soaking by rain for longer than they'd been meant to be so exposed. I wondered when the work had stopped—before or after whatever had put Sterling into his current state of lingering ill health.

On my way to the door, the persistent Grey vision on my left became more pronounced until I was seeing the world as two partially overlapped layers—one of the normal sphere and the other of chilly silver fog and ghostlight. The house seemed to melt away on the left, becoming a gleaming wire frame of light and emptiness through which the mist of uncanny things played around knots of colored energy. I knocked on the door that was half there, half memory. Something flickered at the edge of my vision and I started to turn to look for it, but it fell back before I could pick it out from the general psychic noise of the street and a neighborhood full of kids on summer break. Once again I thought I heard the distant rattle and roar of the Guardian Beast, but I saw no sign of it nearby.

My attention was jolted back around as the door opened with the scrape of loose weatherstripping over quarried flagstone. A blond girl, about fifteen years old, stood in the doorway. She was too thin for her gangly height, barefoot, her hair hanging loose almost to her waist, dressed in ragged cutoff jeans and two layers of T-shirts so thin and clinging that I could count her ribs through them. A pall of surly red and dull olive green energy hung on her. I remembered being that thin at her age and cast a glance down, to see the same kind of knobby, bruised, and calloused feet I still had.

She held on to the door and the frame, making a barrier, and shot one hip, tucking her chin down and staring at me as she did. "Yeah?"

"Are you a dancer?" I asked.

Her head came up and interest sparked in her eyes. "Yeah."

I nodded. "Thought so. Ballet?"

She returned my nod. "And Irish step."

I pointed at the scar on her right foot that gleamed too white in one world and jagged red in the other. "FHL release?"

"Yeah. About a year ago."

"Still hurts, doesn't it."

"Like a bitch. I'm trying to keep it limber by going barefoot, but sometimes it still hurts."

"Your PT doesn't make you wrap the arch?"

She gave a bitter shrug. "Can't afford to go anymore. Dad's been sick and it's eaten all the insurance and most of the cash."

"Your dad's Kevin Sterling?"

"Yeah." She frowned. "Who are you?"

"My name's Harper Blaine. I'm a private investigator."

She rolled her eyes. "Oh fuck. I can't believe you people. Dad's sick. I mean totally ill. He's not sneaking around doing shit behind your backs. He's not faking a coma, y'know!"

She started to shove the door closed but I wedged my right leg and shoulder in between the frame and the door. I'm still pretty skinny even though I haven't danced in ten years or more and I didn't want my too-prominent collarbones or less-than-perfect knees to take the worst of the impact, so I used the hard toe of my boot as a stopper. The door banged into the leather and rubber and bounced back a little, smacking the girl's palm.

"Ow!"

"Sorry," I said, easing through the doorway and putting up one of my hands in a placating gesture. "I'm not with the insurance company or the hospital or any of those people. I don't believe your dad is faking anything and I'm not here to get him in trouble. My client's sister is the same way. We're just trying to figure out what's happening."

"You mean, like, why she's a veggie, like my dad?"

"No—we know why that happened. What we don't know is why she's doing weird things."

The girl narrowed her eyes at me. "What kind of weird things?"

"She paints and she babbles and sometimes she throws things, but she's not awake when she does it; she's still in a coma. Does your dad do that kind of thing?"

She closed her eyes as if a burden had been removed. "Oh, man. We thought it was just him."

Another woman called out from farther back in the house. "Olivia!"

The girl rolled her eyes. "I'm coming, Mom!" She looked at me again, biting her lip and frowning. "I'm not supposed to let you in."

"I understand. But I want to help my client and if I can help her, that may help your dad. The more I know, the better the chances."

Olivia sucked a breath in through her teeth, looking conflicted, her energy corona flashing and fluttering red and orange and pink by turns. She made up her mind. "Mom's going to kill me, but come on. I'll show you Dad."

She led me through the foyer and into a half-finished hallway that went down the side of the house toward the back. "It's kind of messy here. Dad was working on the new garage and stuff when he had his accident and no one's ever finished it. Probably never will."

"That sounds rough."

"It kind of sucks."

"Sounds it. What's your dad do?"

"He's a tunneling engineer—he was working on the waterfront project to replace the viaduct and part of the shaft collapsed and he got buried in the mud."

"Why was he working on your house if he's a tunnel guy?"

"He's Mr. Fix-It. He's always, like, 'I can do that better.' And usually, y'know, yeah. But this time . . ." She shook her head. "Fucking tunnel got him."

"What are the weird things your dad's been doing since his accident?"

Her voice got quieter as we walked and the colors around her became increasingly anxious shades of orange. "A while ago, he started writing stuff and then he started saying stuff. It really freaks my mom out. Well, it freaks me out, too, but I figure even though it's kind of creepy, at least he's trying. Y'know, somewhere in there he's still . . . there, y'know?"

"So it makes sense. He's writing to you and your mom?"

"No. That's the creepy part. It doesn't make sense. He's not talking to us." She stopped just before an open door and turned around to put a finger to her lips. She turned back and walked through the door, leaving me in the unfinished hall. I could hear the mutter and ping of life-support machines and monitors in the room beyond and see the dark green misery that rolled out of the room like smog.

My intrusive Grey vision left me with a strangely overlaid view of the room beyond the wall. Olivia's fluttering colors of anxiety and anger buzzed through the cloud-filled space toward a storm front that boiled with ghosts and was pierced by a tight coil of green despair and fear.

"Hey, Mom," Olivia said.

"What took you so long? Where have you been?" The words came forth strung on spiky orange filaments.

"I just went to the door, like you told me to." Olivia sounded defensive and I could see her energy colors shifting toward red. It appeared that Olivia's resentment burned on a short fuse and I wondered if this uncomfortable relationship was a symptom of stress from Sterling's lingering state or if it had been this way before he was injured.

"You should have come right back. What took you so long and who were you talking to?"

I thought I could hear the eye roll that came with Olivia's reply.

"Mom," she whined, making the word three syllables long. "Don't get all over me. This lady was at the door and she said she might be able to help Dad, so I let her in."

I figured that was my cue to step into the room.

Once through the door, I could see the room wasn't much different from Julianne Goss's—the space that had been a large bedroom was now a sickroom filled with machines—except that instead of paintings, drifts and piles of scrawled paper occupied every vertical space that wasn't filled with equipment or plumbing. Stacks of yellow notepads and boxes of cheap pens lay on one of the rolling tray tables pushed near the large hospital bed. An emaciated form made barely a lump in the blankets on the bed, and had become the focus around which all else flowed, including the churning darkness-and-silver boil of ghosts.

A live middle-aged woman sat alone beside the bed on a desk chair that made her look waifish—not because the chair was so large but because she was so thin. I guessed from her pallor and the way her skin seemed loose over her bones that she'd been much plumper not long ago and her weight loss had been swift and unhealthy. Everything about her had gone dull. As there was no one else in the room, I assumed she was Olivia's mother.

She looked at me as if she couldn't imagine where I'd come from. "Who are you?"

"My name's Harper Blaine, Mrs. Sterling. I work for a woman whose sister is in the same state as your husband."

She frowned at me. "I don't understand."

"I've had information that Mr. Sterling has episodes of strange behavior—writing, talking—as if he were awake, but he remains in a vegetative state—"

Mrs. Sterling jumped to her feet and surged toward me. "Who told you that? It's not true! My Kevin isn't faking being sick!" She slapped me with all the strength she could muster. Her bony hand felt like a giant bird's claw striking my cheek, her fingernails leaving tracks on my skin.

I flinched away from her. She shoved me backward, screaming, "Get out! Get out!"

I'm not easy to move, but her anger added force to her efforts and I took an involuntary step backward. Olivia hopped out of our way and for a moment I could see the man in the bed clearly. Most of the ghosts had drawn aside as if disappointed in their efforts, while two foggy forms lingered, pressing inward until the darker of the two had flowed over the man and covered him like a shroud.

The man shivered and his left hand started scrabbling at the covers. "No soup today," he said.

I stared. Olivia and Mrs. Sterling turned around, frozen for a moment. Then they rushed to the bed. Olivia tried to put a pen in the moving hand, but Mrs. Sterling knocked it aside and clutched her husband's hand. "It's just a spasm," she said, as if she were reassuring herself. "It's nothing. Just muscles twitching. It means nothing."

"No, Mom!" Olivia cried, pulling at her. "He's trying to write. Let go!"

She turned a furious expression on her daughter. "Shut up! Shut up. It's not true. And you get that woman out of here, Olivia Pearl Sterling. You get her out! Now!" Then she cast a look at me, saying, "Leave us alone! Go the hell away!"

I was already backing into the hallway. I'd seen what I needed, and Mrs. Sterling wasn't going to be any help, even though the situation seemed the same as at the Goss house: A seeking cloud of ghosts circled the room, each waiting for its chance to occupy the body of the patient, trying to say something that we couldn't understand. It wasn't all I wanted to know, but it was enough for now.

Olivia brushed past her mother in a flurry of frustration and anger, striding to me and pointing down the hall. I half expected her to leave me to find my own way out, but she came along.

At the front door, she stopped me with a hand on my arm. She was breathing heavily, as if we'd run to the door. "My mother . . . I'm sorry—she doesn't understand. She's afraid."

"Of what?"

"Of losing Dad's L&I case. If they decide he's not really . . . vegetative"—she clearly hated the word—"they'll take back the benefits and we'll lose the house and stuff."

I was familiar with the state Labor and Industries Board and their often hard-nosed and by-the-book attitude toward long-term injury cases. I'd investigated plenty of suspected frauds for them when I was a lot hungrier. They weren't as bad as some insurance companies, but they weren't easygoing, either, and a case like this had to seem hinky to them.

I patted at the stinging fingernail-scrapes on my face. No blood now, though they itched and irritated my skin.

"I'm sorry—about your face," Olivia said.

"It's nothing. Aren't you worried about the L&I case, too?"

Olivia bit her lip. "I am, but I want to help my dad. You saw—"

"I did. He writes a lot, doesn't he?"

She nodded. "Mom used to let him, but now she tries to stop him. She can't. He keeps on doing it. If he can't use a pen, he'll just use his fingers like he's drawing in the sand. I don't understand most of what he writes, but it's not nonsense. You said you could help him—can you?"

"Not right away. I need to know more."

"Is this like the other lady? Like your client?"

I nodded. "Yes."

"What is it? Don't tell me it's just muscle spasms. I know what a muscle spasm is and that's not it."

I peered at her. "Do you believe in God?"

She gave me that look of incredulity and disgust that teenage girls are so good at. "What? Are you some kind of religious nut?"

"No, I just wanted to know how to express this. I take it you don't go to church much."

"No. So what?" she added, crossing her arms over her too-thin chest.

I returned my best professional briefing expression. "My client believes her sister is possessed. She's a religious woman and that's the word she understands for what seems to be happening. But when I say 'possessed' I don't mean that a demon has taken over the body, but that some other entity is momentarily in control. That's what I think is happening to her and to your dad. Some other spirit is pushing through, trying to say something but not making itself clear to us."

"But what about my dad? Isn't this my dad trying to talk to us?"

"I think he's unable to shove the others aside—they're stronger than he is and there are a lot of them. They're very upset and if I can find out why, or who they are, I may be able to solve their problem so they'll go away and let your dad come back on his own."

She pursed her lips and scowled, thinking. "How do you know this shit? How do you know what's happening to my dad?"

I sighed. "I can see them—the ghosts."

"You're some kind of psychic, like that chick on TV?"

I almost laughed. "No. I'm not like that at all."

"You can't make my dad come back? Like, call him to his body or something?"

"No. That's not how it works. At least not for me. The human spirit is stubborn. We're a troublesome bunch. We don't like to shut up and go away, even when we're dead. We reshape the whole world to suit us, even the world we can't see. And something has made these lingering spirits so frantic to speak up that they are bullying people like your dad—the ones who are kind of in between here and there."

"You said there's more people like my dad. How many?"

"Just two that I know of, but that's a lot, if you think about it."

She gazed at me, her lower lip pugnacious and downturned, thinking hard. Finally she said, "Are you going to help us or not?"

"I'm going to help all of you. But I need help *from* you, too."

"What kind?"

"I would like to see some of the papers your dad has written and, if you can remember any of it, a transcript of what he's been saying. I need to know where he was injured and how long he's been like this."

"I'll get the papers. Mom won't care if I take them. I don't know if I can remember the things he's said but I'll try. And he was working on a site down near King Street and Alaskan Way when he was hurt. What else?"

Something had been bugging me and I had to ask, "How long has your mom been sick?"

"She's not sick. She just can't gain weight."

"And that doesn't seem strange to you? Wasn't she . . . fatter when your dad was hurt?" I chose the word because I knew how dancers felt about the subject of weight and body form. To someone who starves herself, overexercises, and may even do drugs to keep her weight down, any normal degree of plumpness represents the hated "fat." There's nothing so cruel as telling another dancer she's over-weight and I couldn't imagine Olivia had never been angry enough at her mother to shout that mean little word.

Olivia started, tears sparking a moment before she looked horri-fied at the direction of her thoughts. "Mom was never . . . *fat*. But she has lost some weight. I'd swear she eats like a pig, but she never gains an ounce—always been jealous of that. We're all thin in this family."

"That's not thin, what your mom is. She's skinny like someone starving herself."

"But I told you: She eats all the time!" She threw her hands up in exasperation.

"All the time?"

"Like, five meals a day. I think it's 'cause she's stressed over Dad." Olivia scowled for a moment. Then her face softened as she gave it some thought. "Oh, man . . . that's so weird. I hadn't thought about it. . . . Maybe she's got, like, a parasite or something."

"Maybe. You need to look after her—and yourself. Do you have brothers or sisters?"

She nodded. "Yeah, two brothers. They're older than me. They help; they're just not home right now."

"Good. Get one of them to help your mom while you come out to bring those papers to me." I handed her my card. "I promise to do everything I can for your dad."

"A real promise, or an adult-to-kid promise?"

I wondered what the story was behind that question, but I answered, "I only make the real kind."

Olivia put out her hand. "Deal. I'll call when I want to come over. I might have to sneak out. Mom's freaky about me leaving the house ever since . . . you know."

"I understand," I said, shaking her hand. "Don't do anything risky. If you need my help, or if you can't come, just let me know. We'll find another way."

She smiled at "we." "Yeah, we will." She cast a glance over her shoulder, then gave me a conspiratorial grin and a thumbs-up. *"Merde!"* she whispered, before she turned and closed the door.

I chuckled. It had been a very long time since anyone had offered me one of the dancer's versions of "good luck." I suspected I'd need it.

As I walked toward my truck, I got the feeling someone was watching me. I turned back and eyed the Sterling house, but I saw no sign that anyone observed me from there. Still . . . I felt like prey—something I don't care to be. I considered dropping into the Grey and looking for the observer in the bright mist, but there was no guarantee that would put me at an advantage. If my stalker was paranormal, I might be giving them an opening I'd regret. I kept walking, stretching my senses as far as I could while remaining in the normal world and without making it too obvious that I was aware of my tail. I doubted they thought I was clueless, but I didn't see a point in putting them on alert.

I was pretty sure they'd have to break for their own vehicle once I got into the truck—or make it obvious there was a second team on me—though I found the idea of a major surveillance team following me around Seattle ridiculous. Who'd be interested in a small-time PI who sees ghosts? I wasn't working on anything sensitive or significant that I knew of. In spite of Mrs. Sterling's worries about L&I, there wasn't any real intrigue about the case in hand. If someone was observing the Sterling house on a fraud investigation, they would just make note of my presence and drop in for a chat if they were really interested. But as I moved away, the sense of being observed persisted. I stopped and dug around in my pockets for my keys, taking a moment to scan the area and peep back over my arm as I gave up on my pockets and began rooting in my bag instead.

Something moved in opposition to the delicate breeze rippling the leaves overhead and left a thin trail of red-gold in the corner of my damaged vision. Yeah, someone was following me. I sighed, annoyed. I don't have a great tolerance for being tailed, watched, bugged, investigated, or eavesdropped upon. It makes me cranky. The only quandary was whether I wanted to shake them off on general principle more than I wanted to know why they found me so fascinating.

Screw it, I thought. Let them be bored a while; I had more important things to do than wound their feelings by blowing them off now. I'd lose them later and then see where they popped back up— as they would do if they were seriously interested. If it was a casual tail, what did it matter if they dragged along? I was only heading back to my office to see if anything had turned up about Jordan Delamar and to manage some paperwork for other cases. Hardly an exciting afternoon.

SIX

I didn't get a good look at my tail, but I got enough of a glance as I stepped up into my truck to know it was human—or humanoid at least. The tangled energy around the dark-haired figure in shapeless clothes was a mess of colors restrained in tight white bands that made me think of prisoners bound with rope. The colors weren't any combination I associated with a specific paranormal creature or magic-user—it certainly wasn't a vampire of any stripe—but I haven't seen everything and some ghosts and monsters are complex enough to look convincingly human in such a short sighting. It was more likely to be a normal person than a denizen of the Grey, but if so, whoever it was had an unusual degree of control over their feelings—judging by the strange constraint of the aura.

I got back to the office, half wishing I could stay out in the sun, and keeping an eye out for my shadow as I went. Once I was upstairs, I took a look out of my tiny window, but I couldn't see anyone on the street who seemed to be watching my building. I gave it up as a waste of time and got on with trying to find further information on Delamar, sorting through e-mails, typing up notes, and generally catching up on the boring necessities of my job.

Still nothing on Delamar. I'd probably have to go stake out the guy's mailbox at this rate—which is about the least interesting job on the planet. I wondered if the three patients were connected in some way besides their extraordinary medical condition. So far, I had nothing to link them except that they were all vegetative. That in itself was disturbing, since Skelly had said PVS was so rare that the occurrence of three cases simultaneously stretched probability. I thought it was more likely that the ghosts were causing or prolonging the patients' condition than that they were just lucky enough to have three outlets instead of one. Clearly, the ghosts wanted to be heard—were possibly desperate enough to exert considerable energy to keep the rightful owners out of their own bodies. But there were a lot of ghosts, which gave them a significant energy reserve, and I was afraid that the longer the living were unable to fully occupy their bodies, the less likely it was that they would survive or awaken from their strange state. The thought gave me a momentary surge of panic: Where were the ghosts getting this energy and how could I break this condition before the patients under their sway died?

Possession wasn't one of my areas of expertise, but from what I'd observed, it obviously took a substantial force to keep a soul—for lack of a better term—out of the body it was meant to occupy. Many things in the paranormal realm cleave to their rightful place with the tenacity of limpets. Grey energy tends to return to its assigned path, be that a ley line, a spell, or a ghost. Once you release whatever is holding them out of place, they move back where they belong pretty quickly. As I understand it, fighting that inertia is one of the things that makes working magic of any kind a ton of effort. It was what made walking through the Grey so tiring for me, even though I'm a naturalized citizen. But the ghosts I'd seen at the Goss house and at the Sterling house hadn't shown any inclination to slide away. They acted like they were waiting for an opportunity to act; they fell back when they had no chance, but didn't leave the area, in case it became available again. Such behavior implied a collective consciousness, compulsion, or need strong enough to overrule the usual routines of the Grey. That kind of urge had to have some basis other than simple opportunity, or every ghost in Seattle would have been hanging about, but that wasn't happening. Seattle's phantasms were mostly right where I'd last seen them—those I took note of, at least. I hadn't seen any drop in the number of spirits just hanging around Pioneer Square or anywhere else. So it wasn't a general draw, but something specific. If I could figure out what linked the patients, perhaps I could find a common cause I could attack to change the situation. . . .

I didn't yet know what had happened to Delamar, the third patient, but I could try to find similarities between Sterling and Goss and check them against Delamar later. With that thought I picked up my office phone and called Lillian Goss.

Eva Wrothen answered the phone in a clipped tone of annoyance over background noise. I identified myself and asked to talk to Lily.

"She can't come to the phone. She's with her sister."

"So I hear. Is everything . . ." I paused to pick my term. "Is everything normal over there?"

She snorted. "As normal as ever."

"Ms. Wrothen, I know it's inconvenient, but I really do need to speak to Ms. Goss about her sister's illness. I know you can't discuss it with me and you aren't a secretary, but can you let her know I'm on the phone?"

"I'll see what I can do."

I heard her put the phone down on a hard surface while the din continued in the telephonic distance. I waited through it for several minutes, typing desultory notes on my computer. Then silence fell, cracked in a moment by the sound of hurried footsteps and the scrape of the receiver being moved.

"Hello?" Lily Goss said. "Ms. Blaine? I'm so sorry—"

"There's no need to apologize. Ms. Goss, I wanted to know how and where your sister was injured."

"Injured? Oh, the cause of the coma, right?"

"Yes."

"Well, I don't really know where, exactly, but I'd assume it happened near the market, since I can't imagine where else she'd have come in contact with a mosquito."

I blinked. "A mosquito? I'm afraid I'm missing the gist here. What happened to your sister?"

"She contracted meningitis from a mosquito bite."

Mosquitoes are fairly rare in Seattle. In spite of the continual rain, there's not a lot of standing fresh water for them to breed in—Seattle has pretty good drainage, existing as it does on a series of hills and streets raised above the tide line specifically to encourage sewage to head one way only: down. That's not to say they don't turn up—especially in the suburbs and small towns of Washington's agricultural areas—but they aren't something the city is noted for.

"She got bitten at work?"

"Yes—well, after work. She works—worked—at an architectural firm on the Pike Hill Climb. You know—below Pike Place Market."

The Hill Climb scrambled from the waterfront near the Seattle

Aquarium up what had once been a steep bluff covered in fir and cedar trees to the city's famous farmers' market. The wide stairs of the Hill Climb are broken by terraces that connect to buildings full of tourist shops, hidden apartments, and offices. Restaurants dominate the open ends of the buildings, spreading tables out on the terraces when the weather allows. It's a nice place to linger over a drink on a summer evening—just when the mosquitoes come out.

"What did your sister do at the firm?"

"She is—was—a computer modeler. She ran the system that created the wire-frame and simulation models of the buildings they design. She was always the math whiz in the family, which is another reason why this painting thing is so weird—Julie never liked drawing as much as drafting and she never learned to paint."

I thanked Goss for the information and sat frowning over it for a few minutes. No common cause except trauma and buildings, and I wasn't sure how a computer modeler at one firm would connect to a tunnel engineer at a different one. Both Goss and Sterling had been near the waterfront when the events that put them into comas occurred, but two points of similarity didn't constitute a particularly strong argument, especially since one was on the job but the other wasn't and the types of injury were completely dissimilar. I needed to find Jordan Delamar and discover what had happened to him and where. First, however, I was going to take a look at the tunnel-construction site where Sterling had been injured. It wasn't far from my office—an easy walk even in unlovely weather. I wrapped up my notes and left the office.

The sun was still shining, though some clouds had rolled in from the north looking threatening. Typical first of July. It would probably start raining once the sun went down and remain overcast all day tomorrow, just to remind the tourists that this was, indeed, Seattle—the land of seasonal depression and rental umbrellas.

I had gone about two blocks toward the waterfront when I noticed my tail again. The foot traffic was a little thicker through Pioneer Square, but it thinned around the construction under the viaduct and to the south. There are a few parking lots in the area, so it wasn't unusual to see pedestrians looking intense or confused, but only one of them had the same tightly bound aura I'd spotted near the Sterlings' house. I might not have seen him so soon without that edge, but I did. My observer was definitely male, but just to be certain that he was following me, I crossed through a parking lot in the middle of the block and turned onto Post Avenue instead of going all the way down to Alaskan. There's no cover on that block unless you have the key to one of two alley gates and few people have any reason to walk any farther than the first parking lot. My shadow hung back, but followed me nonetheless. I wished I could turn and get a better look at him, but I needed to get into an area where I had the chance of cornering the mysterious follower. If I was going to blow somebody's cover, I wanted to get more information out of the encounter than just a glimpse at a face. I walked south toward King Street and the tunnel section that had collapsed over Kevin Sterling, hoping the construction would give me the opportunity I wanted.

The tunnel construction area was huge—about the size of a commercial parking lot—crammed in under the slowly disappearing viaduct between a row of old buildings and the industrial straightaway heading south on Alaskan Way. A yellow-striped plywood barrier had been erected around the project boundaries just south of the ferry terminal, forcing pedestrians to cross the road with the blind hope that Seattle's drivers would actually obey the signals and signs temporarily put up around it. Honking, cursing, and scampering demonstrated that neither the pedestrians nor the drivers were willing to play by the ever-changing rules at that location.

Most of the pedestrians came from the water side of the road at the ferry terminal and headed down the row of buildings on the landward side or toward the stadia farther east. I was on the other side and I figured any route into the construction would be on the water side off the straightaway, so I crossed the street, staying close to the plywood barriers and their confusing profusion of signage.

I went quickly around the water-facing side of the barrier and came to a hard stop on the other side of it, between the blind plywood wall, painted like a school-bus-colored zebra, and the southbound traffic. I'm tall, but still under six feet, and the barrier hid me completely. My tail peered around the barrier as he walked past the end and I snatched him into a headlock, dragging him behind the upstanding plywood and then pivoting, propelling him past me with our mutual momentum and into the next plywood frame head first.

He got his arms up and slammed himself back off the wood as it started to topple, spinning around to face me. He drew his hands across his body and flicked one outward. A steel baton telescoped out of his fist. I turned to keep my good eye on him, not wanting to lose him under the visual noise of the Grey.

He took a step forward, raising the baton, and said, "I can tell you're going to be trouble, Harper Blaine."

It was the voice as much as the dark brown hair and the slim, athletic build that put the pieces together for me. I hadn't seen him in almost a year, and then it had been fleeting as he'd shoved me down in my own living room and bolted out the door. He still looked essentially like Quinton—a similarity he had enhanced at the time with hair dye, clothes, and facial hair. Now he had let his natural gray thread through his hair and had shaved off the beard. His voice was as colorless as air and chill-neutral. Now I understood why his aura looked the way it did. "I'm surprised it took you so long to figure that out, Papa Purlis," I said.

His energy flushed red. For a moment the bands of his control flexed under the strain of his anger and I had the strong impression that he hated me but wasn't going to give in to it. He feinted forward, but I didn't take the bait and flinch. Behind me was a train of cement trucks and I knew better than to go toward them. He swept the baton at me—not very seriously, but I still had to turn aside to avoid an unpleasant contact.

"Now, now," I chided him. "If you break me, Quinton will be very upset with you."

"Then he might stop playing games and do what I tell him."

I snapped a hand at his face. He caught it and pulled me to him. I dove forward as he pulled and rammed my shoulder into his chest. I heard him gasp and his grip on me loosened. I ducked and rolled my shoulders down, hoping to pull him under me. Instead, he let go, rolling to the side and scrambling back to his feet. He was quick, had great instincts, and was in fantastic condition for a man in his late fifties. I suspected he didn't spend much time behind a desk. This wasn't going to be as easy as I'd hoped.

I swept one booted foot under him and he hopped to avoid it. I spun with the movement and came back up, grabbing and turning him with me to put my back to the plywood barrier while nearly throwing him into traffic. He clutched my jacket and shoved one leg between mine, using my own weight and momentum to trip me up.

I got a heel and a hand on the ground to break the fall and we both went down in a heap. A cement truck roared past, inches from our heads, blowing its horn. I tried to keep hold of him, but he had retained the baton and rapped hard on my knuckles. I let go and scampered backward, rising to my full height against the tilting barrier. I was taller than he was, but that wasn't necessarily an advantage.

He glared at me, his eyes almost glowing with ire, then pushed the emotion away and straightened up, taking a step back and sideways out of my reach. Standing still, contained and focused, he looked very much like his son. Except that I loved Quinton and I felt no such thing for his father.

"Why have you been following me, Purlis?"

"I just want to know what J.J.'s been up to—and who he's been sleeping with." He looked me over as if I were an insect caught crawling on his dinner plate.

The sneering didn't bother me, but I wasn't used to anyone calling Quinton by his initials—or his real name—and it threw me off for an instant before I said, "Just fatherly concern, then. Nothing about trying to get him to return to the fold and play spy with you." Quinton claimed that misplaced hero worship was what had gotten him into government work to begin with, but I had never been sure there wasn't a good dose of naive delight in cracking codes and solving problems all day involved as well.

"He talks a good game, but J.J. knows what he needs to do. If I have to remind him what's best for him—and what's not—I will," his father said, his voice dead calm.

"You'd better think hard before you do him any harm, Pops."

He laughed and it wasn't a pretty sound. "It's not my son who'll get hurt first."

"Is that a threat?"

"Absolutely. Persuade J.J. to stop fucking around and get with my program and we'll get on fine. But if you get in my way, or hold him back, I will go through you."

"I'm a lot harder to get through than you think."

"Everyone has soft spots."

I gave him a cold smile. Then I lunged and snatched him by the shirt, yanking him toward me. He pushed and we hit the barrier behind me. The baton swung around again and I ducked as the plywood crashed down into a pit behind us.

I shook him and pushed him off me, backward toward another of the endless line of cement trucks. "Piss off, Purlis."

He caught himself, just out of my range, eliciting another horrified screech from the nearest truck's horn. "Or you'll shoot me, like Bryson Goodall?"

I laughed. If he had any idea what had actually happened the night Goodall died, he would never let me out of his sight again. "I won't need to shoot you. You would be wise to stay out of Quinton's life and out of my sight."

"Oh, you won't be seeing me again. I know what I need to about you."

"I don't think you do," I said, starting forward one more time.

SEVEN

Someone started shouting from behind the downed barrier. "Hey! What are you two idiots doing? Get the hell out of here!"

I turned around, letting James Purlis slither away—I would have other chances to make my point to him and find out what he was up to with the vampires. I was pretty sure I'd have no trouble finding him when I was ready.

A slim woman with curling auburn hair pulled back into a serviceable ponytail was jogging across the city block–sized wasteland of dirt and machines toward me with two big guys in hard hats and safety vests coming along behind her. "What's the idea? This is a restricted area—it's dangerous. We have an open excavation down here!" she shouted at me.

"I'm sorry. I was looking for the tunnel site and I stumbled into the barrier. Those trucks are really close."

"Next time walk on the sidewalk side. What are you, suicidal?"

"No, just lost."

The woman sighed and turned around to wave the construction

workers away. "It's just a tourist, guys. I'll take care of it." She turned back to face me. "What were you trying to find?"

"The initial bore site for the tunnel project."

"The launch pit. Well, this is it. Thoroughly unexciting. Why are you looking?" she asked, wiping her hands on her coveralls and then resting them on her hips. She was petite and had the sort of elfin features that had probably been called "cute" often enough to gall their owner to fury. Her coveralls, work boots, and mud smears only added to the impression that she was a visiting sprite trying to pass for normal.

"I'm trying to find the location where Kevin Sterling was injured," I said.

"Who?"

"He's a tunnel engineer. He was on the project until a few months ago when the tunnel collapsed on him."

"Oh. That. Well, yeah, this would be the place, then. The official digging ceremony was really just for show and that's the section of pit wall that collapsed. We've been doing everything right, I can assure you."

"I'm not sure I follow you," I said.

She shook her head and rolled her eyes. "You don't just dig a tunnel. I mean you do, but not just like any old hole. You have to do all sorts of soil tests and structural analysis, ground stabilization, water removal, staging-area creation . . . and, of course, archaeology. Which is where I come in—or rather the Washington State Office of Archaeology and Historic Preservation."

"I'm still not sure I'm following you. Look, I'm a private investigator and I'm afraid I don't know anything about tunnels or how you build something like this, so I can't understand what happened to Mr.

Sterling and I thought I could get a better idea if I came down here and saw the site." I offered her my hand. "My name's Harper Blaine."

She wiped her hand on her coveralls again and shook mine, leaving a bit of grit behind in spite of her best efforts. Being a woman who often works in messy situations, I didn't mind. "Nice to meet you," she said. "I'm Rhiannon Held. I'm the archaeological site monitor. I wasn't here when the launch pit collapsed, so I'm not sure how much I can help you."

"I'll settle for whatever you can tell me—how the collapse might have happened, what an archaeologist is doing here . . . that sort of thing."

She looked intrigued and glanced around. "I don't think anyone's going to care if I'm not watching them insert bracing sections for a few minutes. Why don't you come with me? I'll find you a hard hat and I can give you a general idea of what's going on—if that will help. It's got to be more interesting than watching dirt get shoved out of the hole."

She waved me through and manhandled the plywood back into place between us and the traffic. She may have looked adorable, but she was no weakling. On the other side of the plywood barrier stretched the site of the tunnel's southern mouth. Right now it looked like the human equivalent of an anthill—a long open pit supported by poured-concrete walls and walkways across the top that was the focus of furious activity by men and excavating equipment in the middle of a huge expanse of mud about a block wide and three city blocks long. The ground shivered around the hole and a distant growling sound issued from the opening. I noticed that we were several feet below the level of the pavement outside the barriers.

"So," I said, "this is the famous tunnel."

"It will be once it's done. This is the launch pit—it's where the excavator entered the ground to start the dig. It had to be shored up and angled so the boring machine could get into position to make the tunnel without risk of the mouth collapsing and burying the machine—it'll also be the basis of the ramp into the southern end of the tunnel once the project is ready for traffic. The small collapse you were talking about happened before the excavator was brought in. The area is a little wetter than everyone hoped it would be. We also found some bottles and other debris at the historic level, but no significant artifacts. All that's been cleared away long ago, though. The project is into the serious tunneling now and that's actually kind of dull to observe. But that's my job—watch the site and keep an eye out for anything that the department will want to take a closer look at." Held led me to a trailer and went inside to grab a hard hat and a sort of coverall coat, which she handed to me.

"Put these on," she said.

As I did, I asked her, "Why do they need an archaeologist on site to look at bottles? Couldn't they send them to you?"

"Legal complications. This area is mostly landfill over tidal mud flats that the local Indians used to fish and go clamming on. The original landfill is kind of interesting on its own, too, so there's potential historical interest and artifacts. Ever since the Kennewick Man find and all the legal wrangling that went with it, Washington has had pretty stringent requirements about working in areas that may present anything of significant archaeological interest. So much of the area around Puget Sound was populated or used by the local tribes that all construction projects have to be investigated and cleared before any work can go ahead—we already did that stage here—and then there has to be a monitor standing by during the construction in case they dig into something unexpected that could be significant. Usually they don't, but that's the bread and butter that keeps most archaeologists employed and in Washington there are enough projects to keep a whole lot of people busy year-round. There's really not a lot of work for us, otherwise. It's not all whips and fedoras out here, as you can see," she added with a derisive snort. "Mostly it's either preparation work screening buckets full of mud for significant items—that's the fun part—or it's sitting on a site like I am, waiting to see if anything pops up. Lots of tedious sorting and grubbing around or sitting and waiting and looking at more buckets full of muck. And I mean a *lot* of muck.

"The excavator—which is named Bertha, incidentally—is about five stories tall and it'll remove about eighty-six thousand cubic yards of mud before it's done. And I get to look at every yard, just in case there's something interesting in it. The hard part is figuring out what's significant and what's just grunge. Mud's not as bland as it seems, though this stuff is pretty cold and nasty. It's mostly seawater here, you know."

"It is?"

"Yeah. The seawall leaks. It's over a hundred years old and it wasn't the best construction to begin with, so that's being replaced— that's another part of the project. The whole area's unstable due to seawater infiltration and the type of fill they used. First they dumped in sawdust from the mill, then they dumped in mud from when they did the regrades. People threw in all sorts of junk and garbage. There's a small artificial island of old ships' ballast stones that was completely buried between Washington Street and Main—we just found some of the cores and minerals that aren't native to Washington, so now we know right where the island was—parts of the buildings that burned down in the Great Fire were thrown in, and there's even a shipwreck in here somewhere at the north end."

"You're kidding."

She glanced up at me and grinned. "No. Some old wooden sailing ship—not a big one—that was beached before they built the seawall. No one wanted to pay to move it, so they just buried it. This part of the harbor was below the mill and the original sewer outflow, so it's got a lot of weird stuff in it that came down from the bluff in the sewage as well as the landfill and junk that was dropped or lost over time—the prep team found some old patent medicine bottles and things like that at the historic level."

"What's that?" I asked.

"Oh, before you get to anything interesting, you have to get past all the modern debris, roads, dirt, and so on that builds up or gets dumped on top of older layers. About ten feet down is where you get to the historic level in Seattle—you'll notice the whole site is about six to ten feet lower than the streets around it. That's because the prep and investigation teams had to basically scrape off the modern layer and look for deposits or sediment that would indicate an area of archaeological significance. That was done back in 2010. For instance, there used to be a coal wharf here before the first seawall was built, so the early team found bits of old anthracite coal and ships' hardware. That kind of stuff is interesting, but the work going on now should be well below even that level. I don't think they've found any of the bodies, though."

I was startled. "Bodies?"

"Yeah. This is where the bad part of town started. It's pretty awful, but during the diphtheria epidemic of 1875, a lot of people died—especially children—and they couldn't bury them fast enough, so they dumped a lot of the bodies that went unclaimed or whose families couldn't afford a burial into the landfill down here. People used to get killed in brawls and accidents around the brothels and saloons, and the poor died of disease and starvation, and the bodies got put in the graveyard here or thrown in the bay. Sometimes they washed out and then floated back on the tide, so the city offered money to any mortuary that would pick them up and bury them. So there was an upswing in 'accidental deaths' for a while down here. Sometimes people who wanted the cash would ambush or drug a sailor or a lumberjack or someone like that and then tie the body under the piers so they could 'find' it the next morning. Then they'd take it to one of the mortuaries in town, like Butterworth's, and split the fifty bucks the city paid the business for dealing with the bodies. Not very nice. This is a great place for gruesome stories—like the car that went down around here."

"Hang on—a car went into the bay?"

"Yes, but it was a long time after the seawall was completed and way out there," Held replied, pointing nearly due west toward the waters of Elliott Bay. "Before the container docks, the bit straight out from here used to be the King Street pier. I think it was 1929 or '30 . . . the family who owned the dock came to look it over and left the car in gear, so the car drove off the end of the pier by itself. The husband and both of the boys who were in the car got out, but the wife drowned, along with their dog. Horrible." She closed her eyes and looked a little ill. Then she shook herself and added, "Anyhow, they pulled it out later, but I always wondered what might have drifted out of the car and into the mud there. I guess it's the morbid streak in me. Probably an archaeologist thing. We're all a little creepy that way—we want to dig up dead people and their homes and find out how they lived and died. There's a lot of freaky things to be found in the mud—it's waterlogged history with teredo worms. This end of the old shoreline is fairly wet and it'll take a while after the new seawall is in place for the landfill to dry out and solidify."

"How long?"

"Years. Personally, I plan never to drive through this tunnel once it's finished. Ugh. I even shudder at the idea of taking the train while they're building this. Everything built on the fill or supported by it would be undermined by a tunnel collapse. They had to insert miles of micropiles to keep the historic buildings down here from shifting or collapsing and they're always fighting water seepage that could interfere with the dig here."

"But the train tunnel isn't in the fill, is it?" I asked. I'd been in the southern end of the tunnel and it had seemed pretty solid to me.

"No, it's bored through the bluff, but it's so old that they grandfathered it out of the current inspection and maintenance standards. It's always damp, and it doesn't even have any lights, modern ventilation, or escape routes. You wouldn't want to be stuck in it if the ground at either end subsided a lot."

"No," I said as much to myself as to her. "I can see how that would be bad. But you guys haven't had any problems now that the excavator is working, have you?"

"Oh, a few hiccups, but nothing worth mentioning. They've hit water in a lot of places, and the investigation teams working on the early seawall part of the project found some areas we'll have to work around in the north end where the local tribes used to camp and that kind of thing. There are always areas that will need more stabilization than originally thought, but the monitoring stations will help pinpoint those problems before they get out of hand."

"What monitoring stations?"

"Technically they're called 'monitoring wells.' The project group installed about seven hundred of them along the tunnel route to measure, record, and report things like subsidence and tectonic movement. The well shafts were drilled about three hundred feet deep, but you can spot the covers in the streets and sidewalks from here to Northlake—they look a bit like small manholes that are painted white and there's a black metal seal in the middle that identifies them as monitoring wells. Take a look around and you'll find them once you know what to look for."

"What would they do if you guys found something significant or the monitors showed movement?"

"Oh, I doubt we'll find anything much at this point, but on the subsidence issue, I'm not sure—I'm not a geologist—but I'd guess they'd try to shore things up like they did with the micropiles installed along the Alaskan Way footing. Probably they'd just throw money at it and keep on going. This is Seattle, after all—the town that graft built."

"Would you say, then, that whoever's in charge of this would have no reason to delay and every reason to clear things up and pay off any claims?"

"You mean, like the businesses that are complaining about loss of customers? Or like your client who was hurt?"

"Either. Both."

"Oh, yeah. There's going to be a lot of money to be made out of fancy condos and new hotels with waterfront views built where the viaduct is now. Personally I think the idea of a tunnel through landfill is crazy, but some people obviously want it and they have the influence to get it. If they have to pay a few claims and kiss some extra babies at election time, they're not going to quibble. If you're working for the family of the guy who got hurt, I don't think they have anything to worry about on that score."

She pushed a lock of hair out of her face with the back of one hand. "I think I'd better get back to watching mud before someone gets pissed off. So . . . y'know . . . if there's nothing else you want to know. . . ."

I caught the hint. "No. I'm satisfied. Thanks for the information. I really appreciate it."

"No problem. Here, let me show you the easy way out." She led me south past the pit and back to the trailer, where she reclaimed my hard hat and coat, then went around the trailer and pushed back a narrow door of plywood, revealing the exit route. "Don't fall in front of any trucks this time, OK?"

I smiled and chuckled. "OK. Thanks again."

"You're welcome. 'Bye," she added, closing the door.

I looked around with care, letting the Grey side of my vision range wide, but I saw no sign of James Purlis.

I checked my watch and figured I had enough time to snoop around the area a bit more. I started back up the street under the viaduct, keeping to the sidewalk this time, looking through the Grey for any sign of why Sterling was being badgered by ghosts. From what Held had said, there should have been plenty of spirits in the area, but I didn't know why they would have attached themselves to Sterling—and certainly not to Julianne Goss, who had been quite a few blocks farther north when she met with a mosquito that had probably come from one of the pools of standing water Held had mentioned. Unless the sheer disturbance of the ground had caused some kind of paranormal upheaval I hadn't detected or understood yet, the connection between the two injuries was so thin as to be useless. . . . There had to be something more. I wished again that I knew what had happened to Jordan Delamar—or even where he was right now. My sense that time was precious was strong, though I didn't have any reason for this feeling.

Then I saw her from the corner of my injured eye—a willowy figure in 1920s clothes standing in front of the Hanjin Shipping compound across the street—and dropped all other thoughts from my head as I turned to see what was happening in the Grey. But even when I faced her and used both eyes, the phantom woman remained clear in my vision. Her beautiful face wore a tragic expression that drew me to her. I crossed the road, dodging trucks and cars, and stepped onto the sidewalk in front of the long concrete walls of the warehouse. Giant red cranes loomed in the background, like strange metal horses waiting to feed on a few of the cargo containers stacked around their legs and on the ships moored in front of them.

The ghost did a slow pivot to face me, her body turning without any movement of her limbs. A few strands of dark hair waved around her face and her clothes rippled as if caught in a gentle current. "I fear for them." Her voice had the softest hint of cultured Southern accent.

"For whom?" I asked.

"The fat ones. I would not like more company in my watery den. My dog is somewhere near and he will suffice to chase away my loneliness."

I frowned in thought, tickling out something Held had said. "Are you the lady who drowned here? In the car?"

A tiny smile flickered over her face and vanished again as she nodded. "I am Cannie Trimble. It is good of you to remember me. Few still do."

"The city tries to remember, but it's not easy with so much change. Things get broken and lost."

"Indeed they do. I do not like these newcomers—they frighten me. They are so hungry, so greedy. . . . And they will break the new things to feed their mistresses." Cannie shook her head, making her hair float and fan out in the unseen water. "It will be much worse than their deaths, much worse than the first time, by trickles, one by one. In the market. In the market where the ashes lay, where the player played, that's where the truth lies. Do not let the wheel roll, do not bring me company—I want none here. I am enough."

Ghosts have a bad habit of speaking in riddles—their minds are focused on different things than ours are and without their context, nothing they say makes sense. The "market" reference I thought I understood—Pike Place Market—but the rest meant nothing. Wheels and ashes, players and truth that lied or lay . . . ? Maybe the wheel was something to do with her car that had rolled off the pier . . . ? "Cannie, what wheels, what ashes? Please tell me where to find them."

"Start in the market, end on the pier. Find the boy who played." She turned her head aside, glancing at something I couldn't see. "Jiggs! I'm coming." She turned her face back to mine. "I must go. Please don't let them roll the wheel."

And she vanished as if a cloud had covered the sun and blotted her out. I reached for the temporacline—the shattered planes of time that float in the Grey, recording history in place—but she wasn't there. She was a true apparition, because she had never existed in exactly that state, in exactly this place. I could not reach Cannie Trimble here, I could only take what she'd offered and hope it led to something more.

I would have to start with Pike Place Market—it was the only piece of her puzzle I understood.

EIGHT

It was twelve blocks to the market Hill Climb if I continued on the waterfront. I'm not usually bothered by that sort of distance, but it was nearly five o'clock and while the summer sun might linger, the vendors at the Pike Place Market didn't. Everything but the restaurants and bars would be closed by seven and I'd burn up thirty to forty minutes if I hoofed it. Parking and traffic would both be terrible, so I took a bus. Seattle's mass transit is adequate in downtown, so it didn't take long and I got to the market with about two hours to spend looking for wheels or ashes or whatever Cannie Trimble had been alluding to.

The market used to be one of my favorite parts of Seattle. The old buildings, the crooked little streets and alleys, the bustle, the people, the mix of old and new, residents and tourists, farmers and artists all charmed me—until I became a Greywalker. Now those layers of time and human occupation so densely packed make it a churning sea of Grey that I cannot ignore or travel through with alacrity. It's about as haunted as a place can get without being a battlefield or a hospital. People have lived, died, loved, hated, and committed politics all over the area, and that sort of activity tends to leave memories that play on as ghosts. It's also as twisty and layered as a rabbit warren, which adds to the difficulty of getting around even with the clearest of senses, and mine were currently slightly impaired. Walking into the market was, for me, like walking into the noisiest, most crowded party ever, where half the guests ignored me while stepping on my feet and shouting in my ears anyhow. The incorporeal dead and their ice shards of history pushed into me, turning summer into winter and bringing a fog of silvered vision and darting, colored light. I couldn't sink into the Grey to avoid the worst of the mess, since I needed to talk to living people as much or more than to ghosts—not to mention that I was pretty deeply submersed anyway. I plowed deeper into the market, threading past bodies that breathed heat as well as those that didn't, feeling them nudge and push and grasp. I kept my bag tucked tight against my side to fend off living pickpockets, and hoped nothing less human was going to run its light fingers through my stuff, either.

Pike Place Market is actually a collection of buildings that house shops and stalls coming off Pike Avenue and turning onto Pike Place and Post Alley for several cramped and colorful blocks as dense as a box of bricks. Originally it was a true farmers' market—a place where local farmers, ranchers, and fishermen could bring their fresh goods in the morning and go home with empty baskets and heavy wallets in the afternoon. Now it was as much a collection of permanent shops and restaurants as it was day stalls. Shop owners, day vendors, artists, craftspeople, and entertainers catered to the tourists as well as the locals in a cacophony of pitches, catcalls, and music, carried on the smell of fresh fish, hot grease, new bread, garbage, and sweat.

I wasn't sure where to start looking for "the boy who played," or for ashes and wheels, but I knew I couldn't canvass every vendor and shop clerk. There are always a few people who've been around forever and know everyone—local characters like Artis the Spoonman and the guys who throw fish—I just had to find one who might be able to tell me if there was a connection between the market and Jordan Delamar—which was a far more pressing problem than cryptic references uttered by a lonely spirit on the waterfront.

I made my way toward the pig. Everyone starts at Rachel, so I figured I would, too, since metal and glass often cancel a bit of my Grey vision. The life-sized bronze piggy bank is supposedly a dead ringer for a real pig that used to live on Whidbey Island—though how that connected to the market, I'd never been sure. But there stands Rachel the Pig—steadfastly collecting money for the Pike Place Market Foundation—come hell or high water or runaway taxi-cabs like the one that nearly knocked the quarter-ton metal porker over a couple of years ago. Seattle's eccentric metal structures seem to have a magnetic attraction for out-of-control vehicles. But the pig was on its hefty bronze feet as usual at the outside corner of Pike Avenue and Pike Place, in front of City Fish—home of flung fillets and slung salmon.

I felt a little dizzy negotiating the heavy tide of Grey that my one overly sensitive eye saw slightly out of sync with the other. I stumbled a little as I reached the pig, missing the short curb in the ghostly mist around my feet. I turned, catching my balance as I took a step backward and bumped into the piggy bank.

"Careful there, dear. You'll give that poor piggy a bruise with that skinny butt of yours."

I glanced to the left and saw a stout woman in a voluminous

purple skirt and a hat made from parts of beer cans crocheted together with bright red yarn. Her hair stuck out from beneath the hat in gray tufts, brushing the shoulders of her blouse, which was covered in pins bearing racy slogans such as I USED TO BE SNOW WHITE, BUT I DRIFTED. She was giving me a sly smile.

"Early in the day for celebrating, isn't it?" she asked.

Seattle is known for its passive-aggressive friendliness, so I was a little taken aback. Then the woman laughed. "Oh, there, I'm just yanking your chain, girl! You looked so serious, I thought you needed a good poke in the funny bone. You only live once, you know, but if you do it right that should be more than enough. Now, what's making you so grumpy-faced? Anything I can do to help?"

"I'm trying to find out about a guy who might have worked around here or had some connection to the market recently. . . ."

"There's a lot of people working here and hanging around. What's his name?"

"Jordan Delamar."

She shook her head. "Not ringing a bell, but I haven't been around much in a while and I don't know all the new folks. What's he do?"

"I'm not sure. I think he might be 'the boy who played' if that means anything. . . ."

"Played what? Because a boy who plays might be one of the kids down in the ramp, or it might be one of the buskers, or—if we're lucky—he might be a playboy and carry us off to his Playboy Mansion. I bet you'd be quite a bunny, honey." She laughed at her joke.

"I don't think I'd fit in very well," I replied. "I'm not polite and subservient. I'm more the poking-things-with-a-stick type."

She laughed again. "Well, that makes two of us, sweetie! I'll tell you what—you try the ramp, and if that doesn't work out, try the buskers. They know *everybody*. You tell 'em Mae sent you," she added with a gleeful cackle.

I nodded, a touch overwhelmed but willing to take the suggestion, since it was all I had at the moment. "All right."

She grinned, but it faded quickly and she peered at me. "You do that. But just one thing, Miss Pokes-Things-with-Sticks—can you tell me what I'm doing here? I haven't been around in such a long time and yet . . . here I am again."

"I'm afraid I don't know. Where have you been until now?"

"Dead, honey. I'm *plumb* sure of it," she said, turning away, cackling and fading from my sight.

She'd seemed pretty solid for a ghost—solid enough that I hadn't been certain right up until the end of the interview. I had a feeling I should have gotten a joke, there, but I hadn't. I hoped I'd figure it out eventually—unresolved questions always bug me.

I had to ask around to find it, but it turned out "the ramp" was an actual ramp inside the area of lower shops. That section of the market starts about fifty feet below on Western Avenue across from the Pike Hill Climb and spreads up the cliff like some kind of wooden vine to the original shopping area at the top of the bluff. The market folks call that section "Down Under." Since I was so close, I headed downstairs first, plunging through the flood of ghosts and the tipping icebergs of temporaclines.

At the stair landing is a doorway to the washrooms on one side and the hallways of the shops on the other, but no ramp, so I went down farther. At the bottom I came out onto an open area that connected the market buildings on my side with the former LaSalle

Hotel building on the other and a staircase in between that walks down to Western Avenue. There was a large red musical note with a yellow number painted on the ground in front of a mural of the market. I'd seen these signs around the market, but wasn't sure what they were for, and whatever this one was meant for, it wasn't in use at the moment—at least not by anyone alive, though the red spot was so deeply awash in ghost-stuff that it was difficult to see with my left eye. Layers of memory lay over the spot, crystal-strewn with shards of temporaclines enclosed in a wide blue net of light. Peering through the Grey sideways I saw a ley line as bright as Las Vegas shooting straight through the site and arrowing for the Hill Climb below. Whatever happened on that red note, it was magical. Reluctantly, I turned away from it and headed into the building, looking for the ramp.

I found it in a moment, just inside the market building on my right: a narrow wooden way between two sets of shops that dropped steeply to the next floor and led into a crooked labyrinth of passages to a large atrium over the main hub of Down Under. Stepping onto the ramp I smelled hay and horse dung and could hear the jingle and stamp of long-gone horses in harness. Large shadow shapes brushed past me, whickering and blowing wet, oat-scented breath into my face. Smaller shadows, some solemn, others laughing and running, raced past, some with the ghostly horses, others from some other time, after the horses had gone. "I want to catch him," one whispered.

I stopped, looking around in the normal world as best I could with one eye firmly in the Grey. I was alone on the narrow ramp. I closed my eyes and dropped down into the ghost world, letting my fingers spread and float forward, feeling for the layers of frozen history that laced through the place like rutile in quartz. A cold edge fluttered under my touch and I opened my eyes, peering into the misty place between the worlds, confronted with stacks of ragged time. I pushed on one, tilting it until I could see without falling in.

The ramp was dusty with bits of straw and dirt knocked from the hooves of the dray horses led by young boys. The lower level was now filled with stalls around a central work area where the massive beasts stood to be dressed up in their bits of harness or blankets. Apparently Down Under had once been a stable for the cart horses that had brought the farmers' goods in to market. But none of these memories of boys was the one I wanted to talk to. I touched another temporacline and pulled it back. . . .

This time it was not the atrium or shops I was seeing, but some other place, its crystallized moment of history displaced by some strong will or association. A large room, packed with cots and people dressed in dirtied white clothes and thick gauze masks who moved among the shivering, miserable patients on the beds. Almost half of the shapes I saw beneath the thin blankets were too small to be adults. One of them retched and turned in its cot, huge fevered eyes catching sight of me. It—I couldn't tell if the child was a boy or a girl—raised its hand an inch or so off the bed, as if it wanted to touch me, but hadn't the strength. I walked forward, unable to resist that sad plea, and crouched next to the bed, as incorporeal to the shadows that passed around me as any other phantom.

"Are you an angel?" the child whispered. "I don't want to die."

"I can't stop that," I said, thinking my heart would break. "This time—your time—is past."

"My mother already died of the influenza. My sister, too."

"I'm sorry."

"Did you take them to heaven? Will I see them?"

One of the nurses had stopped and turned toward the child, staring with wide eyes, stricken but unable to see me. I didn't know why anyone could see me on the icy plains of a moment's history—sometimes they do, sometimes they don't—but I knew nothing I did made any difference. This had happened. Some child had seen a ghost or an angel or just a flicker of desire for comfort given momentary flesh as he or she lay dying in a makeshift ward near the market, the smells of soil and fish, produce and garbage, hay and horses slipping in with the sounds of commerce even under the stench of carbolic acid and vomit and the whispering pleas of the dying.

"You'll see them there. In heaven," I replied. What else was there to say?

And it smiled at me, this ghost of a child. Smiled and turned its head aside, breathing softer, softer, and then not at all.

I ripped myself away from the horrible piece of history and dropped a bit, stumbling, onto the atrium floor only feet from where I'd stood a moment—a century?—before. A man caught my arm and steadied me.

"Are you all right?" he asked. He peered at my face. "Are you—? Oh my. You're not all right at all, are you? C'mon. Come with me."

This total stranger propped me up with his shoulder and walked me into the magic shop under the ramp, steering me through the displays of toys and tricks, into a corner. He helped me into a chair.

"Sit tight. I'll be right back."

In a moment, he returned with a bottle of cold water and a box of tissues. "Here. Are you doing OK now?"

I took the tissues and wiped unexpected tears off my face. "Yeah. I'm OK. I was just . . . upset about something. It's nothing."

"It can't be something and nothing."

I glanced up at him—a skinny guy in his thirties wearing pressed trousers and a striped shirt under a brocade vest, trendy glasses, and a handlebar mustache that was carefully waxed into a stiff curl on each cheek.

"It was something, but it's not anything anymore."

"Did you see it, then?"

"What?"

"Did you see the ghosts?"

Startled, I stared at him. "Ghosts."

"Yeah, the market is haunted. Sometimes you see kids down here who aren't actually here anymore. It's kind of perturbing."

"Have you seen them?"

"Me? No. I hear them once in a while, when there's no one around. And once, our display of dollhouse furniture was all rearranged and the glass on one side was broken when there was no one here to break it. But that's about all. Maybe the occasional levitating stuffed toy, but nothing really amazing. What about you? You seemed really upset."

"I thought I saw . . . patients—medical patients. Little kids in cots."

"Oh, there used to be a tuberculosis clinic around here, somewhere. Way back when the market was new. And I heard that the Market Theater was used to hold sick people during the flu epidemic. That would upset anyone—seeing something like that."

"You believe in ghosts?"

He bit his lip and made a crooked face. "Ehhh . . . I'm not sure. Things happen around here that certainly seem to be unaccountable, and it's romantic to imagine it's ghosts. But I haven't ever seen an apparition per se. And there could always be some other reason things move or make noise or seem . . . kind of weird. We're on top of the train tunnel, you know. And things have been a little disturbed since they started construction on the Route Ninety-nine tunnel. There have even been a few accidents because of tunnel construction stuff. So maybe it's not ghosts. Maybe it's just guys in overalls digging holes."

"You don't have to humor me. I *do* believe in ghosts."

"Oh. Well then. Yeah, the place is practically a ghost hotel."

I just *looked* at him. He glanced aside, giving a rueful smile. "Really. You work here long enough, you start to believe in the strange." He looked back at me and offered his hand. "Hey, I'm Derek Russell. I didn't mean to tease you. Sorry. Apology accepted?"

I reflected his smile. "Yeah. Apology accepted." I took his hand. "Harper Blaine."

"Nice to meet you, Harper. Were you looking for ghosts or for something else? I've got a lot of interesting tricks and toys in here." He picked up a fuzzy, bewinged green thing with a face full of tentacles. "Plush Cthulhu, maybe?"

I shook off the adorably dreadful Lovecraftian horror. "I was actually trying to find a guy who might have worked around here. Jordan Delamar. Someone suggested he might be a busker . . . ?"

"I don't know him, but maybe. There's a lot of buskers in the market and they don't all come every day."

"How could I find him—or find out if he worked here?"

"Oh, you'd have to ask at the market office. They issue the performers' badges, so they would have a list of who has a badge, but they'd have no way to tell who was here when. The buskers just set up on the notes and do their thing when they want to and move on to the next note if they want to stay longer. I think the limit's an hour before they have to move on. They can put out a tip jar or hat or whatever. Some of them sell CDs if they have them."

"What do you mean 'they set up on the notes'?"

"The red music notes painted on the ground. There's one just outside the ramp—you must have seen it, since I don't hear anyone playing out there—the wall reflects a lot of sound into the market from that location. It's a favorite spot, since it's got such great acoustics and plenty of space for a large group. Most of the spots are pretty small—just a one or a two—so the larger groups, like the Andean guys, can't use them. There are a few spots that are very popular regardless of how big they are and others that aren't as much, but they all get busy in the summer."

So that's what the red note on the ground had been. It certainly explained why it was not only rife with memories and spirits but right on a ley line—music and the Grey have a lot in common and strong emotions and powerful actions are always associated with ley lines. "What did you mean 'a one or a two'? Is that a measure of popularity or priority or something?"

"Oh no. There are numbers painted in yellow indicating how many can work on that location. Any performer can work any location solo, but bigger groups can only work where the number is the same or higher than their group size."

"Clever."

"Yeah, it is."

"But what stops the buskers from just wedging in as many people as they can?"

"Aside from the fire marshal? It's not practical in a lot of spots even if it looks big enough. You want to slow traffic, but not stop it.

Most of the buskers are good about sharing and keeping the spaces clean and not overloading the area. There are always a few who don't play well with others, but they don't last."

"Do you know a lot of the buskers?"

"Not so many. I don't have an assistant most of the time, so I don't get to go out of the shop much to meet folks. Andy's here today, or I wouldn't have been out there to catch you."

"Oh. And thank you for that. Do you know if any of the buskers have been injured in the past . . . six months or so?"

Russell shrugged. "I'm afraid I really don't. You'd have to ask them. They'd know. A lot of them will have gone for the day by now—though they might move down to the waterfront until it gets dark."

"Is there anyplace they hang out?" I asked.

"Oh . . . I'm not sure. If you're looking for someone, your best bet would be to ask at the market office, or just start asking the buskers at the notes. Someone will know, eventually."

A high-pitched whistling cut through the air of the shop. Russell looked toward it. "Oh . . . damn. I have to go find out what Andy's broken this time. I'm sorry to bunk off. Are you OK now?"

I smiled and stood up, offering the tissues and water bottle back to him. "I'm fine. Thanks, Derek."

He took the tissues, but waved the water bottle away. "You keep that. And good luck with your search. If you ever need a magic trick or a stuffed elder god, drop back by. OK?"

"OK."

I suspect he was just as glad to see me go—spooky women who believe in ghosts can be bad for business.

I got out of the shop and up into the market proper without being sucked back into visions of the past, though I was rushed and bumped by torrents of ghosts, including more children and gruffer adults who seemed preoccupied and confused, even for the dead. I chose the longer route out of Down Under, coming up the stairs on the west side of the building that overlooked Western Avenue, rather than braving the ramp again.

NINE

A s I walked up the steps, I heard violin music. Emerging into the open space between the buildings once again, I saw two musicians standing on the note in front of the market mural—a young man and a young woman, both with short hair and dark clothes, their violin cases open on the ground in front of them. One case held a hopeful dollar bill, the other a few CDs in plastic cases with a hand-lettered sign that read CD's $12 EACH—SUPPORT CORNISH STUDENTS TRIP TO EUROPE. Their music soared upward in the resonant space, each bow sending a tendril of song and colorful energy twining around its companion's thread, flowing into the road behind them and up into the market as if alive, seeking a path to the sky. People lined the rail of the staircase landing above, listening for a few moments while they waited for friends to emerge from the washrooms or what have you. A few passersby dropped coins into the case, making muffled clanks that reminded me of the harness chains of phantom horses.

I stopped to listen, letting the music flow over me with the re-membered thrill of elation I'd once had for dancing. I had loved it once—even when it was a misery imposed on me by necessity and my mother—and this feeling was why. And for the first time in a long while I didn't mind the memory. I guess I was finally growing out of my resentment and anger—I'm stubborn that way. I felt an odd pressure in my feet and legs and realized I was stretching up, hampered by my boots, as if my legs wanted to dance, even when the rest of me resisted. I took a breath and calmed myself down, settling back onto my heels, not because I refused to dance but because now wasn't the time. And it's dangerous to roll up en pointe in hiking boots—I hadn't had to undergo the surgeries Olivia Sterling had been through during my student days or professional career, and I didn't want to head that way now, either. My odd relationship with the Grey seemed to have granted me preternatural health and longer life than the average human—or so I'd been told by the only other Greywalker I'd ever met—but even that wouldn't fix foolishness or damaged tendons. When the violinists paused, I stepped forward, picking up one of the CDs.

The girl smiled at me, taking her instrument off her shoulder. The boy followed suit in a moment, his eyes hazy as if the music held him in a daze while a kaleidoscopic mist of colors swarmed around him, touching the girl, then coiling back to him. The girl's aura was pure gold that burned like a steady flame.

"Hi," she said. "Would you like to buy a CD? We're raising money to spend the fall quarter in Europe."

"You're at Cornish College?" I asked—it was a pretty safe bet they were students and not from Cornwall, but I asked anyhow.

"For now."

"How long have you been busking down here? Is this a regular gig for you two?"

She shrugged. "Not so much. We're both pretty busy during the school year. We only get down here in the summer and occasional weekends. Sean doesn't like to play alone."

"I see." Judging by their energy, Sean was the more brilliant of them, but not as strong-willed or focused as his partner, so I understood his reluctance to do this gig by himself. I looked at the disc cover and pointed at the names of the performers. "You're Selena?"

She smiled and nodded again, her aura flickering a touch of orange annoyance before she tamped it down. "That's me."

I dug a twenty-dollar bill out of my pocket and offered it to her. She took it with another professional smile and tucked it into her own pocket as I refused change and put the CD into my bag. I wasn't as interested in the music as in their goodwill and that was little enough to pay.

"You don't know another busker named Jordan Delamar, do you?"

Selena shook her head. "No, I can't say I do. Sorry."

I shrugged it off. "Not a problem. Thanks for the CD—you play beautifully."

Now she beamed. "Thank you!"

I stepped back, letting them go back to work as she obviously wished to do. I noticed she had to nudge the dreamy-eyed Sean to attention as I started to leave. I carried on, hoping to find some other buskers before the market closed, since I'd already missed office hours. The music followed me up the stairs.

Back on the street level, I waded into the swirling ghost fog of the market's main street and made my way with care across the road to the Sanitary Market Building, sure that I'd seen musicians and other performers in several locations along that block of Pike Place and

Post Alley. It was hard to pick out specific strands of music or patter above the general hubbub of cars and trucks, shoppers, ghosts, and vendors that flowed all over the street and sidewalks like a river flooding its banks while the fish tried to swim any direction they could. I felt distinctly like a salmon trying to get upstream.

At the first corner, next to the Greek take-out place, a man dressed head to foot in bright blue was bending balloons into hats, animals, and flowers for the amusement of small children and their parents standing in line for a quick bite to eat. Next to him, a ghostly double made a balloon poodle and wafted the finished phantom animal into the air, where it dissolved into sparkles that rained down on the creations of the living man beside him. A little boy in a striped shirt scampered over from his parents, waving a dollar bill, and offered it to the man in blue. The man bent down to listen to the boy's whispered request.

He laughed and straightened up to inflate some balloons and begin shaping them. The spirit beside him did the same. I watched from the crowd-eddy created by a spiral staircase behind them as the living balloon man shaped a monster's head and added goggly eyes by scribbling black pupils on two small white balloons, which he then tied onto the green monster face. Done, he showed it to the boy and asked, "How's that?"

"Great!" the boy yelled, jumping up and down in excitement and causing a few people to step off the sidewalk to continue onward in safety.

The balloon man laughed, once again mirrored by his incorporeal double, and put the monster onto the boy's head as a hat. The boy growled and pranced back to his parents, saying, "I'm a t'ranasaurus! Grroww!"

The boy reminded me so much of the Danzigers' son, Brian, that I laughed myself, and then felt a pang that my friends were still in Europe and I hadn't seen them in a couple of years now. I hoped they were doing well, but I still missed them—even troublesome Brian, who would have been starting school this autumn if I remembered correctly. I sidled closer to the balloon man as he started on a long-stemmed balloon flower for a little girl.

"Hi," I said.

"Hi there, pretty lady! Be right with you."

"I don't need a balloon. I just wanted to ask you a question."

"OK, then. Fire away." He bent a long red balloon into loops and twisted it around a green balloon to make the blossom, without looking at me, concentrating on his creation and sending an occasional wink to the little girl in front of him. His ghost did the same, ignoring me completely.

"Do you know another busker named Jordan Delamar?"

"Not sure. What's he do?"

"That's what I don't know. But I think he was injured a few months ago."

He stooped and handed the balloon flower to the girl and received a few bills from her parents in exchange before he turned to me, absently twisting a balloon between his hands into crazy loops.

"Oh . . . yeah. Didn't know his name. About . . . six or seven months ago, I think that was—around December. Part of an awning in the slabs came down and hit a guy. Knocked him flat. They had to take him to the hospital."

"Do you know what happened to him after that? Is he back?"

"Umm . . . I don't know. I haven't heard any more about him. I'm not here much in the off-season—not a lot of call for balloon animals when the kids aren't around. I do a lot of theater stuff and private parties then, instead. I get some good gigs around Christmas to keep kids entertained while their parents are shopping or waiting in line for photos with Santa. That sort of thing." Another child tugged at his pants leg and he smiled down before he gave me a quick glance, saying, "Sorry—I have to get back to work here."

"Oh, just one more question—what's 'the slabs'?" I asked.

"Oh, that's the outdoor vendor area at the north end of the main arcade building, near Steinbrueck Park. Doesn't get much use in the winter, except for the wreath vendors around Christmas." He turned his attention to his young admirer.

"Thanks for the help," I said, dropping a bill into his balloon-bedecked tip jar.

"Thank *you!*" he called after me as I shoved my way back into the diminishing stream of shoppers, heading northwest, toward the world's first Starbucks store and the slabs.

But by the time I reached the row of horizontal cement tabletops attached to the wall where Western Avenue swept up to meet Pike Place and Virginia Street, it was nearly seven and the only people willing to talk to me were the vendors who hadn't yet started packing up for the day.

A thin, long-haired man wearing sunglasses and sitting in a cloth lawn chair beside a selection of small paintings and T-shirts of cartoon cats committing dastardly deeds nodded when I asked about the accident in December. "Yeah, I remember that. There was a big awning over this area because of the rain—we all chipped in to put it up so we could do some holiday business. There was a work crew up here doing something about the tunnel. Some kind of study about vibrations or sound waves. They were drilling a hole. . . . I don't remember exactly why. Anyhow, whatever they were up to, it was real messy and made the awning collapse at the far end. This guy was standing under it at the time, so he took a nosedive into their dirt pile and got clonked on the head pretty good by the falling awning."

"Did you know him? The man who got clonked on the head?" I asked.

"Not particularly—I mean, like, I didn't know his name or anything. Mostly we called him Banjo Guy."

"Have you seen him around since then?"

He shook his head and started folding T-shirts now it was obvious he wasn't going to make any more sales today. "Nope. Not that I can recall. I suppose I might not recognize him without the banjo. He wasn't an unusual-looking guy. Black guy. Kind of average, kind of not too distinctive one way or another. Young—mid-twenties maybe. Sorry I'm not much help."

"No, no—the information about the awning was a lot of help. Thanks." He clearly had no more information to give me.

Jordan Delamar had been injured about the right time according to the insurance billing records I'd been able to snoop. But whether he was the Banjo Guy or "the boy who played" I wasn't yet certain. The only thing I was pretty sure of was that he wasn't an engineer or architect or computer modeler, so that wasn't the link between the three patients. I'd have to come back in the morning and see if he owned a performer's badge and if he did, verify that he was the person who'd been injured here. Then I'd have to find out where he was. I didn't think I'd be lucky enough to catch any of the buskers on their way out of the market for the day. Most of the vendors and shopkeepers were already closed and the buskers had disappeared while I'd been talking to the man with the bad-kitty pictures.

I started to turn around and go up the steep block of Virginia Street to First to catch a bus back to my office—where I'd left the truck—but paused as I thought I saw a familiar face. Across the street on a small promontory of the old bluff that the market stands on was Victor Steinbrueck Park. Against the Tree of Life homeless memorial—backlit by the summer sky that was darkening with unusually black clouds—was a skinny, restless figure that rocked from foot to foot, flapping its arms as if cold. I knew him—a homeless man I'd met on a case in Pioneer Square a few years back and continued to see around—though I couldn't recall when I'd seen him last. He was called "Twitcher" by almost everyone—he suffered from a rare neurological disorder that set him in constant motion. I frowned and walked toward the park, thinking I could ask him if he'd relocated up to Steinbrueck Park and if he'd been around when the awning accident had occurred.

Twitcher stood near the glass "pool" around the memorial that had been installed last October. He turned his head as if he saw me, and I paused for a moment, shocked at how emaciated he'd become. Twitcher was always nervously thin, since he was literally never still. Most people thought he was crazy, or stupid, or both. He wasn't either, but he was afraid of doctors and he had difficulty making his needs known between his spastic motions. He'd given up and begun living on the streets when the state stopped paying for his treatment.

A car blared its horn at me from my blind side as I started across the street and I turned to shout at the driver for running the Stop sign. When I turned back, Twitcher was gone. Not a hint of him could I find, even when I ran up and down Western for a block in each direction looking for him. There was nowhere to hide—and why would he when he had seemed to be waiting for me? I'd have to

ask his friends Sandy and Zip—fellow Pioneer Square homeless people—if they knew what Twitcher was up to. Tomorrow.

As I waited for the bus to take me back to Pioneer Square, rain
began to fall. The clouds that had rolled in as I searched for information about Delamar—or "the boy who played"—let down a steady
drizzle that thickened into a summer downpour by the time I had to
exit the bus. It looked as if we'd have the usual gloomy, wet Fourth
of July that we'd had more often than not since I'd moved to Seattle.
It wasn't my fault, though; the occurrence was common enough to
rate a joke that summer didn't start here until July fifth, just to make
sure we all knew where we were. I wasn't really dressed for the rain
and my thin jacket was soaked through by the time I got to my office
building, but the sudden storm had one bright side: James Purlis
wasn't too likely to be tailing me in this weather.

I really needed to talk to Quinton about his father's interference.
I didn't like being the rope in this tug-of-war and if the situation
didn't improve soon, I'd have to make my position a bit more clear
to Papa Purlis. I suspected he still thought I was mostly harmless—
he struck me as overly confident or maybe he was just a misogynistic
ass—but I had no problem with proving him wrong. In a way, I was
looking forward to it. . . .

TEN

I headed upstairs to my office, yanking off my wet jacket as I went and shaking the worst of the water out of my hair. I thought I should make sure I didn't have mail or messages pending, but what was waiting for me was Olivia Sterling.

She was plopped on the creaking wooden floor of my historic building right outside my office door, doing split stretches, but she bounced up as she caught sight of me, wincing slightly as she put her weight back on her feet. "Ms. Blaine, I'm so sorry—I should have called, I know, and I was going to, but I had the chance and I just dropped in. I was going to leave soon, but I thought I could wait just another minute and—"

She was so preoccupied by her story that she didn't seem to notice I was wet. I put my free hand up between us to stem the fast flow of her words. "It's all right, Olivia. You don't have to excuse your presence and you don't have to tell me everything in five seconds or less. Slow down."

She caught her breath, nodding and sending her long blond ponytail bobbing and swaying, leaving trails of color and mist on my Grey vision. "You asked me to call, but I couldn't," she said. "I got one of my dad's scribbling pads, but the reason I didn't wait is that he did something really, really bizarre today and it freaked my mom out. I had to call the nursing assistant to come and help with my dad and then Mom was still freaking, so the nurse said she'd stay for a while to calm her down, so I snuck out with both pads."

"Both pads?" I asked as I unlocked my office door and waved her inside.

She nodded again, still seeming breathless in her excitement, and scooped a large shoulder bag up from the floor. She followed me into my office, saying, "Yeah. I picked up some of the more recent ones to bring you, but the thing Dad did today was on a new one, so I wanted to bring that, too, and I had to be kind of sneaky to get it and then leave most of the others so I could get out without anyone noticing I had them. I didn't want Mom to freak out more and you really need to see this."

She started digging in her bag, looking down, and stumbled into the client chair, stubbing a toe. She winced again.

"Why don't you sit down first?" I suggested as I hung my dripping jacket on the coatrack. "Then I can see what you've brought without you falling over." I turned on the heater, which rattled as it started up.

Olivia slid into the chair and put her bag on her lap, then dug back into it. She pulled out two pads of lined yellow paper—one dog-eared and the other still crisp and sharp-edged except for the top few pages, which were bent and creased. She held out both of the pads to me. "This time, I think Dad is writing to us—or to my mom at least. We used to think he was when this started, but then we figured out that he wasn't and most of what he wrote was just crazy stuff, but this is not like that. Here."

I took the pads and sat down so I could study them under the stronger light from my desk lamp rather than the diffused room light. I had to hold them at an angle so my hair wouldn't drip on them while I read. I counted myself lucky that my shirt was only damp and might dry before I had to head out again.

The first two pages of the newest pad were the same mad scribbling I'd seen at the Sterling house, but the third page, written crosswise, read, "Mary. We die by inches in the noisy dark. If not soon, I will not come b . . ."

I looked up from the page into Olivia's face. Her eyebrows were high and her eyes wide as she bit her lip, trying not to pant. "My mom went crazy when she read it. That's her name—Mary. And the writing is Dad's, not like most of the other writing. He wrote it with his right hand. All the other stuff he did with his left." She watched me for a moment, waiting for my response.

I was stunned and it took a few seconds to figure out what I wanted to say to her. "You're certain the writing is your father's?"

"I saw him do it," she replied.

"No. I meant to ask if you checked the writing against a sample to be certain. You said the rest of the writing on these pads isn't like his. How are you sure of it?"

"I know what my dad's writing looks like! But yeah, I did check, because it's been a while and I . . . was trying to calm Mom down, but it only made her worse." She hung her head. "He's trying to talk to us and it's just making things worse!" She began crying, her ponytail flopping over her face as her shoulders shook with the spasms of her weeping.

I came around my desk and tried to soothe her, but I'm clumsy and self-conscious with kids of any age and I wasn't quite sure what I should do and what I shouldn't.

Olivia threw herself against my chest, flinging her arms around me and squeezing hard enough to shorten my breath, wailing her turmoil. "It's not fair! It's not fair! He's dying and there's nothing I can do!"

She had me trapped, so I put my arms around her waist and let her hold on and cry. I felt her warm tears soaking through my shirt and figured it was just one of those things—I wasn't destined to be dry today. "Olivia," I whispered. "Olivia, there's still hope. Don't cry. Dying isn't dead. Not yet. We'll find a way to help your dad. I promise."

I knew I'd regret it, but I had to say it, even if it ruined me.

"Real promise?" she asked, snuffling against me.

"Real promise. He broke through long enough to leave a note for your mother—and you. He's just like you and your mom—stronger than he looks. I will find a way. You'll help me, won't you?"

She loosened her grip and leaned back to look up at me. Her face was red, swollen, and streaked with tears and snot—she looked frightful, but she wasn't crying now. "Me? How can I help you more than I did? I don't understand."

"You brought me this note. I'll read the rest of the pages. I know they have clues, but I may need to ask you questions or I might need you to do something to help your dad."

She looked hopeful, then wary. "Like, what kind of thing?"

"I don't know yet. Nothing gross or inappropriate. Probably nothing big—it's almost always something that seems trivial that turns out to be the key."

"You're sure?"

"No. I'm making my best guess, but I have done this kind of thing before."

She let me go and sat back in the chair, wiping her face with the backs of her hands. "You have?"

"Once or twice."

She stared at me, biting her lip again, and probably trying to decide if I was crazy or not. She started to nod, making up her mind, but squeaked when a sharp little tune squealed from her bag. She dug frantically and found her cell phone. She glanced at it and moaned. "Oh no! I have to go!"

"Do you need a lift?" I asked as she scrambled around, getting up and heading for the door.

She glanced back over her shoulder. "No. I can manage. I have a friend downstairs. . . . I—do you really promise . . . ?"

I nodded. "I do."

She gave me a trembling smile before she turned and bolted out my door. I could hear her running down the stairs until her footsteps died away. I hoped I wasn't going to disappoint her—it sounded as if Kevin Sterling was fading, as if he were already a ghost himself. I doubted Julianne and the mysterious Jordan Delamar were any better off. I had to find Delamar and the thing that linked all three patients soon or none of them would ever wake up.

In spite of my discomfort in my damp state, I threw myself at the notebooks and Stymak's recordings for hours, until I was dizzy and exhausted from fighting my Grey vision and beating my brain against the apparent nonsense of the sounds and the words. I was drier, but no wiser. I gathered up what I had and took it home, hoping I'd find my lover there, teasing the ferret and ready to show off. . . .

*   *   *

Still no Quinton when I got to the condo, nor later that night, and no reply to messages. I was frustrated and starting to worry and only the thought that James Purlis wouldn't have been shadowing me if he already had his son's forcibly bought attention gave me any solace. I hadn't considered how much time Quinton and I spent together these days. We hadn't for the first two years we knew each other. Even after becoming lovers, we were more often apart than together, since neither of us was comfortable changing our lives to that extent. But since then things had evolved so slowly I hadn't noticed that we now saw each other nearly every day and he slept with me more often than we slept apart. Without any intention, without realizing how we had changed, we had become a couple and I liked it more than I would have imagined. More than I would have liked it years ago when I felt I needed no one but myself—could trust no one but myself—to make my life what I wanted. The downside was this worry I had over what might be happening where I couldn't see and shouldn't intrude in his life. No matter how much I loved him, or how much our lives had become entwined, each of us had our own needs and our own problems that couldn't be changed by the other's desire for it. I still didn't like sitting it out, though. Eventually, I'd have to go looking for Quinton or his father and put a stop to the battle of wills that had me in the middle—and I knew whose side I'd be on.

I played with Chaos for a while and tried to sleep, but did a lousy job of it and got up in the morning grumpy and still half-blind. Besides my work, Quinton and I were supposed to have dinner with Phoebe Mason tonight. Right now I wasn't sure he'd make it. Uncomfortably aware of my aloneness, I decided to take the ferret with me back to Pike Place Market. The main arcades are, by default, open to animals because it's impossible to close them—the Sanitary Market Building is called that not because it's any cleaner than the others but because it used to be the only building people couldn't take their horses into. These days, horses are about the only animal you *won't* see passing through the market from time to time. I doubted anyone would have a problem with Chaos peeping out of my bag as she likes to do. Not to mention, she's more of a "people person" than I am and today was going to be a long round of talking to strangers. A little edge in the conversation would be welcome.

Last night's unexpected downpour had already been swept away on the morning breeze—even if the gray sky hadn't been. The air was cooler, but not enough to frighten off the tourists, so I was reasonably confident I'd be able to find some buskers around if the market office wasn't able to give me a line on Delamar's whereabouts. I wasn't foolish enough to go out without my coat this time, though. I've gotten used to getting wet, but that doesn't mean I like it.

I got to the market office just a few minutes past opening. Like the rest of the place, the office was thickly haunted and looked fogbound to my vision. One tall female ghost with a hard face under a pile of dark hair glared at me as I entered and watched me the entire time I was there. I chose to ignore her—I'd have time to figure out her problem later, if I gave a damn.

The office was as busy in the normal plane as in the Grey. When I entered I found a frantic secretary and a handful of other people dashing in and out of the front room with an odd assortment of objects, paperwork, and problems. One of the problems was a monkey at which Chaos took one look before she dove to the bottom of my bag.

The woman holding the monkey tried to put it on the secretary's desk, but each time she put it down, the monkey jumped back onto her chest and climbed up to sit on her shoulder, wrapping its arms around her head. "Get this damned thing off me!" she yelled. "It's been crawling all over my stall and throwing fruit on the ground since six a.m. and if I'm stuck with it for one more hour I'm going to drown it. And if that means drowning myself in the process, I will!"

"Where's Animal Control?" the secretary asked the nearest person passing by. "Didn't anyone call them?"

"We did, but they said they can't come for the monkey until they deal with a bear out in Crown Hill," came the reply as the person vanished behind a wall.

"Oh God . . . is this some kind of hoax? What is this, Animal Planet?"

"City Fish lost a monkfish this morning, and a bunch of shrimp got loose in the main arcade stairway, too," the absent person called back, accompanied by a lot of rattling and clanging.

The glaring ghost seemed to find the hullabaloo amusing; she smirked at me as if, somehow, this was all a joke I should have gotten. I stared blankly back until she was distracted by something else.

"Please tell me the monkfish wasn't alive when it went AWOL," the secretary said.

"It was still flopping. . . . Ah! I got it!"

The woman with the monkey on her head unwound the creature's arms one more time and held it at arm's length. "Please let it be a shotgun. . . ."

A man with a pile of cloth in his arms came out from the other side of the wall. "Monkfish was apprehended in the women's bathroom on Down Under One. And, yes, we have no shotgun—also no bananas—but we do have a tablecloth! Hold the monkey where I can get it. . . ."

"If it were that easy, we'd have wrapped the little bastard up hours ago!"

The man threw the large, dirty tablecloth toward the struggling monkey. The monkey tried to dodge by biting the woman holding it and scrambling up her arms again. It nearly made it, but one side of the cloth got over its head and the woman, now screaming and trying not to move back or sideways, juggled the miscreant up and down, bouncing more of the fabric over the beast's head. "Get it, get it, get it!" she screeched. "Oh God, just get the little monster off me!"

The man who'd brought the tablecloth grabbed at the wriggling shape under the folds of dirty linen and wrestled it free of the woman, wrapping the extra bits of fabric around and around, imprisoning the monkey in the folds.

"Don't suffocate it!" the secretary exclaimed.

The monkey, realizing it was trapped, began to howl and let out an unpleasant stench of an origin I didn't want to think about.

The man fighting with the cloth gave the secretary an exasperated glare. "I don't think there's much chance of that. Someone find a damned cage or a box."

One of the other milling people dragged a large plastic file box into the room, hastily emptying the contents in armfuls onto the secretary's desk. Once the box was empty, the cloth-bound monkey was dumped into it and the lid slammed down and latched.

"Do you think it'll be OK in there?" the secretary asked.

"I hope it dies!" said the woman who had recently been its perch.

"Oh, you do not!" The box thumped and rattled, but the lid held tight. "I think it'll be fine so long as someone punches some air holes in the box," the man said. "It's us who'll be nervous wrecks. Someone get the first-aid kit for Gabby."

Gabby, the now de-monkeyed woman, looked down at herself. "Oh . . . holy fish guts. It bit me and I'm covered in monkey poo! Gross!"

"I've changed my mind," the man said. "Forget the first-aid kit. Someone get Gabby to a shower."

The secretary grabbed her desk phone. "I'll call the hotel—they'll have something."

"Good." The man sat down on the corner of the desk and blew his disheveled hair out of his eyes while another woman came out from behind the wall and ushered the distraught Gabby somewhere less public. The annoying ghost seemed disappointed in the return of relative sanity and the ferret took one peek out of my bag and decided it still wasn't safe to come into the open—maybe she didn't like the look of the ghost any more than I did.

The secretary was busy with the phone, so after a moment of my standing there like a stork, the man looked up and said, "I guess it's all me then, is it?" He held out his right hand. "Hello, how are you? I'm John and I don't usually wrangle monkeys and shrimp first thing in the morning. What can I do for you? And does it involve livestock, because if so, I'm afraid I'll have to run screaming from the room."

"No livestock," I replied.

"Thank God." He glanced at the secretary, who was putting the phone down. "Emily, make sure you punch some holes in the box for the monkey."

"With what?"

"I don't know . . . a letter opener? You can't let it smother in there."

The secretary seemed unimpressed with his argument. "Oh . . . all right. But don't blame me if it gets poked."

"Just don't let it out," John added. He looked back to me as Emily got on her knees wielding a wicked-looking letter opener. She looked dangerous. "What was it you needed again?" he asked.

"I'm trying to find out if a certain person has a performer's badge. Is there a list?"

He looked blank for a moment, then blinked, pursing his mouth as he thought, and then raising his eyebrows high. "Oh. I suppose there is. Ah, just a minute. I'll go look it up. What's the name?" he asked, getting to his feet again.

"Mine or the performer's?"

"I'll take both, if you like." He started toward the back half of the office.

"My name's Harper Blaine and the guy I'm interested in is named Jordan Delamar," I said, following him around the obscuring wall. The nosy ghost tagged along and loomed over John's shoulder. Against the dark wall, the details of her face and clothing were a little easier to see. She had a long, slightly hooked nose and wore clothes from the early 1900s. She was striking, and I imagined that in the right circumstances she'd been considered quite beautiful, though her expression soured that for me. I found her disturbing.

"All right. Let me just get to the computer here . . ." John said, plopping down into a chair at a workstation that was too cutely adorned with photos in Hello Kitty frames for me to think it was his.

He typed a bit and then peered at the old-fashioned CRT screen. "No. Jordan Delamar does not currently have a performer's badge. He let it lapse in April—that's when the sign-ups are."

"But he had one until then?"

"Yes."

"Do you know if he was involved in an accident at the slabs in December?"

"That?" His aura flushed a sickly green, fading until it was barely visible. "Umm . . . yes."

"Do you have a contact address or phone number for him?"

"If it's in connection with the claim, I would prefer not to . . ."

"It's not something you have a choice about if it's connected to a public claim," I said—which isn't really true, but I leaned a bit on him through the Grey, pushing for his cooperation.

John visibly deflated and looked glum. "All I have is an address." He rattled it off. It was the same one I already knew, but I wrote it down anyway.

"Thanks for the help and I'm sorry about your animal problems."

"Oh . . . thanks. I swear this place is getting weirder by the minute lately—and it's plenty weird to begin with."

"Really?"

He made a face. "I'd rather not talk about it. Shouldn't have said anything." I felt him mentally pushing back against me as he gathered his wits.

I backed off in the Grey and the normal, taking a step away. "I do appreciate the information, though. Best of luck with your monkey."

John sighed and waved me out. I went, giving the still-rattling box of monkey and the grimly ventilating secretary a wide berth as I passed, and looking to see what had become of the tall ghost.

The apparition stood at the doorway, watching me again, and her finger brushed over my arm as I passed. I shuddered at the touch and felt a pang of hunger and dizziness as if I hadn't eaten in days. I staggered a little and got away from her as quickly as possible, not turning back to look for her until I was safely standing on the bricks of lower Post Alley. She remained in the doorway, her chin tucked down and her eyes boring into me. She pursed her mouth a little and for a second her face took on a raptor's aspect with her hooked nose and sharp eyes. Then she turned around abruptly and vanished with an audible swish of her long skirts.

I shivered and declined to pursue her. I had something more pressing to do than being drawn into the games of bad-tempered specters. I now knew something about Jordan Delamar—he was the "boy who played" and he'd been injured at the market—and it seemed the best way to find out where he was now would be to question more of the buskers. I wasn't thrilled with the prospect of spending precious hours questioning people about his whereabouts, but I had no choice. At least it wasn't raining at the moment. The tourists were already wandering around, breakfasting on hot pastries from the bakery and paper cups of famous coffee, which meant that the buskers were out, too, hoping to gather some of those tourist dollars for themselves. I just had to find the ones who knew Delamar. . . .

I decided to fend off the lingering sensations of the ghost's touch by getting some breakfast for myself. There was a busking spot across from Sisters café in Post Alley and another just around the corner from that on Pine Street, so I started there.

A young, dreadlocked white man in motley clothes was singing old protest songs from the early 1970s from the tiny stage of a tiled doorway across Post Alley from Sisters. I listened to him while I rushed through some food and fed the ferret crumbs and tried to keep her out of my coffee cup. The musician was an adequate guitarist and indifferent singer. I caught him as he reached the end of his hour and started to put his guitar away. A pair of men with a collection of rough-looking hand drums and harmonicas were waiting to take his place, so I addressed all three of them.

"Hi. I've been looking for a performer. Have you guys been playing around here long?"

The men with the drums blinked at each other before they shrugged and one replied, "Since April—technically."

"Technically?" I echoed.

The guitarist leaned into the conversation as he picked up his case. "They mean they weren't officially here until April. No badge," he added, pointing to the small round pin he wore on his own shirt. He cut the men a collective dirty look. "Sneakers." The silvery mist of the ghost world around him flushed red, spreading over us all like blood in water and in a moment his aura flared the same color. A real "angry young man," I supposed and wondered what he was so mad about. . . .

The man who'd spoken first rolled his eyes, the energy corona around him flickering as if he were fighting the impulse to respond with equal belligerence. "It's not like we didn't try to get a badge before, but you almost gotta wait for someone to die before space opens up."

"Almost as bad as the vendor list," the remaining man said.

I held up my hands to slow them down. "Hey, I'm not familiar with the system. Is there a limit on the badges?"

The guitarist kept his eyes on the rival musicians as he answered me. "Yeah, unless you know someone's badge is going to be up for grabs, it's pretty hard to get a new act in."

The first man scowled at the guitarist. "You implying me and him had anything to do with that guy getting hurt just so we could get a badge?"

"Not implying nothing. Just saying," the guitarist retorted.

The first guy spit and narrowed his eyes at the guitarist. "Maybe you better travel on, Dylan. You're over time."

The guitarist huffed and spun away, turning his back on the other act before stalking off.

"Jack-off," the first man muttered under his breath.

"Shine it on, man. We got music to play," his partner said.

I wedged myself back into the conversation. "So, you guys didn't know the guy who was hurt?"

They blinked at me again as if they had forgotten I was there. "Well, yeah, we knew him. We've been coming around off and on for a couple of years, trying to get a spot. Always seemed to be too late, no matter how early we went to the office to get a badge."

"How well did you know him?"

"Just like 'Hey, man, how y'doing?' kind of thing. He was a nice guy. He let us play with him a couple few times Down Under 'cause the spot's good for more than one. We split the take. He was a good guy. Feel kind of bad we got his badge. Kind of."

Sounded like all the performers I'd ever known: sorry for the misfortune of one of the fraternity, but not enough to refuse the chance to take the spot if it were offered.

"So, you guys wouldn't know where I could find him."

They shook their heads. "Nah, sorry," the first one said.

"It's OK. Thanks for the help anyhow," I said, turning to go after the guitarist and leaving them to make the most of their chances.

By the time I'd rounded the corner out of Post Alley and was heading to the next spot half a block downhill, I could hear the two men laying down a complex rhythm on the drums followed by the wail of a harmonica. They were better than the guitarist, but it was strange music with roots that reached to unquiet parts of my mind. I hurried to get away.

The guitarist wasn't at the next spot—it was occupied by a blond man with a small piano on wheels. He played a jazzy, upbeat tune, keeping his head tucked down a little as if concentrating on the keyboard and avoiding the eyes of the crowd. He was good and a shallow basket of CDs sat on the top of his instrument with the obligatory price sign—this one, however, not claiming any special reason for the offering. I waited for him to finish his piece, but he wasn't any more help than the drummers had been. He knew Jordan by name, knew about the injury and that he had been in the hospital for a while, but he didn't know where he'd been moved, only that he was gone. Once again I paid for the information by purchasing a CD and moved on before I took up too much of his time.

I walked toward the next spot, fighting my way once more through ghosts and tourists, and found the guitarist again, playing in front of the original Starbucks shop with its brown sign and two-tailed mermaid. Same song, different crowd. I leaned against the wall, letting Chaos crawl out of my bag and up to my shoulder as I waited for a pause in the performance. I figured that anyone as pissed off as this guy had been about the badge transfer probably knew Delamar.

He noticed me at once when I stepped up on the next break. "You again?"

I nodded and Chaos rumpled around under my hair, making me restrain a twitch. "Yes. I didn't get to finish our conversation earlier. Do you know Jordan Delamar—the guy who was injured?"

He gave me a wary look, his eyes shifting from my face to the ferret, no doubt thinking I was a bit weird and possibly dangerous. "Who wants to know?"

"I'm a private investigator. I'm working for another patient."

"I didn't hear that anyone else had been hurt. . . ."

I just gave him a thin smile and repeated myself. "Do you know Delamar?"

He heaved a sigh. "Yeah. I know Jordy. Look, I don't have time to chat. I need to make some money here."

"Understood. Can I meet you later? I can pay for your time." Chaos stuck her nose out from under my collar and wiggled her whiskers at him.

His expression brightened. "Oh. Well, then yeah. Um . . . I'm going to work my way around to Lowell's in a couple of hours. See you up in the loft? Noon?"

I agreed and moved on. As I passed near the slabs, I looked across the street for Twitcher, but I didn't see him this time, so I crossed the road and asked a few of the guys hanging out near the memorial if they knew him. None of them did and none of them recalled seeing him in the area. I'd have to go down to Pioneer Square later and find out what he'd been doing up here the day before.

I continued to ask around, killing a couple of hours with the same questions, but I didn't have a lot more luck. But then I got one more "meet me at Lowell's" offer from a woman in a ridiculously large hat whose act involved a talking parrot and a stuffed cat. Chaos had been very interested in the parrot, which had forced me to cut the interview short even though the woman seemed to know something.

"I'll see you at Lowell's," I said, backing away.

"I'll be there when I'm done here," she replied, tossing the stuffed cat into the air.

I hadn't realized how quickly time had passed—it was nearly eleven thirty already. I worked my way through the crowd to a washroom to clean up and then onward through the lunch crush to the restaurant inside the main market arcade. They'd filmed some scenes for *Sleepless in Seattle* there and the photos were still displayed near the entrance. Tourists always seemed to cluster around the doors, staring at them for a moment or two, though I imagined many had no idea what film they were from or who the people in the photos were. I felt old thinking of it.

I smuggled the ferret into the upper dining room at Lowell's and found the woman with the stuffed cat—but no sign of the parrot this time—sitting with a cup of tea at a table near the windows with a vertigo-inducing view of Elliott Bay and the waterfront. I could see the Great Wheel—a giant Ferris wheel similar in design to the London Eye, but about half the size—revolving slowly at the end of Pier 57 and the aquarium's roofs just across the road from the Hill Climb immediately below us. I couldn't see down to the tunnel construction, but I knew it was there, just beyond the edges of the window. I wondered if Julianne Goss had turned to admire the same view on the day a mosquito had bitten her and wished I could figure out the connection between the three patients who might be running out of time as I sat and drank coffee with buskers and fabric cats.

I took a seat on the other side of the table from the woman and was about to say hello again when two more people approached us, carrying trays of food from downstairs. "Hey, Mindy! Can we sit with you?" the male of the pair asked.

The Cat Lady waved graciously for them to join us and then reached up to remove her hat, which she put down with care so it stood flat against the wall. Her revealed hair was faded strawberry blond and she appeared older without the shade of the hat brim on her face.

She looked at me and started to speak but was cut off one more time by the arrival of the guitar player I'd met in Post Alley. "Hey, make some room for me, too," he said, pulling a chair over from another table and wedging himself between the unnamed lady and myself. I scooted my chair next to Mindy to make room for him.

Mindy rolled her eyes. "Sure thing, Fuso. Don't mind us."

"Ah, don't be such a bitch, Mindy. I need to talk to the Private Eye, too."

The couple to whom I'd not been introduced yet gave me a startled look and seemed about to pack up and leave, but Mindy patted the man's nearest hand and they settled back into their seats.

"I thought your name was Dylan," I said to the guitar player.

He shrugged. "Nah, they were just making remarks."

"As is only fitting, considering how often you do the same," Mindy said.

Fuso blew a raspberry.

I leaned forward and said, "I'm sorry for the inconvenience, but I did promise to meet . . . umm . . . Fuso here, too."

"That's all right," Mindy said. Chaos stuck her head out of my bag and sniffed at the odors of food. Mindy noticed her and smiled. "Better keep that under the table, just in case," she suggested. "I leave Beaker with the folks who run the bird store on Western. They spoil him, of course." Then she looked at the couple who had joined us. "Are you two comfortable? You don't mind . . . ?"

"No problem," the woman of the couple said. "Fuso's always a rude pain in the ass." Then she stuck her tongue out at the man named when he looked as if he would object.

Mindy looked around the table while I closed the zipper on my bag to keep the ferret from running amok in the restaurant.

Mindy waited until I was done, glancing at me one more time before saying, "Well, I'm Mindy Canter. Fuso you know—Ansel Fuso. And these are Nightingale and Whim Sonder."

The male Sonder reached across the table and put out his hand to shake mine. "William, really, but it's Whim to most."

I had seen their names on flyers around town—Whim and Nightingale created children's shows with all sorts of puppets, mimes, musicians, and wild costumes. "I thought you two were big-time producers," I said.

Nightingale pulled a rueful face. "Unfortunately, puppetry is not the easiest gig to make a living at if you're not willing to travel. Whim is utterly terrified of planes."

"Not terrified, just not convinced they're going to stay aloft," Whim said. "And we can only afford to mount one show a year—the Christmas show at the Children's Theatre." He glanced away. "Our son would have been six this year. . . ."

I looked at Nightingale, who bit her lip as tears welled in her eyes. She met my gaze and shook her head. She didn't want to talk about it. Silvery faces boiled around her in the Grey, one in particular whispering something I couldn't catch.

Into the awkward silence, Fuso blurted, "But you want to know about the Banjo Guy, not Whim and Nightie's kid."

Mindy gave him a cold glare. "Yes, she wants to talk about Jordy, Fuso. You could be a little more sensitive."

"Me? I'm the most sensitive guy in the world. Didn't I give those two guys who snaffled Banjo Guy's badge the rush? *I'm* not running around acting like he was never here."

"No one acts like Jordy was never here. We just don't use it as an excuse to be mean to other people."

Fuso rolled his eyes and blew a noisy breath into his hair. "You say so."

Mindy gave him one more hard look, then turned her attention back to me. "What did you want to know?"

"Well, I have a mailing address for him, but I really need to talk to his caregivers or family in person. I need an actual address where I can find him."

"Why?" Nightingale asked.

"He may have something in common with a client of mine who's also in a coma," I said. "I'm trying to find out what happened to him and other patients with the same symptoms and see if there's a connection that might help us understand and possibly correct their conditions. So far all the patients' injuries seem to have some association with the tunnel construction zone, but that's very vague and the longer it takes to find Jordan and possibly a common cause, the worse each patient's chances become. I need more information and I think I can get it if I can see Delamar and talk to the people who are taking care of him. Do any of you know his address or anything about his condition or his accident?"

They exchanged glances before Mindy looked at me as if they had elected her their representative. "I have Jordy's address. He's been unconscious ever since the awning fell on him. Whim and Nightingale and I went to see him while he was in the hospital, but when Levi couldn't afford it anymore, they moved him to a different facility and it's been hard to go see him. We all work long hours in the summer. I have another job as well as this one. So do Whim and Night." She cast an exasperated look at Fuso. "Ansel is just a bum who sponges off his mother."

"Hey! I do my bit. Don't go dissing me."

Beside him, Nightingale gave his shoulder a token smack. "Don't be such a whiner, Fuso. Learn to take a joke."

Fuso grunted and snatched a handful of French fries off Nightingale's plate and shoved them into his mouth in a wad. Nightingale shook her head and Whim made an exaggerated face of disgust. "You're such a delicate flower, Fuso. I'm going to make a puppet just like you: Its mouth will reach all the way around to the back of its head."

They poked fun at Fuso for a few minutes, diffusing the tension that had risen between them earlier. I waited for them to wind down. Then I said, "Tell me about Delamar. What's he like? What did he do?"

"You mean his act?" Mindy asked. "He plays banjo."

"He also makes them," Whim said. "It's part of the shtick. He has a real nice Gibson resonator, but he's always got a couple of specialties around. Like . . . he has one made out of a dried gourd and a yardstick and another he made out of a cooking pot."

"I remember that one!" Nightingale said. "He sold it to some guy from a restaurant supply company. Remember the cigar box?"

Whim laughed. "I do. That was a classic."

"He made them all himself?" I asked. "So his act is some sort of gag?"

The Sonders looked appalled. "Oh no!" Nightingale said. "He was just so talented he could make a playable instrument out of almost anything. He made a three-hole chicken-bone whistle once, but he wasn't a very good wind player, so he gave it away. He made things all the time—mostly out of junk he found around the market. He'd play them for a while, but if someone liked the instrument, he'd sell it to them. He was probably better at making instruments than playing them, but he only really liked banjos. I think selling the instruments brought in more money, but he liked to play. He thought of himself as a musician, not an instrument maker."

"You speak of him in the past tense," I noted.

Nightingale drew in her breath as if to rebut me, but stopped. "I—guess it's just been so long . . ."

Whim put a hand on her shoulder. "It's been a long time since we saw him and every show's yesterday's news. Once you go home for the day, it's over and past."

Fuso rolled his eyes. "What he really means is no one thinks he's coming back."

Mindy jabbed a finger into Fuso's arm. "Fuso!"

He turned to her. "It's true! You can pretend all you want, but we all know it. He was a good guy, but there ain't no Prince Charming going to come along and wake him up." He glared at the Sonders. "You know that better than anyone."

Nightingale turned in her seat and slapped him. "Shut up, Fuso. Shut up."

Fuso stood up with more self-possession than I'd have expected, and walked quietly away. Nightingale pushed her tray aside and got up from the table. She looked down at Whim, her face white and the energy around her flaring red, then yellow, then green. "I need to leave." She looked at me. "I'm sorry I can't help you. Jordan is a very nice man. He deserves better friends than Fuso. And us."

She turned and walked off, Whim hopping up to follow her without looking back.

Mindy closed her eyes and shook her head. "I should have known better than to let Fuso open his mouth."

"I get the impression he'd open it anyhow and you couldn't have stopped him."

"He's such a brat."

I thought that was too mild a sentiment, but Fuso wasn't my problem. "I'm sorry to have raised such a stink."

"It happens. Especially if Fuso is involved. He liked Jordan. I think he's a little jealous, really, because he wants to be liked just as much, but he doesn't know how. He's immature and even younger than he looks, so he hasn't learned to keep his temper in check. He's not very good at making friends."

I wasn't either and I felt a niggle of shame since I was older than I looked and should have learned better by now. "I do know how that goes."

Mindy gave a tight smile. Then she picked up a napkin and asked me for a pen. "I'll give you the address where you can find Jordy. He won't be able to talk to you, but someone there may."

As she wrote the information down I watched her. "I have one other question," I said.

She nodded without glancing up.

"Have things been . . . strange around the market lately?"

"Strange? This place runs on strange." She raised her head. "What sort of thing are you really after?"

"I mean has it seemed haunted or like there have been more accidents or that things are unsettled lately?"

"Oh," she said, her eyes lighting with recognition. "There has been more . . . disturbance than usual. It feels like . . . something's broken. People are snappish, strange events have become more common—it's always odd here and some people won't work in the main arcade when that sort of thing starts happening. I won't, for one."

"Why?"

Mindy studied my face in silence before she answered. "Spirits.

You can feel them, sometimes, watching you. All the people who lived on the bluff before the market was here, all the people who've been here since. Usually they're just there, and it's no problem. But sometimes—lately—they seem . . . agitated. Ever since Jordan was hurt. Do you think the ghosts are mad about that?"

"I don't know. But there was a monkey in the office this morning and I was told things have been going badly a lot. I just wondered if that was a widespread impression."

She peered at me, her half smile holding steady. "It's not an impression. It's true. What made you think of it?"

"I met a woman named Mae. . . ."

"Purple skirt, beer can hat?"

I nodded, watching her closely. She returned my intense gaze.

"That was Lois Brown. They called her Mae West because of her bosom and her salty language. She used to be a regular in the market and she lived in one of the low-income apartments here until she died in 1995. Her ashes were buried under the white plum tree in the secret cemetery. The tree put out purple blossoms after that until they pulled it up in 2007. There were a lot of other people buried there—Indians, other market people. Since they started working on the tunnel, the tree they planted there hasn't bloomed. If you saw Mae, maybe she's not the only one of those buried in the market who can't rest."

"Where is the secret cemetery?"

"Across from Kells, in the Soames-Dunn courtyard." She handed me the napkin she'd written on. "If they're unhappy, maybe it's the ghosts who are causing these problems—like the one that hurt Jordan."

The idea hadn't crystallized to that degree in my own head until

Mindy spoke it, but it had been forming there. I wasn't certain, but it did cast an interesting light on the relationship between Sterling, Goss, and Delamar: They'd all been injured in ways associated with the tunneling under Pike Place Market and both Sterling and Delamar had been in contact with the dirt from the tunnel. I wondered if the same was true of Goss. . . .

I took the paper with a frisson running down my back. "Thank you."

Mindy nodded and picked up her hat. "You're welcome. Come back and tell me how Jordy's doing, won't you?"

I said I would and watched her go, discomfited by my thoughts.

ELEVEN

The address Mindy gave me led me to a small long-term care facility that was not quite in Capitol Hill. I parked outside and looked at the building without enthusiasm. Hospitals are not fun places for me; their complex layers of history and emotional residue make them look nearly black to my Grey sight. Even a brand-new facility quickly accrues a burden of anxiety, fear, and pain and the places where we hide people so we don't have to watch them die are among the worst. I squeezed my eyes shut for a moment, trying to ease the discomfort in the injured one before I plunged into the darkness that lay before me. Nothing changed except that I wanted eyedrops.

I took Chaos out of my bag and put her in the small travel cage in the rear with a bowl of water and some kibble. She danced a bit, frustrated that I was leaving her, and I wished I wasn't, but hospitals were not good places for ferrets and I knew she'd be fine for an hour now that the drizzle was starting up again. With a sigh, I got out of the Land Rover and headed inside to find Jordan Delamar.

Since I had the room number, I didn't bother with the front desk, but walked straight through to the elevators and into the heart of the facility, concentrating on my good eye to keep me out of the swirling eddies of ghost-stuff. No one stopped me, but then, it was midday and well within visiting hours and I didn't look like a troublemaker or a vagrant—in this neighborhood both were common enough.

Delamar's room was a single, but I still crept in like a penitent into a church. I invade people's privacy as part of my job, but I don't enjoy it much and the hospital made me more aware of my trespass than usual—all those angry phantoms staring at me as if I should have done something for them. Ghosts don't understand the apparent indifference and inattention of the living. They also have no sense of time. The ugly apparition that loomed in the doorway didn't even know it was dead, badgering me with a roaring complaint as I passed through it, trying not to flinch.

"Hello?" I said in a low voice, noticing a figure sitting beside the bed that was wreathed with a ring of anxious ghosts in a boil of Grey mist.

The young black man in the chair raised his head, blinking as if he'd been asleep, though I knew he hadn't. "Hello? Can I help you? Are you the social worker?"

I shook my head. "No, I'm not. I am trying to find Jordan Delamar, though. I'm a private investigator. My name's Harper Blaine."

The man stood up, seeming confused. "I don't understand. What do you want with Jordy? He's . . . he's not well. You can see that. Is it the insurance?"

I shook my head again, smiling reassurance. "No, nothing like that. Nothing bad. I'm trying to help another patient like Jordan. I just wanted to talk to you or his caregivers about his condition."

In the bed, Jordan Delamar rolled his head to the side, but gave no other sign of animation. His arms lay on top of the covers, pale brown skin slack over too-prominent bones.

"His condition? You mean the PVS?" the man asked. "It hasn't changed. He's still . . . just like this." He waved at the angular shape under the blanket. His lower lip trembled very slightly and he blinked too rapidly. "What could you possibly want to know that would help anyone?"

"I want to know about the episodes—the strange things that can't be happening, but are."

The man sat back down, hitting the chair seat hard. "No. There's nothing going on. Nothing." He shook his head.

A shadow as dark as oil smoke pressed down over the bed and the rest of the ghosts broke away, floating out toward the corners of the room. Delamar stirred slightly and his lips parted with a small wet sound. The other man looked down at him and then rose as he lunged forward, trying to cover the patient's arms with his hands. Delamar's limbs were so thin and his protector's hands so large that it almost worked, but I could still see the eruption of blood red words that scored the patient's skin, flowing as if they were being written before my eyes.

"What does it say?" I asked.

The man shook his head frantically. "Nothing. It doesn't say anything. It's just . . . it's a rash."

I stepped closer, coming up next to the man beside the bed, and looked down at the script now scribbling itself up Delamar's arms and vanishing under his pajama top, appearing swiftly in the collar opening and glowing through the thin cloth across his chest.

"It's dermographia," I said.

The man stared at me. "It's what? Is that a disease?"

"No," I said, amazed. "It's ghost writing. It's a technique fake mediums used to use in séances. They scratched their skin and the scratches would swell up and turn red."

The man turned on me, glaring and pushing me back. "It's not fake! Jordan's sick! These rashes—they're not his fault!"

I put up my hands and didn't resist him. "I know that. I can see it. I know it's real."

The man dropped his hand from my arms. "You do? Everyone else thinks I'm doing it to him. They tried to bar me from the room for a while but I won that fight. I wish—I wish this wasn't happening."

"I know you do. No one would want this."

"You believe me?"

"Yes. I see the same thing you do." I wished I could read the whole message, but the script was difficult to begin with—spidery and shaky—and the words were mostly under the patient's shirt. All I could see were the words "Limos tribu . . ." on one arm and "broken wheel" on the other. At least I now had another reference to wheels and I thought I might understand Cannie Trimble's reference to ashes, too—the ashes of the dead scattered in the market's secret cemetery. "How long has this been happening?"

The man backed away from me and fell again into his chair, letting out a sound like a sob of relief as he put his head in his hands. "Months. Since April at least. It's hard to remember. Every day's the same. . . ."

I spotted another chair and pulled it up beside his so I could sit with him. "You come here every day?"

"Since the beginning. It's been hard. . . . I had to lie about our relationship so they wouldn't throw me out, but no one asks you to prove you're a relative."

"What's your name?"

He stared at me, frightened. "Why do you want to know?"

"Just to be polite. My name's Harper Blaine," I repeated, offering him my hand. "What can I call you?"

He hesitated, shivering, then took my hand in a grip that was cold with sweat. "Levi. Levi Westman. Jordan—called me Westie."

"I'll stick with Levi, if that's all right."

"That's fine." He was trembling harder and his control was crumbling. "You really believe me? You believe I'm not doing it?"

"I can see you're not doing it. I know what it is. It's not you. I believe you."

He broke down and cried quietly for a minute before mumbling through his fingers, "Thank God. Thank God someone believes me. I've been so scared—too scared to tell anyone what's been going on in case they made me leave. They almost made me go once before but I . . . I tricked them into letting me stay. They don't know about us. They'd make me leave if they knew!"

"You and Jordan are partners."

He nodded, trembling, fighting to regain his self-control. In a moment he wiped his eyes with the hem of his shirt and raised his face. "Yes. We—we're partners."

"Then why would they make you leave?"

"We didn't get married. That stupid election . . . we were going to, but then they put the referendum for affirmation on the ballot and we couldn't. And then it was affirmed, but . . . Jordy was injured before we could do it. And I'm not legally a spouse, so I don't actually have any right to be here. But he doesn't have any family in the area, so . . . no one questioned me at first. Now, I just keep on lying. So I can stay with him."

In 2011 Washington's voters had passed the Marriage Equality Act, which gave same-sex couples the privilege to marry legally and enjoy the same protections under the law as heterosexual couples. A religious group had called the law into question before it went into effect and the referendum had gone back onto the ballot for affirmation in 2012. In spite of strong lobbying by the political right, the law had been affirmed by a solid margin, and gay and lesbian couples had rushed to make their partnerships legally binding. Without the paperwork, however, Westman didn't technically have the same rights to visit his spouse or make decisions about his care. With no other family in the area to back up his decisions, Westman was walking a very dangerous line.

"What would happen to Jordan if you were forced to leave?" I asked.

"I don't know. I suppose they'd need to talk to his folks or . . . they might make him a ward of the state. I don't know what would happen then, and it scares me. This is awful. And then this strange thing—these messages—started. I don't know what they are or what they mean."

"Have you been keeping copies of them?"

"No. It's too freaky. Why?"

"I think it's connected to two other cases with similar events."

"What does that mean? 'Similar events'?"

"There are other PVS patients who are manifesting strange activity, like the messages on Jordan's arms. It's not the same thing, but I think it's of a piece." I didn't want to raise his anxiety further, but I knew time was short. "I'm sure Jordan's doctor has told you that the longer a patient remains this way, the less likely his recovery becomes. One of the other patients seems to be failing, so there is some pressure to figure out why this is happening as quickly as possible. If I have all the pieces to the puzzle, we might discover what's causing it and come up with a way to help all of them."

"Really?" Westman grabbed my hands. "Will it make him better?"

"I don't know. It may be that all I can do is make the messages stop. But wouldn't it be worthwhile to try?"

"Yes! I'd rather have Jordy back, but it would be something, at least, not to see him in this state," he said, waving at the angry marks that lingered on Delamar's skin.

"Would you be willing to copy this message down for me?"

"Yes! But we don't have to write it all down—I can use my phone to take pictures if you'll help me. . . ." He seemed uncomfortable asking for a favor, the energy around him flickering orange and green.

Assisting with the photos was uncomfortably intimate and I wished I could look away, not invade their privacy or witness the wasting state of Delamar's body and Westman's painful sadness at revealing it piece by piece, moving sheets or the shirt aside with care and then covering him again gently. We closed the door and worked in methodical silence until every line of swollen, bloody words had been recorded.

Then we sat down again, not speaking, not looking at each other. Westman stared at the photos, checking them. He frowned and put the phone down on the tray table that we'd moved to the side of the bed.

"What is it?" I asked, watching him reach for a pad of paper and a pencil.

"I'm not sure," Westman said. He wrote something on the paper, looked at the photo again, and crossed something out before writing a new word over the excised one. He held the pad out to me. "It's hard to make out—the writing's so bad. . . ." He held up the camera next to the pad for me to read and flipped through a series of pictures. "I'm not sure I remember right, but . . . this message—or a lot of these words at least—may have appeared before. Do you think I'm reading the words correctly or just . . . wanting them to be familiar?"

I glanced at the sentences—just two—that he had written down and compared them to the photos, looking back and forth from the long, spidery lines on Delamar's skin to Westman's transcription. "The writing is hard to read, but, yes, I think you've copied it correctly. 'Given as Limos tribute, those who wasted away. Given to the wheel of death and birth, to break the wheel we are driven.'"

I frowned over the strange message as Westman said, "It doesn't make any sense, does it?"

"Not yet. It may eventually, though, in context with other messages."

"Other messages?"

"If you remember any of the other writing you've seen. . . ." I was reluctant to be too blunt about the surface on which these messages were appearing—it seemed invasive and uncouth.

"Oh," he said, crestfallen. "I thought maybe there were other messages from . . . the other patients."

"There are."

"Do any of them say something like this . . . ?" he asked.

"So far, no, but I haven't read or listened to them all." I changed tack slightly, since this conversation seemed destined only for frustration. "Can you tell me what happened to Jordan?" I didn't want to rely on the vendor's version of events alone.

"There was some work going on around the market—something

about the tunnel or monitoring the tunnel. . . . Anyhow, whatever they were doing caused some temporary structures to collapse. He was hit on the top of the head by a falling awning pole. His doctor said something about cranial sutures . . . the place where the skull grows together when you're a kid. He said the intersection is weaker than the rest of the skull and that's right where Jordy got hit. He had some kind of swelling or clot pushing on his brain and they had to operate to remove it. But he—the surgeon—said that after they removed the clot the damage was like a bad concussion and Jordan should be fine. But he didn't get better. I mean, his head healed up and they say everything's fine, but he won't wake up."

"And where did this happen?"

"At the market—at Pike Place Market. Jody's a musician and he performs there."

"Did he fall onto a hard surface or down some distance?" I asked, to be sure it really was the same accident that had been described to me before.

"He landed in some dirt the workmen had dug up. It got in his mouth and nose, but the doctor said it didn't contribute to the damage—it might have made the impact softer, actually. But he still got the clot and was unconscious." He gazed at Delamar a moment before adding, "I haven't seen him looking back at me since that morning. I was on my way to work and he was still in bed, smiling at me . . . and that's the last time. . . ." He squeezed his eyes closed, forcing tears to roll off his lower lashes and creep down his cheeks. His breath was ragged and he didn't say anything more until it eased back to normal. "I'm sorry. I get maudlin. . . ."

"It's OK," I said. The conversation stalled on the awkward moment.

After a bit Westman sniffed and sat up straighter. "What else did you want to know?" he asked, making an effort to act normal and do something.

"Did he have another job as well? I know performing can be rough financially."

He looked a little uncomfortable. "No. I supported us a lot of the time. I'm a programmer. The money's good but that's another reason I'm worried—I've taken a lot of time off or been working from home, and his health insurance doesn't really cover this. I do. I don't know how much longer I can make this stretch. . . ." His eyes widened in alarm. "You're sure you're not from the insurance company? You're not going to cut us off—!"

I turned my palms out in a calming gesture. "No, no. I'm not working for the insurance company. I work for the sister of one of the other patients who's exhibiting similar behavior."

Westman sagged in his chair. "I can't take a lot more. I live in a state of fear every minute. 'What if they find out?' 'What if they drop us?' 'What if he gets worse . . . ?'"

"I don't know if it will be a consolation, but at least you aren't alone in this and I'm going to get to the bottom of it, I promise."

He grabbed my hands. "Don't promise. I couldn't stand it if it fell through. Please. Just . . . do your best."

"I will. Would you keep on photographing the messages for me? Maybe writing them out again if they're hard to read? If they're not all the same, it will help to have that information."

He nodded. "I'll get as many as I can. I'm not here all the time, but I'll see if I can get anyone to help me record them. How can I get them to you?"

I pulled a business card out of my pocket and handed it to him.

"You can e-mail them to me, or call and I'll come to you—whichever is easiest for you."

"E-mail. Definitely. When I'm not with Jordy, I'm at the computer."

That didn't surprise me in the least. I offered a reassuring smile and my thanks before taking my leave. It was growing late and I had a few more things to manage.

I was sure now that each of the patients had been injured at sites associated with the tunnel project, though I still didn't understand what the defining link was. Mindy and John from the market had both commented on the rise in strange occurrences and the appearance of Lois "Mae West" Brown's ghost seemed to be part of that same phenomenon. Tunneling, by its nature, disturbs the ground it passes through and this particular bit of ground was full of artifacts of the dead as well as the usual dirt and bugs. Was it any wonder if there was an upwelling of ghosts, just as there'd been a rise in rat and insect infestations? Or if those ghosts were confused and creating havoc? I wasn't sure what they wanted to say, but I was reasonably certain they were trying to say *something*. I wished I had more of Sterling's writing and understood more about Goss's paintings. I wished I knew if Goss's accident had involved dirt from the tunnel just as Sterling's and Delamar's had. I doubted I'd change my evaluation once I had any of that information, but it might help me figure out what would make these spirits lie back down.

TWELVE

I had agreed to have dinner with Phoebe Mason a few weeks earlier and I knew she'd never forgive me if I missed it—not even if I was working on a case she'd sent to me. I took the ferret home first—disappointed that Quinton wasn't there—and then drove up to the Wedgwood-area restaurant the Mason family owns. I couldn't remember ever having a meal with Phoebe in her own home, since it was easier to eat at the restaurant, which was always lively with the comings and goings of her large family.

Quinton was sitting in the back at the family table with Phoebe's father when I came in and I had to admit I was a little surprised. With my boyfriend's current preoccupation, I'd half expected him to blow this date off in spite of his reassurances. On the other hand, Phoebe would have been as unhappy with him for missing it as with me, so it had probably been no more an option in his mind than it had been in mine. No one risks the wrath of Phoebe lightly—she's short and curvy and would rather make a joke than an enemy, but woe betide you if you piss her off. But Quinton's presence still warmed me and sent a tingle of happiness through my whole body. I suspect I was smiling like a fool.

I threaded my way through the busy dining room and slid into a seat next to Quinton. "Hi, there, you," I said to him, pressing a quick kiss on his ear. "Hi, Poppy," I added, smiling at Mr. Mason.

"Hey'm, Harper," Poppy said, raising his glass of warm water in a tiny salute. "Been a while."

"Yes, it has," I agreed as Quinton returned the kiss on my cheek.

"What you been doing with yourself?" Poppy asked, his Jamaican accent still thick and musical even after decades in the United States. He never seemed to change, though I'd known him and his family for years—he was still the slim, bent, weathered old black man I'd first met, his bald head shining in the light and the ever-present glass of tepid water in his knobby hand. Still making sly comments, directing the lives of his children and grandchildren with gentle verbal nudges and the occasional good-natured barb. It would be hard to dislike Poppy. He was one of the few people I'd ever seen whose aura remained steady and bright at all times, shining a cool pale blue and sparkling with white lights as if the very air around him was effervescent.

"Oh, just working," I replied. "You know me."

Poppy nodded. "I do." He looked at Quinton and nudged him. "You making her leave them bad things alone, now?"

Quinton shook his head. "I couldn't if I tried."

"Where's Phoebe?" I asked, breaking up the conversation about my work habits before it could get properly started.

"She back in the house, putting babies to bed. They do love a story from their Auntie Phee."

Phoebe's oldest brother, Hugh, shared the house behind the restaurant with his parents and it seemed there was always one relative or another dropping by with kids in tow who had to be watched over and tucked into bed by someone who wasn't busy in the kitchen or the dining room. Since Phoebe was the oldest, the only daughter, and unmarried, she was often stuck with visiting-baby duty, though I don't think she minded. For a woman who swore she was never, ever getting hitched, she had an unlikely affection for children, as well as a huge mental store of tales to tell them at bedtime. I suspected Phoebe of reading every children's book that came into Old Possum's before she put it out on the shelves to be sold.

A few more members of the Mason clan whisked by, set down more glasses of water, or dropped in to sit at the table while we waited for Phoebe, each one offering a smile, a story, or a greeting to Poppy and us. One of the cousins sat down long enough to tell Poppy a joke that got the old man roaring with laughter—he's past seventy, but hardly shows it and doesn't find his age relevant except as a wellspring of wisdom and funny stories.

Poppy wiped tears of hilarity from the corners of his eyes without ever putting down his water and shooed the cousin on his way with a grin. "Go tell that to Momma," he suggested, eyes atwinkle with mischief.

"No way, Poppy," the cousin replied, jumping up in fake alarm. "Auntie Miranda'd smack me silly and tell me to wash out my mouth. And then supper would taste so bad! 'Sides, I gotta fix the espresso machine."

Poppy sighed as the cousin escaped to chores rather than risk the disapproval of his aunt over a dirty joke. "I swear, boys ain't got the heart they used to do. Time was I'd have gone told Miranda that story myself."

"Yeah, Poppy, but she's married to you—she'd just flick you with that towel of hers and tell you to get out of her kitchen. Ty would end up wearing curried goat," Quinton said.

Phoebe finally bustled in, waving at us before she ducked into the kitchen for plates of food and was chased back out by her mother wielding the snapping towel. Phoebe and her father laughed as she settled down with us at last.

"Hey, girl, you made it! And the handsome man, too," Phoebe noted, nodding at Quinton. In spite of the friendly atmosphere, there was still a tinge of reserve in her tone to me and her aura was slightly redder than usual. I had a bad habit of leaving Phoebe in the lurch or worse—I'd almost gotten her shot once and she hadn't quite forgiven me.

"Hey, Phoebe," I replied, having to turn my head to keep her in my normal sight since she'd chosen to sit on my left, where I was still constantly trying to see through the Grey.

"What you been up to?"

"Work."

"Not the kind that includes nasty men with guns this time?"

"No."

"Or ghosts that kill people?"

"So far no killing people, but a few ghosts, yes."

"What you into this time?" Phoebe said with a sigh.

"Some accidents around Pike Place Market."

"Oh, now that's an interesting place for ghosts. You know Chief Seattle's daughter haunts the place. She used to live there until they built the market and knocked her little shack down."

"Chief Sealth?" I asked, double-checking that I knew who she was talking about. "He had a daughter?"

"Sealth, Seattle—he's the man," Phoebe replied flapping her

hands at me. "Yeah. He had a daughter. I can't remember her native name, but they called her Princess Angeline. She was a very old lady by the time they built the market. There's a famous photo of her somewhere. . . . I probably got one in a book in the store. You seen a little old Indian lady ghost? Maybe it's her."

I shook my head. "No little old Indian ladies yet. Though I did see a little old lady named Lois Brown."

Phoebe shook her head. "I don't think I know of her."

"I guess people called her Mae West. She used to live in one of the apartments around the market. The place seems to be pretty lively where the ghosts are concerned."

Phoebe snorted. "There's all sorts of stories about that place. You talked to Mercedes yet?"

"Who is she? Another ghost?"

"No! She runs the ghost tour. She wrote about some of the spirits that haunt the market."

"I haven't met her yet," I conceded. I wasn't quite sure if Phoebe was making fun of me or offering real information. We'd never quite resolved the question of whether I saw ghosts for real or was just dangerously crazy, even though she'd apparently spoken well of me to Lily Goss. I supposed this dinner was Phoebe's way of offering me a chance to finally put that question to bed for her, one way or another. She wanted to believe me—there was plenty of evidence in my favor—but it's a hard thing to swallow.

Quinton and Poppy just watched us chatter. Quinton ate quickly, seeming anxious to get back to whatever nefarious schemes he was executing to cause his father grief. Poppy just drank his tepid water and nodded as if nothing came as a surprise to him—and I was pretty sure it didn't.

"I think I have a copy of Mercedes's book at the store. I'll get it for you," Phoebe offered. "If you're talking to ghosts down that way, you should know who they are. Some people get upset when they aren't treated with respect." She gave me a significant look I couldn't miss even through the Grey, raising her eyebrows.

I put down my fork and turned toward her so I could see her better—that is to say without her being half silver mist and tangled light. "Phoebe, I'm sorry. I know I said it before, but I mean it now and I meant it then. I seem to attract bad things and I shouldn't have put you in the middle of any of them. You're my friend. I . . . I don't want any harm to come to you or your family or your friends. Or even the cats. The five million cats."

It wasn't really five million cats, but it was at least half a dozen—like Simba—who lived in or around the bookshop, wandering overhead on their own feline expressways and dropping down onto the shelves to file themselves under N for "nuisance" or F for "foot." Old Possum's was famous for them.

"Why don't you like my cats? They like you just fine and I never said a bad thing about that stinky stretch-rat of yours."

I laughed at her description. Chaos does have a distinctive odor, I admit. But so do six cats. "I prefer to think of her as the carpet shark."

"She's a little bundle of trouble. All slinky and sneaky like that. No wonder you see ghosts: She probably knows them all by first name!"

"She might. If only she spoke English, my life would be so much easier. I'd just carry her around everywhere and ask her to tell me who these incorporeal pains in the ass are."

Phoebe snorted again. "You better take her with you if you go to Kells. That place is so haunted even I get the creeps in there."

"I don't think it's so bad . . ." I said, but I hadn't been in the Irish pub off Post Alley since I'd started seeing ghosts and monsters.

She shook her head as if I were particularly dim. "It used to be Butterworth's mortuary. Downstairs was the place they fixed up the bodies—or burned 'em into ashes. Now, don't you tell me that's no place to find a few ghosts." She shivered. "Can't imagine how many dead people be hanging around wondering where their body got off to."

Butterworth was the oldest and largest funeral home in Seattle. The building the business had moved out of in the late 1990s was now a law office in the front and a bar in the back, so I guess there was some attraction to serving spirits where there might be other spirits lingering. Oddly, I'd always thought that there was no good reason for a ghost to attach itself to a church or a funeral home since they're rarely places the dead visited in life or died in. Still, I suppose they might be attracted by the presence of friends and family at the funeral. . . .

"That's the place Dr. Hazzard sent her victims to be cremated, you know—right down there in the saloon," Phoebe said.

"She had them cremated in a saloon?"

Phoebe smacked the back of my hand lightly—a soft-pedaled version of her mother's corrective towel snapping. "It wasn't a saloon then! You know what I mean."

"All right, all right. Who was this Dr. Hazzard?" I asked. I knew she was dying to tell me.

"Linda Hazzard. She was a starvation doctor. You know how crazy rich Americans were about getting healthy back before the First World War? That's how Kellogg and Post got so famous—not because of the cereal but because of the health resorts they had where they made people *eat* the cereal to get healthy." She scoffed. "They thought all sorts of crazy things then. This Linda Hazzard, she thought people could be cured of diseases by fasting. But then she'd make 'em fast until they died and steal all their valuables. She had an office right there in the market—in a hotel—and when the patients died, she sent the bodies to Butterworth's to be cremated before the relatives could see what had happened to them. They say she might have killed forty people!"

"Well, that's a lovely thought," Quinton said, pushing his plate aside.

I made a face at him. "You never think it's gross when I talk about dead people."

"No, but I'm used to it from you. Phoebe's usually got much nicer things to talk about."

"You see," Phoebe interjected. "I am a much better conversationalist than you, Miss Skinny Butt."

"Not tonight," Poppy said. "I swear you two gone and spoiled my dinner. And I ate it hours ago. You two talk about something nicer, now. Or I'm gonna tell Momma on you and you won't get no dessert."

Not that I had room for dessert, but the idea of being banned from the Mason dinner table was daunting. I turned to look at Phoebe and she looked back at me like a naughty schoolgirl caught in the act with her co-conspirator. For a moment we stared at each other, smiles starting to tug our mouths upward until we spluttered into laughter.

"All right, Poppy. We'll talk about something nice. Like the weather," Phoebe said, grinning at me. "It's been mighty fine weather, lately, don't you think, Miss Harper Blaine?"

"I agree, Miss Mason. It's been wonderful. Except for that rainstorm yesterday."

"Wasn't that the strangest thing?" Phoebe said, continuing her teasing and giving her father a sly look from the corner of her eye.

Poppy gave us an agreeable nod. "There, now, you two get on just fine. That sure was the strangest thing. Raining in July."

"Like that's unusual," Quinton remarked.

Phoebe leaned over to me and grabbed my hand while the men were nodding to themselves. "I'll get those books for you—I got a whole bunch at the shop about the history of Seattle and if you're working down around the market, you'll want to know."

"Phoebe," Poppy scolded. "Now what I just told you?"

Phoebe sat up and gave her father an apologetic smile. "Yes, Poppy. I'll talk about something nice. Or I don't get to talk at all." Then she looked back to me. "Hugh's wife had twins!"

I flushed with embarrassment: It had been such a long time since I'd last seen the family that I'd lost track of Sonja's pregnancy. "Ack!" I sputtered, imagining the horror of chasing after two little terrors with her sister-in-law's brains and her brother's magic touch for mischief. "The world won't be safe."

"Ain't that the truth!" Phoebe agreed. "Barely crawling around and they already made the house a wreck. But they got the cutest little expressions! Just like those kitty pictures on the Internet—I swear they'll be saying 'I can has cheezburger' before they say 'momma.'"

"More likely 'I can has Auntie Phoebe wrapped around my little finger,'" said Poppy. "You such a soft touch, girl, and even the babies know it. We all going to be their slaves before long." He gave me a sideways look. "Even you, Harper. Even a old spinster like you."

"I am not a spinster, Poppy. I have Quinton."

Poppy looked at the man beside him. "When you going to make a honest woman of this girl, boy? Don't you know she's one of the special ones? You let her get away, you going to regret it."

"I'm afraid I'm not capable of making Harper into an 'honest woman'—she's honestly all the woman I can take already." He winked at Poppy and the old man guffawed, elbowing him in the ribs as he rocked back and forth in his mirth.

I found myself blushing as the whole table full of Masons laughed. It was goodhearted laughter, not unkind. I had to turn my head to glance again at Phoebe, who was laughing just as hard as the rest. She grinned and winked at me. "We're going to be all right, girl. I knew we would."

I felt a prickling under my eyelids and had to bite my lip to keep from making a bigger spectacle of myself by crying over having my friend back—really back. I'd have to work harder to make sure I kept her this time.

Dinner was delicious and we enjoyed ourselves. Phoebe promised to call when she'd found all the books she'd mentioned, which I hoped would throw some light on what I might be dealing with and why the tunnel construction was causing such havoc. But things went a bit sour as Quinton and I said our good-byes and headed out the door.

Quinton paused on the stoop outside the restaurant to kiss my cheek and swing his backpack on. "I'll see you later, sweetheart."

I blinked at him. "Later? You're not coming home now?"

"No. I have to get out to Northlake and fix a few things—or more to the point, break them. It will probably take most of the night. I don't want to disturb you, so I'll catch some sleep on my own and see you tomorrow. OK?" he added, turning away to walk off into the settling summer night.

"No."

He turned back, looking genuinely puzzled. "What?"

"It's not OK. I haven't seen you in two days and I think we need to talk."

"When did my being independent become a problem?" Through the Grey side of my vision, I could see he was letting off annoyed red sparks.

"It's not. But your father is. You have put him at the top of your priority list to the degree that you aren't paying any attention to anything else. You're not acting independent—you're acting obsessed. And I haven't even had the chance to tell you he popped up on my trail yesterday."

"He what? Where? What did he want?"

"He didn't exactly say, but I got the impression he was taking my measure to see if he could use me against you. Or drive me off if he thought I was a threat. We had a little argument. With fists. Did you know he carries a combat baton and isn't shy about using it?"

Quinton was appalled, his energy corona jumping with bolts of red, orange, and green, and he grabbed my shoulders. "Jesus, Harper! Are you all right?"

I nodded, pulling back from him so I could keep an eye on his face. I felt fatigued by my vision and our argument and my voice was sharper than I'd intended. "I'm fine. It wasn't that much of a fight—he wasn't trying very hard and, like I said, he was mostly taking my measure."

"Did he say anything about the project . . . ? Did he know about you?"

"You mean the Greywalking stuff? He didn't seem to. I didn't give him any cause to find out, but if he's still following me around or has set someone on me, he may twig to it, especially if the friends-with-fangs get me involved. The current case is pretty deep into ghost country and you've said that all things paranormal are his current interest. If he's even half as savvy as you were when we met, he'll figure out my connection."

"You have to stay away from him." His anxiety was turning the air around him fiery orange.

"That is not up to me. If he wants to follow me, or if Cameron and his people call me in, all I can do is try to shake the tails off when they appear. I can't go into hiding. He has to back off on his own."

Quinton started to say something but was interrupted by a couple of restaurant patrons trying to get out of the door we were blocking. He took me by the arm and led me a few feet down the block, out of sight of the restaurant and into a shadow where we would be hard to observe. "Harper, my dad is dangerous. I know you can't take him out, but you need to be wary of him."

I had to close my eyes for a second, the injured one uncomfortable and itchy from my straining to see without the veil of Grey fog between me and the world. "I'm well aware of that," I said as I reopened my eyes. "But short of going straight at him and putting an end to this—which would signal an escalation on our part and make him more anxious to either control us or break us up—there is little I can do to stay out of his way. I'm not asking you to do anything about it. I'm only telling you what happened, since I haven't had the chance before now. If you're working on some way of getting out of his reach permanently, you need to have all the facts about what he's up to."

"I appreciate that, Harper. But I'm going to worry and freak out, anyway. You don't want to see some of the things that he's doing to the paranormals he's managed to get hold of."

"Like what? And how did he 'get hold' of anything?"

"I don't know how he got most of them. Some he brought back from some other project in Europe—don't ask about it because I don't know. Here he's directing experiments. It's like something out of a horror movie. And he's not alone—he has a support unit. He's a monster and I don't want him near you."

I was taken aback for a moment, but that didn't change the situation. "Then find a way to stop him. He's not going to give up keeping tabs on me as long as I'm of any potential use to him—which will be as long as he still wants to force you to work with him. I'm trying to give him no reason to tag me, but it's unlikely, given his interests, that I can dodge him completely. And I certainly can't lower my profile as a person of interest while I'm hanging out with ghosts and people who are manifesting mediumistic behavior. He wants to know more about ghosts and monsters and, sorry to say, I'm one of the resident experts. When he figures that out, he'll press you even harder."

"He might not figure it out." His aura had gone an uncomfortable shade of green.

I gave him a disbelieving stare. "Right. He's going to be stupid and blind where I'm concerned. Because he's been such a big blind idiot up until now. Gods, I'm tired," I added, not really meaning to say so aloud as I put one cold hand over my injured eye. "So tired of this . . ."

Quinton put his hands on my shoulders and tried to pull me to him, but I resisted. "Harper . . . what's wrong?"

"Aside from this whole situation with your dad . . . ? I can't see normally out of my left eye at the moment. It's all Grey all the time, which is making my life and my work a lot more complicated than usual."

"You didn't say—"

"You haven't been around enough."

He threw up his hands and glared up at the sky in exasperation. "I'm never around! You're acting like an abandoned spouse! That's not how we operate, is it?"

"It wasn't. But for the past six or eight months, you've been at my place more often than on the street like you used to be. Didn't you notice that's where your dad found you? And I *am* your damned spouse. May not have the paper, but we have the relationship and the magical tie to prove it."

He seemed to ignore the deeper implications of my statement. "Are you saying you're a liability . . . ?"

My turn to thrash my head in exasperation. "No! I'm just trying to get you to recognize the pattern we *both* established. I don't want it to change—I'm annoyed at how little I've seen of you while acting as if it's my due when I know it isn't—but we have to factor that into any plans for stalemating your father."

Quinton took a deep, angry breath, the energy around him turning dark red before it bled away on the exhale. "I'll take care of him."

"Don't do anything foolish," I warned, a chilly sense of doom settling over me.

He pressed his lips tightly together, stubborn and not willing to discuss it further with me.

"Quinton, I'm with you, no matter what. Just . . . respond to messages more often, will you?" It wasn't what I wanted to say, but anything else was either stupid or a waste of breath. For all that he seemed an easygoing guy, Quinton was as devious and stubborn as his dad and wouldn't take kindly to any demands of mine where that sneaky bastard was concerned.

He relented a little and gave me a hug, whispering into my ear, "I'll take care of this. I love you. And I'll stay in better touch. I promise. Just be careful, sweetheart."

I kissed his cheek, unenthusiastic about the situation. "I'll be as careful as you are. And I'll come after your ass if you get yourself in dutch with Daddy."

"Don't you dare," he whispered.

"You won't have any say in the matter." I backed away from him, my face feeling stiff with a lack of warmth. "I'll see you later."

He just looked at me a moment, then shrugged—not a truly insouciant shrug, just a faked one—and turned away.

I wanted to cry or scream, but I wasn't going to. Sometimes you have to let your other half be a stubborn fool. He'd let me do it often enough.

I shook my head with disgust all the way back to the Land Rover—weaving a little as the Grey flitted in and out of my vision—and decided I was too keyed up to go home yet. Work was about all I had to distract myself and since it was night, now might be the time to visit a haunted bar. . . .

THIRTEEN

Pike Place Market is creepier at night. Even if you can't see the shades of the dead among the wiry lines of energy that rush off the bluff like a waterfall, the buildings and arcades take on a menacing air when empty. Sounds echo across the road and along the alleys. Awnings flap in a breeze that is always cold, raising monstrous crow shadows lit by the neon clock over the main entrance. Clouds had begun to roll in again, covering the stars and drowning the moon. The bars and restaurants attract just enough people to emphasize the emptiness rather than fill it and I found the sound of my rubber-heeled boots too loud as I walked along the tilted streets toward Post Alley. It didn't take long to realize someone was following me.

For a moment, I thought it might be Quinton, keeping an eye on me in case his patriotic psychotic father was stalking me, but a quick check of the Grey revealed nothing like either man's energy signature. Instead, something tangled in red and black with trailing tentacles of cold white light lurked just beyond any easy view, as if it knew exactly how to stay out of my normal sight. Not quite vampire-like, but not something I knew. It plainly wasn't normal, whatever it was, and I hoped it wasn't part of the conspiracy of ghosts that were plaguing my client's sister and the other patients I'd seen. If it were somehow connected to Purlis, well . . . that was a different problem altogether. It couldn't keep tabs on me without showing itself once I went into Post Alley, however, since there were no cross alleys in the stretch where Kells Irish Pub was. And it couldn't assume my destination, since two other bars or restaurants had doors onto the alley, too. It would have to close up a bit. . . .

I got all the way to the tavern's door before I caught a fleeting glimpse of something human-shaped beneath the distinctive aura. I paused and considered trying to catch the tail, but a small band of pub crawlers came noisily around the corner and sent my observer back into deeper shadow. I hoped I'd have another chance to "chat" with it when I came out. For the time being, I was going inside to see what ghostly things might be lurking about in the former mortuary.

The first room was the classic low-ceilinged pub with dark wood and tiled floors. The tiles might well have been original, since my Grey-adjusted vision saw the room as it must once have been—filled with cold slabs on which the bodies of Seattle's dead were embalmed. I shuddered and passed through a short doorway to the other half of the bar, where the ceilings were higher and the decor more modern. The paranormal setting, however, was much worse: I'd found the former crematory.

To me the room was uncomfortably warm and a storm of spirits rushed through it, swirling like ash toward the back of the space, where a storage room or refrigerator now occupied what had been the oven. I cringed and turned aside, stumbling into the edge of the bar that was hidden by my Grey vision on that side.

The bartender looked up at me with a touch of alarm. "You all right?" he asked.

"Just dizzy," I croaked back, fighting to put the sight into literal perspective and shut down the double image of the past and the present.

"It takes some people that way," he said.

I got myself onto a barstool. "What does?"

"This room. Some people find it uncomfortable. Even frightening."

"Former funeral home. Yeah, I suppose they might."

"You know the story, then?"

"No, but I have heard the general outline."

"Do you like ghost stories, then?"

My desire was to say "not particularly" but I would never get any information if I did that, so I said, "Maybe. Are they true stories or just hogwash and hokum?"

The bartender laughed. "It's hard to say sometimes, but this being a former funeral home, some of 'em are probably true. They say the original owner used to have hearse races so he could beat the other mortuaries to dead people. Might even be true."

"I heard this place was connected to a certain doctor. . . ."

"Dr. Hazzard? Oh yes. She used to have her patients cremated here and the owner would give her somebody else's diseased organs to show to the distraught relatives to prove the patient had died of something other than starvation. Quite a racket, eh?"

Judging from the phantoms of the emaciated dead rushing through the room, it wasn't just a racket, it was an industry. I nodded, still a bit queasy.

"And there's the little girl some people claim to see here. She stays near the back and she likes the dancing. The theory is that she died of influenza and was cremated here. It's quite likely true. When they were renovating, they found shelves full of tiny urns with no names on 'em, just numbers. Child-sized urns."

"Down here?"

"No. Upstairs. The bar's owners are turning it into a space for catering parties. Used to be the sales room and the chapel."

"What is the attraction of bars in former funerary chapels?" I asked.

"Not sure. Spitting in the face of death, maybe?"

Something tinkled and scraped and the bartender spun around just in time for a bottle to launch itself off the shelf behind him and crash to the floor. "Ah, Christ. There they go again." He glared at the back bar and whispered at the bottles, "Didn't I tell you you could help yourself so long as you didn't break anything? Now, was that nice?"

The mist-shape of a woman oozed out of the racks of liquor and wafted through him to me. She put her incorporeal hand on the bar beside me and then dissolved into the howling storm of other spirits. A small button remained on the bar where her hand had been. As I stared at it, an old-fashioned key dropped onto the bar beside it as if it had fallen from the ceiling. And then the stub of a pencil. Each object was shrouded in trailing blackness. Another phantom woman came toward me from the outside door. She glared at me and her face flickered from fully fleshed to a naked skull. It was the woman who'd lingered in the market office earlier in the day and she exuded malicious intent. All the other ghosts in the room seemed to pull back from her, leaving a clearing around the two of us.

Her face seemed to melt, as if she, too, were starving into a living skeleton before my eyes. For a moment, what stood before me, clothed in only the raging energy of hunger and fury, was nothing that had ever been human. It glared at me and then seemed to turn that baleful expression inward. Then the moment's horrible vision faded.

I felt a burning pain running up my arms where I thought the woman's ghost had touched me earlier in the day and I winced, looking down to see if some creature had snuck up onto the bar to bite me. But what I saw was blood.

I gasped and yanked at my sleeve, but the narrow cuff hitched up and stopped me. I got to my feet and whirled, heading back into the short hallway between the two bars to get to the washroom. Inside a narrow stall, I yanked off my jacket and pulled off my shirt, expecting my clothes to be ruined, but the blood was an illusion. The words burning onto my arms were not. "Tribute does not feed the servant. Leave us be, until your time."

I'd never been warned off with tricks of this sort before. Most ghosts who wanted me gone were more direct, though the phrase "until your time" made me think they had some plan for me I hadn't sussed out. I stared at the words and saw more slowly crawling across my belly. I felt each letter forming as if pushed up from inside my skin. The sensation sent me retching to the toilet.

I got hold of myself eventually and put my shirt back on. I was rinsing my face with cold water when the hostess from the first section of the pub came into the restroom. "Are you all right?"

I nodded. "I'm fine."

"Do you need a cab? I can call one to the hotel at the end of the alley if you do."

"No. Thank you. I really am all right. Bad food. Not drink." I hated maligning the dinner I'd had, but "ghost poisoning" is not the clever explanation you want to offer for barfing in a bar.

She nodded, but her eyes were narrowed and I was sure she didn't quite believe me. I washed my face and hands again and killed a few more minutes until I felt steady enough to venture back out. The ghosts had reconvened, so I hoped that meant the intimidating phantasm had gone for the time being. Before I could escape the room, the bartender flagged me down. Reluctantly I walked through the ectoplasmic storm to the bar.

"Did you want these?" he asked, pointing to the objects on the bar. There were more of them now.

"No. They fell from the ceiling. They don't belong to me." I should have taken them—I was sure the ghosts had left them for that purpose—but I didn't want to touch them at the moment on the chance that they were . . . hers. "Maybe you could put them somewhere in case the owner comes back for them?"

He peered at me as if he, too, was gauging my sobriety and then swept them into a small container, which he put beneath the bar. "All right. If you change your mind, though . . ."

"Yeah. OK," I said and got out as quickly as I could without appearing to run.

Outside, the terrifying phantom woman with the melting face was waiting for me, looking even more skeletal and less human than before. "You cannot take them from me," she said, her voice sighing through the alley on a wind that stank of death. "Tribute is given. It cannot be taken away."

I didn't have a ready reply, though she seemed to expect one, studying me as she was through empty eye sockets with her head cocked slightly sideways. I slid a step backward on the old brick alley floor, my boot soles picking up grit and emitting a slight grinding sound. The revenant lurched toward me and I ducked to spin away. . . .

Something cold and vicious struck me hard from the left—my blind side, knocking me into the railing over a sunken courtyard on the far side of the alley. I fetched up hard and tried to dig my feet in, but there was only hard brick and empty air. I felt myself tipping over the railing and I scrabbled to get a grip on it, or loop my arm around it as something scraped at my face and neck.

I started to scream, but the shout was choked off by an ice-cold hand that clamped over my mouth. But one hand busy meant one less to grapple me with and I hunkered down, pulling out of the remaining grip on my shoulders and wedging myself under the rail. Tucked into the metal bars, I kicked out at the man-shaped thing that attacked me and hit it hard in the knee. It staggered, then turned to take a second swing at me. . . .

Suddenly it spun and bolted away at inhuman speed—it looked like the vampire-ish thing that had followed me to the alley. A second black shape trailing an aura of blood and pain pursued it up the alley and everything Grey fled ahead of it, leaving a vacant eddy of mist and empty ghostlight for me to stand in.

I crept to the nearest bench attached to the railing I'd nearly toppled over and sat down, huddling into myself and shivering as if it were midwinter instead of the first week of July. The melting-faced horror was gone, as was the vampire-like man—if it wasn't the one that had followed me into the market, it was something of the same type.

I breathed hard, catching my startled breath and calming the instinct that urged me to run far and fast as the darkness that had pursued my assailant returned. . . .

Some things never leave your memory; this stomach-turning smell and oppressive clot of dark energy were indelible in my mind. Even though he made no sound and my vision was a mess of Grey overlaid on normal like so much static on a television picture, I knew when he stopped next to me and I raised my head. "Hello, Carlos. Thanks for that."

It's a bit difficult to describe the relationship between Carlos and me. We're friends of a sort, but our history is tangled with unsavory details like death, madness, and vampire politics. I hadn't seen him—or most of Seattle's vampires—in quite a while. Not that I minded: Vampires literally turn my stomach and they always have an angle. They're a frightening lot, but Carlos was much worse than most. He was also a necromancer and he worked as the chief advisor to Seattle's top vampire—a former client of mine. Carlos and I had done some horrible—if necessary—things together and our secrets bound us in silence and uneasy respect.

"Thanks are unnecessary. I didn't catch him." His quiet voice resonated in my chest.

"Maybe that's as good a reason as any to be grateful." I hated to imagine what Carlos might have in mind for any member of the uncanny who'd offended him. He, after all, was a creature who killed for power.

"No. It was he I was stalking. Driving him off you was not what I'd had in mind. But Cameron would not like to hear you'd been injured by one of ours—even if that one has gone rogue."

I shook off some of my discomfort and studied his face. It wasn't just his dark hair and beard that made Carlos difficult to read—his expression is subtle and chilly at the best of times. "You have a rogue vampire on the streets?" I asked, taken by surprise—it hadn't quite looked like a vampire in my Grey sight, but I didn't know everything about that terrible species. Between them Carlos, Cameron, and his inner circle don't miss much and it seemed unlikely that they'd have no idea of it if one of their community was turning against them. "How did that slip by?"

"Not a slip. A theft. My assistant was foolish and fell among evil companions."

I raised my eyebrows. It's hard to imagine companions much more evil than vampires, but given what Quinton had said about his father, I didn't doubt it was true. I chose to address the less frightening half of the statement. "You have an assistant now? Well, I suppose Cameron did sort of graduate out of that job. . . ." I hadn't taken time to wonder how that situation had been resolved, but obviously it had. Cameron had, technically, still been Carlos's protégé when the vampire hierarchy came tumbling down and Cameron stepped into the void.

"It would be inappropriate for the Prince of the City to stoop and carry for me, but I must still work—work that you know requires considerable labor. Inman was only a dhampir, so I cannot be surprised if his mind has been persuaded against us."

I guessed that was the situation Quinton had been warning me about when he said the vampires had a problem. "When did this happen?"

"A few weeks ago. The half-converted can be difficult to track since they walk the daylight as well as the night."

"And you didn't come to me?"

"I felt it would not be in our best interest to be seen to rely on your help too frequently, Greywalker. The current cabal is still young in power."

Considering I'd helped put that group in power, I was well aware of how sketchy the underpinnings of the regime were and how quickly the situation could have turned into a bloodbath at any hint of weakness.

"How—?" I started, but Carlos cut me off with a look.

"This is not the best place for conversation. And I have things I would ask you, too."

I was more shaken than I'd thought if I hadn't the presence of mind to realize that chats with vampires are not best pursued in public places, like famous alleys in front of famous bars. I nodded. "Where would you prefer? I'm on the job, but, to be honest, it's not going well. . . ."

He made a humming sound and motioned for me to follow him down the alley, blending into the night as only a vampire can. I came along behind, trusting him not to lead me into danger—which says a lot about our relationship in spite of the fact that Carlos is the most frightening thing I know. He went down the alley and ducked across Stewart Street, heading to a bench in a tiny courtyard behind the Inn at the Market. It was probably a lovely place to sit and talk during the day. At night it was secluded and dark in spite of its proximity to streetlights and busy roads. We sat uncomfortably close, his aura of death and pain lying over me like a blanket of horrors.

Once we were seated, posing like lovers conversing, I asked, "Why didn't you come to me when your assistant went missing? You know I would take any case of yours as a priority."

"I do, which is why I did not. Cameron suggested it, but he was dissuaded. We cannot be seen to run to you with petty internal problems."

"But a rogue vampire is not a petty—"

He cut me off. "No, but we did not want it known that such a thing had happened. And I prefer to hunt those who defy me myself."

I didn't like the sound of that.

"Defy you? That sounds . . . complicated." I wouldn't have thought a demi-vampire could do other than obey the vampire to whom he was tied by blood and power. Purlis had managed a very dangerous coup. No wonder Carlos hadn't wanted word to get out. It also gave me a new perspective on my ambitious and unpleasant nearly in-law.

"It is," Carlos said. "Inman was not the first of our number to go missing. But he has been the first to come back."

I shook my head, not so much confused as amazed at what I was hearing.

"He came back to spy," Carlos explained. "The others may still live, but they remain wherever their captors keep them and we dare not risk an assault to recover them at this time. So we have allowed the situation to lie as it is. So far it has caused little trouble, but that won't last. With Inman's return, we face a problem that I had hoped to keep you out of. I would not like to ask you to choose between our faction—which you have protected and supported, however much you dislike our kind—and your mate."

I felt exhausted by this skulduggery and closed my eyes, tamping down my anger at Purlis, Quinton, and the whole damned situation.

Carlos spoke into my protracted silence. "You see the difficulty I faced."

I opened my eyes and looked at him, steeling myself against the effects of his gaze. "I do, but you shouldn't have hesitated. Neither of us supports his father's project. Or his ambitions. He's been trying to drag Quinton in for a year, but it's a no-go. Quinton won't do it."

"Because of you?"

"Because his father is a psychotic with an agenda that gets innocent people killed."

Carlos nodded. "I see. I'm sorry that we hesitated—that *I* hesitated to come to you. But we should talk to Cameron. This changes the situation."

He rose and expected me to come along, but I held my place, not least because I still felt disoriented and ill from the swift passage of events. "Wait. I have concerns of my own here. I can't just abandon my inquiry to accommodate Cameron. Time is short on this one."

He arched a brow. "You require something in return."

"I will, yes."

"What will you demand?"

"A favor—when I'm ready for it."

Carlos chuckled, a rumbling that shook my chest and skull. "One to be named at another time. You well know that we owe you many times over."

"Can you speak for Cameron in this?"

"No, but I doubt he'll balk. Come, we'll go to him."

And this time I didn't have a choice. I got up and followed Carlos. He went straight to my Land Rover and leaned against the side with a sardonic smile. "I prefer not to walk, as would you." Which let me know Cameron wasn't in downtown Seattle as his predecessor had preferred to be. Interesting . . .

I don't like to transport vampires. Their presence makes me queasy under the best of circumstances, and the filtering effect of the big truck's glass and steel doesn't work on things already inside it. This was not going to be a pleasant drive . . . wherever we were going.

At Carlos's direction, I drove out of the market and up through downtown and the University District to Laurelhurst—a neighborhood filled with sprawling, well-appointed houses that rolls along the lakeshore between Union Bay and Wolf Bay. Carlos sent me up a twisty street that terminated in a long private drive and a solid gate. I wasn't surprised that he had a keycard for the gate. Nor was I entirely surprised that the gate didn't open immediately. An athletic young woman with a swirling aura of crimson and indigo stepped out from behind a bit of landscaping and paused to look us over. She wasn't wearing a uniform, but something about her outfit hinted at an organization. What she was wearing was a gun—something bigger than a handgun and smaller than a rifle that I didn't get a good look at—on a quick-deploy sling. I guess the vampires were finally giving up arrogance in favor of safety, since even a top-level predator is only as good as his combat reach. Carlos turned a baleful glare on the guard but she didn't flinch. Once she'd satisfied her curiosity, she keyed a radio resting on her collar like a cop's and said something into it. Her energy corona flared and sparked as she spoke and I wasn't able to understand her, though I knew she was speaking English. I was almost glad my left eye was still stubbornly seeing only in the Grey or I might have missed the spell in action. I wondered who'd cast it—the woman or someone else?

The gate opened and I ceased speculating and drove through. I cruised the truck down the long driveway to a dark gray house that stretched along a bit of the hill crest overlooking the Laurelhurst Beach Club and Wolf Bay. The view was spectacular even from the wrong side of the building.

The interior was equally impressive. An eclectic collection of art was casually arranged throughout the rooms in the way most people would display curios and family photos. The carpet in the living room was white—a rather daring choice for a vampire. The furniture was more traditional: black and arranged to face the floor-to-ceiling vista of the bay. Cameron was standing in front of the windows, tall and slim and blond as a young lion. He would always appear to be twenty-one—his age when we'd met a few weeks after his death—but he seemed older. He gazed out at the view with a melancholy posture.

"Don't you find that a bit disturbing?" I asked, recalling that vampires and water don't get along well.

He shrugged without turning. "I like to keep an eye on things that can easily kill me. It just seems like a good idea." His voice now silvered the air with small charms of comfort and relaxation when he spoke. It appeared an effortless performance, though the deep red-and-black energy around him flickered very slightly as I noticed it. He was certainly being more thorough than his predecessor in controlling his environment—right down to how his visitors felt about him. It was masterly, but I didn't like it.

He turned then, flashing a smile that went a long way to dispelling the roiling discomfort that I usually detected pouring off of vampires. His eyes were a deeper violet color than I'd remembered—or maybe that, too, went with the glamour from his smile. I shot Carlos a glance, but saw no magical workings on his part.

"Your former student has come along nicely," I said.

He gave me a small nod of satisfied acknowledgment. "He comes into his own."

I looked back to Cameron. "Very impressive."

"I had the best teacher death could buy." Cameron made a show of taking a deep breath—he'd stopped breathing about five years earlier, so it was strictly for effect—and changed the subject. "It's a pleasure to see you, Harper."

"Is it?"

"Yes. I like you. I owe you . . . pretty much everything."

"That doesn't always lead to joyful reunions and fond remembrances," I said.

"Not for some people, but I'm not exactly *some people*. Am I?"

"No."

He almost smiled. "Since you're in Carlos's company, can I assume this visit has to do with our sudden loss of membership?"

"A bit. Carlos seems to think we have things to discuss."

"If he thinks so, then it's so. Please sit down. Make yourself comfortable."

I'm rarely comfortable around vampires, but with these two I'd do my best to fake it. Nevertheless, I was careful to sit where I could watch them both, which I knew they knew. Cameron's mouth quirked a bit at one corner, but that was all the notice my caution warranted.

Vampires don't have the same sense of time pressure that living humans have. But in this case, they had an immediate problem and I wasn't yet sure if it was more or less urgent than my case in hand, so I kept a bland expression and waited them out.

Cameron sat down at last, in a chair at an angle to mine so he wasn't in my space but still close enough to talk without raising his voice. Carlos kept to his feet, staying within a degree or two of Cameron's shoulder. Cam leaned forward, resting his arms on his knees, the light reflected off the water illuminating one side of his face with wavering blue light.

"In the past month or so, several of my people have disappeared. It isn't unusual for the weaker members of such a tribe as ours to move on or to fall away. Even we die, and accidents do happen. There have been other indications that something's been a bit . . . off with some of our associates. Carlos said he saw signs of interference with magic—small things, but of interest and possibly dangerous to us. And I began to notice fewer homeless people on the streets."

"You watch the homeless?" I asked, my cynicism coming through, while some other part of my brain wondered if he knew anything about Twitcher and if his death was part of the pattern Cam had detected.

Cameron met my eyes and looked disappointed. "Yes. While it's true that the people who fall through your society's cracks may become prey to the desperate and unscrupulous of mine, they aren't cattle. They are human beings, as we were once human beings. We must coexist without drawing attention to ourselves and that means using every resource wisely. Something Edward didn't always appreciate."

He put one hand up as if warding off a comment he knew was coming. "Yes, I said 'resource.'" His eyes narrowed a little and his face hardened with a touch of cold anger I'd never before seen in him. "The past few years have been a hard education for me. Ours is not a society apart from yours. We're predators, but we're also parasites. We are dependent on normal humans and creatures of magic to maintain us and to keep our existence secret. Unless human society changes in vast and significant ways, we'll always be things that live in the shadows—nightmares, dreams, things half seen by moonlight. Phantom lovers who melt away at dawn," he added, scoffing. "That is the fairy tale we perpetuate for our own interests—thank the gods for the pliant imaginations of Bram Stoker and Stephenie Meyer."

He paused with a rueful half smile and made a slight change to his position in the chair—more for my sake than his, I thought—before he went on, his expression growing harder. "Because there are few of us, we're ruthless. Because we're long-lived, we're acquisitive. And if we're not clever and tricky about it, we're dead. We have to tread lightly on the earth and we have to maintain the balance by husbanding resources, by being careful, abstemious, and—when warranted—manipulative, underhanded bastards. So, yes, I keep watch on the homeless, the transient, and the insane. They're like a pack of idiot cousins—an obnoxious, smelly, drooling horde most of the time, but a few are quite likable. A decent custodian doesn't just stand aside and let them all jump off cliffs. Or push them."

I found his use of "our" and "your" startling and unsettling, but it was an eloquent speech and not at all what I would have expected of the chief vampire of Seattle. I had not given much thought to how much the terrified and confused living-dead college student I'd once rescued from a parking garage would be forced to change by taking the reins. I was pleased to detect a touch of student-activist-style passion there. Some things are, apparently, not exclusive to the living.

I bowed my head a little. "I hadn't given it that kind of thought. But . . . much as I don't like to sound petty, could we focus on the more immediate problem? I do understand the larger context, but for now, we both seem to have pieces of a larger puzzle and I'd like to put them together."

Cameron chuckled. "Yes. I'm sorry. I get carried away on this topic lately. As I said, people have gone missing. Among the homeless it's not uncommon for them to move on and we can't always track what becomes of them. I didn't pay that much attention at first, but when a few of my people disappeared, I began to worry. Initially it was our support people—catspaws, blood-bound, day servants— then a few demi-vampires and the ascending. Those are always dangerous stages, when it's very easy for something to go wrong—you remember what I was like. But the apparent mortality rate was a little too high and then I started to notice that no one could positively say that any of these missing had died—it was just assumed. There should have been bodies, but there weren't. No funerals, no rise in suspicious deaths reported to the coroner's office. They were just gone. Like they'd been taken. But there was a lot more ghost activity—according to Carlos." He indicated the other vampire with a small gesture. "I don't have his acuity, so I can't confirm it, but I'd assume you can."

"I have noticed more ghosts, but only in some areas," I said. "And I can't be sure it's really more activity so much as my spending too little time some places and not being familiar with the normal activity levels any longer."

"Are you sure? Carlos seems to think there's a profound disturbance. . . ."

Carlos took a step forward. "It's not what I *think*. It's an observation."

I gave it a moment's consideration, mentally cursing James Purlis but holding back my ire. "When did this start? This rise in activity? And did you notice a geographic pattern?"

"Near the end of the year there was a change," said Carlos. "It has surged twice since then. There are a greater number of animate ghosts active in Seattle now than last year, and yet there has been no significant rise in deaths to account for it. There has been no great cataclysm or disaster here in the right time frame. The activities of your lover's father have also had an effect on the weft and warp of magic. He draws the things of magic to him through mechanical contrivance and he has drawn our own away from us—as he did with Inman."

Of course Carlos would know what the normal death rate was in Seattle and what effect Purlis's activities were having on the local Grey power grid. "Are you certain that he's responsible for the disappearance of the demi-vampires and others like that?" I didn't want to overlook some factor, though I also thought that Purlis was behind the changes Carlos was describing. It fit with what I knew of his project through Quinton.

"I have cast spells and questioned the dead and I am sure of it."

Cameron rejoined the conversation. "We would have brought this to you much earlier, but when Carlos discovered that Quinton was involved, I thought it would be better if we didn't mix in family politics."

I gave a harsh laugh. "James Purlis is not the sort of person I consider 'family.'"

"But he is your . . ." He hesitated and cast a glance at Carlos.

"He is the blood father of your spouse-in-soul. That is a complex relationship in matters magical."

"As far as I'm concerned, the man could die unseen and become food for crows without my shedding a single tear. Except that his corpse might poison the poor crows."

"Not if he were to die by magic or by the hand of creatures bound to you. As Cameron and I are."

I scowled in confusion. "I don't understand. We have no bond."

"Indeed we do, Greywalker." He put his hand out into the air between us, whispering, and touched one finger to a barely glimmering thread of energy. It flared bright, revealing a gossamer-thin line of perfect whiteness that made a web uniting the three of us, with two more tendrils vanishing into distance and darkness beyond the room. Then he let it go and the line faded back to being near-invisible. His expression when he spoke again was solemn. "You were witness to our bond of fealty. You made it so, and so you are tied to us. Were either of us or anyone we controlled to kill your father-in-law—for lack of an easier term—there would be consequences. As the Hands of the Guardian, your family weighs on the fabric of magic—not so heavily as you do, but they are not insignificant. They cannot be wiped off the face of the earth casually."

"My family? I have a mother—who drives me crazy—and Quinton. And that's all."

Carlos laughed at me. "I think you don't quite understand what a family is."

It shouldn't have disturbed me, but his statement seemed to set a weight on my chest and I felt suffocated as a swarm of icy chills prickled my flesh. I didn't see magic at work, but something I had pushed away in a dark closet of my mind was breaking out. . . .

FOURTEEN

Carlos stepped closer to me and I flinched as he raised a hand to touch the side of my face. "I won't hurt you, ghost girl." From him, that was very nearly an endearment. But I still loathed his touch—there's nothing like the sickening in-flooding of history, death, and emotion that comes with the touch of a necromancer—and wanted none of it, nor of whatever my brain was trying to serve up. He settled back. "What have you done to your eye?"

The distraction relieved my panic and I was able to reply in a dry voice, "I got paint in it."

He stroked the air over my shoulders and arms but he didn't actually touch me. "You have been in the company of dangerous things."

"I'm in the company of dangerous things right now."

He grunted and looked me over, ignoring my flippancy. "Their ties and remnants complicate my view, but I can't clear them off now." I didn't know what he was referring to and it seemed a bad time to ask. His hand rose again, toward the center of my chest, and stopped, hovering over my sternum. "I should have known you'd have a romantic streak," he said, rubbing the tips of his fingers against his thumb as if he were balling up some tiny filament, muttering more words that dripped into the air.

From his fingers a tiny glowing strand of pink light emerged and stretched away, reaching for the window, and splitting in two as it spun out. It was so thin that it was hard to see. Carlos blew on the strand and it fluttered brighter for a moment, lighting into a spreading spiderweb with me at the center, radiating unevenly in several directions. I imagined I would see more if I turned around, but I didn't want to put my back to Carlos and Cameron.

Carlos held up his other hand, a small blade gleaming in it. "If you would oblige me, I can show you more."

I narrowed my eyes at him in suspicion. I knew what his knives were capable of.

"Only one drop."

"No sucking up my soul or anything like that."

"I would find it a particularly sweet token, but no. I have no need for that. Today." I had the distinct impression he was teasing me and I had to give it some thought before I held up my left hand and offered him a finger—one particular finger, which he found amusing, but he still pricked it quickly with the tip of the knife.

A tiny drop of blood welled on my fingertip. He caught it on the edge of the knife's blade, whispering to it, and touched the blood to the dulling gleam of the web he had drawn from my chest.

The web flared bright, glittering with sparks of rose and gold that raced into the distance of the reaching splines. More than I would have thought, yet so few, and stretching in so many directions. . . .

"That is family." Carlos said. He pointed his finger at the pink strands. "These are ties of affection. And these," he added, pointing to rare thinner, darker strands that wove among the brighter ones, "are ties of blood. You have tried to cut these, but some persist. They are not like the ones you forge yourself but they are as strong, and each binds you, flows from you and back to you. That is family, this web, this complexity. This binding. Yours burns with the power of what you are, and cutting those strands sends shocks throughout that web and everything it touches, calling darkness to fill the voids. There are always forces opposed to order and control, opposed to the Guardian and to you. They will revel in that darkness and use it for their own ends." He moved his hand with care, not touching any of the complicated, twisted threads of light, until he pointed to one that was brighter than the rest, hot pink, glittering, twisted with other parts that spun away in perpendicular and obtuse directions, fading faster than the rest as they stretched away from me. "There is your beloved and the filaments of his own family, his blood kin, that bind to him and through him to you. You see the intricacy of it all. How twined and knotted as it grows closer to you. How beautiful and terrible."

His gaze was soft, lit in the glow of this strange display, and then he flicked his fingers and the light show vanished. "You see."

I nodded, but part of my brain was trying to rebuild parts of that web, to burn a permanent vision of the ties and clues, the hints of things that had momentarily burned so clearly and now were gone again.

"We haven't been able to stop him," Cameron said, breaking the shivering moment of dazzled darkness. "We don't know his plans, but he sent Inman back to spy on us—"

I had to shake myself back to the conversation at hand, remembering that it was Purlis he was talking about. "Probably to find a way to grab a full vampire for his project—whatever it is," I said.

"You don't know?" Carlos had fallen back again, letting Cameron take the lead, but he continued to watch me with that unsettling stare. I refocused on Cameron—it was easier, if more cowardly.

I shook my head. "Not really. He calls it the 'Ghost Division'—which I think is as much an Intelligence-community pun as it is serious—and it's something to do with studying paranormals and possibly using them but I don't know how. Maybe as spies, maybe as assassins, maybe as guinea pigs for developing something else. . . . Quinton knows and he says it's horrifying, but he's busy staying out of his father's hands while doing all he can to monkey-wrench the whole thing, so he hasn't been forthcoming with details. I suspect the project protocols include some rather gruesome practices, since Quinton's father doesn't consider most paranormals to be anything but dangerous lab animals and he thinks of humans who display paranormal ability as 'freaks' to be studied, analyzed, and used as he sees fit—which probably includes killing them and taking a look at their brains and insides. Do you think he's taking the homeless, too?"

"How or if they are connected to Mr. Purlis is still a mystery. I have the name correctly, don't I?"

I nodded. "Yes, James McHenry Purlis—I had to pick at Quinton for quite a while to get that information, though it hasn't done me much good. He's very deeply buried in the Intelligence machine and I haven't been able to make any connections to him—he's a deliberate blank."

Cameron gave a thoughtful grunt. "We've had no better luck. We can't seem to track him except in general directions. If his mind is set on taking others of mine captive, we may have to strike, even though the fallout won't be pleasant."

"And it appears he's temporarily redirected Inman to harass you," Carlos added.

"Inman won't be as much of a problem now that I know he's out there. Don't make a move yet. Purlis thinks I'm obstructing him— which is probably why he's set Inman on me. He doesn't seem to know what I am. Yet. Once he figures it out, though, we'll be in some deep kimchee. Well, I will. Your kimchee remains about the same." I shut up and thought for a moment. The vampires stayed preternaturally still and let me.

As my brain ground on, trying to put pieces into place, my skin began to itch and burn, my eye stung, and my left hand ached. I tried to shake the sensation off, but it grew quickly and I felt like I was falling out of my body. I groped for the arms of my seat and could see the spiked and bloody darkness of the two vampires flash and flow toward me as my vision darkened. I tried to tell them not to touch me, but it came out garbled. The blacker shape reached toward me. . . .

I jerked in my seat as cold rushed over me, pushing back the burning sensations and easing the pain in my hand. Carlos lifted his own hand away, but hovered, waiting for my momentary debility to return.

I shook my head and took several deep, quaking breaths, feeling hollow and chilled inside while my skin itched. I didn't want to look, but I pushed back my cuff and saw curls of reddened script swelling on my arms. I swore under my breath and hoped Delamar was not conscious enough inside his sleep-imprisoned body to feel the same sensations I'd just had. If this kept up, I'd start to lose my mind. I didn't even want to know what the writing on my flesh said— especially since that would involve taking off my shirt in front of Cameron and Carlos, which creeped me out.

"That should not have happened here," Carlos rumbled. I'd forgotten how close he was and I jumped at the sound.

"I'm not sure it's bound by location," I said.

"One of these strange things has attached itself to you. These injuries allowed a spirit to tie itself to you. The protections on this house should have been proof against such an attack." He glanced at Cameron. "I apologize—this ward is failing."

Cameron shook his head and I spoke up before they could go off on a discussion of who had screwed up and how to fix it. "It's something I brought with me, I think. No fault of yours."

Carlos glowered at me—he doesn't take correction well. "Where does it come from to attach itself to you?"

"I think a ghost touched me at the market yesterday and somehow brought this on. It's the same kind of manifestation I've seen recently on a . . . not quite a client. He's one of three vegetative patients displaying old-school séance effects, but these aren't happening during fake telephone calls to the dead. All the patients are connected to one another in some way that's also related to the tunnel project and Pike Place Market."

Carlos nodded. "The case that took you to Post Alley and the spirit whose conversation with you Inman disrupted."

"Yes," I replied. "That particular . . . thing also seems to have some relation to the case, but—again—I'm not certain of what it is. What I am sure of is that the anomaly of three patients with the same incredibly rare condition is not a coincidence. I believe that whatever magic links them is also keeping them in their current state or may have brought them to that state to begin with. I don't think they're supposed to be locked in this coma-like condition—and the longer they stay that way, the less chance they have of awakening.

One of the patients seems to have broken in long enough to express that fear and the idea that he's weakening to the point of some kind of nonbodily death. I think time is running out for all of them. They aren't in their own bodies, but they're dying."

Carlos glanced at Cameron, who was frowning in concern. Then he turned his gaze to me and said, "I'm unfamiliar with your case, but the principle is correct. When a living soul is unnaturally separated from its proper vessel, it dwindles and dies out like a flame without fuel. It would be beyond the realm of chance that your displaced souls have no common cause with the magical disruptions I've noted."

"I have to agree," I said, "but what is the cause and what the effect? What I've seen so far, aside from the state of the patients, is disruption of temporaclines and a rise in magic and ghost activity associated with the tunnel project, which is definitely connected somehow to the patients; James Purlis's Ghost Division, which I can't connect to the patients because I don't know exactly what he's up to; and the disappearance and death of homeless people, which I can't connect to anything magical yet, but you seem to. If Quinton were here, he'd probably say it's a system of some kind—but not necessarily erected deliberately. There's too much energy in the system—I've seen temporaclines out of place, repeaters far from their tied locations, ghosts that can hold a soul out of its body. . . . The energy required to make those things happen is massive and it has to come from somewhere. Disruption releases ghosts and other energy—both the tunneling and Purlis's project are disruptions but I don't know if they are connected. If they aren't, which disruption is powering which anomaly? If they are, what's the connection?"

Cameron waved Carlos aside so he could see me better without the other vampire in the way. I appreciated the relief from the stomach-turning proximity. "Isn't it more likely that these problems are all of a piece? If you apply Occam's razor it would seem they should be—it's the simplest answer. That would imply that solving one part of the problem will make the rest reducible."

"You sound like Quinton," I said. "If you're suggesting that 'solving' Purlis will break the problem down to something easily managed, I'm doubtful. It certainly couldn't hurt to get him off our collective back, but that could make the situation worse, judging from what Carlos was saying earlier."

Carlos nodded. "It would be best to avoid killing him—much as it may pain me to say so."

"I appreciate that. I'll keep an eye out for your missing dhampir and if I get any ideas about Purlis's location, I'll let you know, but for now I'm going to concentrate on the problem of the spirit manifestations and let the rest come as it may. I have to help my client and the other patients—time is against me on that. Besides, I keep thinking I'm hearing the Guardian Beast rattling around nearby and that's the last thing I want coming down on me for not fixing this problem." Dead pseudo-relatives and their repercussions in the Grey held considerably less horror for me than the thing that prowled the verges of the world between worlds.

Cameron yawned and looked startled by it. A glance at the view beyond showed the sky just the least bit paler to the east than it had been. "Perhaps—" he started.

"It may be a good time for me to leave," I said. "I'll be in touch if anything comes up on the Purlis front, but I don't know when."

"That'll do. We'll continue to gather information from our sources, too. And I'll keep your case in mind."

I stood up, feeling shaky but trying to hide it. "Oh. If I need to contact either of you, how should I do that? I assume you don't drop notes at the shop anymore. . . ." When I'd first met them, Carlos had been managing a porn store in the Denny Triangle area, but it seemed unlikely he spent any time there now. The length of the sunny summer days complicated the situation by shortening the vampires' operating hours as well.

Cameron stood and took a card from his pocket. He glanced at it, then offered it to me. "Any of these will do." I had an old cell number for Cameron and I was a bit surprised to see that still on his card, though it was well down the list.

Carlos gave me a wolf's smile. "You know mine."

I shuddered to remember, but I did. I hoped to avoid ever going near his place again. I accepted Cameron's card and saw myself out, wanting to avoid any intimate conversation with Carlos about my ghostly manifestations. His fascinations were strictly morbid and I would have enough trouble sleeping in spite of feeling nearly somnambulant.

I didn't see the guard on my way out. Had I not known there were people with guns loitering in the hedges, I would not have guessed it. Seeing my rearview mirror flood with the rose-colored light of dawn, I wondered what had possessed a vampire to own a house that faced east, into the killing sun, but I didn't imagine I'd ever know.

As I rolled down the hill and headed back through the university, I thought about the tangled strands of attachment that Carlos had said linked me to Quinton and to all of his family besides. I didn't doubt his identification—Carlos had the skill to do it and no need to lie to me—but I did consider the direction in which the line had pointed—two primary strands running together while two or three others, more slender, wound off to the east, vanishing in the darkness of distance. Wherever the two thicker threads ran, I would find the elder Purlis and probably Quinton nearby. I didn't like the implication that he was so closely entwined with his devious father, and I didn't know how to see the thread again or in such detail, so I hoped it wasn't a permanent situation. It might have been a bad idea to cut a thread off completely, but surely I could pick a few apart. . . .

At home I let the ferret out to romp while I showered, improbably imagining I could wash the traces of the message off my skin. Mostly the too-hot water made the rest of me equally red, which was almost good enough. Chaos bounced into the bathroom and hoisted herself onto the edge of the tub, taking a stroll along the shower curtain, chuckling at me for my folly and sounding remarkably like she was chiding me.

Still feeling itchy, but at least a bit more warm and pliable, I put on a fluffy bathrobe and wandered barefooted into the kitchen, pursued by the ferret. I mourned for the dinner I'd lost and warmed up some soup to fill the void in my middle. I ate and fended the ferret off from my bowl, but lost a chunk of bread to the marauder as we wrestled for control of the slice of chewy seven-grain. "Pest," I said as she danced around her prize in glee. I still felt hungry, even though I'd eaten plenty of food, but I didn't have more, since I hoped to fall asleep soon. The state of my nervous energy was unlikely to allow that, but I wished for it anyhow.

In spite of myself, I fell asleep on the couch while the morning selection of talking heads jabbered about the upcoming Independence Day festivities and what we should all be cooking on the grill. Chaos has no interest in people on TV, so I didn't get a dose of her tiny cold nose or tickling whiskers in my ear until someone started talking about protecting your dog from being frightened by fireworks and she felt I needed to pay attention. Not that she had ever paid any attention to fireworks, but she apparently felt I should take note in case our neighbor Rick needed them for managing Grendel, his pit bull. Grendel was easily upset by things that went "bang."

The whiskery snuffling in my ear woke me and I put the carpet shark back into her cage and dragged my suddenly listless self to bed. Alone. No sign of Quinton—not that I'd expected him after he'd said he wasn't coming . . . or I had and I was lying to myself. I was far too used to his presence and I had to admit that one of my primary reasons for despising his father was the way he stirred up Quinton's sense of imminent danger and pulled him away from me. Pure resentment, that's what I felt—well . . . and disgust because Purlis Senior believed in Ideals without pausing to think of people. No. On second thought, I just didn't like him. I wasn't up to hate yet, since that required a depth of passion I didn't feel for the man at this point, but "healthy dislike" was well in the ballpark.

My thoughts went round and round as I lay in bed, not quite sleeping and not quite awake. After a few hours of nonsleep, I gave in and got up again. My injured eye didn't ache and itch as it had the night before, but the annoyingly persistent Grey vision remained. I used my ointment and drops and thought I should probably call Skelly—once this case was over.

I considered taking the ferret along, but I thought it was going to be a long day and didn't like the possibility of her getting hurt if I had any other confrontations with monsters or ghosts, so I put her back into her cage before I left. I got a glare for my trouble. "I'm just trying to protect you," I said. Chaos was not impressed.

I drove up to Pioneer Square and left the Land Rover in my parking garage so I could walk around and find out if any of the street people had seen Twitcher recently or could tell me why he'd relocated to Steinbrueck Park, or who else might be missing. Or if he was dead, as a small part of me I did not want to listen to kept suggesting. Cameron's mention of the homeless had made me worried. I knew quite a few of them—by sight at the very least—and had spent a lot of time with some a few years back when I'd been looking into some deaths in the area. A few of them were criminals, some were injured or addicted, and some were crazy as a quilt full of mice, but most had just been screwed over by circumstances and were doing their best to get out of the situation. I was fond of some of them. Others I'd be happy to leave alone. Pretty much the way anyone would feel about any group of people. These were just more transient and desperate than most. I grabbed a cup of coffee from the bakery and started on the rounds.

The historic district was looking pretty decent these days. A lot of junk, rickety kiosks, and general bad design from the eighties had been cleared off and in spite of the economy the place seemed a little cleaner and more prosperous than it had in a while. There was still plenty that was old and dirty and scary, but the overall demeanor of the area was not as broken down as it had once been. The construction of the new seawall and the tunnel, as well as the phased demolition of the viaduct, was taking a toll, and in spite of the summer boom, it wasn't as crowded as it usually was this time of year. The merchants were doing enough business to keep their doors open, though—for the most part. There were more empty shop fronts than there had been in 2008. Clouds overhead scurried by in a haphazard parade, casting shadows that passed on after a few minutes to let the sun through. It wasn't a bad day to be outdoors, looking for people.

I had some luck pretty quickly, since the bakery has a door onto Occidental Park—a popular place for the homeless with its high tourist flow and its odd nooks in which a smallish person can easily hide from the persistent rain. So long as the homeless are clean and don't cause any fuss, the cops around Pioneer Square mostly leave them alone during the day. The authorities step in if someone complains or if the situation is dangerous, and they make a point of checking on the "regulars," if they can, since it's useful to have the homeless community on your side when you need information about things happening on the street. Things still looked odd to me since my left eye continued to see through the Grey more than the normal, but when the sun cut through the clouds, the effect was much easier to ignore. I found one of my best informants leaning against the wall outside the bakery door: Sergeant Sandy. She's an elderly woman with a small wire shopping cart always in tow who claims to be an undercover police detective, but no one at SPD has ever heard of her. So she's either the deepest-cover agent in the Western Hemisphere or she's just a half bubble off plumb. She would have made a good detective, though: She's observant, patient, and almost unnoticeable. On seeing her, I ducked back inside and bought a cup of tea and a roll stuffed with ham and cheese.

I walked outside and held out the cup of tea to her. "Hello, Sergeant Livengood. How is your duty going today?"

She took the cup with a grateful nod as the sun hid for a moment behind a cloud. "It's a little slow. This unpredictable weather's been keeping the subjects indoors a lot. How are your cases doing?"

"Pretty much the same. I was looking for Twitcher. I'd swear I saw him up at the market a few days ago. Did he move on?" I took the roll out of my pocket and offered it to her.

Sandy sipped her tea and took the roll. "Thank you." She took a discreet nibble and thought while she chewed and swallowed before addressing my question. "Twitcher . . . ?" she confirmed, then shook her head. "Couldn't be. I'm afraid he died a while back."

I had hoped to hear something else, but I hadn't really believed I would. Confirmation of suspicion saddened me. "It must have been someone who looked like him. What did he die of? Was he outside?"

"Oh yes. He went back to Western State for a little while, but they let him go again and he came back, but he seemed to be having some kind of problem with his digestion after that—they may have poisoned him, you know. They don't like admitting how many folks they kick out to fend for themselves."

In my experience, all homeless develop a streak of conspiracy theory if they're on the street long enough, whether they start out a little paranoid and freaked out or not. The hard part is figuring out when they're right and when they're confabulating. It was entirely possible that Twitcher had been poisoned—and equally possible that he hadn't. I'd have to check with other sources to find out.

"Has anyone else moved on or died recently? Like, since December?"

"Oh, there's always a few on the move all the time. As you know. There's been a few deaths, though. Winter was rough and with the economy so down, it's been a little harder to stay fed and dry."

"Who died, aside from Twitcher?"

She kept her eyes moving, watching everyone but me as she answered between sips of tea. "Samuel died a few months back, and Ron—you know, the one with the stick people."

"Any idea how?"

"Not sure about Samuel, but Ron was hit by a truck in the alley behind the Indian place. Not a great loss. Upset the poor trucker something awful, though. Wasn't his fault, of course. Ron was lurking around the trash bins, probably planning to rob the cab when the driver got out to make his deliveries—he'd done that before—and stepped out before the guy'd set his brakes. Got crushed into the wall, the fool."

I made an acknowledging sound. No one had been fond of Ron. He'd been a leering, unpleasant man who made figures out of sticks and scraps and intimidated tourists into buying them so he'd leave them alone. Such a death wasn't pleasant, but it was hard to feel much sadness for the passing of a man who'd stolen from anyone he could take advantage of and had the habit of groping any woman he could reach. He'd been in and out of jails, just skirting a long sentence several times. He was, as Sandy had said, not a great loss. It appeared I'd get no more from her, though; she was focused on other people and giving me only the selvage of her attention.

"Who is your subject today?" I asked as a polite segue to taking my leave.

She tipped her head very slightly toward the corner of the park, where some crafts booths were being set up. "Fella in the jacket. Dark hair, short, Hispanic."

I looked and snorted back a laugh. "That's Rey Solis. You know—Detective Sergeant Solis."

She nodded. "Yup. Been acting odd lately."

I've known Solis for years, but we'd only recently become friends. He was as far from odd as I could imagine—though I could go for "subtly intriguing."

"Odd how?" I asked.

"Just out of character. Gotta keep an eye on that."

I was pretty sure I knew exactly why Solis was acting out of character, but I wasn't going to say so to Sandy. I gave her a sideways look. "Internal Affairs?"

She nodded again and went back to watching Solis and the people at the booths.

"Well," I said, "I need to speak to him myself, so if it won't cause you any trouble, I'll be on my way now."

"No problem. Good luck."

"Thanks. Good luck to you, too."

Armed with names, I walked across the park toward Solis as a sunbeam cut through the cloud for a moment and blazed a trail along the brick plaza, slicing away the glimmer of silvery mist in my left-side vision. The light passed over the booths with their canvas roofs and cast a softened glow on the people working inside, making them strangely radiant in my overlapped vision. I strolled around a display of paintings on pieces of found wood arranged next to jars of arty hand cream and rounded a corner, nearly running into Rey's back.

He turned around sharply. "Oh. Why am I not surprised to see you?" he said.

I shrugged. "Not much surprises you?"

"Not much about you surprises me."

"All right, I'll buy that."

"You have business down here this morning, Blaine? Or do you just enjoy the walk?"

"Business. You?"

He pulled at his jacket as if it didn't fit the way he wanted. "The same."

"Should I go, then?"

"No, no. We're canvassing about some thefts in the area. Seems to be a gang of kids causing a disturbance so their friends can take goods off the counters. You have any ideas about that?"

"I haven't been in the area much the past few days but I'd suggest you hunt down a street rat named Mimms. If he's not in it, he knows about it."

"I have been looking for Mimms. So far, no luck."

"Try the back door at Cowgirls an hour or so before opening. He had something going with one of the waitresses there a while back. If they're still together, he may walk her to work, and if they aren't, he may drop by to flirt with her coworkers just to spite her."

"Ah. That sounds like his way," Solis said.

Mimms was one of those good-looking, fast-talking, low-rent troublemakers girls find charming until they get to know them. I'd dated enough of them in my turn to recognize them at a distance now. Mimms was one of the least offensive variety—more charming than vindictive and smarter than his impulses, but still too brass-balls stupid to ignore them. He might clean up all right if he survived.

"I had not heard about the girlfriend. I'll check on it. Thank you. And you?"

"I heard a couple of homeless from the area died in the past eight months or so. Anything on that?"

He gave a tiny shrug. "A few do in the winter. What aspect of these deaths interests you?"

"I'm just wondering how they died."

"Nothing as spectacularly disturbing as the last time you pursued that question. I would have to look it up, but I believe it was one vehicular accident, one untreated infection of the lungs, and two starvation. Very upsetting that people can starve to death on the streets of a major American city. . . ." He furrowed his brow, but his eyes were more pensive and sad than angry and his aura shifted slightly to a dark blue-green that seemed to run over him like drips of paint. Then it pulled tighter to him, easing back toward its normal yellow color.

I was startled by the list. "One of the latter wouldn't be a guy named Twitcher, would it?"

Solis shook his head. "I'm not sure of the nickname."

I stirred my memory for Twitcher's real name. "Umm . . . Davis Thompson. Had a neurological disorder that caused him to twitch and gesture compulsively. Forties, brown hair, brown eyes, about six feet."

Solis listened to my description and considered it, but shook his head. "I cannot be sure. That sounds correct, but you may have to look into the death records to confirm it."

I didn't really need to; my heart sank with final certainty. "I'll do that," I answered.

Solis peered at my face. "I am sorry. You knew him."

"Yeah, I did. I thought I saw him recently, but apparently not."

"Is this . . . one of your particular cases?" He asked. Solis is well aware of the nature of my "particular" cases, but since he wants to keep his job with the Seattle PD, he's been circumspect about it. Especially since he came along on one of my cases last year. Before that, he was suspicious about the frequency with which I seemed to be in the middle of investigations featuring bizarre and inexplicable circumstances. Not so much anymore.

"Yes," I said. "Quite the woo-woo creep show, complete with mediums, ghosts, and haunted bars."

"Can I expect to see any of this cross my desk?"

"I hope not. So far, the worst things have been some on-the-job accidents. Nothing criminal, no suspicious deaths—at least not modern ones."

"A haunted bar, you said."

"Kells in the market. Lovely place—too bad about the mortuary."

His eyes lit with understanding. "Ahhh . . . I see. I'll look into your homeless reports when I get back to the office. Call me later."

He didn't have to do that—probably shouldn't have offered—but I wasn't one to say no. I smiled and thanked him. "I'll keep an eye out for Mimms."

He nodded, a small smile cracking his face. "Thank you."

I waved and turned away, catching a familiar shape moving at the edge of the crowd. I adjusted my path to keep just behind it and out of sight while I got closer. It was a bit tricky weaving through the vendors and the morning tourists, but while they were an obstacle, they also provided cover. I managed to work my way onto the sidewalk less than half a block behind James Purlis without his seeing me.

FIFTEEN

I'm taller than a lot of people. I'm taller than Quinton and I'm taller than his father, so I could stalk along behind him, able to keep his head in sight at a longer following distance than usual. He must have known I was following him, though I never saw him give any indication. After all, he'd been in the business of following people longer than I had and I would have spotted me by now. Still, he led me up First Street in the thickening crowds of workers and tourists—and then he disappeared.

I was a little startled. He was in front of me and then he just wasn't. I dropped into the Grey, feeling a bit vertiginous as I slammed through the barriers of the ghost world, looking for signs of his unusual aura. I spotted it sinking through what I knew was the street. I flung myself back into the normal, stepping on toes and body-checking a few people as I regained solidity and shoved my way forward to the spot where he must have vanished.

It was an old street-access elevator used by the utilities people to take equipment from the built-up sidewalks down to the original street level, about thirty feet below. Most of the devices weren't in use anymore, closed up permanently as unsafe or impractical, but one or two lingered. The diamond-patterned steel plates over the lift clattered as I stepped onto them, settling back into position after being disturbed just minutes ago. He was fast; I had to give him that. I looked around, marking the area in my mind, and thought this was far too close to Quinton's old bunker under the Seneca Street off-ramp. I had the urge to run and see if Quinton was there, but I wasn't sure that Purlis wasn't watching to see if I would do just that. From this vantage, I could no longer track his energy with any ease and I wasn't sure where he was in the storm of mist and colored light that muddled half my vision while I stood amid the moving crowds on the sidewalk. There were plenty of places where he could have come back up to see what I was going to do. I hoped he hadn't noticed my sudden vanishing act as I'd slipped into the Grey if that was the case.

To chase or not to chase . . . This had to be a feint to draw me into revealing Quinton's lair. Quinton would have twigged to something like this elevator and its tactical value or vulnerability fairly early on since he had lived under the streets here for years and knew the buried sidewalks and passages better than anyone—including me. He wouldn't have let his father get this close without having a way out.

If he'd felt threatened, he would have abandoned the tunnel bunker and—I shook my head at my stupidity—he'd been staying with me since his father had shown up in town. Apparently love *is* blind, because I'd missed the connection until now. While my condo was an obvious place, it was one that was much harder to approach unseen than Quinton's subterranean hideout. I might have been miffed at his not saying anything about it, but since I'd just made an ass of myself on that point, I had no cause for complaint. He liked to keep his problems to himself, which was a familiar mode of operation for me, too.

I made a show of looking around and concluding I was out of luck before I turned back, retraced my steps half a block to the corner, and crossed the street. I worked my way down toward the waterfront, checking for a tail, but finding none this time. I paused long enough to send Quinton—who still carries a pager in preference to a more easily tracked cell phone—a numeric message with the code for "call me" before I started back up toward the various hidden doorways and utility accesses that led to the tunnels connecting with his hideout.

None of the doors or manholes looked recently opened but I couldn't get too close without arousing Purlis's suspicions if he was still watching me covertly. And I supposed he was, since I couldn't imagine any other reason for his luring me up near Quinton's lair. I kept looking for any sign of Quinton but I couldn't find one. While that annoyed and depressed me in some ways, it at least meant that his father hadn't found him, either.

I made one more round of the locations where I would expect to catch some indication that Quinton had been there and checked my phone again, but there was still no message. I'd walked all the way up to the southern entrance to Post Alley without any glimpse of him or the little markers he sometimes left.

My stomach made a gurgling sound and I felt a bit queasy, remembering that I'd had nothing to eat except coffee at the bakery since the soup I'd had last night. No matter how worried and off-stride I felt, I still needed to eat. But maybe not this close to Pike Place Market. I turned back and took myself out for lunch at a Chinese deli on Western. The food was mediocre, but the staff was nice and I could look out the windows at Western Avenue and the traffic working its way around the snarls of construction under the slowly eroding viaduct.

I'm not a total klutz with chopsticks, but I'll certainly never be taken for a native user. Still, I should have had less trouble picking up noodles and conveying them to my mouth. After the fourth missed mouthful, I put the chopsticks aside and sat still for a moment, catching my slightly labored breath and trying to steady the growing quiver in my hands. I felt dizzy and hot and too big for my skin—as if another me were writhing around inside it, pushing and shoving to make it bigger. The vision on my left side blazed up too brightly while my right seemed to fade slowly. My flesh felt as if it had been rubbed with sandpaper and soaked in alcohol while my hands ached and trembled. I sat back in my seat, hoping these sensations would pass quickly and that it wasn't the first wave of another manifestation like last night's two episodes. I couldn't take time to be ill, but I'd have much preferred that this was just a sign that I was coming down with something prosaic—like the flu.

The deli was busy enough that no one was paying me any attention, but not so crowded that anyone was hovering over me, hoping to snag my table the moment I was done. I tried to pick up the chopsticks again, but I fumbled them and one clattered to the floor. As I leaned down to retrieve it, the lights went out and I felt the Formica tabletop press against my cheek just before I lost consciousness.

But I wasn't unconscious, not really. I had been pushed aside, violently, inside my own body and felt cold, weighty things shoving into me. Not like sharp edges or pointy objects tearing the skin, but as if great balloons pressed past my fragile shell without breaking it, pushing in and stuffing me down into a corner I didn't even know I had—a little dark closet of hell I had lived in once upon a time, when I believed the degrading, thoughtless things other people said about me. I couldn't break out, even though I struggled, and I experienced sensation at a distance. I felt my hands close and move, felt words express themselves on my skin as if a drypoint pen was pressing from beneath the surface, scribing looping lines of script that my closed eyes couldn't see. And always the pushing, pressing sensation of weight, moving, squirming inside me.

It felt like I was in this remote, tortured state for hours, unable to cry out, or even to breathe, unable to move or fight back. For a moment I did not fight, but let myself fall away, further into the Grey and the darkness that it had become. Now I saw nothing in my Grey sight but at the deepest level, where the power grid of magic roared in channels of searing, colored light and I could hear the murmur of the Grey talking to itself, of the souls in transition that were neither ghost nor human singing with the music of energy flowing through the world. I tumbled and soared to the grid and looked back, searching for the forms of the presences that had shoved me aside.

Silver and foggy black clouds—the half-life forms of the dispossessed dead—boiled through a wire-frame human form of white light that spun a full spectrum of colored strands in all directions until it looked more like a tiny sun than a woman. A rope of twisted colors shrouded in black tied me to the incandescent shape. I stared at it; I'd never seen my own energetic form before, yet this was clearly it. This was what Grey creatures saw, what drew ghosts and trouble to me like moths because I was, to them, as bright as flame and sun, moon and stars in cloudless skies. I'd been told this, but it's not the same to be told as to see it for yourself.

I wanted it back—wanted my whole self—and I pushed with the only weapon I still controlled. I vaulted back toward the shape of me, thrusting with my mind against temporaclines and shadow shapes of things gone or yet to come, climbing back to it by will to drive the ghost shapes away. I could not grip them, but in this deep plane of the Grey I could exert myself as force, drive them out, thrust against their incorporeal weight with the vigor of being alive. I had so much more to lose than they did and though I was rough with them, I didn't hesitate any longer. I pulled the burning flow of the grid into my mind, feeling it swell and howl through me, and then propelled it out and up to sweep them away on the gust of power. The ghosts scattered like autumn leaves before wind and I rushed back toward the gleaming shape of my self, passing again into darkness as I went.

I sat up with a gasp, dizzy from the transition back to normal. A young Chinese American woman jumped back from me and I thought she must have been bending over me as I'd lain across the tabletop. She was usually behind the cash register and I hadn't seen her come over.

"You OK?" she asked, quivering a little from surprise. "I thought you fainted." She looked frightened.

I shook myself, settling back into the feel of my own body. "I'm fine."

I'm a good liar, but she wasn't convinced. She stared at me with wide eyes and raised one hand to her cheek. "Your face . . ."

I touched my own face and recognized the stinging heat I'd felt the night before at Cameron's house. This time the dermographia had scrolled up my neck and onto the side of my face, just in front of my ear, then vanished again under my hair. I could sense the burning tracery running down my back as well, like a trail of fire ants.

I pawed my brown locks down over my cheek. "Cat scratch," I said, then stopped to stare at the tablecloth, scrawled with a soy-sauce-and-chopstick sketch of the same cliff I'd seen in Julianne Goss's paintings. Beside it were the barely legible words "beach to bluff and back." I dropped the stained chopstick from my left hand as if it were hot.

The young woman's fear wasn't appeased. "Are you sick?"

I forced myself up from the table, containing my rising panic for the moment. "No. No, I'm just very tired. Didn't get any sleep last night. I'm so sorry I disturbed you," I added, digging money out of my pockets and dropping it on the table so I could run away without feeling quite so guilty for disrupting the place.

And run I did. Frightened and adrenaline-fueled, I darted out of the deli as fast as I could without causing any more upset and hurried back toward my office, feeling horribly conspicuous, branded, pursued, and under threat. A cloudburst dampened my escape, rain erupting from the sky just long enough to wet everything and soothe the acid-burned sensation on my flesh. Though I felt oppressed by watching eyes, no one stared at me as I darted along Western toward Pioneer Square; they were all doing the same thing—running for cover.

I bolted into my building and up the stairs to my office, locking the door behind me as I looked around, just in case there were any little friends of Purlis's—or anyone else's—lurking about. All clear.

I'd thrown off the worst of my horror and panic, though I was still breathing too hard and quivering. I forced myself to calm down, breathe in mindful cycles, clear my mind before I did anything else. I knew I was safe enough here and that panic was unhelpful. I wasn't vulnerable and helpless like Goss, Sterling, and Delamar—I knew what was happening and I could do something about it. This time I made myself undress enough to photograph the writing that had appeared on my skin, since there was no one to see but a handful of ghosts too remote from life to stare at me. I almost wished I'd stopped to photograph the drawing on the table, but I didn't think I could have managed it. I could always see it again in Julianne's room.

Standing in my tiny office, shirtless and chilly in spite of the season, I followed Levi Westman's example and took photos of the dermographia with my cell phone's camera. Photographing my back was difficult and I hoped I'd not ended up taking out-of-focus snaps of my butt. I hustled back into my clothes the moment I was done and sat down to examine the photos, hoping to decipher the text that had appeared on my skin. Naturally, some of the images were useless and others out of focus or not very good in other ways, but I could read parts of the text. I'd be able to see more when I looked at them at home, with the more powerful software that Quinton had loaded onto my home computer—I didn't see any point in keeping a high-end machine in my office, since the building was more than a hundred years old and far too easy to break into.

My phone rang as I was trying to decide if I should send the photos to myself or keep them where they were on the off chance that Purlis Senior was monitoring my e-mail. "Harper Blaine," I answered.

"Hey, girl. I got some books for you."

"Hi, Phoebe. Thanks. That was fast."

"I know what I got in stock. I'd have called you sooner, but I got to reading one of them and forgot the time. Anyhow, you going to come up and get these?"

"I am. In fact, right away." I couldn't think of anything less likely to interest Quinton's father than Phoebe and the cat-house-that-books-built.

"Good. I'll make you some coffee."

Phoebe knows all about my coffee addiction. I thanked her and hung up, repacking the phone into my pocket after sending the photos to myself. It was a risk, but I hoped Purlis was too busy to be interested in an e-mail I'd labeled with the name of a well-known auto insurance company and a long case number.

SIXTEEN

Old Possum's seems never to change. Phoebe occasionally rearranges the shelves and reorganizes the stock, but the air of everything having been, forever, as it is right now and always shall be is as permanent as the musical wooden floors and the cat hair on the doormat. The sign over the coatrack still read HE WHO STEALS MY COAT GETS TRASHED, and there were still fake dinosaur skulls on the walls, as there had been since I first arrived. One of Phoebe's employees—eternally referred to as "the minions"—stood behind the cash desk, folding hardcover books into plastic covers, while Beenie, the dumbest of the shop cats, supervised. If Beenie stayed true to form, he would end up half-wrapped in plastic before the books were done and wandering through the shop in a daze, unable to fathom how to get it off. The shop wasn't busy at this early-afternoon hour, so I just waved to the minion as I passed and headed toward the back, drawn by the scent of coffee.

Phoebe was waiting for me in the coffee alcove where I'd first talked to Lily Goss, cups of coffee—hers iced, mine hot—sitting on the painted table between the comfortable chairs. Simba, the giant cat, was curled on top of an ancient unabridged dictionary and overflowing the sides. They both looked up at me as I walked over to the unoccupied chair. Simba stared hard and I wondered if he could smell the ferret's recent presence in my bag.

I fixed the cat's defiant stare with one of my own. "This is not a large snack," I said. "So don't get any ideas, because next time I'll bring Chaos with me and the tube rat will kick your furry butt."

Simba put on a haughty expression and turned his head away as if he couldn't be bothered with peasants or ferrets. Phoebe snorted. I just sat down.

"Hi, Phoebe," I said as I reached for the coffee cup. "Thank you for the coffee. And the books."

"You haven't even seen them yet. How are you so sure you need to thank me for them?"

"You have never given me a useless book. A few weird ones, but never useless."

"What was so weird?"

"That Christopher Priest book was pretty strange."

"Oh, you haven't seen weird if you think Priest is it."

"Please don't attempt to prove that to me. At least not today."

"I just try to broaden your horizons, girl. You always reading those mystery novels. Don't you get tired of that? It's like reading about work."

"No it's not. Real detective work is never that interesting or exciting."

She snorted again. "So you say, Miss I-Talk-to-Ghosts."

I glanced down, a little put off and still a bit worried about her reaction to what I was going to tell her. "Usually I'd say that's not how it works—they come to me—but in this case I *have* been talking to ghosts. A couple of them, at least."

I glanced at Phoebe sideways to see how she was taking it. She was staring at me and nibbling on her lip. "Do you truly?" she whispered. "The things that happened, they seemed like . . . just bad people doing bad things."

"Do you remember when Mark died?"

"I'll never forget that."

"That experiment was all about creating a ghost. Which they did."

"It was a fake ghost."

This had become so ordinary to me over time that explaining it was hard. Getting my understanding of the what and why of the Grey, ghosts, and monsters into the air on a stream of words was like trying to sculpt smoke. "The ghost existed, even if it wasn't the revenant of a human who'd really lived. What we call ghosts aren't always the lingering spirits of people. Some of them are more like a memory that won't fade or a habit that's so much a part of a place that it keeps on repeating even when the people who performed it are gone. And some are things we make out of our own minds."

"You mean they're our imagination."

"Not quite that. More like the animation of things we believe."

"If that's the truth, then why don't we see angels and devils all the time?"

I looked her in the eye. "Do you really believe in imps from hell who cause all our misfortunes, who torment and tease us constantly? Or do you only want to? To have something to blame. Do you believe an angel stands watch over you night and day, to guide you through life, even when things go to hell in a handbasket?"

Phoebe bit her lip again. "I did when I was a child. I believed in all the spirits, devils, and angels Poppy told me about. I told you about the duppy, remember?"

"I do. But now . . . ?"

"I don't."

"Why not?"

"I never saw them. And why didn't I? You say I just need to believe—"

"That's not quite what I said. It's not just the things you accept and it's not just you. And even when the idea has form, it may not be revealed, or it may not come to us in a way we can see or understand. Some things that we believe are, when we face them, too horrible or too awesome or too large to take in. And so we just don't see them. Most of us adults filter them out so we can keep on going ahead with our lives without losing our minds. Can you imagine the impact— the disorienting mental shock—of actually seeing God or an angel in our world full of science and machines and humans who believe bone-deep in self-determination? We may claim something is fate or destiny, but we almost never truly believe it—not Americans. If we did, how could we run around feeling so . . . guilty all the time? If we didn't believe that we caused the worst things that happen to us and our world—that it's all our fault—we couldn't also believe that we could fix it. We're so arrogant, so filled with hubris that if there were any gods still paying any attention to us, they'd have to wipe us out like so many fleas for our presumption. We have to believe that we are ultimately in control of the earth, of our destinies, of our lives, and that makes it very hard for any god to speak to us. It's a little easier for ghosts—we only have to remember them or something of them."

Phoebe sat still, watching me and thinking, the energy around her flaring and shifting. This idea I'd just planted in her mind made her mad and sad and thrilled and it made her curious and frightened all at once, to judge by the colors that burned and sparked around her. I wondered which emotion was going to win.

Simba screeched and whipped himself into a puff-furred arch, batting at something on the floor. Phoebe and I both jerked out of our fugue to stare at him.

One of the other cats was crouched on the carpet in front of the dictionary with a guilty paw in the air. Simba swiped at it, issuing a guttural, gurgling moan. Then he spun around and crouched to leap away, but the attempt was ruined by the sudden pounce of his adversary.

Simba shook the other cat off and turned back around to slap the miscreant on the head. Then he gave a snarky-sounding yawp and bounded away to the top of the fake fireplace, nudging a small gargoyle so it rocked for a moment on its chipped base. The other cat hopped onto the vacated dictionary and huddled into a self-satisfied loaf, with its tail wrapped around its feet and a tiny cat smile on its furry face.

Phoebe sighed. "Troublemaker." Then she looked at me, quirking her head to the side and studying me as if I'd suddenly changed in front of her eyes.

"What's that on your cheek?" she asked.

I was puzzled and frowned over her question. "My cheek . . . ?"

She pointed at the same bit of my face that the woman at the Chinese deli had. "You got a scratch or something. You been in a scrap?"

"No," I said, shoving my hair back. "It's something a ghost wrote on me today. Can you read it? I can't."

She was taken aback and gasped a little before she leaned in and stared at the curling letters on my skin. "It's so fancy. . . . It looks like a tattoo, but I know you better than that."

"You don't think I'd get a tattoo?"

"I know you wouldn't—you don't like to be noticed. Don't get a lot more noticeable than tattoos on the face."

"Oh, I don't know. I could pierce my nose. . . ."

She gave me a mocking slap on the arm. "Oh, girl! You would look like a skinny rhino!"

"Why? My nose isn't big."

"No, but on you a pierced nose would stand out like a big ol' horn. You got that kind of face that says 'You don't really see me' to everyone."

"Bland."

"White. You are *so* white, girl."

I looked down at my hands, the marks of the dermographia fading to pale pink scratches. "White. Like bread. Like a mid-America, middle-class, WASP. Which I am."

"That's not what I meant at all."

"But that's what *I* mean. That's what I want people to see. Most of the time. Someone nearly invisible—someone unremarkable."

"Then it's a good thing most of them never get to know you, because you are remarkable. I remark on you all the time!"

I tried on my Phoebe imitation—which is to say a terrible phony Jamaican accent. "Dat Harper, she nothing but trouble, dat girl!"

I got another smack on the arm for it, which I deserved, but it came with a smile and a laugh. "Stop that! We all be trouble—ain't nobody in my family boring."

There was that word again: "family." It seemed like I couldn't move without running into the idea or some member of someone's family. At least I liked Phoebe's—couldn't say as much for my own or Quinton's, though I'd met only one member of his. I wished I could see the web Carlos had shown me last night, but even without the visual, I was reasonably certain that a line of affection bound me to Phoebe and her clan of laughing, loving lunatics.

I felt the warmth of a blush on my cheeks. "It's a very nice family to be allowed into."

"Oh, girl, you don't get permission to be family; you just are. Oh! That reminds me," she said, bending down to pick up a pile of books from the floor beside her chair. "Talking of family, I found this book with a photo of Princess Angeline—Chief Sealth's daughter." This time, I noticed, she used his tribal name, not the Americanized version.

Phoebe settled the pile of books on her lap and sorted through it until she found a slim brown paperback. She opened it with care, not bending it at the spine or the covers, and held it out to me. "There she is! Some local photographer—Edward Curtis—paid her a dollar to let him take that picture and he wrote a book about the Indians and got rich selling the photo to newspapers and magazines. She was an old lady then."

I took the book and studied the photo of a very old native woman that was dated 1907. Her strong, square face was folded and creased with wrinkles and had sagged at the brow and jaw, pulling the corners of her wide mouth down and nearly closing her dark eyes. She seemed to be dreaming something sad. Tired, but undaunted, she had sat erect and still while the photographer had done his slow work. Thick gray hair peeped from beneath the bandanna she'd tied over it and the arched top of a well-worn cane pressed to her chest just above the bottom of the picture. "Kikisebloo" was the name the caption gave her.

"I haven't seen her," I said and wished I had. I wondered what she would have said about Seattle now.

"She used to live by where the market Hill Climb is now," Phoebe said. She turned aside to dig out another book and I flipped idly through the one in my hand until a face seemed to jump off the page to glare at me. A handsome, if hard, face with a crown of dark hair and a slightly hooked nose. It was the woman I'd seen in the market office and again in Kells, where her face had melted away to show a skull that wasn't hers. I bent the book open to get a better look at the photo and try to read the caption.

"Hey, be kind to the books!" Phoebe said, stopping in midsearch.

"This woman . . . I saw her ghost at Pike Place Market. She seems . . . very unpleasant."

Phoebe raised her eyebrows at me and blinked. "Not surprising. That's Linda Hazzard. That doctor that I told you starved all those people to death. See, it says there she had an office in the hotel at the market." She pointed to a bit of text on the page. "Says back then it was called the Overlook. Now it's the LaSalle, right in the main arcade corner. It's all low-income housing these days and offices for the Market Foundation and that."

"Yes," I said, nodding absently and trying to fit the terrifying spirit of Linda Burfield Hazzard into the puzzle of this case. She'd starved people—calling it therapeutic fasting, but the difference was semantic. How many people? The book said it was unknown, but guessed at forty or more. But I'd seen more than forty ghosts, hadn't I . . . ?

Phoebe interrupted my thoughts, holding up the book she'd been looking for. It was a large-format hardcover full of photos and she flipped it to a particular page and pushed it toward me. "See, this was Princess Angeline's shack."

Reluctantly, I closed the first book and put it on the coffee table, smoothing it down to undo any damage I might have caused. I accepted the new book and looked dutifully at the photo. I felt electrified and I sat up very straight.

Phoebe gave me a curious stare. "What?"

"I've seen this before."

"The photo? A lot of people use it in books about Pike Place Market and old Seattle."

"No. The place." The picture showed a small white shack near the bottom of a long bluff covered in pines. A steep slope of trees ran from the stony beach below toward another rickety-looking building that sprawled along the top of the bluff. "I drew this place this afternoon—not the buildings, just the area." It was the same scene my hand had sketched on the tablecloth. It was also the same place I'd seen in so many of Julianne Goss's paintings. The long bluff of mist-shrouded fir and cedar over the curving, stone-strewn shore.

Phoebe frowned. "Why would you be drawing that if you didn't know what it was?"

"It's a strange, disturbing little story."

"Then you'd better tell me."

I told her a little bit about the case and the patients I'd seen. Then I told her about the incident in the Chinese deli, about my fainting but not being quite unaware, about the drawing and the dermographia. I didn't talk about the sense of being displaced from my own body—that was a little too much for me at the moment and I suspected too much for her as well. She stared at me in silence and I thought maybe this was the limit at last. That this time I would not be believed, forgiven, or invited back to dinner.

Finally she asked, "You got that writing all over you?"

"Not *all* over . . ."

"Well, then, where?" She tugged on my shirtsleeve. "Show me."

I found myself squirming and feeling uncomfortable, batting at her hands rather than just pushing her away. "I'm not taking off my shirt in your shop. Stop it. I have pictures."

Phoebe sat back and goggled at me. "You got what?"

"I took photos with my phone. They aren't very good shots, but the marks are fading quickly this time, so it's a good thing I took the pictures when I did."

"What do you mean, they're fading quickly *this* time?"

"It happened before but it was just a short message—on my arms. This time it's all over my upper body and I can't read it—it's on my back, too." I pulled the phone out of my bag and poked around until I got to the photo gallery. I handed it to her. "There. Take a look and if you can tell me anything it says, I'll be thrilled. I can't make much out of it."

I'm not the most modest person in the world—after years spent in dance troupes, backstage in cramped conditions with dozens of other dancers, I'd shed any shyness about people seeing my naked body—but handing over those pictures to Phoebe felt strangely intimate and I found myself holding my breath, waiting for what she would say. She flicked through them, going back and forth, enlarging some, skipping past others with a snort of dismissal. . . .

She looked up and said, "You are a terrible photographer."

I laughed in relief. "You try and take a decent picture of your own back."

"I can't hardly read any of this. And what's this . . . like a picture here?" she said, pointing at a photo that showed part of my back below my left shoulder blade. The looping text had run up into an arc, like part of a large circle that had been cut off by the angle and the curve of my body under my arm. The circle appeared to be segmented like a pie by more lines of text.

I took the phone and enlarged the section of the photo to peer at the words. " ' . . . Great Wheel where tribute comes to make a meal for . . .' I can't make out the rest. Then the lines say 'Limos comes within . . . the mistress of death . . . hunger calls to hunger.' Terrible grammar, but I can't say it makes much sense. . . ."

"It does look a little like the Great Wheel, though," Phoebe said.

"What does?"

She put out a finger and traced the shape the trail of words had taken. "This. It's a Ferris wheel, with the spokes here, and the loops in the words make the—what do you call 'ems—the gondolas for people to ride in here."

As she touched the image, I could almost imagine her touch on my skin and I shuddered. I put the phone down on the table between us.

"Harper? You all right? You look like a goose walked on your grave."

"No, but . . . I'm starting to get a picture in my mind of this whole case and I don't like it at all. I see these ghosts . . . and among them is Linda Hazzard, but she's not quite like the rest—there's something more going on with her and she seems to be more autonomous than the others. This writing talks about hunger calling to hunger. It says something about the Great Wheel and even makes the shape of it on my skin. . . . It's all of a piece, but . . . too much of it's still missing. Mistress of death . . . that's got to be Hazzard, right?"

"I suppose. . . ."

I was thinking out loud, my brain just too frantic to contain my thoughts in silence. "How does all of this connect to the patients? They all have a connection to the tunnel project, to accidents associated with construction. . . . Wait," I said, snatching my cell phone from the table.

Phoebe glared at me—she disapproves of cell phone use in her store—but she humored me as I called Lily Goss.

When my client answered I identified myself and asked, "Did Julianne's job put her in contact with dirt from the tunnel project?"

"What? Dirt from the tunnel . . . ? I think so. The firm was designing a hotel that's planned for one of the reopened lots under the current viaduct. She was on the team and they went down to the site to do some planning work. Julie went to photograph the area as a reference for the models. That was earlier on the day she was bitten by the mosquito—or maybe she was actually bitten then. . . . The site is down near the water and the tunnel site, so I guess it could have happened that way. Why?"

"I just had a feeling there was a stronger connection to the other patients. They all had contact with dirt from the tunnel project."

"Is it a pathogen, then? Some disease . . . ?" Goss asked, excited for a possible solution that was so very ordinary.

"I don't think so—the doctors would have found a virus or something like that. But this gives me more information to attack the problem with. How is Julianne doing?"

"Badly. She doesn't seem to rest at all. If she's not painting the same things over and over, she's shouting or crying. It's so awful.

I—I had to get out of the house for a while. I'm just on my way back from church. I had to pray for her and I talked to Father Nybeck, but . . . he still can't offer any more help. She just doesn't get better and I'm . . . losing hope. When is this going to end? Can you send these horrible spirits away from her? Have you figured out how?"

"Not yet, but I think I'm close." I hoped I was, though I really didn't know what the animus of the possessions was. I felt like the answer wasn't far away, but it was still only a dim and shapeless idea. I had to put the pieces together soon or Julianne and the others might never wake up, their living souls fading away while they were pushed aside. "I will have it very soon, though."

I could hear her breathing raggedly, as if she were close to tears. Finally she managed to speak again. "I'll be waiting to hear from you." She disconnected abruptly and I was sure she'd lost her battle not to cry. I felt terrible for lying, but I couldn't let her give up—I would find the solution in time because I simply had no choice.

Phoebe reached for the phone as I finished, and I handed it over, feeling grim, but at least I now knew the link. I just had to connect it to a driving force. I scowled a moment in thought.

Phoebe poked the phone until she found the photos and frowned expectantly at me when I looked up again.

I tried to explain as my mind tumbled it around. "All three had accidents, all three came into physical contact with dirt from the tunnel on the day they were injured and went into a coma. They're all haunted by these ghosts . . . these strangely obsessive ghosts who try to say something we don't seem to be getting. The patients—or rather, the ghosts speaking through the patients—write strange things about tribute and hunger and food. . . . Everyone connected to the patients and the ghosts is thin, too thin, and too hungry—

even me. The ghosts come from the market and they are connected to Hazzard, who believed in extreme fasting. They keep showing me the market like it used to be—before the city grew up all around it—when the shore was right below the hills and bluffs, not buried under the seawall and waterfront. . . . I keep finding the phrase 'beach to bluffs and back.' That's the tunnel route—from the edge of the original strand in the south end of downtown up into the bluff where the market is. And something about the Wheel . . . but there wasn't any Ferris wheel when Hazzard was around. And I don't see what the Great Wheel can have to do with three bedridden patients who can't even wake up. Cannie Trimble said something about a wheel—she must have meant the Great Wheel—and I didn't get it. I still don't. I just don't understand how the Wheel is connected to the ghosts! And now to Hazzard . . ." I slapped my palm against my head as if I could jar the puzzle pieces together and make out the whole picture, but it wasn't coming.

Phoebe put the phone down and grabbed my wrist on the fourth smack, arresting my hand. "Stop that! It's not going to solve the problem for you. You got to think, not beat yourself up. You take these books and you go home to that man of yours and you think it out with him. He's a smart one. He'll help you figure it."

I met her earnest gaze, biting my lip. "Phoebe, you believe me, don't you?"

She scoffed. "Girl, what kind of lackwit you think I am? Of course I believe you. I can see it right here," she added, tapping my phone as it lay on the table. "I could think you were crazy, but I know whatever crazy you are, it's the good kind, not the psycho, lying kind. Now you go home before you knock your brains loose beating on your head like that."

"I—" I started, but she cut me off, rising to her feet with the books bundled in her arms.

"No. No excuses, no thank-yous, no rattling on. You got work to do and you are going to go do it. Now," she added, nudging my nearest foot with her own, "go on. What've I got to do, throw you out? Go on. You're going to do it anyhow, might as well get on with it." She prodded me to the door like a mother hen and loaded the books into a bag, which she shoved into my arms. "Now, out you go, Harper. And you come back for dinner next month. Poppy's got to fatten you up for that man of yours."

She winked at me and nearly pushed me out the door.

SEVENTEEN

It wasn't raining, but it was thinking about it again. I hurried to the Land Rover with my bag full of books, not wanting them to get wet before I could look them over. Not to mention that Phoebe would skin me if they were damaged. I was troubled by the image of the Great Wheel, too. What we'd deciphered indicated some connection between it and the ghosts and the phenomena that the patients were experiencing, but it didn't lie on the tunnel route per se, and damned if I could understand what the link was. It was on the waterfront and the accidents were all associated with the tunnel. The waterfront would be deeply affected by the construction and the tunnel, but . . . so what? How did that concern ghosts? What was Linda Hazzard doing in the mix—something about hunger, but what? Purlis was probably linked to all this, too, but that was another connection I hadn't been able to discover yet. I just wasn't seeing something and in the meantime I was chasing my thoughts in frustrating circles.

It was still early enough to ask a few more questions and going home would only remind me of Quinton's absence. I headed back to the market to take another look at the bluff I'd drawn, above where Princess Angeline had lived and near where Linda Hazzard had killed her patients and had their bodies cremated without ceremony or tears.

It was sufficiently close to dinnertime that the streets were busy, but the parking lots were in flux, with the morning shoppers leaving and the evening revelers not yet arriving. I managed to find a parking place for the truck on one of the steep streets next to the market. The back-in angle parking was tricky and I almost thought the Land Rover would tip onto its side and roll down the hill to fall off the edge and onto the waterfront below, but it didn't. I hurried down the sidewalk toward Steinbrueck Park.

I crossed the road to the park and sat down near the homeless memorial, imagining that this must have been almost directly above Angeline's shack. I wondered what it was like to live at the edge of the city then, when ships lay at anchor to be unloaded by smaller boats and the goods hauled up the steep hills in carts.

"Bad clams," said a voice beside me.

I turned my head sharply. "What?" The woman next to me wore a white garment that wrapped her in light. She wasn't so much a ghost as a presence with a vague shape and a face hard to see in the luminance that shone from her.

"The city made the water dirty. Bad water made the clams bad. Not all the time, but enough."

"Are you . . . Kikisebloo?" I asked.

She nodded. "You shouldn't be here. The land is riddled like the timbers of old ships and the vileness comes with strangers. It rises, a tide to sweep away the new and the old. It will sweep you with it, if you cannot manage the ones you cannot love."

"I don't understand. Do you know how this all goes together? The ghosts and the patients and the tunnel and the Wheel? And my not-quite-father-in-law?"

She gazed at me as if looking inside my soul. "What stands may fall like the great forests fell before the ax. Look to your own. The answers you truly want are there. This moment passes. The Wheel may turn or it may fall into the sea. Who knows?"

"I think someone must know. What's the connection between the Wheel and the ghosts who are haunting the sick people?" I demanded.

"I cannot say. There was a way here, long ago. Up through the pines from stony shore and mucky strand. Up from the boats, up from the hoardings of men who are blind to what they do."

She began to dim and age before my eyes, becoming the old woman in the photo taken in 1907. "I do not like the future that I see. The worms have eaten till the wood is rotten with them. It is like my old shack and cannot stand much longer if they remain. I miss my father and mothers. I miss my brothers and sisters and my little daughters, my Mary and Enie. You should not miss them. But you must look in the graveyard. Look to the graves. Look to your own, to your husband, for answers. It is a dark thing to be alone and hungry."

She shimmered away and left me on the bench, looking back toward the market. I wasn't sure I had anything more than I'd started with, except she seemed worried and she wanted me to ask Quinton something—something about his father, I imagined.

I muttered under my breath, annoyed with the obtuse conversation of spirits. Graves . . . There were graves—or at least a cemetery of sorts—in the market. What if Angeline had meant the secret cemetery in the Soames-Dunn courtyard where Lois "Mae West" Brown was buried—among others?

It took me a little while to figure out which building I wanted—the names on old historic buildings are sometimes obscured by newer signs and additions, like awnings. But I found it nearby and went through the arcade, lured by the watery sunlight visible at the end of the hall. I stepped out into a deep courtyard, a high wall in front of me scaled by a staircase that led to Post Alley. I could barely see the sign for Kells hanging in the alley above. Those iron balusters were the rails that Carlos's assistant, Inman, had pushed me against and nearly tipped me over. I stared at the distance from the rails to where I stood and shivered at the idea of falling from there to this flagstone courtyard, already stained with fist-sized blotches like the remains of small homicides. I doubted I could have survived that fall headfirst, Greywalker or not.

The stairs were partially wrapped around a large sort of planter with a low, rambling plum tree growing from it up against the wall. I laughed, suddenly understanding Lois Brown's joke—she'd said she was "plumb" sure she was dead—dead and buried under a plum tree. This was the secret cemetery—this quiet little courtyard with its tiny tree. I started up the steps to where I could swing over the rail and get onto the earth beneath the tree.

That was when the rain came. I could hear people dashing along the alley overhead and a few shouts and squeals of dismay as shoppers and tourists scurried to get under cover. I thought of backtracking into the building behind me—better that than the haunted bar up the stairs—but I was already getting wet, so I just zipped up my jacket and tucked my hair under the hood and down the collar to keep it from falling into my eyes.

I climbed the rest of the steps and over the rails to crouch on the soft ground beneath the tree. A few other plants had started up on a bit of grass, but for the most part it was barren except for an array of small objects strewn randomly across the ground. I crept around, looking at the objects. Some had plainly been put there by other people—the remains of a bunch of flowers, a cheap plastic ring with a note tied to it that read "Forever," a handful of coins—but others seemed to have dug themselves from the dirt and wisps of ghost-stuff clung to them.

I carefully collected the Grey-touched things. I found another key much like the one that had fallen from the ceiling in Kells, two more buttons, a bit of old jewelry chain, and a funny little tool with a dull point at one end and the other end flattened into a disk a little larger than the end of my thumb.

There was also an old "flair" button with a rather naughty suggestion on it. I picked it up and rubbed some of the dirt off it. "One of yours, Mae?" I asked, looking it over. She didn't respond, but I wouldn't have been surprised if she had.

The ground under me shifted and I scrambled a little to stay on my feet, lurching closer to the railings and clutching them to keep from falling off the planter. For a moment, my Grey-sighted left eye showed a flicker of ghostly hands reaching from the soil, but they faded as I moved away.

A man stepped out into the courtyard, shielding his face from the rain with one hand. "Hey," he called, "get out of that! It's not safe up there—the planter almost collapsed a few months ago!"

I put my collection of odd treasures into my pockets and scrambled back over the rails and down the stairs.

The man scowled at me and shooed me inside, saying, "What the hell were you doing up there?"

"I dropped my key," I said. "I didn't know there'd been any problems with the planter."

"It was months ago, but they had to shore up the wall afterward and I'm not sure it's going to hold if the tunnel people keep on poking around. They buried some kind of sensor to monitor the tunnel there. Just making more messes than fixing them so far," he muttered.

"It's quite a project, isn't it?"

"It's a pain in the butt. Kind of like you."

"Me?" I objected.

"I need to run my shop, not go climbing around saving tourists from being foolish."

"I'm not a tourist."

He gave me a cool look. "Then you should know better than to go climbing over rails around here. Now, go on. You're dropping dirt on my floor."

He turned his back to me, but I noticed he kept an eye on me in a mirror mounted by the cash desk until I left. The market's tiny, cluttered shops must have been prime targets for thieves and pickpockets. I hoisted what little dignity I had left and took off through the back, defiantly, to trot up the stairs to Post Alley.

Taking a deep breath at the top, I braced myself for trouble and entered Kells. This time no horrifying vision of women with melting faces assaulted me. The worst scare I got was the ghost of a small girl who ran through me and then turned back to stare, saying, "Dance with me! No one at this party will dance with me."

I put out one hand and she put a thin wisp of cold into it. It didn't feel like a hand, but I closed my own over it anyhow and walked her into the hallway between the two rooms, making a slow circle as if I were just looking around. In the unobserved corridor between the larger rooms, I executed a couple of pivot turns and a swing out that let the little girl spin into the larger room that had once been the crematory. She swirled away in a spiral of smoke and glitter, giggling as she vanished. I walked through to the bar and caught the bartender's attention, though he was already giving me an odd look.

"Hi," I said. "I seem to have lost some things out of my pocket the other night. I was hoping they'd been picked up."

"What sort of things?"

"Oh, an old button, a key, a pencil stub . . ."

His brows drew down. "Funny bunch of things to come back for."

"Part of a scavenger hunt," I said.

He shrugged and ducked his head a bit to look under the counter. "Huh." He pulled out a cardboard box and set it on the bar. "Let's see . . ."

The box had a ragtag collection of small objects that included quite a few car and house keys, car alarm fobs, some safety pins, a length of broken chain, one dirty pearl bead, buttons, a pocket-knife, a brooch shaped like a dolphin, two wedding rings, a thimble, a button hook, six or seven pens of varying quality, a large metal grommet, and several lighters. There was one pencil stub and I picked it up, feeling a cold burn on my fingertips as I did. This was the right one.

"Anything else look familiar?" the bartender asked.

I picked through the trove, closing my right eye and looking only with my left for the black gleam of the ghostly artifacts. There were several more than I'd originally seen, and I picked them all up. The bartender squinted suspiciously at me, but didn't object when I took the brooch and the grommet as well as several buttons and the old-fashioned house key. Neither of the wedding rings had any ghostly haze to it, for which I was grateful—I doubted I could explain taking one of those when I hadn't mentioned it to begin with. I did wonder where the thimble had come from, though. Who carries a thimble into a bar? The button hook was intriguing because although it was an old object, it had no Grey gleam at all. I supposed it was something bought in the market and dropped by accident. Maybe it went with the thimble. . . .

"That it?" the bartender asked, looking at the small pile I'd made on the bar.

I glanced up at him, opening both eyes. "Yeah. That's it."

"Weird. OK, they're all yours."

I shoved the objects into my pockets with the ones I'd found outside and thanked the man as I left. I didn't see any further sign of the little girl ghost or Linda Hazzard and I was grateful. But I did feel a renewed tingling and burning where my skin had been scribed with phantom words. Being near the market was becoming a liability for me. I needed to solve the puzzle and get away from this as quickly as possible. I didn't have all the pieces I needed, but Carlos might be able to help on that score and at the moment he owed me, though I wasn't excited about collecting.

I also needed to find Quinton, which meant finding his father. Quinton had mentioned Northlake when I'd seen him last and it was in that general direction that the convoluted and knotted line between us had stretched when Carlos showed it to me. I already knew Quinton wasn't downtown, and his father obviously wasn't operating out of that area himself—much too easily observed by his government colleagues and others. I might also find Inman in the area, since a demi-vampire doesn't wander far without orders from whoever is holding his leash. Carlos would be more inclined to do what I wanted if I had a lead on his missing dhampir.

I had to admit, I was curious as to how Papa Purlis had subverted the dhampir—the ties of blood and magic between creator and "child" vampires are strong and usually broken only by destruction of one or both vampires, though dhampirs are rather unusual cases. Purlis had discovered something very dangerous and I wondered if he recognized it or even knew what he'd done. Sending Inman after me had been risky and foolish. It made me think he wasn't aware of the importance of what he'd accomplished. But since I hadn't seen any sign of Inman today, it was possible he'd figured it out. His Ghost Division needed to be discredited and burned to the ground before he had any more breakthroughs. Not to mention I was running out of patience with Quinton's obsessive absences. I was the unreasonable, obsessive member of this little party and I didn't want to share the distinction.

I trudged back to the Land Rover and drove through the thinning traffic to the north end of Lake Union, thinking about where I might find Quinton or his father.

Northlake is a light industrial area, bounded by famous neighborhoods: Fremont on the west, Wedgwood to the north, and the University District on the east. It's an area full of boatyards, marinas, workingmen's cafes, and incongruous condos. My very first Grey case had started at an old naval architecture warehouse in the area—and now I was back. The area had changed a bit more in particulars than in general. The Lake Union Kite Shop had gone out of business.

The moldering Kalakala Ferry had been moved to Tacoma, where its Art Deco superstructure could decline in silence, but the Skansonia remained, still hosting parties but never leaving the dock. Ivar's Salmon House still squatted on the edge of the U-District, putting the scent of salmon and woodsmoke into the air. The remains of the old gasworks still stuck its rusted metal fingers into the air at Browns Point, surrounded by parkland and the kite-flying hill that hid the wreck of its old buildings, now buried in sod and environmental plastic to keep the seeping chemicals of sixty years of coal gas production under wraps.

If you want to hide something like a secret lair or a questionable government project, it's better not to put it in the middle of nowhere. People will notice something new where once there was nothing and they'll notice you coming and going, too. It's far better to put your "secret" where people won't question it. Spies work fairly well with industrial neighborhoods. No one thinks it's strange if they soundproof a building, or have guards with guns around, or come and go at odd hours. No one pays attention to trucks bearing crates or large pieces of equipment, or to cars with blacked-out windows, and absolutely no one finds subterranean garages with security doors odd. Most won't pay any attention to odd sounds, either—even sounds that mask screams—since there are plenty of other noises in the area.

Northlake is not heavily industrial, but it's on the lake, next to the canal mouth, so there's plenty of coming and going, plenty of din, plenty of distractions, and a fair number of buildings that aren't fully leased. I figured I'd start at the park and work outward, since the most likely places were on the water. I left the Land Rover in the parking lot between the Adobe building and the rowing club and started walking, paying more attention to my Grey vision than to the normal—figuring I'd be more likely to spot an illicit bit of magic or a lurking monster that way. At first I ran into a tree along the Burke-Gilman Trail, but I got the hang of it after that.

The area around the park turned out to be the most active in the Grey—not that that should have surprised me. I drifted that way, trying to get a better idea of what was going on. Old factories are often scattered with ghosts, loops of history, and shredded tempora-clines, and the coal-gas-cracking towers of the gasworks hung with mist that had nothing to do with the unseasonable clouds. I concentrated my search along the bike trail, looking for a likely building or entry to something Purlis might be using as a base of operation.

I walked past the loading docks for Fisheries Supply and noticed a sign at the edge of the park's driveway. I strolled across to it, not bothering to hide, since there really wasn't anyplace to go. It appeared to be an old notice that no one had removed claiming that the state Department of Ecology would be doing maintenance and upgrades to the ecological barriers in the northeast corner of the park, followed by regrading and restoring the area. The project was supposed to have been finished in the spring of 2013 once the grass was established. I didn't see any signs of ongoing work, but the sign and a bit of temporary fencing remained. I assumed it was just an oversight that no one had bothered to fix, but as I strolled on, it struck me very much like the misdirection Quinton had used to create his secret bunker under the streets of Seattle, using the excuse of a construction project to carve a bit of space out of the underground and then keep people from investigating it by creating signs that didn't say what it was but gave the impression it wasn't safe.

Quinton was a clever guy, but he must have picked up a few things from his coworkers and mentors in Intelligence—maybe even from his dad. I walked up the hill beside Fisheries and then down another street, looking for a good place from which to observe the area. It didn't look like much of an access, but there was a slope and a bit of old building within the fencing that could easily conceal a way deeper into the gasworks. And who would even think twice about odd sounds at an abandoned gasworks? The wind that made kite flying off the hill so attractive also made a whistling and howling sound as it passed through the many ladders, walkways, trusses, and towers of the old industrial site. I spotted a good vantage point where the corner of a condo building met the sidewalk and the builders had poured a small slab to make a level platform for the trash and recycling bins on the edge of the steep street. The fencing around the bins was woven with strips of bamboo to mask the unattractive little corner, but it didn't obscure the view completely. I moved to the farthest part of the fence, where I couldn't be seen from the park, and climbed over it.

Seattleites can be a little obsessive about garbage, so the area wasn't too rotten, but it did have a bit of a smell to it. I was thinking I might have to give up the surveillance as a bad job when someone spoke nearby.

"Hey there, beautiful."

I turned toward Quinton's voice, but could see only a shadow behind the fencing. "Hey. How'd you find me?"

"You and I have the same taste in observation posts."

"Ah," I said. "How come you're not replying to pages?"

"Kind of busy lately. I'm sorry."

"I need to talk to you. Your dad seems to have snatched a demi-vampire from Carlos and Cameron. They aren't happy about that. And I've got the impression that you or your father knows something connected to my own case. What's going on here?"

"Details are still pretty sketchy. I knew he'd grabbed a few paranormals, but at first I didn't know he'd gotten a vampire. I don't know how he managed that. At least not yet."

"What other paranormals has he got?"

"I'm not sure. There was something . . . I called it Pandora's Box, since it seemed to have something in it, but now it doesn't. Not big enough for something living unless it was insect-sized. Kind of like a . . . folding shrine. I didn't get to examine it or get a good close look, so I don't have much information except that it had been stored in dirt for a while. I got a sample of the dirt and I asked Fishkiller to look it over." Ruben Fishkiller was a forensic pathology technician who'd exchanged a few favors with me over the years. Quinton went on. "But he says it's local, which kind of surprised me, since I know the thing came from Europe. Whatever was in the box or attached to it is gone, but it looks like Dad put the container in the tunnel dig for a while—that's where the dirt came from, according to Fish— and I'd guess that Dad set the thing from the box loose there, or it escaped. He doesn't seem very worried about it, so I imagine he let it go himself. Anything new running around town aside from your pushy ghosts?"

"There is definitely some strange stuff going on, but neither I nor the vampires have spotted any new paranormal players in the area. Doesn't mean there isn't something, though, and that might be the connection between your dad's project and my case. . . . Quinton, please be careful. You're focusing on your father, but there are a lot of other interests watching this."

"You mean Carlos and Cameron."

"Not just them. And not just the paranormal end of the spectrum. What your father is doing is only barely on the reservation, so when it goes wrong—as you are bent on making sure it does—there's going to be a lot of fallout. I don't want you to be in the blast."

"I'll be all right."

I wanted to argue with him, but it wasn't going to do any good and I'd only be doing exactly what I didn't like done to me. I settled on "Be careful."

"I will. And I'll try to stay on top of the messages."

I made a face. " 'There is no *try*,' " I quoted.

He laughed. "I'll bear that in mind, Master Yoda." Then he slunk off and left me to extricate myself from the trash bins.

I wished I had Quinton's skill with electronics—not to mention his ever-ready stash of parts—and could leave some kind of monitor behind, but I would just have to make an opportunity to come back later. At least I knew I'd found the secret lair. Now I just had to find out what Purlis had let loose on my city and what the hell it was doing to so terrifyingly empower the ghosts in the market. Mentally cursing, I crawled back over the fence and took myself home for cleaner clothes.

EIGHTEEN

With no other leads to chase, I felt there was no option left but to contact Carlos and ask him to "read" the objects I'd collected from the secret cemetery and Kells. I hoped that if I knew who the ghosts were I might be able to contact them and make the connection to Purlis and whatever was happening between them and the PVS patients. By the time I got back to my place, dusk was falling and I was pretty sure I could reach Carlos at one of the phone numbers Cameron had provided, if not his own.

Chaos wasn't pleased with me for leaving her alone all day, but ferrets have the memory of clams and she forgot to be angry as soon as she was on the living room floor with her favorite toy, a squeaky anthropomorphized eggplant with massive feet and a nose that resembled a ski jump. Quinton had christened it "Nixon."

While Chaos bit and wrestled Nixon, I took a shower and heated soup for my dinner. Then I put in a call to Carlos's voice mail. I always find the idea of vampires with voice mail odd, though I can't really say why; maybe it's that the idea of something as far removed from the technological world as a vampire just runs counter to the concept. I was barely seated to slurp down my dinner when he called back.

Even over the phone his voice sent an unpleasant crawling sensation up my spine. "Blaine," he said.

"I have some objects that I believe are connected to the ghosts in this case of mine. And I think I have a line on where your missing assistant is. Can you take a look at these things and tell me about them?" I wasn't telling him the whole story just yet, but I'd get to it once I had his agreement.

"If you will tell me where Inman is."

"Afterward."

He was silent for a moment, thinking about it, I assumed. It was possible for him to get around me—by some magical trick, by force, or by setting another of the vampire community's helpers on my tail until I showed them the way. But all of those strategies were wasteful and Carlos didn't approve of waste—necromancy is the ultimate expression of the phrase "Reduce, reuse, recycle."

"Very well. Where?"

This was a problem. I didn't want him in my place and I had no desire ever to return to his. "Where are you?" I asked, thinking I could find a location conveniently between.

He was silent. Vampires don't breathe and Carlos had the trick of being utterly still, so the only sound that came through the phone was a very distant whispering that might have been the voice of the grid or just people in some other room. It was unnerving.

"Ten Mercer. Upstairs."

"Thirty minutes," I said.

He chuckled and hung up. I frequently have the impression that he's humoring me—and considering how easily he could wipe me off the face of the planet, he probably is.

I finished up my soup as quickly as I could without wearing it. Then I rounded up the ferret, put her back in her cage—much to her consternation—and headed out again.

Ten Mercer is one of those places that a lot of people thought would die with the market crash—and yet it is still hanging on, a couple of blocks from the Opera House and Intiman Theatre, on the north end of the Seattle Center complex. One of those undecorated New American cuisine places that manages to seem sparsely elegant rather than empty and barnlike. The upper floor is the dining room, while the larger lower floor is the lounge. Floor-to-ceiling windows on both floors between the exposed red brick of its building front allow the world to see others drinking and yet no one looks, except in a general way. The lowered lights hint that you, too, might be able to come inside, but it would just be uncouth to stand outside and stare. Ironically, there's a bus stop right in front of it. No one stares in. No one stares out. And it's rarely busy before ten p.m., when the theaters let out.

When I arrived and told the hostess I was meeting someone for dinner, she gave me a thoughtful little frown and asked whom I was meeting. I gave Carlos's name and she wordlessly led me up the stairs to the empty dining room. She tucked me into one of the few booths, far from the windows and isolated from the room full of tables by a low, curving wall of slatted wood. The table could have seated six with room for their winter coats. I would have felt conspicuous but for the half wall.

Since I'd had dinner and didn't really want to linger with Carlos, I didn't order anything more than sparkling water with lime. It's never safe to drink alcohol with vampires—even the ones you think you know. Carlos kept me waiting for another fifteen minutes and came up the stairs alone. The hostess didn't return and Carlos sat down across from me, bringing his cloud of darkness and death. He didn't speak; he just sat and studied me for a while.

A waiter passed, as if casually on his way elsewhere, but he slid an appetizer plate of smoked sturgeon onto the table before he walked on. I peered sideways, looking for signs that the staff was bespelled in some way, but aside from being preternaturally good-looking, they seemed normal.

Carlos unrolled his silverware and spread the cloth napkin out between us. "What did you bring me?" he asked.

I dug the objects out of my pockets and put them on the napkin, each separate from the next rather than in a pile. They nearly covered the thick cloth square. Carlos made a thoughtful growl in his throat and leaned forward to look at them. He pushed the plate of food in my direction. "Make this look eaten."

"Why?" I asked.

"Because I say so."

"I'd rather not. Food doesn't seem to be a good companion to me lately."

He snorted but kept his gaze on the collection I'd presented. "Interesting. Are these connected to your 'conspiracy of ghosts'?"

"I think so. The artifacts . . . came to me around the market."

"Hmm. There is a strange thread binding these, yet there should be none," he said, glancing at me. "There is someone in this. . . ." Then he went back to his examination of the objects on the napkin. He picked them up one by one, muttering over them and to them, peering at each one, holding some close to his face, holding others away. Each one gave off a wisp of color that cast the shadow of someone else's face on his before disappearing. He put them down again, but not always in the same place he'd taken them up from, segregating them into three piles.

I picked at the sturgeon as he continued. It was delicious, but while I felt vaguely hungry, I also felt a touch queasy. Vampires do that to me, and Carlos worse than most. I had to push the plate aside.

Carlos looked up and gave me a slow, unpleasant smile, glancing from the plate to me. "My mistake."

"Very funny."

His expression became serious. "No. It was not my intention to cause you distress. I forget the effect my kind have on you—it's rare. But I should have given greater thought to what these things"—he waved his hand over the collection on the napkin—"might portend."

"What do they portend?" I asked, mocking his formal tone.

"Each of these people died of starvation."

"All of them?"

"Every one. Some quite recently. Others as much as a century and more ago."

I felt myself scowling as I took that thought in. "But . . . they couldn't . . . They can't all be Linda Hazzard's victims if they died more recently than the early twentieth century. *Are* they Hazzard's victims?"

"Hazzard. Yes. The name comes from these," he said, stroking his finger over the smallest pile, which included the keys, some buttons, and the odd little tool. He touched the pile that included the dolphin brooch. "These are more recent. These are of the same age or older than the first and yet they do not speak that name." He indicated the last pile. "But they all died of the same cause."

"All these artifacts came from people who starved to death."

He nodded. "They did."

"But not all Linda Hazzard's victims. Were they all murdered?"

"No. Most simply died. They were too poor or too lost in mad-ness to find food. But they all have the thread of this Hazzard woman binding them."

"She's been dead for most of a century. How could she have bound them—especially those who died after her?"

"It is not precisely she who did it."

"You've totally lost me," I said.

"You call them a conspiracy of ghosts, a cabal haunting these patients, manifesting through them."

"Yes, but it's like they're fake ghosts. You know about the Spiritu-alist movement, specifically the fad for what they called 'table tap-ping' in the early years of the twentieth century. Most of it was phony—charlatans claiming to speak with the dead or channel them during hokey séances and producing all sorts of ambiguous messages and signs that convinced people to give the 'medium' money. People believed ghosts talked to them through these false channels."

"I'm aware of this diverting human folly. Not all were liars and cheats, however," he said, giving me a meaningful stare that sent my stomach on a slow roll.

"And *I'm* aware of that. But the techniques—no, the manifesta-tions these ghosts are using are straight out of the fakery handbook."

One corner of his mouth rose and brought an unexpected glint of amusement into his eyes. "Do you think they would know the differ-ence between that which is false and that which is true now that they're dead? Few spirits are aware of the world outside the prison of their unending existence—you know this; why do you question it? If they know that they are dead, that they continue in life only as shadows, how would they choose to speak except as ghosts? As they have been told that ghosts do? By automatic writing, by speaking in tongues, by backmasking, by dermographia, by spirit manifestation of visions and sounds. This is what they knew and all they know. They come to their unwilling channels as the vagrant souls they believe they are bound to be. If Linda Hazzard has, even after death, gathered them, it is her victims who will dictate the path no matter how many other souls they drag in train, like slaves in chains."

"But how did they come to be gathered up and bound by or to Linda Hazzard?"

Carlos shrugged. "I don't know. These things don't reveal that. You will have to ask the spirits. That is not my forte, though it could be done. By blood and magic you would despair of."

I already despaired of solving this problem in time. "I can't allow that. There has to be some other way. . . ."

"Of course there are other ways. How have you become so blind? This power is drawn and flows differently for each of us. For the witch, for the mage, for you. Perhaps, knowing the time they occupy, you could go to them."

"I haven't had any luck with that so far. The temporaclines are shattered and displaced around the market and I don't even know where these guys died."

"Have you tried? Perhaps taking the objects that belonged to the dead with you?"

"Me? I don't see how that would make a difference with the temporaclines. . . ." But I was thinking. Maybe it would work. . . .

I picked up the odd little tool and edged out of the booth, moving farther from the windows and sinking toward the Grey.

The broken and tilted edges of temporaclines fluttered against my reaching hands, cold and razor-edged. Concentrating on the tool I held, I riffled the edges, looking for one that seemed brighter or more open, but they were all much alike and nothing felt right. I tried simply shoving one open enough to look, but it wasn't even remotely the right time period and the sheet of frozen time hung without invitation until I let it slide shut.

I tried several more, but even when I found one of the right period, it had no affinity for the object in my hand and stepping into it took me nowhere and into no time that helped me. Frustrated and chilled, I stepped back from the Grey and returned to the booth, where Carlos was watching me, frowning a little, the darkness around him swirling and swelling like ink in water.

I put the tool down with a sigh. "No luck. I couldn't even find out what this thing is."

"A very old pipe cleaner."

"What? No, a pipe cleaner is a fuzzy piece of wire."

He gave me a look that said he was indulging a particularly slow child. "The narrow end is for clearing the unburned tobacco residue and buildup from the bowl of the pipe and the mouthpiece. The flattened end is for tamping down the new tobacco before igniting it."

I blinked at him. "I have a hard time imagining you smoking a pipe."

"So did I. A nasty habit I could not afford when I was alive and had no use for once I died."

I had never been certain of his age, but if tobacco was still an expensive luxury item at the time of his death, Carlos was even older than I'd thought. I changed the subject. "Let me try another. . . ." I said.

I took one of the keys this time, hoping its connection to such a large object as a house might put more weight into the temporacline it came from, but again I got no response from the planes of frozen time. I wasn't close to the place where I'd found them, but time—even noncontiguous time—tends to link to objects of significance in the Grey. But it wasn't happening. The objects must have had no significance for the time they came from. If none of the people who owned them had been important, their weight could be negligible in the well of the Grey. And yet the things had come to me as tokens of the people who had owned them. Surely they were not entirely insignificant?

I tried holding on to all of the objects associated with Hazzard's victims—assuming that they would occupy a similar time and that the weight of all of them together might be great enough to influence one of the temporaclines to flash or warm to my touch. But there was no such response.

I backed out to the normal world frustrated and ice-cold.

Shaking my head, I sat down again and put the things back on the napkin. "It's just not working. I think I'd have to be in the right location or know the names of the people each object belonged to. I might be able to make a connection at the market, but I'd rather not go back there until I have to."

Carlos cocked an eyebrow at me. "Indeed?"

"I'm having a lot of trouble there. Hazzard seems to know when I'm in the area, and the manifestations are uncontrollable there. I can barely stand to be close to the place because the dermographia begins to burn my skin and my hands cramp and convulse. I'm afraid I'll pass out again or lose control. I need to find a way to contact these ghosts without reentering the market area. At least not until I know what's happening and have a way to counter it or break it down."

"The simplest thing would be to bring a medium into this."

"There's already a medium involved. I've been trying to listen to some recordings he made of my client's sister—the first patient I encountered—but they're extremely garbled. She's doing automatic painting of the bluff where the market currently stands, but she started speaking recently and none of it makes sense. I've been able to pick out one phrase, but the rest is total gibberish. Or it seems that way, since I doubt anything about this case is just sound for the sake of sound. It must mean something. The paintings did. The writings probably do, too—both the dermographia and the automatic work the two other patients are manifesting."

Carlos raised his eyebrows. "Three unconscious patients and each manifests a different phenomenon. This intrigues me. I will go with you to talk to the medium."

"Why? Not that I'm not grateful for the offer, but I don't get the attraction."

He chuckled. "Very little is new to me anymore, but I have never seen spirits behave as you are describing. I could manage the magic myself to discover what they want and what the cause of their distress is, but my way would be destructive and dangerous to you. That I do not want—and nor would Cameron. But I do wish to see this through." He paused before adding, "If you allow it."

I wasn't thrilled at the prospect of spending more time in Carlos's presence, but I wouldn't say no to the extra magical muscle he represented. I'm no mage or medium, so I would need help no matter what the solution was. I could probably recruit other assistance, but, to be honest, Carlos was about the most powerful that I could hope for. He's dangerous and occasionally unpredictable, but we're friends of a sort and I wasn't fool enough to throw his offer aside lightly. I hoped he would have no temptation to go further than necessary, though; Carlos's whims tended to have horrifying consequences.

"All right. I'll call the man in question and see if he'll play along."

Carlos curved his mouth into something less a smile than a smirk.

I got my phone out of my pocket and called Richard Stymak. When he answered I could hear Peter Gabriel's "Games Without Frontiers" playing in the background. "Hey," he said.

"Hi, Stymak. This is Harper Blaine. I'm working on the Goss case. . . ."

"Yeah, I know. Hi. What for you can I do?" His words came out a bit slowly and with an odd flourish of inversion, as if he were a little high or quite tired.

"I've found some objects I think belong to the ghosts manifesting through Julianne and other patients—"

He interrupted me with an odd, drawling excitement. "You did find them? The other guys? I knew there had to be some."

"Yes. But the thing is, Stymak, I can't seem to make any contact with these spirits, even with the objects in my hand. I was hoping you might be willing to help me."

"Sure! When?"

"Tonight."

"Like . . . now?" His voice squeaked and I could hear him scrambling about. "Umm . . . I'm not exactly ready for this." He sounded less dreamy now that he was panicking.

"How long would it take for you to get ready and where would you like to do it?"

"Um," he started, still making shuffling noises and possibly shaking himself to greater clarity—I could hear something being whisked about that passed over the phone in sudden whispers. "I could probably do it in an hour or so. I'm . . . well, I'm naked at the moment and while that's a good guarantee I'm not faking anything, I'm guessing you don't really want to see that."

"I'm quite sure I don't and neither does the other guy."

"Other guy?"

"Independent witness. He's helping me out with the identification of the objects."

"Oh, like . . . a psychometrist? Never met one of those . . ."

"Yes. I'd like to bring him, too, so we have corroboration."

"Oh. OK. Well, definitely don't want to be wagging my willie in that case. I . . . uh . . . um, do we have to do it at my place? It's small and kind of a mess."

"If you're comfortable elsewhere and can get set up by"—I glanced at my watch—"say, ten o'clock?"

"Ten? Yeah. I can do that. Umm . . . we could meet at the Goss place. . . ."

"I would prefer not to," I said, thinking it might not constitute neutral ground for all the spirits and I didn't want to introduce Carlos to Lily and let him into her house. Vampires don't really need permission to enter your home, but it's just better to keep them at a distance when you have the option.

"Oh. Oh! Hey, do you know the CalAska Pub in West Seattle?"

I certainly did, since I lived just a few miles from it. "Yes, I do."

"The owner has a back room he'd probably let me use for an hour or so. He's an old roommate of mine. He's cool with the occult and all that. Kind of owes me."

"If you're sure you can get the space . . ." I replied, a little wary, but since I was asking Stymak for a favor on short notice, I wasn't going to fuss much.

"Sure, sure. I'll call him and call you straight back, all right?"

"OK."

"Cool." Stymak hung up.

Carlos gave me a questioning look.

"He has to check on his work space. He doesn't want us in his home."

I assumed Carlos understood the idea of not letting magical strangers into your private space. He nodded and made a silent "ah."

In a few minutes Stymak returned my call.

"Yeah, Harper, so . . . yeah. John says it's good to go. Meet you at the bar at ten."

"Will do. Thanks, Stymak."

"My pleasure. Want to get to the bottom of this thing myself. And I wouldn't mind meeting your psychometrist—that's a cool skill."

"I'm not sure how much you'll like it once you've seen it up close," I warned.

"Man, as long as we're not sacrificing puppies, I'm good."

I gave Carlos the eye and said, "No. No puppy sacrifices."

"Cool. See you at ten," Stymak replied and hung up again.

Carlos returned a long, thoughtful look and then cocked his head with an amused half smile. "Puppy sacrifice? Some people have the strangest ideas."

"You're talking about a guy who plays telephone with ghosts. Strange won't even start in this race."

NINETEEN

I have no idea how Carlos gets around on his own. He doesn't seem to drive and I can't imagine him taking public transit— unless there's a paranormal bus system I'm not aware of. Usually he just turns up where he agrees to meet me, but this week I seemed to be playing chauffeur to the undead.

We had about an hour to kill and I thought I could skim through some of the books Phoebe had lent me while we waited at the pub. I didn't want to get sucked into some compelling bit of research and then miss our appointment with Stymak, but since I had the opportunity to glance through the books, I figured I should grab it while I could and Stymak or Carlos would drag me out whenever one of them was ready to work.

CalAska was one of the early self-contained boutique brew pubs in Seattle. It's small and has changed names and owners several times, but continues to serve decent house-brewed beer and pub food that's a cut above the usual commercial-grade sandwiches and greasy fish-and-chips. I pored over a book about Linda Hazzard's career as Washington's first serial killer with a glass of root beer at my elbow.

Carlos had a pint of stout in front of him, but he wasn't drinking it. Not that vampires can't drink alcohol, they just . . . don't. Why bother with something that doesn't affect you? To be intoxicated you'd have to have blood flow to the brain to begin with and they don't. I figured the token beer was like the smoked sturgeon: a polite deception and a sort of payment for taking up space. Personally, I'd have liked to have a beer myself by this point, but I was having enough trouble keeping the soda down. I'd noticed the unhealthy thinness of everyone involved in the case and suspected it was now affecting me, too—the connection Carlos had mentioned in passing the night before might have had something to do with it, but I wasn't certain.

My reading material wasn't really helping on the digestion score, either. The more I read about her, the less I liked Linda Hazzard— and I hadn't had a soft spot for her at the beginning. The author wasn't sure how many people she'd killed in two U.S. states and New Zealand, but estimates ranged from a dozen to forty. Hazzard had believed fervently that fasting would "purify the blood," improve health, and cure anything from shingles to cancer—and, of course, obesity. She'd left her home state of Minnesota for Washington in 1906. At least one victim of her fasting regimen was already in the ground by then. She hadn't been prosecuted for that one, since as an unlicensed practitioner, she couldn't be tried for malpractice under Minnesota law at the time. Apparently, killing a patient you had no right to treat wasn't malpractice or murder.

Ironically, the opposite was true in Washington. She'd had no advanced medical training, but due to a quirk of state law, she was licensed as a doctor in Washington in 1907—where she was also im- mune from prosecution for the death of patients so long as they had been undergoing her "therapy" willingly. She wrote a book about her curative process and published it in 1908. She killed her first Seattle patients the same year—among them the mother of Ivar Haglund, the founder of Ivar's Acres of Clams and the Salmon House in Northlake. Most of those who died under Linda Burfield Hazzard's care had never had a chance to protest that they wished to quit the regimen of watered-down tomato broth, daily enemas, and violent "massage" that left fist-shaped bruises on their backs and foreheads, since she kept their friends and families at bay by locking the patients up in hotel rooms in Seattle or in cabins on her property in Olalla. When the patients died, their relatives rarely saw the bodies, and all valuables they'd owned vanished into Hazzard's coffers. Sometimes she even billed the family for her services.

Enough patients simply lost weight, felt better, and left her care that she continued to attract more, even when her failure rate was suspicious—the richest patients tended to go home in urns. One went home with a bullet in his head. Whether he'd been killed by someone on the Hazzard property or shot himself to escape the treatment, no one knew, but it was interesting that though he was technically an English peer, his family was broke. Before she was finally caught and tried, Hazzard had managed to bury at least one Englishman who actually was wealthy, a lawyer, several socialites, a publisher, a civil engineer, and a retired U.S. congressman, among sundry others who were merely well-to-do and foolish.

She was brought to trial in 1912 over the death of an Englishwoman and the near-starvation and imprisonment of the woman's sister. She had a studio photo taken of herself for the papers in which she wore a dress she had "inherited" from the dead sister. The author speculated that the photo was carefully engineered to create a sympathetic image of Hazzard as a beautiful woman who couldn't possibly be a killer, thus softening up the jury to rule in her favor. It must have worked, because while it had taken a nurse and the British vice consul to bring her down, Hazzard had still skipped away to New Zealand with a revoked medical license after serving only two years for manslaughter—because her patients had "taken the cure" voluntarily, even if it killed them. No one seemed to know how many Kiwis had died under her care, only that she'd offered the same "cure" under various titles while she lived there.

She'd returned to Washington in the 1920s and operated her "sanitarium" in Olalla as a "School of Health," until it burned down in 1935. No one else apparently died there except Hazzard herself, who continued to live on the property until she became ill in 1938 and, true to her beliefs to the bitter end, starved herself to death while fasting for "the cure."

I looked up from my book, relieved that such a monster was long dead, and worried about what she might have been up to in the afterlife. I couldn't fathom what the ghost of a fasting quack would be doing with the spirits of her victims and others like them, but it couldn't be good.

Carlos noticed my blanched face and seemed about to speak when Stymak trotted into the pub and up to our table, wafting a hint of Washington's finest weed in his wake.

"Hello! Ready to . . . tip some tables?" he joked.

"Yes," I said. Carlos just looked amused as I stood up to follow Stymak to the back room.

Stymak gave Carlos a glance that turned into a scowl with a side dish of fear. "You're . . . the psychometrist?"

Carlos nodded, but neither spoke nor offered his hand.

I recaptured Stymak's attention as he recoiled—though I wasn't sure if it was the vampire thing that was giving him the heebie-jeebies or the necromancer thing. He looked at me as if he would have said something, but shook it off, upset but trying to hide it.

"Let's get started. Then we can get done faster," I said.

Stymak nodded with the enthusiasm of a bobblehead doll in the back of a lowrider. "Yeah! I'll go get John to unlock for us," he added, almost sprinting to the bar to get a key from the man behind it.

I followed more sedately, keeping Carlos next to me. "He doesn't like you," I muttered.

"A good sign. I had half imagined he would be a charlatan. But I shouldn't have doubted your abilities in reading . . . people," he added, casting a glance at the book I'd stuffed back into my bag.

"I read just fine, thanks," I replied.

"Without doubt. Let us discover what this bitch is up to."

His use of the pejorative surprised me. "You mean Hazzard?"

"Hers is the name that all the artifacts sing. And not in praise."

Carlos is a cruel bastard, make no mistake, but whatever he'd already gleaned from the objects I'd brought him seemed to have convinced even him that Linda Hazzard was as despicable in death as she had been in life. Without further comment I followed him into the back room that Stymak had unlocked.

Stymak had turned on the lights and was keeping busy around the wooden table and chairs in the middle of the room. The space looked as if it was usually used for storage, cleaning supplies, and occasional breaks for the staff. The lighting was harsh, but didn't quite penetrate the corners, where shadows curdled. Stymak was nervous now, fidgeting with a messenger bag he'd unslung from his back and kept moving from chair to floor and back again.

"Um," he started. "I'd usually lower the lights a bit. . . . I have a little electric lamp to put on the table, but if you guys don't feel comfortable with that . . ."

It was Stymak who was uncomfortable, but even as I thought it would be better for him not to see Carlos so plainly, the vampire spoke up for me. "Neither of us is afraid of the dark. Do as you would prefer. We are in your hands."

I wasn't sure that made Stymak feel better, but it at least goaded him to stop fiddling and finish his preparations. He set the small lamp on the table. Then he arranged some chairs and put a few more items from his bag on the table: a pad of paper, some easy-flowing markers, and a large plate that he filled with fine white sand. He placed his digital recorder on the table also and stood back to study the setup.

Stymak looked at me. "I used to use candles—ghosts like the smoke—but I had to give that up when a few things got set on fire. And of course, you can't smoke in bars anymore. Think it needs anything?"

I shrugged. I'd never experienced a true séance before, only fake ones, so I had no idea what might be useful.

Carlos caught my eye. "The objects you showed me. Put them on the table."

I dug them out of my pockets once again and put the collection of odds and ends on the table near the lamp.

"Where did those come from?" Stymak asked, eyeing them with a frown.

"They came from various parts of Pike Place Market," I said. "They seem to belong to some of the spirits who are possessing the patients."

Stymak nodded. "Well, I think that should do it. Would you turn off the room light? Then we can get started."

Carlos beat me to it and we sat down around the table as Stymak turned on his digital recorder and the little lamp.

It cast a dim light—just enough to see the objects on the surface in front of us, but not much beyond. The room was deep in shadow and the muted music from the taproom drifted in, giving the impression that we were far from civilization but not entirely removed.

"We should take hands with the people on each side," Stymak said, but as soon as he touched Carlos, he jerked his hand back, taking a hard breath through his nose. "Ugh! Uh . . . maybe we should just put them on the tabletop . . . unless you guys think I'm cheating. . . ."

"We would know," Carlos said.

"Oh. Well. Good. We can trust each other, then."

I saw the energy around Carlos flicker slightly brighter than usual—I took that as amusement.

"We'll trust each other," I reiterated and put my own hands on the tabletop.

Carlos chuckled but did the same, and Stymak, looking spooked in the dim light, followed suit. His aura had gone a bit green ever since touching Carlos and it was clear that he was very uncomfortable with the vampire. I wondered if he knew what Carlos was. He hadn't said anything. I would have to wait to find out.

Stymak closed his eyes and started off with a nondenominational prayer for assistance and protection. It reminded me of magical ceremonies that called on the four directions—the magical equivalent of a politically correct hedge on religion while at the same time getting the attention of whatever magical thing might be around to do the work required.

In the near dark, I let my Grey vision open as wide as possible without my slipping away. The energy around Stymak had begun expanding, brightening and spreading in all directions. The light it shed into the Grey was white, just like my own had appeared when I sank away from my body. But he wasn't just bright; he was reaching out mentally, concentrating and casting his net outward, trolling for spirits.

Stymak spoke in the same quiet but bell-like voice I'd heard him use at the Goss house as his consciousness ranged outward. "We ask for the attendance of those spirits who have been drawn to Julianne Goss and others like her. Those spirits who have spoken through our friends. Come to us and speak. We are ready to hear you."

He was unnaturally still and very quiet as his energy continued to expand and seek, growing brighter until, to my eyes, the room was awash in white light. He waited for a while, and then repeated his invitation. "Come to us and speak. We are waiting to hear you."

The sand in the dish stirred and a few particles rose into the air, then more, making a small cloud that spread upward in a thin column. I heard a distant rattling and a roar that grew closer, like a train hurtling toward us. The sound reminded me of the rattle and roar the Guardian Beast made when it was bearing down, but here there was an added element: a howling keen that cut me through with dread and raised a churning in my gut that was more nauseating than Carlos's presence nearby.

The cloud of sand hovering over the dish began to spread sideways, growing thicker in some places, thinner in others, taking on form and shadow in the pale light of the electric lamp. The cloud began to resemble a face. The face opened its sand-pale eyelids, the grains rolling away to reveal dark pits containing distant points of fire that dwindled toward more distant stars. It split into several faces, each turned in a different direction, the mouths moving out of sync.

"We come . . ." the faces whispered. "We are gathered."

Something swooped in, screaming and clattering, and dragging a tail of the floating sand across the table to swirl around the edges of the room. The remaining sand billowed upward, coming back together into one large face that glared at us.

"Why do you trouble me?"

Even with his eyes closed, Stymak was frowning and looking slightly ill. Carlos glared at the apparition, his hands rigid and digging into the tabletop, but he didn't move or speak. The sand outside our circle continued whirling around the room, drawing into the shape of a skeletal wolf that stalked the table, watching us.

"We wish to speak to those who are crying out for help. You aren't one of them. Who are you? What is your name?" Stymak said, his voice now choked and rasping as the white energy in his corona faltered and flickered. He'd begun sweating and I saw a slight tremor in his hands on the table.

"Why should I tell you?" the ghost demanded, firming within her shell of sand and rising higher above the table. She was tall, almost stately, and angry, her scowl reddening the hazy world of the Grey.

Stymak was struggling, having difficulty speaking, the far-reaching clouds of his aura diminishing and pulling inward. I didn't think this was how he'd intended the séance to go, but I wasn't sure what to do aside from distracting the ghost's attention from him.

"I know who you are," I said, recognizing her now. "You're Linda Burfield Hazzard. We don't want to talk to you, Mrs. Hazzard. We want to talk to the others—"

"*Doctor* Hazzard!" she roared.

The skeletal wolf howled in chorus, stalking around us faster, hunching closer to the ground.

"Doctor. As you like," I said, letting my disdain for her unwarranted title color my voice.

She turned all of her attention on me. Stymak remained as he was and the circling wolf-thing nipped at him as it passed. He shuddered and made a gagging sound, but nothing more.

"I thought you would be useful," Hazzard said, looking me over. "So thin, so pretty . . . You should be mine, for all I've done." She put out a hand to touch my face and I saw a thin streamer of ghost-stuff rise off my chest and yearn toward her—this must be the tie Carlos had seen. The skeletal wolf rushed toward me from behind her. I ducked aside and felt the strand between Hazzard and me pull uncomfortably tight.

The two forms clashed in a spray of white grit and a crash of bones. The tugging sensation in my chest broke off. Stymak and the sand collapsed to the table, leaving the ghost behind. Hazzard's face deformed, twisting and tumbling, then re-formed as a skull more like the wolf's than the woman's, the illusion of flesh clinging in melting strands over it. The terrifying creature spun and scattered the items remaining on the table, then turned back to me, snarling.

"You disturbed the tribute. Had I known you before, you would have been mine," the monstrous thing said. This was no ghost. It was something else—something much more dangerous. "Perhaps you still shall be, when the wheel turns, when the hunger of the damned is sated."

The creature took another bite at Stymak, who twitched and

jerked away, eyes still closed, uttering a small cry of distress. His energy collapsed toward him and he writhed as if it were crushing him, forcing a word out on his expelled breath. "Who . . . ?"

"I am Limos, the Insatiable! You shouldn't meddle in my affairs!" the creature spat, biting at me, now, too.

I ducked again, but not fast enough and the ghostly teeth ripped loose a shred of light from my shoulder. I cried out from the rending pain that seemed to tear deep into my gut.

Carlos pushed hard against the table and stood up, knocking the furniture over. Notebooks, pens, and the recorder scattered around the room and the dish of sand shattered on the floor. "Enough!" he roared. "It is time for you to go back where you came from." He put one hand out toward me as he kept his eyes on the dreadful thing between us. "Give me your hand," he ordered.

I didn't want to touch him, but if I didn't do something the monstrous, incorporeal thing would tear more pieces out of me or Stymak, and I could see Stymak's light dimming with every nip the creature took. I grabbed Carlos's hand, shuddering at the touch.

"Push!" he commanded. "We cannot tear it apart, but we can force it back. Push!"

I felt rocky and sick, my feet unstable on the shifting sand that covered the floor, but I reached down toward the grid, trying to anchor myself to the energy of the Grey and draw it up through me like I had before. I pulled with mind and will and thrust the rising energy toward the horrifying thing. I could hear Carlos, dimly through the ringing in my ears, muttering words that bled and sparked in the Grey, sending growing ripples outward that tore through the phantasm before us. The power I shoved upward became a tsunami carrying the barbed, coruscating words into the creature, tearing it in two and tumbling the parts away into the blackness between the hot lines of the grid.

The world collapsed on us, bearing me to the floor. Carlos knelt beside me, peering into my face. His touch made me cold and I imagined black coils of stinging vines curling up my arm and digging at the torn part of my shoulder.

I stifled a sob of pain and tried to pull away from him. He stared at me a moment longer, then let go. Heat flooded back into my body as soon as his hand left mine. I gasped in air that tasted of dust and spilled beer as the normal world came back into focus.

"Stymak," I murmured, turning toward him.

Carlos had moved over beside him, his hands hovering a scant half inch above the medium's shoulders. A dim blue glow lay in the thin gap between them as Carlos bent his head and concentrated. The glow sank into Stymak and Carlos moved back, keeping a wary eye on him.

The necromancer turned his head and caught my attention. "Better it be you nearby when he wakes," he said.

I scrambled across the floor to Stymak's side as Carlos backed farther away. I felt like death warmed over and mashed flat, but took the man's hand and felt for a pulse. I sighed in relief when he had one.

"Stymak? Stymak?" I said, patting his hand and bending close to keep my voice low. The sound of music and conversation from the taproom beyond was unchanged, and I hoped no one had noticed any disturbance.

The overhead light came on and I jerked my attention to the doorway. Just Carlos, standing next to the switch and guarding the door.

Stymak moved and groaned, then lifted his eyelids. His eyes were bloodshot and his face was wan. "I think . . . I'm going to be sick."

I grabbed a box of trash bags off the floor nearby and yanked one off the roll. Stymak turned white and barely snatched the bag quickly enough to save his friend's floor. He was spectacularly and noisily ill.

When he was done, he looked at me and asked, "What the hell happened?"

"I'm not sure. I think we got an unexpected visitor."

"God, I feel like I've been hit by a combine harvester."

"I think you're still intact," I said. "It's a bit of a mess here, however."

Stymak looked around and sighed. "Could be worse. I hope my recorder's all right. . . ."

Carlos and I started putting the room to rights while Stymak staggered around, looking for his digital recorder. He found it wedged between two boxes of cocktail napkins and brought it back to the table we had just set back on its feet. Carlos shoved a chair toward him, carefully not touching the medium or looking directly at him. I was too tired to be openly amused at the powerful and terrifying necromancer doing housework. I kept my mouth shut and continued cleaning up.

Carlos slipped out into the bar as I dumped the spilled sand into the trash can by the door and went to sit with Stymak.

"How does it look?" I asked.

"Seems OK." He pressed the Replay button.

A whispering chorus muttered from the device. "Run. Flee. . . . They come. . . ."

Stymak paused the playback. "They? Uh-huh." He nodded to himself. "I thought there was something else along for the ride." He looked up at me. "What happened? I saw the beginning of a manifestation—a face formed in the sand—but things got a bit hazy after that. I had the impression of something . . . foreign, something . . . hungry, grasping. I thought it bit me. . . ."

"It was Hunger Incarnate," Carlos said, a slight frown creasing his brow. "It called itself Limos."

He had reentered the room silently, carrying a pitcher of beer and three glasses. I tried not to laugh at the sight of the vampire as cocktail waitress, but a snort escaped me anyhow. Carlos set down his burdens on the table and reclaimed a chair, arching an eyebrow at me in challenge. I chose not to accept and ducked my head.

Stymak seemed a bit stunned by what Carlos had said, but he was nodding as if taking the idea in while he poured beer into the glasses. He guzzled a mouthful, making a face before he washed the first taste away with another.

I added my ideas of what had happened. "I think those voices on the recording are the ghosts themselves—the ones that have been attempting to manifest through Julianne and the other patients. I don't think they ever really got to us—they never spoke up, even after you'd asked several times."

"They remained at bay," Carlos said. "I felt them outside, but they didn't enter the circle—they were restrained."

"Uh-huh," Stymak grunted, pushing the other glasses over to us. "I had that feeling, too." He tapped his recorder. "This sounds like a lot of the other recordings. Some garbled talk, warnings about something coming . . . but this time something came and it didn't come by itself."

"It came with Linda Hazzard. I thought they were the same thing at first," I said, "but I'm pretty sure it's two separate entities. Hazzard starved her patients, so maybe the sensation of hunger was connected to her. . . ."

Carlos shook his head. "No. Quite separate. Hunger may be what drew one to the other, but the sensation of starving was animate and separate from the ghost of the woman, Hazzard, who killed the voices."

Stymak and I both stared at Carlos.

"Can you not hear the thread that binds them together? Not all were her victims in life, but they are all in her power now."

"That's not what's giving us the creeps, Carlos," I said. "It's the idea of animate hunger."

"You saw it for yourself." He glanced at Stymak, but didn't lock his gaze with the pudgy medium's. "You felt it tear into you. Did it not seem the embodiment of hunger, feeding on your soul?"

Stymak shuddered and turned his face aside. "Ugh . . . I'd like to forget that feeling."

"You would do well to remember it," Carlos suggested, his voice resonating through me. Judging from Stymak's wince it had the same effect on him. "That way you will not fall victim to other hungers, to temptations that consume you in the same unremitting need that burns you to a shell but never lets you go."

Stymak, wide-eyed, gulped beer too fast and coughed, doubling over until the fit passed. "I . . . hope I never go wherever you've been, man."

Carlos inclined his head, but said nothing.

"What did the ghost . . . thing say while I was . . . out of it?" Stymak asked, looking at me and very much *not* at Carlos.

I thought back before I spoke. "She . . . or it . . . said something about tribute—that I had disturbed the tribute. And something about the wheel turning to feed the damned."

" 'When the wheel turns, when the hunger of the damned is sated.' That is what the creature said," Carlos quoted. Leave it to a necromancer to have a perfect memory for the horrible.

"There's some connection to the Great Wheel," I said. "It's come up before. It appeared as dermographia on my skin and other spirits have mentioned the Wheel. Though I'm not sure how turning a Ferris wheel sates the damned. Or what this business about tribute means."

"The souls that are bound together would be the tribute," Carlos said. "They were gathered by Hazzard, but for what purpose?"

"Given to Limos," muttered the voices from the recorder. Stymak self-consciously pushed the button and turned it off. "I didn't do that," he said. "It just came on."

Carlos and I both nodded.

"Typical ghost crap," Stymak continued, glaring at the recorder as if it understood his discomfort.

I tried to think aloud. "No. No, it's not. The ghosts were all people who died of starvation. They were gathered by Hazzard, who starved her victims to death, so she has an affinity for them, even in the afterlife. Gathered as tribute for Limos—some kind of otherworldly manifestation of hunger. And in return for tribute, this . . . thing is going to turn the Great Wheel and sate the hunger of the damned. Does that sound as totally loony as I think it does?"

Stymak nodded vigorously, but Carlos grinned. I glared at him. "What?"

"It's no wonder she likes you."

"Who? What?" I demanded.

"Hazzard. She said she wants you for her own." His wolf grin struck me cold. "Because you are thin. She believed, did she not, that fasting was healthful? She would find a thin but healthy woman like you to be very attractive. Ideal, even. A paragon. She touched you, marked you. And then the messages began, because you were tied to her just like the starved ghosts she had gathered for Limos."

"Hang on . . ." I said. "If I'm tied to Hazzard and therefore to the ghosts she gathered, why are her messages appearing on *my* skin? Shouldn't I be just like another of the ghosts?"

Carlos shook his head. "You can't be like them—you're alive. Hazzard said, 'You should be mine for all I've done.' She thinks you should be her prize once their plan is successful. A victim to torment and starve forever."

I shivered. "I really don't like that idea, but it implies that there's some plan between Hazzard and this Limos to 'sate the damned,'" I said.

Carlos nodded.

Stymak watched our conversation with horror clearly writ on his face. "Who or what is 'the damned'?"

"It must be Hazzard herself," Carlos said, looking not quite convinced of his own argument. "The ghosts are not damned, merely unable to leave this place. The other entity is not human—it cannot be damned, but it can be fed."

"Damned or not, it can't—" Carlos shot me the coldest glare I'd ever seen, cutting me short. He gave the tiniest shake of his head, warning me off what I'd been about to say. I reformed my idea before I spoke again. "Tribute cannot feed the hungry. . . ." I said, thinking aloud. "Hazzard already brought souls as tribute to Limos. So Limos owes her something in return that they plan to get by turning the Wheel . . . ?"

"The fat ones!" the recorder blared.

Stymak hit it on the tabletop. "Stop that! I know you're only trying to help, but this is just not the time."

"The disturbed spirits—that's the extra energy in the system," I said.

Carlos got it, but Stymak was lost. "What are you talking about?"

"Never mind, Stymak, just a tangent. Don't worry about it. Just hold on to the idea that ghosts or death represents energy."

"I know that."

"Someone wants more energy, more food, more tribute. They plan to get it from ghosts, and if you don't have enough ghosts to go around, you make them."

Stymak was shaken. "Jesus!"

"Exactly. There's another phrase that keeps coming up in the transcripts—'beach to bluff and back'—and Julianne keeps painting pictures of the bluffs and the beach in the area that's now the waterfront and Pike Place Market. It's all along the State Route Ninety-nine tunnel route, and the Great Wheel makes a very convenient central point to push energy from once it's been gathered there. All the patients had contact with the tunnel and that contact made them ideal conduits for the ghosts once the patients were injured enough to become comatose."

"So . . . Julianne's persistent vegetative state isn't natural?" Stymak asked.

"I don't think so. I never did—did you?"

He shook his head, but it was a weak movement.

I went on. "The ghosts are forcing it to linger so they can scream for help, not just for themselves but for the people who'll be riding the Great Wheel when Hazzard and Limos put their plan into motion. Hazzard doesn't have any corporeal power to do anything to the Great Wheel, so she has to get someone to help her topple the Wheel and take the lives of the tourists on it."

"Limos," Carlos supplied. "It is no ghost. It has power of its own as well as that of the ghosts gathered by Hazzard."

I felt sick and put my hand over my mouth. Stymak had turned the color of parchment, appalled by only half the knowledge Carlos and I had.

Carlos gazed at me with eyes that smoldered with pain and death. "Very clever, isn't it? Hazzard and Limos will upset the Wheel and dine on their share of the souls drowned in the ever-hungry sea."

"We have to figure out what they're going to do and when," I said. "It must be soon, because once the patients' souls have faded out, I suspect their bodies will die too and we can't let that happen."

TWENTY

I was impatient to talk to Carlos without Stymak around, but I needed the medium's help first, so I reined myself in.

"Given to Limos . . ." The recorder had played that segment again and although I wasn't very comfortable with it, I'd produced the photos of my dermographia. Stymak had looked them over and passed them on to Carlos by putting the phone on the table and pushing it toward him. He wouldn't touch the vampire even through the intermediary of the device.

"Did you ever listen to those recordings I sent?" Stymak asked me.

"I couldn't get more than the one phrase I mentioned. I was going to have my . . . someone try translating them or running them through various decryption and filter programs, but he hasn't been available."

"I don't think it's that complicated, now that we've done this. I think it's just backward. Because you remember the first time we heard this—at the Goss house—there was that phrase, umm. . . ." He searched through his pockets until he found a memory card, which he swapped into the recorder.

He pushed the button and the speaker squealed a bit before it let out the words ". . . Slows row someel vague rot codeth—" He clicked it off and looked up, accidentally catching Carlos's eyes, and then shifting his gaze to mine. "Makes no sense, does it?"

I shook my head. I'd had the same problem with some of the written pieces I'd seen at Sterling's house and the dermographia that afflicted Jordan Delamar.

"But if it's just backward, 'slows' could be . . ." He wrote the word on one of his notebooks and then wrote another under it. "That could be 'souls' and 'row' could be . . . 'oowwrr' . . . 'our' and then comes 'someel' . . . which could be . . . 'leemos' . . . that's got to be Limos—the hunger-monster thing, right?"

"Yes. The ghosts also said 'Given to Limos,' and there it is again," I said, retrieving my phone from Carlos and looking through photos for what I wanted. "Here. The message on Jordan Delamar's skin."

I handed the phone to Stymak, who read it aloud. "Given as Limos tribute, those who wasted away. Given to the wheel of death and birth, to break the wheel we are driven." Stymak put my notebook down and listened to his recording again, writing the message down phonetically and then writing under it, "Souls, our, Limos, gave, tor thedock . . ." He stared at it. "No . . . that's not right. That's got to be 'the doctor,' so the whole thing is perfectly backward."

He rewrote the sentence forward: "The doctor gave Limos our souls."

"They've been saying the same thing over and over—we just didn't get it," Stymak said. "God, how could I have missed that? Backmasking! It's the oldest trick in the book!" Then the color rushed out of his face and he stood up, looking more than queasy. "Holy Jesus." He dashed out of the room.

I glanced at Carlos.

He cocked an eyebrow at me and I took that as permission to pick up the conversation we hadn't had earlier. "I think the ghosts given in tribute account for the extra energy in the system we were discussing last night," I said.

He gave it some thought and nodded. "They could. A few recent cases of starvation might have been required to start the cycle, however."

"At least two homeless people—one of them a contact of mine—died of starvation near the end of last year or the beginning of this one. That's right in the time zone. There could be other deaths that didn't come to my attention, or anyone else's, especially if there was a more obvious cause of death, like cancer or HIV. And here's another thing—Quinton mentioned a box that sounds like it might be some kind of portable shrine his father brought from Europe for this project of his. He says it contained something when Purlis arrived, but was empty when he got a look at it himself. But it had dirt from the tunnel project on it. I've seen Purlis around the square off and on for about a year now, so I think he hid the shrine in some segment of the construction near or in Pioneer Square for a while—probably in one of the monitoring wells—because the area has a high homeless population. There are always a few who don't or won't get enough to eat, so they'd be a nice attraction for this hungry monstrosity. And his presence in the area might help explain how he caught on to your people, too."

"The disruption of the soil accounts for the initial upwelling of ghosts and magic, but the continued presence of Limos would explain why the rise continued, rather than falling back. With Limos loose and fed, she could have been a formidable problem for us, but she hasn't been."

I wondered at his use of "she" but I didn't want to derail my train of thought with that right now, and instead I said, "I think the deal between Limos and Hazzard is not just for their own profit. I think Purlis must have some stake—"

Carlos cut me off with a quick motion of his hand and a glance at the door. In a moment Stymak returned and sat down again, looking pale, smelling slightly sour and wiping his face with a damp towel. "Sorry. This thing is wigging me out." He looked again at the transcript he'd started and at my photos. "Couple of these guys are kind of poetical, aren't they?"

I gave it a thought and said, "A lot of these ghosts are from the early twentieth century—pre–World War I—and fairly well educated, so, yes, they might be inclined to be flowery."

"Yeah, I can see that, especially if they're victims of Linda Hazzard's. But who or what the hell is that Limos-thing? It didn't feel like a spirit, really. Some kind of demon?"

"A god," Carlos suggested.

Stymak and I stared at him. Stymak turned his gaze aside quickly, but kept his attention on the vampire. "What makes you think so? I've never heard of him."

"A distant memory . . . from my childhood." Carlos gave me a sly grin. "Yes, I did have one, Blaine. Greek and fairly obscure, I seem to recall—Limos, the goddess of famine and hunger. However long forgotten, she has the ability to create or destroy—if she can access power."

That explained his use of "she" earlier, but I said, "Why didn't you mention this before?"

He bowed his head very slightly and cut his gaze down. I thought that might have been embarrassment, but it seemed unlike him to be abashed. "I've been teasing the memory from the back of my mind since she gave her name. But even I can't dredge up everything I've ever known."

I hadn't thought about the depth of memory he must have, or how much work it might be to put all the pieces of a disused fact back together. "Do you think she's going to do something more tonight?" I asked, casting a glance toward Stymak, who was looking worse by the minute.

Carlos shrugged. "I think not. She spent a great deal of energy to come here and try to overawe us. She wouldn't do that if she was planning some other action tonight as well. You've annoyed her and she's made a tactical error in attacking you two, wasting energy and drawing too much attention to herself. She would have been better served to let us believe Hazzard was the only spirit we needed to worry about."

Stymak looked ready to scream or faint—I wasn't sure which was more imminent—and I thought I'd better cut the discussion short before he lost it completely. "I think *we'd* be best served to drop it for tonight. You and I can do some research. Stymak needs to rest."

Stymak stood up. "Actually, I think I just need to get away from both of you. I—I can't do this anymore. Tell Lily I'm sorry. I can't . . . touch this anymore. I feel sick . . . filthy. This is . . . this is not what I signed up for."

He tore the page he'd been working on out of his notebook and dropped it on the table, then swept the remains of his materials into his bag and hurried out of the room with his head down.

I looked at Carlos, who returned an arch look.

"A delicate one, your Mr. Stymak."

"Sensitive—isn't that what a medium is supposed to be?"

"He won't last long if he continues this way. He hasn't learned to separate his feelings from what he is told by ghosts. He allows the horror of it too deeply into his mind and it will drive him mad. Or kill him." He peered at me. "I assume that would not sit well with you."

"Of course not. But I suppose *you* would have a certain . . . connoisseur's appreciation of it."

Carlos snorted. "You continue to think little of me after all this time, Blaine. I do not revel in the distress of others. Unless they deserve it."

He was right and I was being unfair. I sighed. "I guess we're out one medium."

"For now. He may recover."

"We may not need him now that we know what we're looking for."

"I doubt this will be so simple. We should, perhaps, arrange some help for Mr. Stymak. . . ."

I narrowed my eyes at him. "What sort of 'help' do you have in mind?"

He chuckled and my stomach flipped. "Nothing of that sort. I'm concerned for him. He has overtaxed himself and is in distress. I'll arrange for someone to look after him and keep him from harm. I doubt he'll be paying much attention to the psychic realm right now, and that could be dangerous for him. Cameron's attention to our wider community makes it in my best interest to ensure that people like Stymak don't fall victim to their own powers."

"Altruism just looks so odd on you, Carlos."

He let out a full, rolling laugh that hit me like an earthquake. "You must work very hard to remain so cynical, Blaine."

"It suits me."

He grinned, but didn't reply.

We left the pub together, seeing no sign of Stymak and getting a strange look from the owner as we went, but no trouble. I wondered if I would be allowed back in the next time I went to the pub. We walked toward the parking lot where I'd left the truck. The séance hadn't lasted very long; it was only a bit past midnight. The sun comes up early in the summer so I knew Carlos would soon want to get to whatever safe place he hid in during the day.

"Where is Inman?" he asked.

"Huh?" I grunted, surprised.

"You promised me the location where Purlis has Inman. I've done your task and now I would like my half of this bargain paid."

"I'm not certain that Inman is there," I hedged. "I didn't get inside."

"But you know where Purlis operates. That will do. Take me."

"Carlos, the sun will be rising in a little more than four hours. I'm not sure it would be wise for you to start on a rescue mission right now."

"That is for me to decide. Take me."

"No. This conspiracy of ghosts has to be broken before they do whatever they're going to do. I can't let people die because you want your pet dhampir back right this minute. And if Purlis is actively involved in my case, it would be better to let me do my job and undermine his position before you go after him."

Carlos grabbed me by the shoulders and turned me to face him. The shock of his touch weakened my knees and drove black pain through me. I struggled against the despair and horror that invaded my mind, trying to push them back, but the closeness of his dark energy was pervasive and I could feel him concentrating on me, driving the sensations and thoughts that made me feel fragile and helpless.

"Don't toy with me, Blaine. You can do no more tonight without my help. And what else you would do can be accomplished in daylight, where I cannot go. Time is short, yes—short for both of us."

I was shaking in his grip, but I tried to break free. I was having difficulty concentrating enough to draw any power from the grid with which to oppose him and the push I gave against his mental weight seemed feeble to me, but he snatched his hands off my shoulders and backed away from me.

"I don't wish to harm you any more than I wish to beg you," he said. "Why must I remind you that you made a promise?"

"All right. I know. But I'm . . . I'm afraid."

"You? Why do you hesitate to trust me now, when we have seen and done what we have together?"

I kept my chin up, though I would have preferred to look away. "My . . . mate is there as well as his father and whatever prisoners and assistants he may have."

"Love is a strange thing. You worry that I'll disregard the harm that would be done by killing your mate's father. I assure you, my desire to mete out some punishment to the man who would enslave and destroy my creatures is difficult to restrain, but I shall. I wouldn't *have* to kill him."

I almost laughed, as awful as that sounds. I steadied my thoughts before I replied, a little ashamed of myself. "I'm sorry. This situation bugs me as much as it does you and I can't imagine how I'll solve my case, and your problem, too, without you. I'm not thinking as clearly as I ought to where Quinton is concerned. I'm a fool to have forgotten what we've done for each other. I'll take you there, now. But swear that no one dies tonight."

"I can and will swear not to kill anyone at this place. I do not promise to do no harm to certain parties, but they will survive it. Will that do?"

I weighed his promise, though I really didn't need to. I'd gotten out of the habit of trusting him, but there was no reason I shouldn't and every reason that I should. I nodded. "Yes. Now let's get out of here."

But this time it was Carlos who stood still. "One thing more: The return of Inman means a great deal to me and to Cameron. If that is accomplished, I will lend you any aid I can with your ghosts—and Limos. If not, I will still help you, but without Inman my resources will be limited to the nighttime—which may not be enough."

It was a considerable concession. Carlos is the most magically powerful ally I have. As much as it gave me a qualm to admit it, I felt more confident that the plot involving Hazzard, Limos, and Purlis could be unwound with him on my side than without him. I stopped and turned to him, risking his direct and dangerous gaze. "Thank you. That's generous of you and I appreciate it."

He laughed, the rolling tide of his amusement shaking in my chest. "I'm a fool to remind you, but I am indebted to you, as is Cameron, unto death and beyond."

I felt uncomfortable; I hadn't done the things I had just to help Carlos or the vampires of Seattle. "Come on," I said, turning to walk to the Rover.

Still chuckling, Carlos came along behind me.

I didn't enjoy the drive to Gas Works Park. I left the truck around the corner from the condo building where I'd last seen Quinton. But he wasn't in the alcove near the trash and recycling now. I frowned and Carlos gave me a quizzical look.

"Quinton should be here. . . ." I felt a tugging, vibrating discomfort in my chest—the vibration of a preternatural connection that Quinton and I shared—and looked down toward the park, dropping toward the Grey.

The ghost world was churning around me, the park an upheaval of paranormal activity, much more so than it had been earlier. I backed out and turned to Carlos. "Something's wrong."

"I can sense that. And Inman is close."

"So's Quinton. But he's down there." I swore. "I was hoping we could sneak up on Inman, but he's probably with Purlis. It appears we're just going to have to dive in and make the best of whatever is going on."

I started running for the bit of temporary fencing—if there was a secret door to something it would be there. Carlos kept up with me easily. I didn't care if Daddy Purlis had eyes and ears on the entrance—I figured that if the turmoil in the Grey was any indication, he was too busy to do anything about it—and so I shoved through the flimsy gate that was hanging ajar. Beyond it lay an old building that had been renovated into a picnic shelter, but a new door in the old concrete structure stood open, letting a blade of light fall onto the recently grown grass. I snatched my pistol from the holster at my back and went through the doorway hard and fast.

There was no one on the other side, just a stairway leading down and distant clangs and screeches coming up. I swept the room just in case and advanced with the HK down, but ready. In the back of my mind I was thinking it was silly to carry a gun when I was backed up by a vampire necromancer, but it's a habit and, to be fair, sometimes a brute-force technique is easier and cleaner than waiting for magic. Carlos seemed to have no problem following my lead. He kept behind me, close enough to whisper but far enough not to foul my movements. I could feel the tingling cold of spells held ready but in check. He was taking no more chances with the situation than I was.

We advanced quickly, but with sufficient care to avoid being unhappily surprised. Our caution was probably overkill, since the staircase led to a long, dim corridor with nowhere to hide and nothing hiding in it. That led to another door that stood slightly open, letting sound escape from whatever lay beyond.

The first room was plainly a remnant from the old gasworks. Rusted bolts and anchor plates, still adorning the concrete floor where equipment had once been secured, were now being used as tie-downs for empty cages with their doors hanging open and a few locked animal crates that rocked and leaked disquieting groans. The overhead lighting was long gone and had been replaced with superbright LED work rigs clamped to the remains of wall brackets or sticking up from tripod floor stands. The lamps cast overlapping shadows around the room and made our trip through it more difficult. I stared hard at each shadow to determine whether it was natural or paranormal.

As I searched the shadows, I noticed I was no longer seeing the overlap of Grey and normal vision simultaneously and wondered when that had changed. My preoccupation made me sloppy and I barely noticed one of the shadows shimmering as it shouldn't have.

Darkness erupted from the shimmer with the crack of leathern wings unfurling and something built of nightmare and scales lunged into the world. I couldn't say what it was—it seemed to have no real form, and yet it had a physical presence that swept toward us with a ripple of muscle under iridescent blackness.

I pivoted, raising the gun, and Carlos stepped forward, pushing me back with a murmur. "Don't shoot. And avoid the claws."

We both ducked as a forelimb trailing black wings like smoke and tattered funeral shrouds ripped through the air where our heads had been. Carlos muttered something and made a throwing gesture that propelled a coil of glimmering midnight toward the creature's diving face.

It was a long-snouted thing with an evil smile full of glittering obsidian fangs. It opened its maw to bite and the spinning, expanding shape of Carlos's spell ripped into its mouth, tearing the thing's head in two. The monstrous shape vanished in a sooty cloud and a skeleton clattered to the floor.

The bones at our feet were pale, acidic green and black talons defined its digits. The concrete steamed with a thin, noxious fume where the claw tips touched it.

Carlos knelt by the remains and carefully picked a few of the claws out of the rubble by their rounded, bone-end attachments. He wrapped them in a cloth from his pocket and stowed them away.

"What was that?" I asked in a low voice.

"Night dragon," he replied. "This is a very small one—young and weak. But where you find one of these, there may be a ley weaver or dreamspinner nearby."

I'd met a ley weaver and would be quite happy never to meet another. I shuddered at the thought. "So it's not a monster—it's a construct . . . ?"

"Yes and no. This skeleton is drachen, but the animation and manifestation of the night dragon is created, not born. They are useful in rousing fear and panic, but not hard to destroy once you know they are mostly illusion—but only mostly."

I wanted to ask more about dragons in general, but I felt the press of circumstance more with each passing minute. The strange connection between Quinton and me brought a sense of growing distress that was not just my own. I nodded and stepped carefully over the skeleton, ready to carry on. Carlos didn't need any prompting to follow me.

We continued through the room and I kept a much more careful eye on the Grey this time. A small flurry of ghosts caused us some disorientation, but as they passed I recognized a face and knew we'd gotten lucky: These were some of Hazzard's ghosts and their energy was too depleted by the séance to do whatever they had been tasked with. But I had no idea why they were here and neither did Carlos.

"Perhaps it is not Hazzard but Limos that connects them here with Purlis," Carlos suggested.

"I suppose, but I'd rather get to the end of this maze and find out what's going on with the people who are still breathing before I worry about the disposition of the ones who aren't."

He nodded and we crept onward.

We didn't see a single living human in the next room, only ranks of equipment and a ragged dead body of something with wispy hair and blue-green flesh. It lay on a steel table, oozing green liquid I couldn't help but think of as blood. Whatever had been done to it had been done in haste and I had to hold back an urge to be sick or cry over it—whatever it was. On another table sat an object that looked remarkably like a salesman's sample case made of bones and stretched skin. The boxy thing stood open, its three sections partially unfolded to reveal a cold sparkle within. A bunch of cables led off the table and away through a hole in the wall. The table was stained a curiously glimmering gray around the box. I paused at a distance to study it only long enough to see if it was an immediate threat to us, but while the cables carried power and the object was enfolded in dark energy, it appeared to be inactive and certainly not alive.

We moved on toward the door at the far side of the room, which let us out into a corridor. Not far away I heard Quinton—or someone who sounded very much like him—arguing with someone who wasn't answering back. "You don't understand this. I thought you did, but you just don't get it, and you can't have it both ways."

Down the hall, light lay on the floor and crawled up the wall across from it. The voice had to be that way, and I assumed Purlis would be the person Quinton was talking to—if it was Quinton talking. I glanced at Carlos.

He nodded toward the light. "Inman is also beyond that doorway."

I just nodded in reply and began moving forward again as quietly as possible. An ache in my chest and a cold feeling lying along my spine told me all was not well with Quinton. My anxiety was growing, pressing on my heart and lungs and sending cold thorns into my skin.

I looked at the floor and the wall opposite the open door, searching for shadows that might give me some idea what was happening inside the room, but nothing was revealed. I forced myself to breathe slowly and let myself drop toward the grid—it wasn't ideal, but at least I'd have some idea how many animate things were in there, if not what they were.

The walls were stubbornly misty even deep into the Grey, as if someone had managed to obscure it from my particular brand of prying. I could make out three or four cylindrical skeins of colored energy—one of which seemed to exist, fade, and then surge slowly back toward existence again as I watched—but nothing more. There weren't any temporaclines here that I could use to slide into the room as a fragment of history and step back out of, so I had no choice but to go through the doorway like a normal human. Carlos wasn't able to discorporate, so far as I knew, so it looked like we'd just have to storm the door.

I eased to a more normal state, looking back at Carlos, but he wasn't looking at me; he was squeezing his eyes shut as if in pain and murmuring under his breath. I put my free hand out toward him, not wanting to risk speaking to get his attention so close to the open doorway.

As my fingertips grazed his shoulder, Carlos snapped his eyes open and grasped my hand in a cold steel grip. Fury blazed in his expression and I winced under the onslaught of his glance and the pain he was inflicting on my hand. He clenched his teeth and glared at me for a moment, as if he could communicate his angry thoughts by will alone. I flinched and crumpled a little, trying not to collapse completely and swallowing my desire to scream.

The voice spoke again. "You've forgotten all sense of service. You've become a thoughtless, selfish little bastard."

Carlos let go of my hand at the sound and I turned back toward the doorway, trying not to nurse my bruises as I crept forward again. It sounded much the same, but I knew that wasn't Quinton's voice.

"Thank you," my love said. "I'd much rather be a bastard than be your son. I think it shows considerable good taste on my mother's part, if it's true. I only hope my sister's a bastard, too, because having you for a grandfather—"

Something screeched and I heard a curse and a heavy thump. A large, dull-edged pain wrenched through my chest. I caught my breath and ignored it.

"Go," I whispered and bolted through the door.

TWENTY-ONE

I cut through the doorway as low as I could and turned sharply, heading for where I'd seen the two stable energy shapes. They had to be Quinton and his father. Carlos flew past me, heading for the strangely surging energy I'd observed in the Grey—by his interest, I guessed that was Inman. I had no worries for Carlos.

Purlis was standing between a dentist's chair and a sort of workbench with what looked like an old-fashioned ham radio sitting on it—lots of dials, lights, meters, and switches—the only thing missing was the microphone and speaker. He had his back to me so he could face the chair. Quinton was in the chair, held fast with an arrangement of straps that looked distinctly unsavory.

Purlis was already turning toward the sound of my running footsteps, reaching for a gun that lay on the workbench. Quinton looked startled and relieved to see me, but he didn't say anything, biting his lip as a dozen clashing colors flashed through his aura and sent sparks into the Grey. I heard something humming, buzzing in my chest and ears, and I wasn't sure if it was real, or Grey, or just the racket of my own pulse.

I wasn't as close as I wanted to be, but I slid to a halt just before Purlis completed his turn and I squeezed the cocking lever on the HK so it made its distinctive clacking sound. "Drop the gun," I said. I wasn't sure if my voice was shaking or if it was just the shuddering of my blood in my ears.

Purlis stiffened, probably wondering if he was a faster, more accurate shot than I was. I adjusted my aim a little to the side and down and shot the big metal box of electronics. It made a howling sound as it collapsed in a smoking pile on the bench. Dark liquid ran out of the box and dribbled to the floor.

In the large concrete room, the concussion rang like a bell and my ears throbbed. I hoped I didn't have to fire again—I would have hated to be more deaf than I was at that second—but I remained steady, returning my aim to the center of Purlis's chest as he faced me. "Now," I said.

He knew the shot would have temporarily messed up my ears, but he was in the same condition. Only Carlos and Inman could have ignored the shattering sound in this enclosed space. But I was already in position and Purlis wasn't. I truly wanted to shoot him and from the look on his face, he knew it. He opened his hands and let the gun fall onto the workbench—I could barely hear the clatter. He was betting I wouldn't shoot an unarmed man in cold blood, which was frustratingly true.

I was dimly aware that the howling from the box hadn't ceased and I wondered where Carlos and Inman were, but I didn't dare look around and give Purlis an opening to move on me. "Walk toward me, *Dad*," I told him. "Slowly. Hands where I can see them."

He took a step, letting one hand fall a little and turning his head toward the other, attempting to misdirect my attention.

"Don't be a jackass," I warned him.

"A bigger jackass," Quinton muttered.

Nettled, Purlis shot a glance over his shoulder at him. "J.J. . . ."

Quinton's face lost all expression. "Shut. Up."

A black blur sped across the room from my left and struck Purlis's chest, knocking him sideways and into the wall on my right with a crunching sound. Purlis shouted as he disappeared from my field of view.

Carlos seemed to just appear a few feet from Quinton, glaring toward the place where Purlis had fallen. "Stop," he said, his voice shivering with command.

The thing that had hit Purlis rose and stood still. I couldn't say I recognized the face, since I hadn't really seen him when he'd attacked me in Post Alley, but I assumed it was Inman. The demi-vampire was bone-thin, wearing only a pair of black sweatpants that barely stayed on his skeletal hips. His hair was an unnatural dull slate color. He quivered as he watched Purlis with hunger and fury in his eyes.

"Stand up, Mr. Purlis," Carlos said.

For a moment, Purlis resisted, glaring defiantly at him, but either he was smarter than he seemed or Carlos was pushing him magically, and he got to his feet. Inman shook and made a chattering noise with his teeth, staring at Purlis. I figured the vampires had that situation in hand, so I dashed to the chair and set Quinton loose.

As he stood up, Quinton put his arms around my waist a bit unsteadily and kissed my left cheek. I appreciated his not obstructing my view—or line of fire—to his father. He whispered into my ear, "Thanks, sweetheart. I'd be pissed you came down here if I wasn't so damned relieved to see you."

"You can berate me later."

I glanced around the room, hoping I hadn't overlooked something I was going to regret soon, but aside from a lot of bizarre equipment, there wasn't much to be seen but a few tables with tools and parts and one with a laptop computer sitting on it. There was a bundle of cables from the wall to the wrecked box and another set of cables from that to a gurney contraption in the middle of the room. I assumed that was where Inman had been until Carlos had freed him. It looked as if the table could be swapped for the chair Quinton had been in. I didn't like the implication of that.

The howling from the broken box had finally ceased and though my hearing was still a bit dulled, I could make out Inman's chattering. I pivoted to look at the rest of the group, turning my back on the wretched gurney and the workbench.

Carlos had placed one hand on Inman's chest, but he was looking at Purlis, who was giving back a poisonous glare.

"You seem to have some difficulty with the rights of others," Carlos said, unfazed.

"Your kind don't have any rights," Purlis hissed back. "You're not humans. You're monsters."

"I was thinking more in terms of property rights. Inman is mine. You took something of mine from me. What should I take from you . . . ?" His gaze roved over the general vicinity, but settled back on Purlis in a moment. "Ah," he murmured, poking Purlis in the chest and then crooking his finger.

Purlis made a choking sound and rose up on his toes as Carlos pulled his hand slowly back. I could see a thin yellow filament of energy drawing out of the man's chest.

"Carlos, no," I said.

He snarled, then rolled his eyes and looked back at me. Our gazes met and for a moment I felt the pressure of his anger and his desire for revenge burning like acid. I didn't back down, but kept my stare on him, disapproving and adamant. He uncrooked his hand.

Inman made a sudden lunge at Purlis while Carlos and I were distracted. Purlis dodged and ducked, snatching something off the floor and ramming it into Inman's chest. The dhampir fell backward, making a gagging, gurgling sound, his hands scrabbling at the steel rod protruding front and back from his ribs.

Carlos dropped to Inman's side while Quinton and I both spun and jumped to pursue Purlis. Purlis, crouched, was running for the door. I went for my gun. Quinton grabbed the bundle of cables and hauled back on it.

The cables sprang off the floor and snapped taut across Purlis's shins. He went down hard on his face and I heard his skull hit the concrete. His energy corona dimmed and he slumped against the floor, stunned or unconscious—I wasn't quite sure which—but certainly not dead. Quinton picked up his father's gun from the workbench and went to check on him while I moved toward Carlos and Inman.

I could hear Inman's wet, gargling cough even though I couldn't see him through Carlos. Demi-vampires aren't as dead as the real thing, so he still needed to breathe, but the rod through his chest wasn't making that easy. I stepped around to where I could see and—if needed—lend a hand. Carlos brushed me aside and put both his hands flat on Inman's damaged rib cage, muttering. The slow blood that welled up around the steel rod crawled across Inman's skin and disappeared under Carlos's hands, but the dhampir didn't seem to be recovering.

"The box . . . box," Inman gurgled. "Feeding . . . Limos."

Carlos seemed shaken and he stopped short in what he was doing, shooting me a glance. Inman's energy corona began fading faster the moment Carlos's attention wavered. The vampire pressed his hands back to the dhampir's chest.

Inman coughed red foam. "The *kostní . . . mágové . . .* move south . . . the bone . . . churches . . ." He put his own blood-coated hands over Carlos's and raised his eyes, going silent, staring at his master while more blood oozed out of him.

Carlos was stricken, a pain-filled expression flitting across his face and then vanishing again. "He's been wasted. I can't—I need more blood." He looked at me and the glance had none of the arrogance or command I expected of him.

It startled me, but I had to shake my head. "I can't. You know I can't."

His gaze darted toward Quinton and his father.

"No," I said, softly but without equivocation.

"Purlis," he suggested in desperation.

I shook my head firmly. "No. If you do that he'll always have a blood tie to Inman. You and Cameron can't risk it."

It was a moot point anyway: Inman was dead. Forever.

Carlos let his shoulders fall. He closed his eyes, head down over Inman's body. If I hadn't known better, I'd have thought he was praying, but I suspected it was something else. I could barely see a thin stream of energy rising from Inman and wafting toward Carlos's downturned face like smoke that the surviving vampire breathed in. It almost seemed he was somehow absorbing Inman's spirit—if a dhampir has a spirit.

Whatever thing, whatever knowledge it was that he received as

Inman passed out of the world, it made Carlos furious. He came back up to his feet in a rage, roaring and rushing across the room toward Quinton and Purlis.

Quinton spun on the balls of his feet, still crouching, braced, and raised the gun. "No! If anyone's going to kill this stupid bastard, it'll be me. You back the hell off, Carlos." I had never seen him look so cold-blooded.

"You don't understand, boy!" Carlos shouted, but he didn't advance any farther. "This paltry man brought the hunger that threatens your home—Limos will devour whatever comes into her path and he placed thousands in her reach, which will only expand to hundreds of thousands, to millions. To bring her here, he planted seeds among the dead places of Europe and what he planted is bearing fruit. He brought starvation, disease, and death!"

"I know that!" Quinton spat back. "You think this little experiment tonight was the first one I've seen? My father believes that what he's doing is right—no matter the cost. He believes the United States ought to rule the world—he believes in a global hegemony with America on top and everyone else under our heel. And he thinks he can make it happen by letting the monsters loose—his carefully tailored monsters, first here, then in Europe. He does not care who gets killed or what gets destroyed along the way because he *believes* in what he's doing. Oh, I do understand."

I felt like I was watching a play and had missed part of the first act. I wasn't quite sure where Carlos had picked up the information he'd thrown out so angrily—from Inman somehow?—because he hadn't seemed to know it when we were wrestling with Limos and Hazzard in the CalAska Pub's back room. And I had known that Purlis believed the end justifies the means, but I hadn't imagined his end to be quite so grandiose. I didn't like being out of this loop.

Quinton and Carlos glared at each other for a moment until Carlos calmed down, but his calm was more frightening than his ire. "No. There is much more to it. What he has unwittingly set in motion will start in Europe, but it will spread. Fanatics who worship the bones . . . I have no time to teach you history!" he snapped. "He brought Limos here and he intended to take her back to Europe well fed after he had caused enough havoc. No doubt he thought a sudden plague of starvation and disease would make a case for whatever expansion of his project he's proposed to whoever holds his purse strings—call it some kind of bioterrorism out of the unstable parts of Eastern Europe and the Middle East and your government leaps to throw money on the fire. But your father can't have known who he was dealing with—he no doubt thought this cabal who told him of the shrine was nothing more than a pack of mad old men who guarded relics of power they didn't understand or dare to use. But they are far from toothless and their age is not infirmity. With power handed to them by Purlis himself, they would starve and burn Europe to scorched earth."

"Who are these men and how do you know this?" I asked.

"The *kostní mágové*—bone mages. I know them of old, in Portugal, when I still breathed. They are not the doddering fools dreaming of myths and magic that they appear to be now. They are ancient and steeped in darkness—I know what they are capable of. They had been stopped, bottled up and made impotent, but they will rise—are rising—because of what Purlis has already done."

I shook my head slightly. "I meant, how do you know what's happening, what Purlis is planning?"

Carlos pressed his hand to his forehead as if he were in pain.

"Inman. He showed me what he had plucked from Purlis's mind. What he knew, I know. That is why I wished him back in my hands. Inman's talent remained intact as he moved toward death—it is exceedingly rare. But it was also his weakness through which Purlis took him from me. Only when passing did he return to my mind. Now he is truly dead. And a fire that should have been ashes in Europe long ago is smoldering back to life. Because of him," he said, pointing at Quinton's father.

Carlos lunged toward Purlis again and it took both Quinton and me together to push him back. He wasn't trying too hard or we wouldn't have succeeded; I wasn't sure why he'd made such a feeble attempt when he could have easily bowled us over.

The commotion had roused Quinton's father and he struggled to his knees while we were busy shoving Carlos away.

Chest heaving, I stood close to the suddenly quiescent Carlos and Purlis, keeping both in my sight, but ready to jump back between them. "We'll take care of Limos," I told Carlos. "Here. Soon."

"It will not be enough," Carlos said in a low growl, watching over my shoulder.

Purlis scrambled to his feet and started running for the door.

"I'll take care of my father," Quinton said, turning, raising the gun. . . .

I don't know if he would have killed him—he looked cold enough and set upon it—but I didn't give him the chance. I swung at Quinton, knocking the gun barrel downward.

Not my best move: The bullet ricocheted and skipped off the floor, tearing through the back of Purlis's leg near the knee. It could just as well have gone through something fatal—or through someone more important.

Purlis crashed to the floor again, writhing and trying to crawl away. Quinton shook me off with a glare and darted toward him. Carlos started after them both but I grabbed him, anchoring myself down to the grid as hard and fast as I could, pulling the vampire with me toward the earth, toward the flow and rage of magic.

Carlos struggled a little and I thought I'd lose him, feeling my own energy draining quickly. Then he gave up and stepped away, turning his back. "Let him die, then." The voice was as much in my head as spoken.

I pulled myself back up from the Grey and glanced toward the door. Quinton was kneeling beside his father and I could hear the conversation between them as bowing and plucking on the strings of the Grey, because my natural hearing was nothing but buzz and whine.

"You shot me."

"I missed. I was aiming for your head."

"I'm your father. You owe me your existence, if not your loyalty."

"I gave you that. You pissed on it. I'm not giving you anything else. Except your life. For now."

Quinton ripped strips off his father's shirt and wrapped one above the gushing wound in Purlis's left leg. He picked something up off the floor and used it as a stick to tighten the tourniquet, which he tied down with another strip of the shirt.

Quinton glared down at him. "There. Now we're even."

"You wouldn't leave me here. . . ."

Quinton gave him a hard stare. "What else *should* I do with you? I can't imprison you—though I wish I could, for humanity's sake, I have no way to do it and it wouldn't do any good to turn you over to the police when there's no charge that will ever stick to you. And I'm not going to kill you and bring the wrath of your agency down on my head. No, you get to stay here until someone comes to find you and I can get well ahead."

"If you leave me here alone, I could die."

Quinton scoffed at the weak bid for sympathy. "You wouldn't die. Your underlings will come back soon enough to find you and save your rotten life. I'll even raise your odds. I'll carry you to the stairs. Which is more than you deserve or would have done for me."

"Son—"

Quinton stood up and away from him. "Call me that one more time and I'll kick you so hard, they'll have to look for your head in Japan. You gave up the right to call me your son. You almost fed me to that thing in the box—Limos or whatever it's called. You believe you're a patriot and the end justifies the means. Well, justify this: I'll see you in Europe, where you won't be threatening my friends, or I'll see you in hell. You choose."

Whatever he saw in his father's eyes convinced him of something and he stooped, picked the older man up, and carried him out of sight.

I turned back to look at Carlos, who had gone so still and quiet I was afraid he'd slipped away.

"We will find Limos," he said. "Her shrine must be here. . . ."

"My head's still reeling. How can she be here if she was with us earlier? And you said she's a goddess of hunger, but a few minutes ago you said something about disease . . . ?"

"She is the goddess of famine. She brings the blight, the failure of crops, the drought, hunger everlasting. Death by starvation. Purlis brought her with him from Europe—I don't know where he found her—and he meant to take her back when he was done here. Somewhere among all these effects is her container, her shrine. She rides Hazzard, uses her ghost to her own ends. To Purlis's ends as long as they coincide."

I closed my eyes, thinking, remembering. . . . "Pandora's Box."

I opened my eyes, sure now. Carlos quirked an eyebrow at me, but said nothing.

"Quinton told me about it. He called it 'Pandora's Box'— something Purlis brought here from Europe. When Quinton found it, it had dirt from the tunnel project on it, which is how I connected it to the ghosts and the PVS patients. Remember Quinton said, 'You tried to feed me to that thing in the box'? He meant Limos's shrine. Well, I'll bet that's what's at the end of these cables."

We looked around the room we were in first, carefully skirting Inman's remains. I tried to follow the cables, but they ended in a coupling at the wall. Carlos followed me out and around to the previous chamber where we'd seen the body of the blue-green creature.

The box of skin and bone was still there, on its own table, surrounded by the glimmer of lives swallowed up in its folding doors. The cable ran to a plate—some kind of resonance emitter, I thought—on which the box stood. I slid the panels open and looked at the miniature shrine within and the glittering wreck of tiny figures, carved in bone and decorated with delicate gems and gold leaf, now all tossed about by the glut of suffering that had been pumped into the box through the device I'd shot in the other room.

"What do we do with it now?" I asked.

"We must entrap Limos in it and then destroy it. Otherwise she will be unbound, and while that will reduce her power, she still holds Hazzard and the tribute of souls. She would have no reason to stop her plans to ruin the Wheel, and every reason to go forward at once."

"Then that's what we'll do. How are we going to catch her?"

Carlos looked amused. "I suggest we lure her to us once again through the offices of your friend Mr. Stymak."

"Why can't you do it?"

"This will be much more complicated than our little chat with Hazzard and her mistress. You and I must be free to act, so others will have to occupy the séance circle. We'll need a circle of protection for them while you and I remain outside it to capture Limos and Hazzard."

"So . . . we need sitters—at this time unknown—to be bait for Hazzard and Limos and we need a medium who doesn't want to be associated with this for a séance we aren't actually going to be part of. Oh, that's going to be a piece of cake," I added in a sarcastic tone.

Carlos laughed—damn him. "I'll leave the arrangements to you on that score."

TWENTY-TWO

I hadn't liked handling the thing, but I took possession of the shrine of Limos. There really wasn't anything else to do. Carlos had refused it, saying he had only enough darkness left to deal with Inman's body, and I wasn't going to stick Quinton with it. In the end, Quinton found a place for it among his many hidden stashes around town where I could leave it for a few hours in the certainty that it would be undisturbed by anyone, including his father.

Daylight had begun to creep across the sky by the time I drove Quinton home with me, since he and I had also needed to clean a few things up before any of Purlis Senior's associates turned up for the day. I hadn't been sure he had any, but Quinton assured me his father had flunkies who would take care of most of the mess and probably squeal to a superior at their earliest convenience that the head of the project had been shot. There wasn't any sign of Purlis when we'd come up the stairs and at first I was worried, but Quinton had assured me his father was safely off to the University Medical Center—since it was the closest emergency room—having his leg attended to before it got worse. I wasn't sure how he'd gotten there and I didn't want to know, but I was pretty sure that Quinton wasn't lying about the hospital. He'd have needed help with the body if the wretched man had gone and died, and Carlos and I had been the only people around to ask, which he hadn't done.

"You don't seem worried he'll tell someone you're the one who shot him," I said as I drove carefully toward West Seattle.

"No. Dad wouldn't want it to get out. It wouldn't make him look good to say the 'top recruit' he'd been working to bring on board was his renegade son who turned on him. He won't tell the regular cops on me, either. Though if he did, I guess I could always go to them first, demand to see Solis, and get a sympathetic ear at the very least. No, Dad will keep his mouth shut, I'll clean up as much of the disaster as I must to keep from being connected to it, and then I'll have to find the rest of Ghost Division and take care of this problem in person."

"In Europe? But—" I started. Then I shut my mouth over my objection and kept on driving.

Quinton let it drop and he didn't say anything even while we were securing the shrine box.

I drove us home and he followed me up the stairs to the condo in silence. I wasn't angry. I just wasn't sure what to say or how to broach the subject that was weighing on my mind even more than the idea of a ghost and a god killing off a few hundred tourists so they could eat their souls. The booming silence of it hung between us and I tried to ignore it by doing normal, trivial things: I let the ferret out to romp while I undressed and got into the shower. Quinton followed me into the bathroom and leaned against the wall, playing desultorily with Chaos while the steam built up.

"I don't want to leave you," he said once he was completely obscured in clouds of vapor.

"But you're going to."

"I have to. What he's doing is terrible and I feel a little responsible—if I hadn't called on his help a couple of years ago, he wouldn't have known where I was or tumbled to what I knew about ghosts and magic and that sort of thing. I wouldn't have felt I owed him and he wouldn't have been able to screw with my life again. This is at least partly my fault and I know he won't fix it—he'll just try to use the current situation to his advantage. Maybe he'll spin the destruction of the lab as some kind of breakthrough or something. He's perfectly capable of it. And he'll have figured out who—and mostly what—Carlos is, so he'll also have realized you're not just a plain-Jane human being. I'm not sure if he saw anything but I think he already suspected you weren't exactly 'normal.' I need to keep him off you."

I stuck my head out of the shower and gave him a hard stare. "You are not my keeper and you aren't responsible for fending off your dad as a result of my own actions. I can take care of myself in that regard. Especially now that he might already know I'm a little more than an average PI and I won't have to pull my punches."

He walked forward, putting Chaos down on the floor. She danced around our feet as he leaned forward and kissed me softly. "Harper, I know you can look out for yourself, but I have to take care of the situation he's caused. It's my responsibility."

"Would you have shot him? I mean fatally?"

"I think I would have. And I guess I should say thank you for stopping me. That would have been a mistake. This way, he'll want to cover it up. Otherwise, his bosses would have come looking for me and I'd never have been free again. I am grateful. I love you. And not just because you came to my rescue like a knight in crumpled armor with your trusty vampire sidekick, either. I just . . . I just do."

I grinned at him. "Then why don't you get your clothes off and get in here?"

He looked shaggy and dirty, his clothes were stained with some things I didn't want to think about, and we were both at less than our best, but I couldn't think of anyone I would rather share a shower with. He glanced down at himself, back at me, and broke into a wicked grin.

He was pretty quick at getting out of his clothes, though dropping them on Chaos wound her up and we could hear her chuckling and dancing around in miniature ire as Quinton joined me under the stream of hot water. We stayed until the water got tepid and then fought our way past the furious ferret to roll into bed and make love until we were both too tired to try anymore. We even forgot to put Chaos back in her cage.

A brush of whiskers on my face woke me at noon. Quinton was already gone, but a note said he'd be back. I picked up the ferret and showed it to her.

"What do you think?" I asked. "Truth or lie?"

She sniffed the paper and snorted. Then she tried to eat it, leaving neat sets of puncture marks in the corner of the page until I took it from her. "I'll take that as a vote of confidence, since you didn't turn up your nose."

Talking to the ferret made me feel less alone, but it probably would have given most people the impression I was completely off my rocker. I put her down and got dressed, then took her out to the kitchen while I made some breakfast and thought about what I'd have to do next.

Carlos and I had determined that we needed another séance in order to capture Limos. The only practical bait would be the families of the patients, since they would attract the ghosts bound to Hazzard and through her to Limos. We'd have to use them to get the goddess to her shrine, then capture her in it and disperse whatever hold Hazzard had established over the ghosts. Once that was done, we'd have to get rid of Hazzard and hope that allowed the ghosts the freedom to rest and leave their unwilling hosts alone.

Not a very detailed plan. We would have to wing it a lot and I'd have to be the one to talk Stymak into trying one more time. I knew Lily Goss would join me in cajoling him, but I really needed someone representing each of the patients to make the circle work. Carlos and I would have to stand aside from the circle to do our work in the Grey once the ghosts and their hungry handlers were present. It wasn't going to be fun and it had to be tonight—before Purlis could make any efforts to get the shrine back or more harm could be done to Julianne, Sterling, and Delamar.

I started with a phone call to Lily Goss. She answered, sounding very harried, and I could hear Julianne's babbling in the background.

"Hello? What? I'm sorry, we're having a crisis, could you call back?"

"No. This is Harper Blaine. I've got a solution to the problem. I think. But it will require a séance with Richard Stymak."

"What? Séance? I'm not sure. . . ."

In the distance I heard Julianne scream, "Somil, somil! Throuf eeluge lew eth drag! Lew eth drag!" I couldn't figure out what she was saying on the fly and that frustrated me, but first I needed to concentrate on persuading her sister to do as I asked. If Julianne wanted me to get the message, she'd repeat it, I was sure.

I said, "I believe we can fix the whole problem, in one effort, tonight, if we can just do this. But I need you to persuade Stymak. He's afraid and I need him. I need you, too—I can't do this on my own."

"But Julie is so agitated. I'm afraid to leave her. She may hurt herself. . . . Her vital signs are very strange. She keeps saying—screaming—that phrase—'throuf eeluge lew eth drag'—over and over since yesterday morning."

"Did you write it down? Why didn't you call me?"

"I . . . I couldn't break free. She's been so bad, I felt I had to stay with her and do what I could for her. But she's getting worse and she started throwing things. . . ."

"I know about the throwing things part," I replied, touching my eyelid. It stung just a little and I thought of the eyedrops I'd been neglecting. The Grey connection may have been severed but the physical damage was still there. "Repeat that phrase for me? What Julianne is saying."

She stuttered, started, stopped, and finally got it out. "'Throuf eeluge lew eth drag.' Or that's what it sounds like. She's been screaming it and then she . . . passes out. When she wakes up, she starts again."

I wrote the phrase down and stared at it while Julianne continued to raise a ruckus in the background.

"Oh, please . . . Julie, sweetie . . ." Lily said, turning aside from the phone for a moment. "Please calm down. I'm trying to help. . . ."

I puzzled at the words. I knew they were backward but knowing and translating aren't instantaneous. "'Throuf . . . fourth . . . eeluge . . . july . . . lew . . . well' . . . no, 'Wheel . . . eth' . . . that's got to be 'the' . . . 'drag . . . gard' . . . 'guard.'" I rewrote the phrase in proper order, just to be sure . . . Guard the Wheel July Fourth. "Oh shit . . . It's tonight."

Julianne fell silent.

"What?" Lily asked in the sudden quiet.

A surge of fear squeezed my heart and my ears sang with the pressure. "Please, Lily. Get Wrothen to sit with her—she's a dragon, but she's a good nurse. She'll take good care of Julianne and if things work out, you'll never need her help again after tomorrow."

"Tomorrow? You want to do this tomorrow?"

"No. Tonight. Please talk to Stymak. I'll call him, too, but he's going to say no to me at first. I need you to persuade him. We can do it at whatever time he wants, but it has to be tonight. Please, Lily."

She hesitated. "I—I'll call him. Tonight. All right, I'll call right away. Oh, dear God, I hope this works. Julianne's so weak when she isn't . . . doing things. I'm so scared."

"It will work. Call Stymak. Then go to church as soon as some relief comes. I want you to go and pray as sincerely as you know how. If God is going to say anything, now will be the time. Trust me." It certainly couldn't hurt to have a god on *our* side, if he was taking any. Lily believed, and I knew just what the power of a believer could do. Purlis's belief—as twisted as it was—had brought Limos here in a box. Maybe it could fight her, too. I wasn't a Christian, but I didn't think Lily's god would turn a cold shoulder to her for that. Even if there was no divine intervention, it would help Lily focus and that would help me. Yes, I'm that hard—I would use someone's religion to my own ends if I had to. I would have prayed myself, if I'd thought anyone was going to listen to me.

"I . . . I will. All right, I will. I'll talk to Richard. I'll be there."

"Thank you, Lily. Thank you. I'll see you there."

I didn't even know where "there" was yet, but I'd be there.

My next call was to the Sterling house, but I couldn't get through to Olivia. I would have to go there and see if I could catch her in person.

I tried the care center Jordan Delamar was in, but the staff told me Levi hadn't arrived yet. I'd have to make that visit in person, too. Damn it! I needed to get a lot coordinated in a very short time and people weren't taking my calls. At least I didn't have to worry about Papa Purlis at the moment, since he was probably still in the hospital for that leg wound and if not, I guessed that Quinton's continued absence was so he could keep an eye on his frustrating father and make sure he didn't come after me before he cut out for Europe and whatever he'd have already put in motion there. For a second I found myself hoping Purlis's wound wasn't as bad as it had looked. Then I forced my mind away from it—I couldn't spare sympathy for my almost-father-in-law right now. I suspected that he was much like the proverbial cat that always landed on its feet one way or another. I still didn't like him and I wished he were long gone without dragging Quinton along for the crash, but that was another thing I'd have to worry about later.

I tucked Chaos into her cage with fresh food and water—I wasn't sure when I'd be home and I didn't want her to breed too much of her namesake while I was gone. I checked and reloaded my gun and headed out the door.

I drove to the Sterling house first, thinking it was going to be harder to catch up to a high school kid on summer break than it would be to find Levi Westman. The neighborhood was busier than it had been before. I saw quite a few families loading ice chests and folding chairs into SUVs and minivans, and there was a surfeit of small humans dashing around on lawns and sidewalks.

As I walked up the driveway to the Sterling house with its tarped-over construction, someone in the street let off one of those annoyingly loud whistling fireworks. I turned around to find the culprit and discovered a smiling young man coming up the driveway behind me, flipping a Zippo lighter open and closed in his hand.

He was as blond as Olivia Sterling, but his face was plumper and less prematurely aged with worry. Which is not to say he wasn't slim; he had the slender, flexible look of an athlete and the confident stride to go with it.

"Hey there," he said as he closed with me. "You here for Olivia?"

I was startled, but played along. "Yeah. Is she in?"

"Yep. She's probably still trying to get out from under Mom's clucking like a hen, but she's ready to go. When are you going to bring her back?"

"Oh. Not too late."

"After the fireworks, though, right? I know Mom was trying to get her home earlier, but I think Ollie needs some more time out of this place, y'know? She's stuck here all the damned time taking care of Dad. So, you're good to go?"

"As soon as I see Olivia."

He gave me a thumbs-up much like Olivia had the first time I'd parted from her and headed for the door. "You wait here. I'll get her and send her out. Mom will be all over you if I don't and you guys will never get out of here."

I stood at the edge of the walkway to the front door, a little stunned and wound up with nerves as the young man went inside the house. In a few minutes, Olivia came trotting out with a backpack in one hand and a tote bag slung over her shoulder. She stopped short when she saw it was me and I watched the conflicting emotions storm over her—surprise, disappointment, excitement, worry. . . .

"Hey," she said. "What are you doing here?"

"I know you're expecting someone else, but I need to talk to you."

She closed the distance to me and bit her lip as she looked up into my face. "I'm sorry—I didn't have a chance to bring you more of Dad's notebooks. Mom hasn't let me out of her sight."

"How's your dad doing?"

"He's . . . well, not good. Really restless. It's been harsh and it makes my mom kind of crazy. She's been really wound up and I swear now she's not even eating—she looks like a skeleton. I'm worried about her. And don't say I need to watch my own weight—I know I'm too thin. I didn't used to be. . . ."

That was a detail I'd let slip my mind again until she mentioned it: All the patients and their caregivers were dangerously skinny. They were all starving, like Hazzard's victims. Even the ones who ate regularly were being drained by the proximity to Limos. That situation would only worsen and spread if Limos and Hazzard were successful. "It's not your fault, Olivia, but I think it's one of the side effects of what's happening to your dad. And that's one of the reasons we need to stop it as soon as we can."

"I'm trying. I kind of feel guilty that I'm going out. . . . My brothers, Peter and Darryl, are here, though, so they're going to hang with her and Dad for a while. Let me, y'know, get some sun." She lit up suddenly. "Hey! I could get one of those notebooks for you now! Peter could help me. That's my big brother, who you met just now—he's totally cool."

The sudden flip in her attitude was something I'd seen before when people try to deny the horror of a situation they can't seem to get out of. I put out my hand to stop her from turning and running back into the house. "I didn't come about the notebooks. I figured it out. What I need is for you to come to a séance tonight. I don't know the time and place yet, but if you can come, I think we can fix this problem. For good."

"Tonight?" She looked stricken. "But . . . it's the Fourth of July! I practically had to sell my soul to get out of the house. Mom's going to freak. . . ."

I felt a stab of panic as I thought of what an excellent opportunity Independence Day offered to Hazzard and Limos, with the hundreds or even thousands of people who would be all over the waterfront to hang out at the park, eat junk food, ride the carousel on Pier 57, and watch the fireworks display over Elliott Bay. No doubt there would be a long line to get on the Great Wheel and see at least a few minutes of the display from the unobstructed height, through the Wheel's swinging glass gondolas. I swallowed my swelling fear before it could infect Olivia and said, "Don't tell her. Do you have a cell phone?"

She rolled her eyes. "Yeah." She gave the word two syllables, somehow.

"Give me the number and I'll call you when I have the details. It'll be later, maybe after the fireworks. But this is important and I'm sorry it's messing up your plans—you need to come when I say. This is the key to everything."

She sighed, her jaw muscles bunching as she fought her fear and disappointment. Then she rolled her eyes and sighed again, settling. "All right. For my dad. But this has to work. Please say it's going to work. . . ." Tears lined the bottom of her eyelids, swelling on the pale fringe of her lashes.

I wasn't sure—I never am—but I lied for her. "It will. With your help."

She bit her lip and then launched a hug-tackle at my midsection. "We're going to save him. Thank you! You're the best!" Then she backed off self-consciously. "Oh. I'm sorry. That was, like, really overboard, wasn't it? Oh, God . . ."

I gave her what I hoped was a reassuring smile. "It's just fine. You're fine. It'll all be good. Now—phone number?"

She was startled, then she gave a nervous laugh and dug a card out of her tote bag. It was a tiny slip of heavy, plasticized paper with her name and phone number on one side and a close-up black-and-white photo of a ragged toe shoe on the other. I DANCE, THEREFORE I AM was printed in white script over the shoe. She handed it to me. "There. That's the number."

I looked the card over with a curious frown.

"I had them made when I thought I was going to be doing a lot of auditions and stuff," Olivia explained, blushing with a touch of embarrassment. "Kind of silly, huh?"

"No," I said. "I've just never seen such a small card before—we didn't do these in my day."

She shrugged and looked uncomfortable. "Umm . . . well, any-way . . . It's going to be really loud out on the pier, so you maybe better text me as early as you can, to be sure I get the message in time."

"The pier? Are you going out to the waterfront?"

"Yeah, to the park with a couple of the girls and one of the in-structors from the ballet studio. Mom wouldn't let me go without 'a responsible adult' to watch us. But it's really just Delphia's mom and she's cool."

Now this was a quandary: I didn't want to frighten her or her friends, but I also didn't want to ignore the danger if things didn't go as I thought they would—I didn't know what time Hazzard and Limos would move their ghosts toward the Wheel. I bit my lip for a second and Olivia noticed my hesitation.

"Yeah? Something wrong?"

"No. But there could be a problem with the Great Wheel tonight. Were your friends planning on riding it?"

"I don't know. Delphia's scared of heights, but that doesn't mean the rest wouldn't want to go up. If the line's not, like, horrendous. Do you know something . . . ? Is it bad?" She looked scared now.

I wanted to tell her the truth and I wanted to lie, too. I wanted her to be safe—which she might not be with or without me. "I don't know," I said.

She studied my face for a moment or two, then she nodded. "If they really, really want to go, I don't think I can stop them, but I'll get them to go early, not later, if that makes a difference."

"It could," I said, thinking an attack on the Wheel would be more likely later, when the crowds were thickest.

"Then that's what we'll do. And I'll come whenever you tell me to—unless I need a ride. Then it might take a while."

"I can pick you up if you're OK with that."

She shrugged. "Hey, I'm already going out ghostbusting, so I guess I'm pretty good with all kinds of crazy stuff. Don't tell my mom, though. She will freak."

I laughed a little. "Believe me, I won't tell her."

She glanced around me and grinned. "There's Delphia! I'm gone! See you later!"

And she darted off before anything could change, embracing the momentary freedom, running from home as much as toward her friend. I had to swallow hard to keep on breathing normally as I watched her go. I hoped with every fiber of my being that I wasn't lying, that it would all be OK.

I trudged back to my truck and headed for the care home where Delamar was. I hoped talking to Levi wouldn't leave me in knots like this. I hadn't thought that Lily would be the easy one. Even convincing Stymak to try again had to be less uncomfortable than telling half lies to Olivia Sterling.

I drove back into central Seattle and parked a few blocks from the hospital so I could walk for a while outdoors in the patchwork sunshine. The weather was typical for Seattle—neither hot nor cold, with clouds that rolled over the sun and then cleared away again after dropping a smattering of rain. It was such a common phenomenon here that the weathermen had a name for it: sun breaks. I was wearing a light jacket and didn't mind the sun's game of hide-and-seek; my confidence was suddenly staggering and even with time seeming to fly away from me, I felt the need to be in the normal world with all its mess and inconvenience for just a while longer before I plunged back into the darkness of the situation and faced the séance and everything that went with it. A misty drizzle came down for a minute or so, then dissipated in sudden steam as a hole broke in the cloud cover and the sun stuck a beam of light through to warm the sidewalk.

I sat on a cement bench beside a little triangle of lawn and closed my eyes for a moment, feeling the sun warm me. It was three o'clock on Independence Day but I didn't feel particularly celebratory or patriotic. I especially felt no connection to James Purlis's idea of patriotism, which had moved him to do horrible things not for his country's sake but for the government and some twisted idea about worldly power. Surely that wasn't what "love of country" was supposed to be?

If some act is wrong it is simply wrong, no matter who tells you to do it or for what grand motive. It seemed to me that a true patriot and decent human being rejects doing wrong and puts the ideals on which the country is founded ahead of the directives of government bureaucrats. If the government is off the rails, you don't keep on riding the train to destruction—you certainly don't push it there on your own; you start hauling the other way as hard as you can. That was what Quinton was doing, quietly and without any help or recognition, trying to pull things back toward that delicate state of balance. It was a strange and huge undertaking, but whether I approved of his Don Quixote way of going at it or not, I had to let him do it. Where would I be if Purlis's ideas won? Branded a monster—a nonhuman with no rights—and put in a cage to be experimented on? That flew in the face of what I'd always taken for granted here—all that high-flown Founding Fathers business about people being inherently free and self-determined, endowed with rights just because they *were* human. I shuddered, imagining the alternative—the end result of what Purlis would do, starting first in Europe and then back here.

As loony as it sounded, it meant I had to do a Don Quixote act myself and dismantle this conspiracy of ghosts. I turned my mind to that, trying not to dwell on my own bizarre and complicated family problems instead of the more immediate situation. I only hoped Hazzard and Limos would hold off tonight until Carlos was available. I thought it was likely that they would, since the ghosts would be exhausted from their exertions the previous night and, although

Limos and Hazzard were also drawing strength through the rest of the patients' families, their energy would be low for a while after their last effort. If they were going to have the strength to do something drastic to the Great Wheel, it would probably be after dark, but I didn't know how long after sunset they would come.

And I still needed to talk to Levi Westman.

I got up and walked on, banishing the sense that I was taking on more than I could manage. I probably was, but I didn't feel there was an alternative to trying. And I didn't have time to formulate a better plan. I'd just have to make the one I had work.

I walked into the building and had no trouble getting up to Jordan Delamar's room. It was a holiday, so I wasn't surprised to find Westman sitting next to Delamar's bed once again. He had the television on, but wasn't paying any attention to it. Instead, he was bending over to study Delamar's arm.

"Hello," I said from the doorway.

Westman jerked upright and turned around, eyes wide. He relaxed when he saw me. "Oh. It's you."

"Yeah, just me. How's Jordy today?"

He shook his head, looking worried. "I'm not sure. He's restless and the . . . rash is pretty bad today." He motioned me in and pointed at the welts on Delamar's arm. "What is that?" he whispered.

I looked at the angry red lines that ran from the edge of the pajama sleeve Westman had pushed up to the shoulder all the way into Delamar's palm where a Ferris wheel had been scribed. Along the arm what looked like clouds boiled and rushed toward the wheel. The coils of the clouds looked disturbingly like anguished faces. Westman lifted the other sleeve to reveal another picture—this one stylized waves with tumbling tops that looked uncomfortably like teeth also facing toward the palm. There was the number ten in this palm. If he had cradled his hands together, the clouds and water would have been converging on the tiny wheel at ten. I didn't need to be very clever to figure that one out.

My expression clearly revealed my dismay. Westman stared at me as if on the verge of tears. "What is it?"

Here was another of those times I debated whether I should lie, but as I needed his help, I thought it would be better not to. "I . . . it's a sort of warning."

"About what? Is something going to happen to Jordy?"

"Something is going to happen to a lot of people, including Jordy," I said. From what Carlos had said about the effect of being forced out of their bodies, I knew there had already been damage done to the living souls of Delamar, Sterling, and Goss. I doubted that they would be able to just slip back into place while the ghosts were busy doing the bidding of Hazzard and Limos. They might even be dragged along and destroyed by the psychic carnage that would reign over the Great Wheel if I couldn't stop this horrifying plan.

My fears surely showed on my face. Westman looked panicked as he said, "Why? Why Jordy?"

"It's not because he's Jordy; it's because he's been . . . occupied by ghosts. And the ghosts are tied to this event. If it goes off as someone plans, a lot of people will die, and the ghosts will be burned up like fuel."

"Jordy's not dead. He's not a ghost."

I was relieved that he seemed to have no problem with the concept of ghosts and possession, but it was a lot to swallow anyhow, and the news didn't get better. "No, he's still here, but . . . without control of his body, he's not really anchored anymore and he may not be able to resist being taken along in this storm." I pointed at the clouds of faces. Then I looked at Westman. Did he believe me? It certainly sounded crazy.

He peered at me with narrowed eyes, his lips pursing and unpursing as he thought about what I'd said. But remarkably, he didn't reject it or me. "You're saying that this . . . this stuff that's been happening to Jordy is ghosts, trying to warn us about something. This event? Whatever it is."

I nodded, giving the smallest of mental pushes to incline him to believe what I was saying. It was cheating and I felt bad about it, but I needed his cooperation and understanding. Was that as bad as what Quinton's dad did? Not in degree but in kind? I wasn't sure, but I hoped it wasn't. I couldn't claim to have no agenda, but I did think mine was better than Purlis's.

"Crazy," Westman said. He sat down, shaking his head. "I'd say it couldn't be true, but I've sat here every day since . . . I don't even know when anymore, and watched this stuff happening, these words showing up on his skin, this restlessness, the helplessness . . . and I know he's begging for help, but I can't seem to give it to him. And you come along and say it's ghosts. And I don't even think that's impossible anymore. But how can I do this? How can I keep on sitting here and watching this when it's not even my Jordy there, reaching out?"

"But it is, in a way. It's not just because Jordan is injured, but because he allows them to come through him," I said. I didn't really know if this was true, but I hoped it was. "He may have had no choice originally, but I think he wants this to end as much as they do, so he lets them come. Look at how clear this is. This writing isn't even like it was a day or two ago—it's stronger and more fluid. We need to help him."

"What am I supposed to do? I've already done everything!" Westman said, his voice thick with frustration and mental anguish.

"I have a plan. It is going to sound totally nuts, but I believe it will work."

Westman gazed at me as if I'd promised him the earth and heaven, too. "What is it? What do I do?"

"You come to a séance tonight."

He pulled back from me, scowling. "Séance?"

"If there are ghosts, doesn't it make sense that a séance is the way to talk to them, to force them to let go of Jordan and change their plans?"

"I . . . I guess," he said with a conflicted shrug.

"This message on his arms," I said, carefully pointing to the whole stream of information leading to his two upturned palms, "appears to say that two forces will converge on this object at ten o'clock. That's my best guess and it fits with information I've had from other sources. This event could kill hundreds of people. And we can stop it if you will come and help me and the other families of these patients to talk to the ghosts. Please."

He seemed dazed and exhausted, blinking at me as if he didn't quite see me. "Family," he murmured. "I wish . . . we had a family. We're a family. This . . . this is killing me, to be cut off from him and from being together by such incomprehensible things, such wild insanity I can't conceive or contain." A tear escaped from his eye and rolled down his cheek. "You have me at your mercy. I can't fight anymore. I'll try anything. Tell me where to be and when and I'll be there."

I felt no elation, only hollow pain at his complete lack of resistance. The situation had broken him and anyone could have used him to their own ends at this point. I hated what I was doing to him and I had to do it. If it worked, maybe he'd get his lover back. I hoped that would be the case and despaired that it might not. And time felt so short, so very short. . . .

"It will be nine o'clock," I guessed, judging from the number in Delamar's left palm and giving us an hour to reach into the Grey and put a halt to this before the situation became too dire to stop. "I'll call you and tell you where in Seattle. Can you work with that?"

He nodded. "I'll do it."

I got his phone number and extracted his listless promise to answer when I called. He let me take photos of the message on Delamar's skin for reference. When I left, he was staring down at Delamar, slow tears falling down his face. He didn't even notice my departure.

TWENTY-THREE

Frustration and a dull-edged panic sawed at my nerves. Time seemed both too short and too long. I'd returned to the Land Rover and was sitting in the front seat, trying to think of where I could assemble this séance when Lily Goss called to say she'd persuaded Stymak to do it. He hadn't been pleased, but for her, he'd agreed. She was also working on the location, but had had no luck with such short notice for something that needed such a degree of privacy. She had already thought of her own place and rejected it for fear of injuring Julianne or upsetting Wrothen. I agreed that wouldn't do.

I thought that we'd want to be near the waterfront if possible and reluctantly suggested my office. The area would still be busy, but more of the crowd would gravitate to the docks once night fell. The fireworks were set to begin at ten—which would ensure that the Great Wheel was fully packed with tourists willing to pay for the best, if fleeting, view. I hoped it wouldn't begin with the wrong sort of bang.

And now things began to move fast—it all had to come together in less than five hours on a major holiday, within blocks of the waterfront and all those oblivious revelers—and what had seemed like a wasteland of empty time became an obstacle race. Lily and I arranged for her to get Stymak and his equipment to my office by eight. I made phone calls to Olivia and Westman, quick calls telling them where to be, when, and how to get there and trying to allay their fears. I rushed to rearrange my office, find more chairs, move my computer to a safer location, and make room for the shrine.

I left a message for Carlos, certain that he'd have no problem showing up on time, but still fearing he wouldn't, since the sun wouldn't be properly down until after nine. Then I paged Quinton and paced around in nervous anticipation until he finally called me back.

"Hey, gorgeous."

I tried not to sound like the ball of nerves that I was. "Hey, yourself. How's your dad?"

"Apparently he'll live. What's up at your end?"

"Oh, you know: Carlos and I get to hold an emergency meeting with the families this evening at my office. I'm there now rearranging things. I don't have room for the computer so I'm probably going to move it"—I paused, worried that Purlis's minions might be listening in—"to that other storage unit we visited, just to keep it from being smashed to hell and gone if anything goes awry."

"Sounds like a pain in the ass. Why your office?"

"I couldn't think of any other place close enough to the waterfront that we could secure on such short notice. Major holiday and all that jazz."

"Cameron couldn't have come up with something?"

I stopped. "I actually hadn't thought of that. But I'm not sure I'd want to do this in any space that was not really under my control, if you follow my thinking."

"Yeah, it's probably best to avoid the entanglements of other people's agendas."

"I'm thinking the same thing. Anyhow . . . no one's trying to kill me today, so this might be easier than I think."

Quinton laughed. "Don't be too sure. Do you think you can get any help from Solis with the waterfront problem?"

"No. The only thing I could ask would be that he shut down the Great Wheel, but unless there's a bomb threat, that's not going to fly. Not today. And one thing I won't do is call in a false report—that's just a little too much since I know I couldn't dodge it and I'd lose my license at best. Or end up in jail. And then how could I run away with you to Europe?"

He paused, his silence weighty in spite of my teasing tone. "Would you do that?"

"What? Call in the report anyway? No."

"I meant would you follow me to Europe?"

I scowled at the phone. "Follow? Hell no. I'd be right beside you all the way. You're—" I found myself without the right word. "Everything" seemed a bit heavy and "mine" too possessive, but both were true.

The silence hung there, stretching, until he said, "Yeah. I feel the same way about you."

My heart bumped around unevenly in my chest, knocking on my ribs and blundering into my throat.

"Do you want me there . . . tonight?" he asked.

I struggled with it, but I said, "Want and need aren't the same. I always want you with me. But tonight I think you need to be some-where else, don't you?"

He was quiet for a second, then said, "Following the family footsteps—at a discreet distance. But it's not what I *want*."

"I know."

"I love you," he said.

"I love you, too," I whispered back, the phone going silent as he dropped the connection.

I finished up at the office—I even dusted and swept up to make the evening a bit less of a sneezing fest. I'm not much of a house-keeper normally, so the pall of dust I'd raised by my rearrangements was significant and as hard to lay as a recalcitrant revenant. Also, I just needed to be *doing* something. Traffic was getting kind of crazy as more and more people flooded the area for the fireworks and other entertainments. I was lucky to have a parking space nearby, but it was still nerve-tearingly slow to move on the streets.

I wanted to scream at everyone I saw heading for the waterfront to go away, far away from the Great Wheel and everything close to it. I wanted to warn them but I knew it was futile and at best I'd get arrested, so I shut my mouth and ground my teeth. Finally I fetched Limos's shrine and tucked it into a corner of the cleaned office, near the door where I was most likely to be able to use it.

I stopped long enough to bolt down some food and noticed it was nearly eight already. I had to scamper back to my building to get there before Goss and Stymak arrived.

Stymak glared at me when Lily brought him upstairs. "This is all your idea, isn't it?" he said.

"Not entirely, but I think once I explain it you'll agree that it's necessary and you're the only medium I can trust to do it right."

I waved him and Goss to the client chairs and stuffed down my own impatience and nerves. I didn't want to frighten them with some of the more gruesome and specific details of what might happen, so I kept my instructions and descriptions deceptively bland as I told them what we needed to do and why and what part I—and Carlos—would play. Stymak wasn't much mollified.

"I don't like your friend. He has a very ugly vibe."

"I'm aware of that and I'm sorry, but you won't have to touch him. He won't even be in the circle. He's mostly helping me with what I need to do. The only people you'll have actual contact with are Lily here, and the representatives of the other two patients. They'll be here about nine, so we need to get any setup done before then so we can get to work as soon as they arrive."

"It's not that easy with . . . civilians," Stymak said, giving Lily a contrite glance.

She shrugged it off. "You mean nonpsychics? We're not as useless as you think."

"I don't mean that. I just mean it's not easy to get into the right state of mind if you haven't practiced. And this is going to require a very clear initial state or we might not get anywhere—or not fast enough to . . . do what Harper wants to do."

Goss made a face at Stymak. "I know how to clear my mind to listen to God. I think the others will know what that's like by now, since we've all had to live with this . . . stress. I think you're underestimating our willingness and ability, Richard."

Stymak nibbled his lower lip. "I don't know. . . ."

She put her hand over his. "Trust, Richard. That's the first thing God asks of us. That's the only thing you need to do." She smiled at him. "It'll be fine." She kept his gaze in hers for a moment longer, still smiling gently. I guess she saw what she wanted eventually, because her smile broadened and she patted his hand. Then she stood up. "Then let's get to it."

I thought I had just caught a glimpse of what Lillian Goss had been like before her sister's illness, before she became thin and nervous and somewhat lost.

Stymak apparently couldn't ignore her charm. He got up, too, said, "OK," and looked around. "I don't think we can work with the desk, but maybe the typing table, if that's all right with you, Harper. We'll have to move the desk and other stuff aside."

I was tired and I found it ironic that I'd already moved it all, but I had no real issue with moving the furniture yet again. We quickly rearranged the room to Stymak's satisfaction, although we had to bring in one more folding chair and put my work chair out in the truck—we didn't want anyone to end up sliding out of the circle if the chair rolled under the pressure of ghosts.

I returned from locking up the chair and met a nervous Levi Westman in the lobby. He looked almost ready to bolt until I put my hand on his shoulder like a friend I was pleased to see and said hello, leading him up the stairs to my office.

"Are you all right?" I asked as we went up.

"Fine. No. Scared. Worried. I'm not fine, but I'm not . . . not-fine, if you know what I mean."

"It'll be OK," I said, opening the door to my office.

When he saw Lily looking solid and calm and Stymak looking slightly nerdy and very unthreatening, he relaxed, the color flooding up higher in his aura, which had closed so tight to his body I'd barely been able to see it.

They were standing and chatting quietly, comparing horror stories of what their loved ones had undergone, when Olivia clattered up the stairs.

She was limping a bit and I could tell her foot hurt, but she looked windblown and red-cheeked—happy and livelier than I'd seen her before. Her quick smile convinced me I wasn't doing the dumbest thing in the world—not if it freed her to wear that look of hope and happiness afterward.

Now we just needed Carlos. . . .

I don't know why vampires don't or can't go out in daylight—I've never asked and I've never discovered the answer on my own, but I've never known a full vampire to be active before sundown or after sunrise. Yet, the sky was only barely black when Carlos arrived and I wondered if I'd just gotten lucky and he'd been sleeping nearby or if he had some strange magical way of moving that I didn't know about. The rest of the group didn't seem bothered by his sudden, silent appearance, but Stymak recoiled and made sure he was as far from the vampire as possible. The rest stared and seemed to sway toward him—pulled by the sexual charm that vampires exude to cover their aura of death.

I turned my head and made a disapproving face at him. He returned the barest smile and seemed to dial down the reach and intensity of his glamour.

I hesitated for a moment about introducing him. Names are powerful things, but in this case I wasn't sure if it was better to have the extra energy or the extra protection. Carlos took the decision for himself and inclined his head slightly, almost like a bow, saying, "I'm Carlos. I'll remain outside the circle with Blaine. We should begin, now that we're all here, yes?" he added, glancing at Stymak, but keeping the contact short.

Stymak nodded, shaking with nerves, and started directing the other three to sit so the small typing table was in the center of their circle, though it barely had room for his equipment.

"We'll have to hold hands around the table, but it's OK if your hands are resting on the chair arms instead—this tabletop's kind of small," Stymak explained. He glanced at me. "The electric lamp died. . . . Are you OK with a candle? Otherwise we'll have to do this in total darkness."

"A candle's fine," I said. I supposed it was possible the typing desk could be set aflame, but I'd live with the risk. One candle was unlikely to catch the whole building on fire even at the worst and the small flame would help the rest of them focus.

He set a squat white candle in the middle of the table and lit the wick. When he was satisfied that it was properly alight, he asked me to turn off the lights, leaving the area illuminated only by the candle's flame and the pale diffusion of distant neon through my window. The scent of vanilla drifted into the room. I felt a weak charge in the air and glanced sideways into the Grey, noting a thin, soft mist rising from the floor near where Carlos stood and spreading quietly, mingling a slight flower smell, like fields of chamomile in the sun, with the candle's sweet smoke. Without any direction to do so, the four people seated at the table fell silent, no longer wiggling in their chairs or shuffling their feet as their breathing slowed and they stared into the tiny flame of the candle. I caught myself smiling at Carlos's subtle aid in spite of the precarious situation. He'd never bothered with such charms when working strictly with me, but I supposed he never felt the need.

They began, again, with a prayer and no one objected, letting the final "amen" fade into the dark as they settled themselves to the task at hand. At first, Stymak just sat still, letting the silence pool and deepen, but as I inched closer to the Grey, keeping watch on both worlds, I noticed that he, too, was adding energy to the room, his cloudy white aura expanding as before, white light seeking outward, while the misty element curved around the room's perimeters, creating a bubble around the séance. All the living people in the room but me appeared enclosed in gossamer webs of color that knitted into one another and wove with the white mist of Stymak's energy. A few illegal fireworks went off outside, making the calm surface of the enchanted sphere shiver, but it didn't break. In the distance of the Grey I heard the rattle of the Guardian Beast, prowling the edges of the world between worlds, but keeping its distance, as it had since the beginning. I wondered for a moment if it would close in if things became dire, but the thought was chased away as Stymak began to speak, his voice low this time but strumming on the threads of the Grey.

"We call on the presence of our loved ones who are lost, but not passed beyond, on the spirits that have come to us through them. We call on you to attend and help us restore order and peace. We call on those who have gathered these spirits against their will. We call on you, Linda Hazzard, and upon the hunger you have brought. We call you to come to us, to bend to our will. Come to our circle."

The floor buzzed and the vibration grew, the walls singing with a tumult of ghosts. The air around the circle grew brighter and thicker, filling with faces of shadow and mist. Among the host, three were brighter and more colorful than the rest, though one flickered and fought to stay alight—the living souls of the three patients. In the rising sound I heard sighing and sobbing, and the howl of a wolf closing in, stalking toward us.

In the Grey distance I could see it coming, loping nearer on its skeletal legs, jaws agape and full of sharp teeth, the shape of Linda Hazzard dragged with it like a cloak trailing across dirty snow. With a roar, it leapt over the edges of the circle, tearing a hole in the protective dome, and the ghosts around the circle cried out.

The four people at the table gasped in unison, shuddering as the wolf landed on the table, raveling upward into the cloaking form of Linda Hazzard, her face as sharp as ice shards pulled from the mist of the Grey. At the edge of my vision I could see the red-hearted darkness that was Carlos reach out and tangle its own slim thread, unnoticed, around the trailing gleam of Hazzard and Limos where they had broken through the circle.

"Why do you call me here again, pest?" the ghost of Linda Hazzard demanded as the slavering jaws of the Limos wolf moved under the mist-skin of her discorporate face.

"We ask you to release the souls of our loved ones to return to their fleshly homes," Stymak said, his voice still soft, but not pleading.

The ghost and its dread mistress laughed, letting out a howl and the chatter of teeth. "After tonight we shall have no further use for them."

"But we do and we will not allow you to use them. Release them now, as we speak."

"Paltry man, I have no use for you and your petty demands. You cannot hold me and I have much to do."

The combined shapes of Hazzard and Limos turned to go back through the hole by which they had entered, but as the creature leapt up, the scent of chamomile shifted to the smell of burning hair and the void slammed shut with a grille of gleaming blackness. The wolf-thing continued through, striking sparks from the contact as if Carlos's magic tore into its energy, but the ghost of Linda Hazzard remained imprisoned in the bright bubble of Stymak's talent.

"No!" Hazzard shrieked as the two entities separated with a short spark of energy arcing and then blinking out between them.

The wolf form bounded away, snarling. The white light around the circle wavered, the colors of the sitters' auras separating and flushing with panicked shades of yellow and green as the ghosts around them suddenly wrenched sideways and began flowing after Limos as if drawn with her like a ribbon through a keyhole.

Carlos pushed harder on the black energy reinforcing the enclosure of light. "Hold hard," he muttered. "Don't let her escape." He turned his head toward me—a blackness denser than the rest—and said, "I hold dominion over the dead, but not gods. Pursue Limos." Only Hazzard and the three bright flames of the living souls remained in the circle.

"Stymak, keep that ghost here!" I shouted, snatching up the shrine and turning to fling open my office door.

Stymak was pale and the candle on the table was flaring upward impossibly high, nearly scorching the ceiling as the wax sputtered and flowed like water. He wouldn't have long to hold Hazzard and his knuckles had gone white as he clutched the hands of Lily on one side and Olivia on the other.

"Hold them," he whispered to the circle. "Hold on to them and don't let them go."

I rushed toward the Grey to chase Limos as the colors of the circle struggled to close again, gathering around the three bright shapes that remained behind as the goddess of famine dashed away with the rest of the ghosts—her tribute—in her drooling jaws. Hazzard, trapped in the circle, dwindled to a thin spark, screaming for rescue.

I dove deeper in the Grey, clutching the shrine to my chest. It felt unusually solid, whereas most normal-world things became as hard to hold as smoke. The Limos wolf rushed toward the waterfront and the hot energy clouds of thousands of revelers, pushing her vanguard of ghosts in front of her now.

The wedge of spirits tore through the mist and light of Grey Seattle, shoving the brightness of living things aside like chaff before wind. The bright shapes fell and rolled and I could not pause to help them or even to confirm that they were people, bowled over by the ravenous force bearing down on the brilliant wheel of dangling soul fire over the blackness of cold water. I was falling behind, relying on my human speed in the Grey while she had no such limits. She was Hunger and moved like a prairie fire.

I concentrated on the Guardian Beast's distant rattle of spines and shouted to it, "Now would be the time, you useless collection of bones! Come and help me catch this bitch or I'll wash my hands of you and your stinking job forever." Not that I could but I'd certainly want to after this. Ugly as it was, I had to rely on the friends and family that I had and the Guardian Beast qualified as much as anything.

It had never answered me before, never come when I wanted or needed it, but this time it let out a roar like a train wreck and swept through the silver mist world toward me, a wave of force and power that pushed me forward faster than I could run.

We raced toward the Great Wheel, tumbling everything aside before us. . . .

A fireworks shell boomed and a rain of red and blue stars spread over the night sky. Another boom and pink planets ringed in green bands appeared in the air, followed by whistling that erupted into showers of gold. Music poured from distant speakers, eerie and thrilling.

I drew even with Limos, barely keeping upright in the eldritch wind, and snatched at the thin coil of silver that bound the ghosts to her. She growled and snapped at me, cutting a gouge in my left forearm.

I gasped in shock, unprepared to be bitten by a spectral wolf.

She laughed, tipping her head upward and howling. Then she spit the ghosts out, propelling them toward the Wheel on the breath of her fury, and turned back to me, snarling.

I needed to break the thread that bound the ghosts to her as tribute. It would do no good to simply imprison them with her in the shrine, since she could use their energy to escape. She had to be severed from them. I feinted right, but still moving too fast from the Guardian Beast's push, I tumbled into the wolf instead.

She rolled from my impact, and spun to snap at me again.

I ducked and dodged toward the line of energy between her and the ghosts that bowled toward the Ferris wheel, screaming and gibbering. I threw myself after them, tucking and somersaulting with my arms around the shrine.

The smell of salt water, old wood, and creosote wafted into my nose both on the cold of the Grey and through the normal world. We were at Waterfront Park, only yards from the Great Wheel. I heard shouts as people were thrown aside by the passage of air and ghosts, but I paid them no attention, rushing down a short flight of steps onto the dock itself. I could see the thread between the ghosts and Limos taut and bright a few feet in front of me and I strove to reach it.

The wolf growled behind me. I turned my head just in time to see her leap for me. I rolled sideways, then scrambled back to my feet, putting the shrine down in the shadow of the strange abstract statue of Christopher Columbus that left a dark shape in the Grey as well as in the normal world.

I spun back to face Limos, moving away from the shrine and into the light, nearing the normal world enough to be thinner in the Grey—something wraithlike and weak in both planes—hoping to tempt her to bite at me and ignore the shrine.

The tangle of spirits struck the Great Wheel, making it sway as a storm of fireworks erupted overhead.

Limos lunged at me and I dove sideways, down into the Grey, reaching for the coil of light between her and the ghosts that swarmed over the Wheel, shaking it and raising a howl of unearthly wind. Water blasted up from the bay as if responding to the cry of the starving souls.

I clutched the thread of energy and it burned into my hands with the fire of Limos's fury and hunger. I wrenched at it with all my might, driving myself down, deeper, into the Grey, toward the grid, stressing the gleaming energy until it blazed too bright to look at and ripped apart.

The broken power recoiled and snapped me away from the grid with the sound of thunder and an explosion of colored fire. I tumbled through the air, in and out of the Grey, back into the normal world, and landed hard on my shoulder against rough wooden dock planks.

The clouds lurking immediately over me tore open above the drifting smoke of the launch mortars and the sparkle of burning phosphor and washed down rain that blazed with reflected color from the distant starbursts of the fireworks.

The Limos wolf pounced from the Grey, dragging me back into the mist world with a snarl and a shake of the head, but the ghosts were no longer hers. They shouted and then rushed outward in a sparkling cloud, vanishing in a sigh and curls of mist. The gust of the Guardian Beast's roar died away with them.

The dock was breathless in the rain, which looked like streams of light in the Grey. Colored tangles of energy—the Grey shapes of humans—lay everywhere, stunned or struggling to rise from where they'd been thrown by the eldritch wind. I could hear and see the Great Wheel's operators as bright, shouting shapes scampering around, securing their giant mechanism and checking to see if it was safe and still functioning or if they should shut it down and try to remove people from the glass gondolas with a crane, their mutterings like distant birdcalls.

I at least knew the passengers were all alive and the threat to the Wheel was past. I was half done. But I needed to get back to the shrine and catch Limos in it before I could call this a victory. And I had to do it before she tore me to shreds and devoured me.

I wasn't used to dealing with gods and I was never sure how much power they could bring to bear on me. This one was well and recently fed, which was a bad thing for me, even without the tribute souls at her beck and call. She was hungry for more and was going to be royally pissed off when she realized her loss.

Startled by the escape of her soul tribute, Limos jerked her head toward the Great Wheel, which stood as a dark shape in the Grey, dangling clustered lights of living human beings from its cold steel arc. I wrenched my leg free of her jaws, feeling those unnatural teeth tearing my flesh, and staggered to my feet. She turned back, glaring at me, her shape fluctuating toward skeletal human, then back toward wolf, the spectral skin melting away and flowing back in streams of quicksilver and spirit fire.

Finally she chose the human form, horrible as it was, and turned back toward me.

"You've robbed me," she said, advancing as I backpedaled unevenly on my injured leg.

"They weren't yours to take," I replied, crabbing sideways and stumbling down a misty step toward the weird statue of Columbus, the silver-light rain ringing dull music off its bronze surface.

She streamed forward, clattering bones and chattering teeth as she reached for me, her burning, uncanny gaze on my face as her own melted continually, her bones in hard relief. She wasn't interested in witty debate. She only wanted to kill me, so great was her fury and disappointment. The Grey didn't hinder her, but it no longer helped her, either.

I threw myself backward, toward the statue, landing short of the writhing darkness that was the shrine.

Limos fell on me, picking me up and throwing me viciously toward the unyielding shape of the statue.

I twisted in the air, riffling my fingers over the temporaclines and pushing on the first one that predated the statue. I fell through it, passing harmlessly where I should have been smashed into the inert bronze shape . . .

. . . And fell out the other side, into the mist and churn of the Grey again, Limos screaming as she grabbed for me. But the statue I had avoided still blocked her and she had to sweep around it, her bones rattling—if the sound was from her at all. I had not seen or heard the Guardian since I'd fallen over Limos at the dock's edge. I was certain it was still watching but I couldn't expect any more help from that quarter. I didn't need it, though. As Limos circled the statue, I scrambled in the shadow and grabbed the shrine. I pulled it to my chest, doors facing outward. I flicked the latch aside and flung the three sections open. The shrine gaped like a maw and I thrust it toward her as she reached down for me.

She screamed as she touched it and I braced the box between Columbus and my hip as I grabbed onto her bony arms, yanking her forward and into the shrine. The box swallowed her and I slammed the doors shut and latched them, sealing off her shrieks of betrayal. It wasn't much of a prison, but she'd be stuck in it until someone opened the doors again. Sweeping it into my arms, I held it tight to my body, then I pushed toward the normal and found myself sitting under Columbus, panting, filthy, and bloodied, with the curiously heavy box on my lap.

It was still raining, but the isolated storm was dying out as the fireworks continued in the distance. A man in a reflective yellow coat ran past, heading toward the Great Wheel. I could see other men in various uniforms approaching—firemen, cops, public safety officers, EMTs. I struggled to my feet and limped away from them into the darkness.

"I could use another lift," I muttered, thinking of the Guardian Beast, but the only response was a chiming of bone spines and what sounded like laughter.

TWENTY-FOUR

I managed to find a pedicab nearby and persuade the owner to take me back to Pioneer Square. He said he'd have to charge me extra for bleeding on his seat, but I didn't fuss.

Carlos and Quinton stood in a shadow near the door to my office building, waiting for me. Quinton stepped forward and held his hands out to help me from the pedicab's seat. I flinched with every movement, but I was thrilled to fall into his arms. "What's a handsome guy like you doing here?" I asked.

"I'd say saving damsels is distress, but it looks like I missed. You're hurt."

"I don't care," I said and kissed him with all the aching passion and relief I contained.

"I can't stay," he said against my mouth. "Will you be OK? I have to get back to Northlake to take care of a few things, but I had to come and see that you were all right. I could feel"—he traced a bruise on my jaw where I'd hit the dock and stroked down to my aching shoulder—"all of this. I wish I'd been here sooner."

"You didn't miss anything good. And I'll be fine."

"But you know how I love a good fight scene. . . ."

"I suspect we'll have plenty more in Europe."

We kissed long and hard enough to garner some whistles from passersby and a shouted "Get a room!" before Quinton let me go to pay the pedicab driver.

"I'll be back. Very soon," he said, looking unhappy to be leaving.

"I know," I said.

He nodded and walked down the street, casting a longing look back before he vanished into the crowd that was beginning to fill the streets again now that the fireworks—real and paranormal—were over.

Carlos was waiting for me by the building's door. "I took the liberty of disposing of Hazzard," he said.

"Thanks," I said, turning to pick up the shrine from the sidewalk. Even that little task hurt. "I didn't think I'd be gone so long, or that I'd end up quite so bloodied and banged up."

He shrugged, making the world roll and shake. I almost fell over and he had to catch me, sending a spike of ice and pain through me that wasn't any better than the pain and discomfort I was already feeling from much more corporeal sources. Without the glow of being in Quinton's presence I was uncomfortably aware of my injuries. My shoulder was badly bruised—though I counted myself lucky it wasn't dislocated—and I had cuts, abrasions, bites, and more bruises all over. My leg was still bleeding, although my arm had stopped. I could be worse off, I thought. I could be blind again.

Carlos chuckled. Had I said that aloud?

"Come upstairs. Stymak is busy with your guests and you may need some new furniture. . . ."

This time I knew I'd sworn out loud even without witnessing Carlos's amusement.

I took the elevator instead of the stairs and entrusted the shrine—filled with Limos—to Carlos outside my office door. I knew he wasn't going to let her out, considering his outrage the night before over what Purlis had started by releasing her to begin with, but I was surprised to see him take a cloth bundle from his pocket and produce a long silver chain from it. The chain smoked and burned when it touched his hands as he wrapped it around the shrine and sealed the wretched thing closed.

"You didn't have to—" I started.

"I do. And the burns will heal eventually. Better to be sure she cannot escape than to be delicate over a few fleeting injuries."

I knew how much they hurt him, but he didn't wince as he closed his hands over the blackened marks on his palms and fingers. That hadn't been ordinary silver, but I didn't ask what it was. I just pushed open my office door and went to see what had happened in there. Carlos didn't follow me.

Stymak was standing, but the other three were seated. Olivia was perched on the edge of my desk with Levi Westman and both looked shaken. Lily, still in her chair, though it was up against the wall now, looked calm, even though she appeared to have lost an eyebrow somehow and a bit of hair at the front of her head. A tower of white light loomed in the farthest corner, the shadows somehow darker by proximity. I started a little at the sight, but no one else seemed to notice it.

I looked them all over as they stared at me. I almost said something about the white light, but somehow it didn't seem the right time. I felt odd in its presence—like I weighed less and the earth barely touched me.

"I'm sorry for leaving you alone," I said and I wasn't sure if I meant the humans or the light. "What happened while I was gone?"

The light didn't reply, but the people all blinked at me for a moment, mute, and then Stymak said, "The candle . . . kind of erupted. I'm afraid it . . . ate your table."

I laughed more than was called for, relieved that it was such a small thing, just relieved in general. "I'll get another. How are all of you? And what happened *aside* from the candle thing?"

"We held on to Linda Hazzard as long as we could, but we lost the other spirits."

"It's all right," I said. "I saw them released. They're gone and free, wherever they went."

Lily Goss sighed. "I thought they were."

"How did you know?" Olivia asked, her eyes huge with an expression of awe and excitement.

"I guess God told me." She smiled. The white light seemed to expand and brush her shoulder, sending a hint of warm summer breeze through my stuffy office. "I think everything will be all right now."

I took a deep breath and felt lighter with it. "Will it?"

She nodded. "Yes. I'm sure of it. Your friend made that terrible ghost leave. Forever, I think."

I glanced at Stymak for confirmation and he nodded vigorously, his eyes bright. "Oh, yeah. Banished like a bad dream. I still don't like him, but he can really pull a ghost's cork when it needs to be done. I gotta tell you, that was the freakiest thing I've ever seen in a lifetime of freakiness."

"I can imagine," I said.

He shook his head. "No. I don't think you can. Unless you've seen it, it's not even in the imaginarium of most people."

"Trust me. I've seen it."

If his eyes had widened any farther, they'd have fallen right out of his head. I gave him a sheepish smile. "I should have warned you about that. I am truly sorry."

"No, no . . . It was . . . Well. It scared the crap out of me, but the experience was worth it. And I will never see something like that again—I hope." He seemed more awed than upset or freaked out.

Olivia and Levi nodded agreement, seeming a little dazzled. Goss sat still and looked beatific.

"What about . . . the others?" I asked. "Jordan, and Kevin, and Julianne . . . ?"

The light brightened just enough to notice. "They're fine," Goss said, her calm unruffled. "They stayed until we were done with that terrible woman. Then they went away. But they're fine, now."

I could only stare at her, agape, a touch awed myself at the calm certainty she exuded.

The whiteness in the corner gleamed and something shot outward from it that was too brilliant to look at. A sound like a clap of wings and thunder shook the office and the radiance erupting from the corner was too dazzling to bear. I closed my eyes, but the searing light could not be blocked. When the flash had died away and I could see again, I glanced at where it had been. The corner was dim and empty and the room was just as it had been before and somehow nothing like it, neither better nor worse yet changed completely. I felt shaken and transparent, but I didn't want to sit down or go to sleep. No one seemed to want to move at all for a minute or so and the expressions on their faces were beautifully stunned.

Eventually the strange feeling that held us captive faded and we went our separate ways. Stymak went with Lily Goss and Westman said he'd get a cab to the care home. Carlos had already taken the shrine away and I knew there was nothing to worry about on that score. I drove Olivia home and we didn't talk on the way.

This time I pulled into the driveway to let her out. The house was lit up as if to banish every shadow that had ever lingered in the world. As Olivia ran up the walk, her brother Peter came out and hugged her and swung her around like a child.

"He woke up! Dad woke up!" he shouted.

Olivia squealed and kissed him, hugging him back so hard she knocked the breath out of him. Then she broke away and ran back to me, her stride free and smooth, with no sign of her earlier limp.

"Did you hear? Dad's awake!"

I grinned at her. "I heard. Congratulations."

She nearly jumped through the window to hug me. "Thank you!" she whispered into my ear. "You did it!"

"You did it," I replied. "I just chase ghosts. You, and Levi, and Lily, and Stymak did it. Now go inside. Go."

She backed away from the Land Rover, grinning wide enough to crack her jaw, then whirled and flew into the house, screaming, *"Dad! Daddy!"*

I sat there and grinned myself for a while, then drove home elated. We had done something—whatever it was, however we did it—that was good and that felt wonderful.

EPILOGUE

I wrote it off to adrenaline, but I didn't feel as sore and ragged as I'd expected to on the way home. But it turned out I really wasn't hurt. When I went to shower, although my clothes were torn, filthy, and bloodstained, I wasn't. My injuries had vanished except for the mildest pink traces on my legs and arms. My shoulder was fine, too. I'd certainly been in a bad way when I'd arrived at the office, but sometime between then and getting home again, the hurts had been wiped away. I never did find out how, though I suspected it was something to do with the brightness that had lurked in the corner of my office.

Lily Goss said it was the work of an angel. She claimed to have felt it standing over her shoulder. Or maybe that had been her sister, Julianne. Of the identity she wasn't sure, but the presence of something that radiated goodness was not a point she would argue. It had been there and that was that. And that was why she wasn't upset that while I had been chasing Limos and the rest of them had been holding tight to Hazzard and the souls of their loved ones, Julianne Goss had slipped out of the world. Of the three patients, only Julianne didn't wake up. She died quietly and with no fuss at 10:27 p.m. Lily seemed relieved and even happy for her sister and I suppose that's the best we could have hoped for. Her doctor said he didn't know how she'd held on so long. He didn't use the word "miracle"—it didn't seem appropriate in the face of death—but it seemed to hover in the air nearby.

Kevin Sterling and Jordan Delamar both improved at remarkable speeds, though even the most optimistic doctors weren't sure how much their lives would return to normal—they'd been injured and bedridden for a long time and it's slow, hard work coming back from such a state. The Sterling family seemed to take the news well and it appeared that Labor and Industry was going to settle Kevin's case without more fussing about the details, so the house might finally get finished, too. Olivia's scars had faded to dim lines and the pain from her surgery vanished completely. She talked about possibly going back to dance class, but she wasn't ready to make that decision yet—she wanted to spend some time with her family first.

Westman and Delamar exercised their legal right to marry as soon as Jordy was able to speak and write steadily enough to sign the paperwork and say "I do." Westman sent me a copy of the wedding photo with a note of thanks, which I thought was very sweet of them. I declined the invitation to their party, held at Pike Place Market, since I couldn't face the ghosts there again so soon—if ever.

The Great Wheel had to be shut down for two days to be inspected, but eventually it was declared mechanically fine and as safe as ever—how safe that was would be open to interpretation. The bizarre winds along the waterfront had caused some damage to parts of the new tunnel construction zone and the dismantling work on the viaduct and a few people had been injured, but none of them worse than a broken arm suffered by a woman who'd fallen down the stairs by the Great Wheel's loading platform. The rest of the Independence Day celebrations hadn't been affected by the wind or the localized downpour and the freaky weather was written off as just the usual sort of Seattle summer weirdness.

A month later I had dinner with Phoebe's family again. I reveled in being around them and their unconditional love for one another. Even when one of them was being foolish or bad, the rest stood by them or cajoled them back into line and generally acted . . . well, like family. My own family was small, fragmented, and fragile, but if Carlos was right that the ties of affection are as strong as the ties of blood, then I was, in my slow and often makeshift way, creating my own family from what I had with Quinton and by the Masons' example.

Though, on the family front, I wasn't seeing as much of Quinton as I wanted to. I hadn't expected to as the situation with his father deteriorated, but it was still a sharp little thorn in my side that just as I was starting to get into the idea, my tiny family was being put under considerable strain by his father. But one thing I was learning from the Masons was that you work with what you have. Quinton was spending a lot of his time preparing to leave the country and fix what his dad had broken—the more we found out, the worse it looked, and that wasn't even considering the hurt and betrayal that was now irremediable between them. I hadn't heard what the final extent of James Purlis's injuries was, but I assumed I'd find out eventually.

I had said I'd go with him, but Quinton asked me not to.

"Why not?" I asked, puzzled more than hurt.

He pulled me close, wrapping me in his arms. I could hear his heart beating steady and calm, the warmth of him enfolding me like a cloak. "Because you are the one and only Harper Blaine and you can't just disappear. I'm already nobody. I can slip through holes in the system. But he'll see you coming. He'll track you and I can't stop that. I don't want him to know you're a threat until it's too damned late for him to stop us."

"What about you? Won't he know you're out there, hunting him down?"

"He might think it, but he won't be sure. He knows I don't want to leave you—he counted on it before and I think he'll count on it again—and so long as you are here in Seattle, doing what you normally do, he'll be unsure where I am and what I'm doing. It'll puzzle him and then it will bother him, and eventually his uncertainty will trip him up. I know him better than he knows me now. And I'm going to use that against him.

"It's a lot to ask of you, I know. I'm sorry," he continued, "but will you play along and remain here until I let you know it's time?"

"It's going to be hard to pretend you're here when I'll be wishing all the time that you really were."

"I'll always be here," he said. He pressed his finger to my chest between my breasts. "I'll always be right here."

"Where?" I asked, teasing and ruffling his hair. "Here?" I kissed him.

He laughed and kissed me back, then kissed my neck and worked his way lower, saying with each kiss, "here . . . and here . . . and here . . ." until we were giggling, and then gasping and not talking at all. . . .

I knew I'd do what he asked when the time was right—I had no choice. There were forces beyond the normal at work and it is, after all, my job to fix that sort of thing. And there is also that other strange thing at work: love.

For now, I was going to treasure what I had and do my best with it. I'd fix the rest of the world later.

AUTHOR'S NOTE

When I started this book I thought it would be fun to write one that was just about ghosts and hauntings. Of course, that's not quite how it worked out. . . . But if you're going to talk about ghosts in Seattle, the obvious places to start are Pike Place Market and Pioneer Square. Since I've done a lot around Pioneer Square, I decided to concentrate on the market this time, and I couldn't have picked a better spot—it's the mother lode of freaky Seattle stories. At the same time, the activity around the construction of the State Route 99 tunnel became an irresistible addition since the area is linked to some of the weirdest and most bizarre events in Seattle's history—and you know how much I like weird events—so I started looking at the proposed route for the tunnel to see what sort of fictional havoc I could wreak on my town. And, of course, Seattle obliged by providing the sites of a tragic accident and the offices of a serial killer on either end of the route, with all sorts of strange things in between. I just couldn't resist stirring them up and seeing what happened.

During the final editorial cycle, I found a note from the copy editor of this book expressing some surprise (or possibly doubt, horror, or curiosity) about my referring to Linda Hazzard as a serial killer. Not only was Linda Burfield Hazzard a real person, she is one of the few women to be recognized as a serial killer and she was the first ever recorded in Washington's unhappy history of them. There are quite a few articles about Hazzard online—including several on my usual haunt, HistoryLink.org. The best known of several books about her is *Starvation Heights* by Gregg Olsen, which is guaranteed to give you the creeps. I also got information about Hazzard from the ladies of the Clallam County Historical Society while I was doing research for a previous Greywalker novel, *Downpour*. I really couldn't have made up anything as dreadful as the details of Hazzard's crimes. Truth is, once again, more outrageous than fiction.

The tragedy of Cannie Trimble is also sadly true and is another bit of strange Seattle history that I picked up initially through an article at HistoryLink.org. She's a bit of a mystery, as there seems to be little information about her other than the reports of her death and the fact that she was married to one of the wealthiest men in Seattle at the time. There's also a debate about her name—some archives and articles list her as Cassandra or Cassie Trimble, but comments from surviving relatives claim that her name was actually Cannie. I made her into a sad but helpful spirit, and I wonder what she was really like—smart and funny and full of life, I hope—but I suppose I'll never know.

I took some liberties with the disposition of Gas Works Park, which actually was undergoing ecological restoration in the first quarter of 2013, but there never has been a secret door into the abandoned coal gas processing plant. However, you can fly kites off the top of the mound that covers some of the factory's wreckage—it's a great location with a fantastic view and constant wind.

Pike Place Market is famously haunted and Mercedes Yaeger has conducted tours of the market's ghostly sites since the early 1990s, as well as written several books on the topic, which I read as research for this book. I also went on the tour with fellow writers Liz Argall, Melissa Mead Tyler, Stina Licht, and Cherie Priest and had a wonderfully spooky time. I didn't have to make up any of the stories about the market that I included in this book—they're all true, as are most of the ghosts. As I write this, Kells is still in the process of renovating the upper floors at the former Butterworth Mortuary building, but you can still get a drink downstairs in the old embalming and crematory rooms, where things do, once in a while, go bump in the night. If you want to experience some of this for yourself, take the ghost tour the next time you're in town, or walk through the market after dark with your ears pricked and your eyes open.

I had some archaeological assistance from my friend, writer Robin MacPherson, but the majority of the archaeological information came from another writer friend, Rhiannon Held. There is a real-life Washington State Office of Archaeology and Historic Preservation, and Rhiannon was able to help me with information about that office's work and responsibilities on the tunnel and seawall projects. I was thrilled she had the time to look over the manuscript and to assist me with it—the line "It's not all whips and fedoras" is one I borrowed from her. And she was still kind enough to let me slip her into the story, even though I had to demote her to monitor.

I also had a lot of help from Dr. Martha Leigh of Swedish Physicians about eye damage from oil paint (as well as help from my minion, Thea Maia) and the facts about persistent vegetative states, which are, in fact, extremely rare. I probably fudged the facts here and there by accident, but I tried to keep them as true to the real world as possible while still telling a good story.

Here and there I had to tinker with reality to make it fit my story; I have to say that anything I got wrong with this or any other detail of fact, personality, or history is all my own fault.

AUG 07 2013